WHEN THE
NEEDLE
DROPS

WHEN THE NEEDLE DROPS

COLIN MacINTYRE

Black&White

Black&White

First published in the UK in 2024 by
Black & White Publishing Ltd
Nautical House, 104 Commercial Street, Edinburgh, EH6 6NF

A division of Bonnier Books UK
4th Floor, Victoria House, Bloomsbury Square, London, WC1B 4DA
Owned by Bonnier Books
Sveavägen 56, Stockholm, Sweden

A CIP catalogue record for this book is available from the British Library.

ISBN: 978 1 78530 513 9

1 3 5 7 9 10 8 6 4 2

Typeset by Data Connection
Printed and bound in Great Britain by Clays Ltd, Elcograf S.p.A.

www.blackandwhitepublishing.com

To my mother-in-law, Margaret "Peggy" Ghuneim – for the encouragement, belief and wind through my sails. Sorry in advance about more swears.

Author's Note

This book is a work of fiction; it is partly inspired by the Great Mull Air Mystery of the 1970s, but I would like to emphasise that the characters are entirely made up. Any resemblance to real people, events or places they might be connected to, I would only wish to be taken as a tribute to a time, a place, a people and an island.

'If I got rid of my demons, I'd lose my angels.'
Tennessee Williams

'And fuck.'
Ivor Punch

INTRO TRACK

STITCHING THE NEEDLE AND THREAD along the flesh of the floppy arms had been less haphazard, less bloody, than anticipated. In fact, strangely therapeutic. It was getting between the fingers that was proving tricky.

Late on a December night, sitting with the body propped alongside on the couch and the house quiet save for the Atlantic wind blowing the arse out of bats, it was easy to get lost in the work, in the company. It was strangely comforting to have the body's presence in the sad house. The thought occurred that the gable end might be the first thing the wind had hit in three thousand miles. It all added to the sense of significance. Of being noticed. Of touching and being touched.

The pinpricks from the needlework had caused the fabric to stain with blood. A clear sign of rustiness. Irritating. That would need to be cleaned up. The final finger on the body was navigated and the thread cut; the needle put aside. The face was not the finest work, but the likeness, certainly to locals, would not be lost on anyone. The length of the arms would seal the deal.

It was time now to dress the body. Folding the shorter arm into the uniform jacket gave the illusion of life being blown back into the floppy limbs, of oxygen circulating within; that even the possibility of a conversation was on the cards. There was the devilish thought of propping the limp body up in the armchair opposite and placing the TV remote within its stitched hand; of liberally pouring it a large measure and attacking the glass with ice; or, more ghoulishly, of fastening the torso into the passenger seat and driving it around Tobermory. It had apparently been done by horse and cart in olden times. A headless horse, the legend went.

The legs were now folded into the baggy trousers. The impression created was of a Hebridean Charlie Chaplin, minus the cane, without the silent damsel in distress. Or a pulse. But that was the thing, the giddy excitement: the inverted delectation of giving life to something, of creating movement, of transforming black and white into colour, silence to sound; it all added up to a power more godly than human. That hadn't been expected. There was a sense of reconnecting with one's earlier, more alive self. This was the first one, but it was hard now to imagine it being the last.

It was time to stand back and admire the work. Adrenaline arrived like a shock wave, like a new element blowing against the house. There was music playing, which earlier had seemed so urgent, so relevant and all-encompassing, but was now reduced to background noise, instantly forgettable, as though

2

washed across the Atlantic to the wrong port. It was *him* playing. Had to be.

It was time.

Time to clean off the blood from the hands. To put a rope around its neck.

SIDE A

TRACK 1

MORNINGS WERE A JUGGLING ACT for Sonia Hislop. She looked in the mirror and sighed at her bleached, greasy bedhead. Twenty years too late for punk. Or maybe it was still to arrive on the Isle of Mull, along with *JAWS* and the Bee Gees too? She couldn't be sure. A single mother didn't have time to fix her hair or fully consider such things. Nor did she have time to roam free on Tobermory golf course at 8.12 a.m. on a Saturday, but that was all she really wanted to do. Now. Right now. Naked, preferably. Sid Vicious linking her arm. Though Barry Gibb in his day ... She wouldn't say no.

It had been a late shift at Macgochans the night before, the pub at Ledaig, on the distillery end of the town's Main Street. The dreaded Friday lock-in, the clear-up, followed by poetry recitals up the Prison Brae from Tinsel, the man in his late seventies with the Samuel Beckett hair, sailor's cap and woollen socks folded over his wellies. He had insisted he walk her home. Unnecessarily, thought Sonia. At first. He was a permanent fixture in the Tobermory pubs,

7

gravitating like a sixty-a-day moth between the lights of the Mishnish Hotel and Macgochans. Tinsel – nicknamed because he was born on Christmas day, which was now only days away – had wheezed his way up the steep brae, his heavy-coated arm locked in hers, and when she released her arm near the top, he had insisted he walk her all the way; *better that I do*, he had said. But she had wanted to be alone, to let all the voices of the evening leave her, all the demands of drinks orders and drunken chit-chat. Her cheekbones always ached like a talk-show host, sore from smiling at unfunny jokes. The Glasgow School of Art hadn't said anything about this.

She had reassured Tinsel's serious, watery eyes that she would be fine, and, for the umpteenth time, before parting, that she wouldn't accept his proposal of marriage. The silly old fool was lucky his cheek, if not his poetry, didn't get him locked up in the old prison for the night, which was reduced to a derelict building positioned at the top of the brae opposite where they stood, with creels and colour-faded buoys outside. It was haunted by the myth of the Grey Lady, according to Tinsel. Sonia had commented on his cute waistcoat, having heard he had once trained as a tailor. True, he'd said, and that was when the mainland almost got its clutches on him, but he'd had to come back when his mother began to fail. To his brother. Sonia was aware Tinsel had a twin called Tonsils, so nicknamed as a result of having once been caught with his tongue down a full cousin's throat when he was a teenager. *Quite a different fellow altogether*, was all Tinsel had conceded. Others at the bar were less kind.

8

Alone at the top of the brae, she had watched him depart further into the night, like a wounded animal in a bin man's coat, the strains of 'White Christmas' arriving like a sixty-a-day Teuchter Bing Crosby. Or, she thought, more like an angel with sideburns.

Sonia had then looked down from the top of the Prison Brae to Tobermory's colourful seafront; with its shoulders partly turned to her, she had the feeling of being backstage again, behind the curtain, imagining the echoes of theatre applause from ... *where*? The mainland? The pastel-hued houses appeared like scale models; she felt outsized and briefly significant above them, relieved to be freed from the beck and call of Tobermory's barflies. The clock had chimed one: a singular, resonant cry that sounded strangely alive. She looked to the dark blanket of sea where she knew Calve Island sat, relieved it was hidden, hoping to feel significant above it too. But that could never quite happen.

The streetlights of the seafront reflected the buildings onto the black sea, including the recognisable triad of blue, red and yellow of the Mishnish Hotel and Royal Buildings, thrown like a giant shimmering, overpriced table mat from the hands of a tourist. She had wished she could still shimmer, still illuminate, throw colour, rage, rage against ... she wasn't exactly sure what anymore. She then felt a presence standing nearby. Heard rustling in the bushes. Had turned, ready to reprimand Tinsel for his septuagenarian tenacity. But no one was there.

'Teeth!' came the voice. And then – 'Check!'

'Christ!' Sonia gripped the sink with both hands.

Iris had arrived like a red flare in the bathroom from the short hallway, returning Sonia to the here and now.

Sonia half expected Tinsel to be standing there, reading glasses on a string, all shabby chic if he only knew what it was. But it hadn't been Tinsel in the bushes, last night, she was sure. It had been *him*, returned, back to watch over her. Or them both?

'Lan-gu-age!' Iris cautioned, as though just discovering syllables and making a play of sizing up her mother, marking her findings with a pencil onto a pad. Sonia noticed the strand of red hair stuck to her daughter's cheek, a hint of toothpaste in the mix. 'Taking the Lord's name in vain means Santa might take you off his list, Mummy. If there *is* a Santa, that is.'

'Sorry, love,' Sonia said, surprised at how much this surveillance felt like a continuation from the night before of the watching glare of the barstools, of Calve Island; it was already unsettling enough to feel the eyes of one island on you, let alone two.

Still, it was nice not to feel totally past her sell-by date, even if the chef – who called her 'honey' and she suspected cooked with Blue Stratos instead of olive oil – was nineteen at most. But that hadn't stopped her from occasionally setting her skirt just a tad higher, or fashioning a provocative rip up the back of her fishnets.

She had felt less free, less secure, than she had imagined she would on Mull, instead experiencing the confinement of the goldfish bowl, the glare from the Co-op queue and the other passengers on the Oban ferry on the rare occasions she went anywhere. But she couldn't leave. Couldn't leave *them*, what she had.

10

'It's okay, Mum ...' Iris said, forgivingly, looking at her checklist and placing the end of the pencil on her lips. She took it and poised it above the page. 'But it's time to do your molars.'

'Oh, okay, love.' Sonia sighed. In actuality, she lived for these daily morning set-plays. They kept her alive.

'And he's real,' Sonia said, into the mirror.

'Dad?'

'No. Eh no. Santa.'

'It's you!' Iris said, waving her arms. 'Along with the Tooth Fairy and the Easter Bunny!'

How Sonia wished she didn't have to play all the parts. Her mind jumped to that first Christmas. *After*. Just the two of them. And then ... inextricably ... then ...

'Your molars ...' Iris said impatiently.

'Okay, love,' Sonia said. 'I mean, Sergeant Major.'

'*Ess*. Mummy! Major-*ess*.'

'Yes. *Ess*. Still waking up my hair.' Sonia ran her hands through her mane, realising it had all turned a bit *Laurel Canyon*, had the scene originated in the valleys outside Oban. 'Kind of early for the inspection, isn't it? I get enough of that from the regulars.'

Sonia allowed the electric toothbrush to vibrate in her mouth. She always liked how it sat in the mug alongside the child's one. That was a detail, a small miracle in her life that no one could take away, which she could never have imagined back in her carefree clubbing days on Sauchiehall Street when even Sid might have given her a wide berth. Her life in Glasgow seemed like another planet ago. Even now, ten years later, the shock of being responsible for

11

another, actual, living being could overwhelm her. So what if her art career hadn't taken off? At least she had created something unique in Iris. And there was still time for the curator from the Tate Modern to step off the Craignure ferry searching her out. Though, in truth, she couldn't even get a print hung in Macgochans. Something she had said to Tinsel on the night previous had stayed with her, in response to his encouragement for her to pick up the fabric, scissors and maybe even her brushes again: I'm not sure what people *look* like anymore.

She couldn't stop her eyes dropping once again to the two toothbrushes. The hardest thing about the mug used to be the missing toothbrush; now it was the one she had kept. There should have been three. She suspected that was why she couldn't really see people anymore: there was too much of *them*, dear *them*, in the way.

Sonia rubbed her forefinger gently over the tattoo of the little number 3 on her wrist. Then took the bar of soap from the clamshell. Rubbed it furiously over the inkwork, harder and faster. She rinsed and dried off. She quickly thrust both hands repeatedly through her hair, Tina Turner-like, and could almost feel his hand still caressing her neck, her hair army-short then, arty, ready for her inevitable breakthrough profile on Channel 4. But, instead, her 'installation' was to be her womb housing the child he would never see; the discovery of the pregnancy coming after he had gone, after they had been told he would 'not have long'. He didn't even get to place a hand on her swelling midriff.

Even the sight of a guitarist setting up in the pub could trigger grief, have her reimagining the golf course with Sid.

12

Though she always thought of him as more Joe Strummer than Sid. He was wiry, ambitious, almost too alive, until he wasn't. The Mull Music Festival every spring had turned into a small nightmare for her. Watching *Later . . . With Jools* had become impossible, that being his final national TV appearance. The expensive bottle of wine from R.E.M. hidden somewhere, which he'd received after supporting them across Europe. Music had become a reminder of everything she had lost, and art a reminder of everything she could have been. He: Sean. She: Sonia. They'd almost rhymed; almost been a lyric. Often she thought of Iris as their song. *Cancer*, the album.

'Okay,' Sonia said into the mirror. 'Schoolbag?'

'Check!' Iris said, finishing off at the toilet. 'Already prepared. Crisps for after ballet too!'

Sonia swallowed a pill and closed the bathroom cabinet on Sean, on the memories. She placed her toothbrush in the mug.

Iris walked out of the little toilet and into the bedroom they shared. The sound of a foreign language arrived, low, being spoken into a phone. From another room. People talking. About her? A woman's voice. Sonia pulled her black coat and bobble hat from the hooks by the entrance and deliberately let the other coats fall to the carpet. She closed the chalet door on it all.

Outside, she and Iris took the longer route up over the golf course, making angels into the wind.

'You may take my hand!' Iris shouted, holding out her hand to her mother. 'Oh, yours is sweaty, Mum! Like holding a bath!'

'Thanks!' Sonia circled down to Iris. 'We'll need to work on your chat-up lines, hen ... Sid would never have said that to Nancy.'

13

'Eh?' Iris said, scrunching her face, causing a landslide of freckles down her nose. *His*, of course. She hummed, not one of his songs. 'Why can't I listen to his voice again, Mum? Daddy's?'

'Oh love. Not now.'

Sean had insisted she take all his CDs and records to the Tobermory dump. It turned out to be the day before the end. She still couldn't fathom how to explain to Iris the reason why they had none of his music to listen to. Not even a radio in their room, in case of an unexpected play.

'Eh, I need to walk the last bit to the school alone now, Mummy. It's not cool anymore. They call me Ira now. I've got a boyfriend.'

'Argh!' Sonia mimicked a dagger through her heart as they exited the golf course onto Erray Road. 'Okay, love. I was your age once too.'

They passed the pebbledash police station. She had heard across the bar that apparently it housed an *actual* jail. Looking at the little building, with the matching pebbledash police house next door, and the police vehicle outside positioned at a capricious angle – as though it had hurriedly parked itself – she wondered where did domesticity end and crime begin? The sergeant had come into the pub the night before for a Coke as he occasionally did, commanding the space, not long before last orders. Assured, unknowable, he had barely said a word beyond pleasantries to the faithful, and left before the keys went into ignitions. They said he was good at turning a blind eye that way. She had projected a bit of the Al Pacino onto him. The dark, silent type, as though moving to his own tune, an island himself. It was said he slept with a horse's head, something more to do with one of his ancestors than *The Godfather*.

Sonia craned her neck back to the station house as she passed, the weeds taking hold out front, and thought of him alone inside, a kind of prisoner of sorts himself. Naked? Part-clothed? Rock music? Traditional? More porn than poetry, she imagined.

She looked to the Christmas tree in the window of the house she was now passing at the start of Creagan Park. Glistening. Hopeful. Expectant. The festive period was always the hardest time for her, a reminder.

'Just me now, Mum. Austin might be watching,' Sonia heard, as she passed the manse and the tree on which she always saw a face. 'That's the boyfriend.'

She felt Iris's hand leaving hers, lost to this Austin who was not Sean. The feeling of a part of her about to be removed was growing again, losing the edges of herself. She watched her daughter run off too soon. Her red hair bouncing, contrasting starkly with the yellow coat, backpack in place, as she hurriedly fled the embarrassment of being seen with her mother. Off to conquer another place: the planet of opportunity, of *two* parents, nuclear families, of more capable mums without genre-defying hair. Sonia took a last look at the faded orange backpack, imagining it merging into other backpacks around it. She caught a final glimpse of the skulls and bones on the fabric; maybe rebellion was alive and well on Mull, after all.

She turned self-consciously to a passing dog walker whose pity behind a smile she felt stitched into her. She turned back up the hill, feeling more hopeless because her tragedy was in full view. Like an artist forced to display unfinished work.

By the time she was back in the chalet her emotions had become a storm in her head. It was then, in the shower, that the policeman returned to her thoughts, his hand down her bare back and fingers moving between her legs from behind. She wearing his police hat, handcuffs and nothing else. Guilty. Guilty.

She threw on the black uniform and dashed down to the Western Isles Hotel, to her housekeeping job, to play at being somebody else again, eking out as much Siouxsie Sioux as the uniform could muster, her wet hair attracting the morning chill, cheeks stinging.

It was there, some twenty minutes later, that, white-faced, she told a workmate she had just received a call.

It was the school secretary. 'Is Iris ill?' she was asking. 'Is that why Iris isn't at ballet today?'

TRACK 2

MOST MORNINGS HE WOKE LIKE this: the endless scratching, the needle searching for the groove. Rotating like an unanswered question as though in pursuit of not an opening chord, but the first clue to a wider puzzle. Rod Stewart's seventies-era rasp still rung in his ears. The golden period. He was never sure on waking if the needle was in reality turning within his hungover head, like the inner workings of an ongoing case playing out, rather than the record player rotating from the night before.

There had been a dream. A plane going down. Again.

The station phone was ringing. He dragged his still-clothed body off the mattress and dropped his booted feet to the carpet, knocking over what was left of the Tobermory Malt in the glass on the floor where there might have been a bedside table. He groaned; *why does it always have to be the good stuff?* He reached as if on autopilot to take the needle off the spinning vinyl.

'Christ,' he croaked, grimacing; there had been more calls from Strathclyde Legacy Division than usual of late, always

17

early like this, as if checking he was out of his scratcher. Performance was down, apparently. He rubbed his temples, feeling more like one of his small flock of rams about to be put to the slaughter than he did the Isle of Mull's senior law enforcer. He lunged towards the persistent phone.

'Better be Rod himself,' he grumbled.

He lifted the receiver with his shorter arm; it was an affliction that gave rise to his nickname on the island of 'The Clock'. Not that anyone dared say it to his face – not if they didn't want a pillow and a cold cell for the night, accompanied by all the early-period Rod they could handle. If torture was required, there was always the eighties material. He had read the singer now had a hobby building vast model train sets, planes, boats and the like. Not the most likely of town planners, unless the Marquee Club was after an extension.

'Punch ...' he answered, clearing his throat; and then, flinching, as though the needle had instead hit a vein: 'Station. Tobermory.'

'Ah yes, hello. Hello! Can one hear me?' A woman's voice, going ten to the dozen. Unfamiliar. Slurring. 'Is one speaking to Tobermory Police Station?'

'It's not the Marquee Club, 1971,' Punch said. 'Regrettably. Take your time, please. Who am I speaking to?'

'It's my ... my ... he's ...' The voice rose in pitch then paused; there was heavy breathing, gulping. In the background, sweeping classical music soundtracked the speaker's urgency.

'Are you okay ... eh?' Punch reached for a pen and a copy of the *Daily Record*. 'Can you tell me your name and location please? Contact num—'

The line went dead.

Punch looked at the handset as though it was a shell and, like a wave, the voice might still be inside. He was aware it was a thing all TV sleuths did, all bad actors really. Biggest crime was to catch eye contact with the camera lens, so they said.

He placed the receiver back on its cradle. Could barely be bothered documenting the call; it was one of those voices that was hard to discern, either English or posh Scots. It was a step up from the usual crank call; often they came at ungodly – *Rod* – hours. A waste of his bloody time. Usually a teenage giggle followed, often from the phone box down on the seafront next to the St Mary figurine, sometimes with the offer of a blowjob. Not usually accompanied by classical music, it had to be said; more like some rap bullshit. But it was better to log the call, especially in these days of performance stats and tables, rather than endure the resulting enquiry from the increasingly bureaucratic head brass at Legacy Strathclyde. Particularly now they had sent a new fresh-faced recruit just out the wrapper from the Police College at Tulliallan to check up on him. He could only imagine the spew of online forms needing filled in should he ever, even jokingly, accept said blowjob. Aye, better to log a name, *any* name, rather than leave the box empty, less chance of time-sapping follow-ups from pen-pushing officers with all the case nous of Cato, never mind Inspector Clouseau. Aye, the quiet life was the endgame; more time for dropping the needle on vinyl.

'Maggie May,' Punch scribbled in the phone log. He squinted up to the clock above the sink in his kitchenette, just visible above the overflowing dishes: monuments to another lived week. He added: 'December 20th, 1998, 8.54 a.m.'

Punch crawled face down back onto the bed like a crocodile re-entering a swamp; reached down into his own natural habitat for the discarded bottle of Tobermory. Writing the date had caused his body to stop feeling. It was just a day away, the anniversary. The unwanted reminder. That was what the dream was all about. But the whisky would help with that.

He would have PC Cluny input the log onto the new database later. 'Guinness' was the nickname he had given his new recruit, he of the shock of blond hair against the black police uniform, recently deployed by Legacy Strathclyde to Lima Bravo Division, Isle of Mull. Like Sting without the tunes, he thought, or the tantric marathon hard-on, if you believed the rumour mill. Punch failed to see what backup he really required for surreptitiously removing a set or two of keys from ignitions outside Macgochans, the MacDonald Arms or the Mishnish. Those at the more salubrious Western Isles Hotel up the hill he would leave. He preferred to be a solo artist. Like Rod leaving Ronnie Wood & Co. He couldn't be sure who he wanted to strangle more: Guinness or the new computer he had arrived with. Though, now Sting was in the frame, it was a close call.

Everybody on the island had a nickname, or acquired one; Punch often felt it kept the mainland, bad tunes, at bay. To a point. Crime too. Sometimes. If not dreams, if not planes going down. Lockerbie – that place he tried to confine to the bottom of a bottle – was looming again. This time with all the dreaded merry-go-round of the tenth anniversary. Why

20

the media didn't know that all he and the families wanted was peace was beyond him. He had arrived at the tenth anniversary eve.

Punch would rather the eighties had not happened at all; preferred that technology had stopped evolving just after Rod had recorded *Every Picture Tells A Story*. But the place name of that significant Borders town made the decade impossible to erase. No matter how much liquid amber he threw down his gullet, the plane still came down. And with it, images of body parts strewn over the golf course. That was the night the island felt like part of the mainland, the sea between them rendered insignificant. He'd lost a part of himself too on that hillside he had never visited. A farmer from the town had plucked the body of a baby girl straight off a hedge for fuck's sake; he'd driven it as his passenger to the local police station. Not a mark on her.

Punch took another hit and grimaced as the fluid burned the back of his throat. He looked out the window to the barmaid walking up the road outside the station from the direction of Creagan Park, which led down to the school. She was alone, as was normal. Even if he didn't already know the details only too well, he would have been able to detect the invisible cloud of tragedy, of loss, around her: that she knew what it felt like to be stared at in the Tobermory Co-op queue, to stand like a stag in headlights, nobody sure whether to talk about the weather, ask how you're doing or leave you in grief. That was if the uniform even allowed you grief.

Punch stood and edged closer to the window. Didn't dare be seen. It came with the job spec. The woman was right outside the station house now. She always seemed smaller than she appeared behind the bar, her hair at angles, cheekbones cutting the cold morning light. He noted how the human face stored loss; it always held loss. There was something out of time about her. Dressed in black, she looked like she was on her way back from the funeral of a New Romantic. Her hand swung as though a child was still attached to it. There was something of the sandpiper in her quick-stepped walk. She progressed out of sight.

Punch moved to check the phone was properly on its cradle, then ran his hand down his black tie and stopped at his buckle. He had a feeling; it was the itch he sometimes got, a sign the world was about to send him a case. Clues, to him, were like grooves cut into vinyl, like songs requiring to be put in the correct sequence, though, crucially, unlike the album format, not as the criminal intended. When deciphering a criminal mind, it was more about being handed a list of seemingly unrelated riffs, melodies and lyrics that you had to consider, order and reorder, then gradually formulate into a coherent narrative. Much like the work of The Faces in their heyday. Guinness, on the other hand, was more of a one-hit-wonder type. Punch was sure the lad wouldn't know where to search for a sniff of a clue unless Bill Gates or Tim bloody Berners-Lee was his DCI.

The phone rang again.

'Was it my Paco Rabanne?' he croaked.

He grabbed the handset.

'Punch. Station.'

Silence at the other end. No music.

'Station? LB division? Tobermory?'

'Bloody hell, Ivor . . .' A familiar voice. 'Am I getting your inside leg measurements as well? Yip yip.'

'Christ, man, talk about pregnant pauses. And fuck.' Punch shook his head at the phone.

It was Randy, one of the barflies.

'Though you've caused a few,' Punch added. 'Pregnancies, that is. And it's *Sergeant* Punch when I'm in uniform. How many times have I told you that, man.'

'How the heck can I tell if you've a uniform on?'

'You think it's the Turkish Baths you've called? What else would I be wearing?'

'Heavy night by the sounds of it, Sarge . . . I'm hearing Tom Waits . . . injected with laryngitis.'

'Compliment accepted. And fuck.' Ivor recoiled from the turbo-driven ceilidh music in the background. 'Struggling to hear you over that racket.'

'My new CD, yip yip. Made it in Oban for a hundred and fifty quid.'

'You were robbed. I'll put an arrest warrant out for the studio engineer. And fuck.'

'Look, you need to come now, Ivor, I mean, Sarge. Was just on my way back to Tob from the Forestry office out Aros Mains when . . . Well . . . You need to come. To see what's hanging here.'

Albums. Days. Cases. Riffs.

For Punch, they all started this way.

TRACK 3

'NECK-WRINGABLE,' PUNCH SCOFFED.

'Called you as soon as I saw it, yip yip.' Randy was standing in his Forestry Commission uniform, pointing eagerly to the body hanging from a tree before them. 'Aye, was just on my way back fr—'

'You said,' Punch said, still gazing upwards. 'Neckringable. And fuck.'

'Can't deny the likeness, Sarge. The police uniform . . . They've even done the badger-like fur around your temples . . .'

'Enough!' Punch said, clearing his throat, shaking off the Tom Waits. He took his hat off and put it on again. 'I've fucking *black* hair.'

'You must be proud as punch . . .' Randy smirked to the uniform. 'Talk about greater police visibility . . . but is it a *crime*? Yip yip.'

'Your puns certainly are. You can forget your stint in Dictionary Corner on *Countdown*. Carol Vorderman would need security.' Punch stared back up to the hanging form. 'It's not a good fucking likeness at all. So yes. It *is* a crime.

To art. I don't *have* fur.' He rubbed with the wrist of his longer arm at his temple, where he couldn't deny grey was emerging a little too badger-like for his taste. He had seen hair dye in the Co-op, but it would be round the town quicker than a dose of syphilis from Randy.

The air was thick, like a breath caught in the mouth. A scent of new-felled pine, mixed with stale lager. He had no clue why the Forestry was called the Forestry anymore, given they seemed to spend most of their time felling the bloody trees. 'I'm too busy for this kind of thing, and fuck. Folks taking the piss.'

'Doing what? Alphabetising your vinyl collection?' Randy looked to the tree and then to Punch, as though comparing notes. 'Yip yip. You're not going to do anything about it?'

'Oh.' Punch stepped towards the effigy. He glanced to the mainland, then turned to the road and back to his doppelganger. 'You can bet your Frankie fucking Millers I'm going to do something about it.'

'The superior voice, to Rod, yip yip,' Randy said, nodding slowly and running his hand through his mane of red, thinning hair. 'Miller.'

Punch looked at him. Placed his hand on his handcuffs. 'You *want* bloody arresting? I can throw you in a cell with Elton if you want ...'

The two men were standing on the outskirts of Tobermory, on the Gally Goo, the passage of road leading from the island's capital to the sleepy village of Salen. They were at the road's highest point above the Sound of Mull, the strip of sea separating the island's east coast from the mainland. It had been immortalised in Gaelic song – famously by the

25

Glasgow Orpheus Choir, which Punch had on vinyl that crackled even more than Rod.

'So should I cut Guy Fawkes down, Sarge?'

Punch looked to the road and then back to the sad face of the effigy.

'Wonder what my replica would look like?' Randy said.

'Axl bloody Rose springs to mind, minus the tunes. And fuck.'

'I've got the 880 Magnum in the back of the truck? Still warm from clearing some trees out round Gruline, yip yip. I'll have this bugger down quicker than you can say Freddy fucking Krueger.'

'No. Leave it,' Punch said. 'Can't go disturbing evidence, man. Save the chainsaw for cutting your locks. Or better still, your instruments.' He turned to survey Randy more closely, this man famed for doing a Mexican wave with his eyebrows; skin stretched tightly across his face like lorry tarp. 'Cut your hair, man, and clean yourself up. Look at you? You'll be living like a hippy on a bloody houseboat next and pouring your shite over the side from a bucket.'

'I'm a bloody good Forestry-man!' Randy said.

'You're an alcoholic,' Punch spat. 'Surprised they trust you with a single tree, never mind a forest. Sting *will* be off the ferry next. I've a good mind to strip search you for a needle and thread myself.'

'Wonder if he's as tight when it comes to his round? Yip yip.'

'Sting? Oh, I'd think so. Every penny a prisoner. And fuck.'

'No. The effigy.'

'Enough.'

'The nose is right, yip yip. Arms too.'

'Enough, I said!' Punch folded his arms. He was more than a little dissatisfied with the pigeon-chested padding.

He looked to the CalMac ferry, moving incrementally like a toy in the distance. Imagined Rod's giant hand coming down to turn it around; though he suspected it might take more to get CalMac running on time.

'Must be from Tiree . . .' Randy said.

'You can tell that how?' Punch scoffed.

'The ferry I mean.'

'Oh? Aye. Right.' Punch looked to Randy and then back to the effigy. 'Thought you were referring to the missing eyebrows on the thing. They'd have them off you in a second.'

'CalMac?' Randy said, kicking the gravel as he puffed. 'Nothing surer.'

'No. The Tirisdichs,' Punch said.

'You weren't long in the pub last night?'

'No. But long enough to hear the usual shite from you and Tinsel. I pity that poor lass. I mean, how many times can you hear grown men burping "The Archbishop of Canterbury"?'

'Never enough.' Randy chuckled, causing a wheezing cough. 'Anything to keep Tinsel off the poetry.' He walked closer to the effigy and peered up at it. 'I'm seeing a touch of the Mr Blobbys about it.'

Punch turned inland to the road and to the light landing pleasingly on the snow tops of north Mull. Nobody from away ever seemed to know this was scenery people actually lived with, that that was enough, its main requirement. He released a trail of smoke. Somehow, he saw it escaping only to one destination: Lockerbie. To Charlie. He shook his head. Couldn't shift the woman's voice from the phone call earlier, maybe a domestic. Tourists up for the Festive. Sometimes he felt more like a marriage counsellor. Her voice reminded him now of the one on his doorstep in 1988 telling him about Charlie: a female officer, well spoken, hat to her stomach. A complete loss of control he had felt, matched only by his inability to show it. The aftermath led to him embracing the uniform even more, moving speedily up the ranks, and then to policing his island of birth. Given his local ties, he had been risk-assessed up the gazoo, and run through the ringer on competences, communication skills and initiative – all Guinness Speak. In the end, the strength of his local knowledge won over fears of nepotism.

'Hope nobody's seen it,' Punch said, glancing up and down the Gally Goo. 'Last thing I need is Guinness getting my gig full time.' He looked back to the effigy. 'Hung like a bull I suspect.'

'Guinness?'

Punch sent a steely stare towards his old classmate; he couldn't think of one reason why they had reconnected as friends on his return to the island, if that's what the arrangement was. He had always felt removed in some way from Mull, largely owing to having left for Inverness as a twelve-year-old. His brother's fate had only rubber-stamped that sense of separation.

'You die twice: once when you actually die, and then the last time somebody utters your name. And fuck.'

'Eh?'

28

'Nothing.' Punch cleared his throat. 'Aye, computers don't solve crimes, people do. It's no wonder about the poor stats since Guinness arrived.'

Records of any sort bothered Punch. And he wasn't sure whether he *did* want Charlie's name remembered. Was it less painful to forget? Even his brother's athletics records, listed every July in the Tobermory Highland Games programme, were a quandary; presenting as they did an equal measure of pride and unwanted reminder. The fact that the island's funeral director, Dave the Grave, hadn't been the one to box Charlie made it even harder to believe his brother was truly dead.

'Argyll & Bute: Scotland's number one hundred and one detective agency!' Randy chirped, interrupting Punch's bleak, troubling thoughts.

'Bugger the tables. Things are different on an island. Methods can't *be* measured. And fuck. Retrospective policing is the way. Now I know how Frankie bloody Miller felt when "Caledonia" came out.'

'Why?'

'Never got higher than eleven in the charts. Christ knows where I plucked that from. Suppose a cop never forgets.'

'Yip yip.'

Punch looked at him and felt a sudden tinge of disgust at the new name tag Randy was wearing on his fleece below the Forestry Commission logo.

'You need a name tag now for tackling the wife too? So Edna recognises you?'

'She recognised me this weekend, yip yip. Strap-ons, the lot.'

Punch's lip curled as he turned away to assess the scruffy effigy once more, making sure his own shirt was tucked properly into his trousers.

'Guinness: never seen such a clean-shaven face,' he said. 'Shoes like mirrors – a tiepin, for fuck's sake. On Mull? It's a wonder he hasn't snapped an eyelash on the job. I've a good mind to toss him and that bloody device of his in the cell for the night. Though of course he calls it a "custody suite". Bugger online.' Punch tapped his badger's temple. 'You can't replace what's up here.'

He thought of the woman on the phone again; how the classical music seemed to be as alive as her voice. He had decided against documenting it.

A crack came from the sky. Punch ducked to the side; his hat fell on the ground. A plane soared over them and out above the Sound.

'Just the RAF boys, yip yip.' Randy chuckled, swigging from a can just plucked from his pocket. 'Drills.'

Punch dropped down for his hat. The sky could have this effect on him. His DCI at Strathclyde would no doubt have him on the couch for this Iraq thing, PTSD. Sometimes he wished he had stayed stationed at Legacy Highlands Division in Inverness, where nobody knew him, or what he had lost. He had assumed his disability would be an issue, but he'd sailed through the police fitness test.

'Big bird ...' Randy croaked, turning his head in the direction of the plane.

'And she'd know what to do with it,' Punch said, replacing his hat. 'Sorry. Thought you were talking about Edna again.'

He drew in the last of the tobacco and flicked the stub towards the inferior mainland. He walked to the effigy and stood directly below it, bent for a stick and, with his longer arm, used it as a prod. His likeness swung liberally in the growing wind in the way of the sheep carcasses he hung in the station lockup come slaughter time, a pursuit he first witnessed in his uncle's small barn behind his house in Tobermory. 'Four days to dry them out. Easier to cut when stiff,' was about all his uncle – his father's brother – ever had to say of the process.

The effigy's eyes were fixed on him, and Punch looked away. He felt a shiver up his spine, seeing it now as one of the bodies hanging from the drainpipes on Lockerbie's Sherwood Crescent. Some still in their seats, for fuck's sake. The pilot and captain strapped upright in the detached, grounded cockpit cone, exactly as they had been 31,000 feet up in the air.

'Local kids, you reckon?' Randy gestured.

'No,' Punch said. 'Something more is my hunch. But leave the Miss Marples to me, man – since when did you wear a Police badge?'

'Or is it the knicker-knocker strikes again!'

'You'd know,' Punch said, referring to the recent case of women's underwear going missing from Tobermory washing lines. A crime he had since solved or, as the red tape brigade would never know, 'made go away'.

Randy walked to his pickup and returned with another can of Tennent's. He jutted the can to the effigy.

'Nah, local kids, I reckon. Yip yip. Getting you back for cautioning them for shooting thon' Rupert and Felicity tourist couple with the air rifle out on the Lighthouse Path.'

31

'Lucky they had no more than a nick on them.' Punch shook his head. He hadn't been out to the Lighthouse Path on the Mishnish end of the seafront since a young girl had tragically fallen to the rocks below, when he was just weeks into the job. The words 'GOD IS LOVE' had appeared not long after, painted in large white lettering on the dark granite cliff face. Whoever it was that maintained the upkeep of the letters was a mystery enough on the island. Passengers on the Kilchoan ferry slip had witnessed the whole brutal thing. Punch recalled cordoning off the incident area and having a sense of nature having been interrupted, of it not being allowed to take its due course. An inviolable line crossed. He knew what that felt like.

'Did you not say the couple who were shot at had their Wimbledon jumpers tied up around their necks?' Randy said.

'Aye, the buggers should've got a night of "Do Ya Think I'm Sexy" for that alone.' Punch angled his head and stood back, still facing the effigy. 'I think it's more. We'll see. This is police work from here on in. You lasted two weeks at catering college and now you're a professor.'

Punch kneeled and lowered both palms flat on the ground, a task that was not straightforward for him. He stared down as though reading something deeper in the dirt than was possible with the naked eye. He looked up and over to the Morvern peninsular, to the different shades of daylight landing on the land like thrown blankets. He would love to pin this on the mainland, but suspected otherwise.

'You're lucky no ferry traffic has passed, yip yip.'

'Let that be your last can till later. And fuck.'

'Fancy a go at thon' barmaid in Macgochans ...'

'Off you go now to count the trees on Tiree. I'm a fucking jailer too, remember. Folk don't realise that. We're police *and* custody officers on the islands.'

Punch was surprised to feel a longing stirring in him at the mention of the barmaid. He couldn't stop thinking how the poor lass always looked so sad behind the bar. No wonder. He heard Randy disrupting gravel on his way to the Forestry pickup. The engine cranking up. Was certain the man would have raised a fresh can as he drove off, but didn't give him the satisfaction of turning.

He stood up and addressed the mainland, lurking as it was like a gossip over a hedge. Even so, it was all quite beautiful and silent really. He didn't like the implication in the hanging any more than he did the puffy face or saggy arse. The noose represented something. That much was clear.

'Who the hell hung you?' he said to it. '*Me*?'

He took in the little coloured buildings in the distance, recognisable the world over. The island had drawn him back from the mainland, in the wake of Charlie. He sometimes wondered if the pull had been the power of the uniform, the control it allowed him over his old island, at a time when he had felt so lacking in it. Or had it been the mainland he had to leave, for it having taken his brother? He would routinely say to victims of crime or bereavement that he was *sorry for their loss* when, in truth, he wasn't, when in actuality he couldn't even let their loss touch his sides, let alone address his own. There was, he felt, probably more heart in the effigy.

A voice.

'Fuck ...' Punch caught his breath, briefly stunned into thinking the effigy had spoken.

The stillness of the Gally Goo filled up with the sound of Guinness's chocolate-coated Bearsden tones.

'L747 to L519. Do you receive? Over. Do you receive? Over.'

Punch looked both ways and crossed the road to his Ford Ranger. He leaned in and lifted the handset off the holder, mildly irritated by the unnecessary use of shoulder numbers; before Cluny's posting such feedthroughs would have come from a control room officer, or the acting shift sergeant in Oban – were he off duty, which was not often; off duty left too much time to think – and been a damn sight less irritating for it.

Mull fell within Legacy Strathclyde's L division, which, within its LB sub-division, policed Argyll & Dunbartonshire, encompassing the towns of Oban, Lochgilphead, Dunoon, Campbeltown and Rothesay. Officially, shifts ran from 8 a.m. to 6 p.m., 3 p.m. to midnight, and 6 p.m. to 4 a.m. at weekends, it being deemed doable to get from Tobermory to Bunessan on the Ross of Mull in time for any trouble after the pubs closed. Forty minutes was Punch's record.

'LB sub-division: L747 to L519. Do you receive? Over. Do you receive? Over.'

Guinness sounded to Punch like he had swallowed his space bar. But he had tuned to the open channel and so Punch lifted the handset and turned the dial to enable a more private conversation.

'Punch. Receiving. And take it down a notch, man, you're not Chris Tarrant on a Saturday night. Use my title not my shoulder number when transmitting locally. Over.'

34

'*A call's come in about a child. A child missing. Over. 11.30 hours. Do you read 51 – sorry, I mean, Sarge? Over. A child missing from Tobermory Primary School. Over.*'

'Right? I read you, PC Cluny. Over,' Punch said. *A child?* He opened the door and dropped to the driver's seat. Looked at the dash: 11.33. 'What age? On a Saturday? Over.'

'*Saturday club apparently. Eight years old. An Iris Hislop. Her mother is Sonia Hislop. She is with me now in the station. Over.*'

Punch inhaled deeply through his nose. He couldn't delay speaking much longer but needed a small moment. Just a breather. His voice, or lack of it, was likely being heard by the woman. Guinness was susceptible to such schoolboy errors. Punch gulped.

'Right. Eh, all likely explanations, school, friends ... favourite places and the like have been checked? Have they? Over,' he said.

'*Affirmative, Sarge. The mother has confirmed this. Over.*'

'Right, and eh ... description? Over.' Punch fixed his eyes closed, in receiving mode, but was not really receiving. Vomit was detectable in his gullet.

'*Red hair, shoulder length, Sarge. Slightly below average height. Skulls and bones on her schoolbag. Over.*'

'*Orange schoolbag,*' Punch heard; the woman's voice. Strangely composed.

'*Yellow coat,*' Cluny said. '*You said yellow coat, Miss?*'

'*Mrs,*' Punch heard.

'*Sorry, eh Mrs,*' Cluny said. '*A yellow coat?*'

'*Yes. I said that already.*'

Punch heard the woman's voice as shriller than he remembered. This Sonia Hislop. The barmaid. And noticeably

35

better spoken at this remove. He wanted to say more but didn't. Couldn't.

'*Sergeant?*' Cluny said. '*First port of call is to prompt special constable units? Over.*'

'Eh ... hold off. I'm heading back to the station now, PC.' Punch was irritated at Cluny's reference to the three locals he'd had trained as support staff as 'units'. 'I repeat. Hold off on any wider alerts, PC. Over.'

'*Really?*'

'Yes. Over.'

'*Affirmative. Loud and clear, Sarge. Over.*'

Punch wondered, could it have been the barmaid calling earlier? If she was Maggie May? The voice had sounded much too clipped, but you never knew with these arty types underneath all those cheekbones. She didn't strike him as a classical music lover, more like one of those dance freaks. Everyone knew her man had been a player in the music game and had chosen Mull as a getaway. Quite a clever bugger, apparently. But that was the thing Punch understood about people on an island: you never really knew them. Familiarity was not the same as knowing. Familiarity *masked* knowing.

He couldn't delay any longer. He flicked his stub out the window and turned the key in the ignition. He took a glance at the hanging effigy as he drove off, annoyed that he hadn't allowed Randy to cut the thing down, now that a bigger moment had arrived. Police work was all about instinct and prioritisation. You could manufacture all the flipcharts and tiepins in the world at Tulliallan, but they couldn't train that into you.

He listened to Cluny now monopolising his radio waves: everybody was on transmit these days, and nobody on receive. Twenty-four-hour news media and shops that never closed. No fucker could get a moment's peace from the hysteria or recognise different levels of importance anymore. Too much airtime to fill. Nothing was significant and everything was. Nothing was news and everything was. But a child missing was both, especially on a place considered as safe as Mull.

Punch had sensed Sonia Hislop's pain coming down the radio. For him, the job was more about the powers of watching and observation; it was about dealing with the invisible parts of people. He felt for the lass. Children were not supposed to disappear in this neck of the woods. A drunk, yes; fir trees off the Forestry land come Christmas, certainly – he was a *tree-scavenger* himself, for Christ's sake – but not a kiddie.

He pushed the accelerator towards the coloured houses in the distance, dotted as they were like a Spanish model town below the big, cloud-strewn Scottish sky, seeing them for the first time as bordering on garish. Maybe everything was fake, or modelled, replaceable with stuffed replicas. Even wee girls.

He felt a brick lodged in his stomach, unsure if it was Charlie or the lassie. Sometimes he wanted to paint the whole fucking town grey.

TRACK 4

PUNCH GRIMACED TO THE UNDECIDED sky as he pulled up outside the station; the pattern above him like a glaze gone wrong on a clay pot. He sighed towards the pebbledash, feeling a growing sense of foreboding. He couldn't let go of the steering wheel. Despite the nascent urgency of the case, all the way in from the Gally Goo he had felt a reluctance, no, an inability, to address it. This one felt personal. Unnecessary. He hated anyone losing anyone, especially more than once. That was like dying twice.

He had driven around the town in the act of looking for the girl. Outside the school, at the top of the Post Office Brae, everything had looked so quiet and not at all like a child could be missing. He had felt a duty to the mother to check the Aes and Back Braes, even scouting along the Main Street in between. But nothing. Really, he had been delaying the inevitable.

He had raised a finger reluctantly, pained, as was normal for him when unwittingly catching the eyes of folk on the seafront. As he turned around the clock tower his acknowledgement had been more genuine to the fishermen, one of whom, John MacLean – who, having the same name as the character played by Bruce Willis, went by the nickname Diehard – was positioned alongside the others at the end of the Old Pier in their garishly coloured oilskins, which did not match their monochrome characters, nor the impression some gave of shyness, of not wishing to be seen, as they dwarfed the hills of Morvern behind them. Punch identified with their daily pursuit of shoals, not unlike clues, as he did their isolation and sense of remove. Was the sea not a puzzle too?

Driving further along the seafront he noticed the squawks of seagulls for the first time since – *when*? Somehow connecting them with raising an alarm for the missing girl. But – unlike those dark December days of 1988 – the sense of a community about to be plunged into the chaos of losing one of its own was in no way evident; everyone appeared to be going about their usual morning business, which was just as well for the woman. He couldn't help wondering which of his fellow islanders had, at some surreptitious hour, been busy with a needle and thread, a ladder and rope, not to mention a paint brush and tin. But that line of enquiry, that particular groove in the vinyl, would have to be put on ice. For now. He had wished he *could* find the girl idling about somewhere, but he was feeling some sense of defeat about that possibility already. The image of Dave the Grave boxing the child was one he fought hard not to entertain.

Punch got out of the Ranger and closed the door quietly. He wasn't yet ready to announce his arrival, nor sure how to play it with the woman Hislop, but knew he couldn't delay any longer. Cluny would be like Taggart with a raging hard-on in there: all spreadsheets and fancy fonts. Punch filled his chest with cold air. In reality, he felt more like a keeper of secrets than he did law enforcer, especially with cases such as this one.

He felt an unwelcome kinship with Sonia Hislop, about such a public thing happening to such a seemingly private person. The embarrassment. The shame. He knew that what awaited him inside the station was going to require another kind of act, a level of subtlety he wasn't sure he possessed without a hit of Tobermory Malt. Nobody realised how difficult it was to move on from a day that the world seemed to want never to forget. How could you explain that to somebody while buying toothpaste or toilet roll, grief pulling on your face like fishhooks on gills?

He always had the feeling when around the woman Hislop, whether at the bar or even driving past her, that there were lines he should have learned in advance and marked positions he should know to be standing at; camera lights that if he could only detect them would instruct him where to look. The beginning of any case was akin to how he imagined walking onto a stage or film set. You had to be sure you were prepared, your composure set. His audience, which was how he thought of the residents of Mull – not to mention new deputies acting as stage-prompts despatched from the city with their mammies' saliva still wetting down the downy hair of their scalps – had to be in no doubt *he* was in control. He had once heard Laurence Olivier on an episode of *Desert Island Discs* on the BBC talking about how half his life was taken up observing people; how even on the London Underground or walking the streets of New York he was 'working' in a sense, which Punch had associated with his own acts of quiet surveillance, whether that be on the CalMac ferry, at Tobermory's petrol pump or in the Co-op opposite the clock.

Punch walked briskly to the station door. He wanted to push the other door instead, to the police house, to silence the world, to drop the needle on some early-era Rod and forget how much could be taken away from people. He wanted a little girl never to have landed on the rocks, a plane never to have fallen out of the sky. He pulled at his tie to loosen it, making sure it wasn't rope.

Cluny stood when his sergeant entered – a bit too eagerly, thought Punch – while continuing to input into his computer.

'Sarge!' Cluny said.

'Right . . .' Punch removed his hat and rubbed his badger's temples. 'No sign on the way in. Not yet. Anyway. No.'

Cluny waved his arms towards Punch as he turned to the woman.

'Miss Hislop, this is Sarge—'

'She knows who I am,' Punch said. 'And it's Mrs. She told you that already.'

The woman took a sharp intake of breath. She was sitting on the black plastic chair between the two desks with a glass of water by her lips, facing the window from which Punch, only hours earlier, had watched her passing, arm swinging. Punch noticed her glass was very slightly shaking. A tissue clutched in her fingers. The dark rings around her eyes and contrasting pale skin gave the impression of a dairy cow.

41

Still – strangely calm, he thought, for a missing wain, which Cluny had somehow failed to notice.

'So—' Punch said, unable to sustain any length of eye contact with anyone, and relieved he hadn't ordered a drop of Oban from her and a packet of salted peanuts. 'Can you, eh, tell me when you last saw her?' He turned to Guinness instead of the woman. 'I'm sure you'll have told PC Cluny here, but it would be helpful to hear it again. You know, in case it stirs anything in particular, well, eh, unusual ...' Punch motioned in the direction of Cluny and mouthed: '*Go. Search.*'

'Special constables are already out looking,' Cluny said. 'The school and other hot spots.' He scrolled down his screen. 'Okay ... already earmarked for lines of questioning we have ...'

'Nineteen ninety-two,' Sonia said.

'Right. Right.' Punch nodded, placing his hat from one hand to the other and then onto his desk.

'Sorry?' Cluny looked up from his screen to the woman, and then to Punch.

'When I last saw her ...' Sonia said into her glass. She was looking at Cluny through it. 'You asked the question?'

'But that's ...' Cluny pushed back from his keyboard, jutted his blond head back and forced an exasperated smile. 'Six years?'

Punch wished he would shut up. He also would prefer his deputy hadn't gone against his wishes and deployed special constables, but hopefully they would show some decorum given their local knowledge. There was a strange presence with her in the room. As though she owned the space, and he and Guinness were stagehands, or worse, prisoners. Punch had noticed it was the same with her in Macgochans. The Co, too.

'Eh ... the school?' Punch said, trying to salvage things for the woman in the headwind of Cluny's eagerness. He sat down at his desk, which had no photos on it unlike Cluny's busy array. Punch wondered if there was anyone in Scotland the man *wasn't* related to. 'You should go there now, PC Cluny. The school.'

'They've been prompted to call if anything transpires,' Cluny said, looking to his screen. 'There was concern about raising alarm with other pupils in the clubs.'

'My fucking God!' Sonia stood. She addressed the floor. 'Other pupils? Other fucking pupils! My wain's missing!'

'Look. Eh, I'm sure she'll be, eh, she's fine. Just fine,' Punch said, uncertain whether he was meaning the woman herself or her daughter. He turned to Cluny, knowing he needed to get rid of him pronto. 'Buses?'

'I've put a call in to central office,' Cluny said.

'Quicker if we do it. Try Bowman's at Scallastle. CalMac?'

'Notified,' Cluny said. 'Though ...' He checked the clock on his screen. 'Next ferry won't have made it to Oban yet, but we have LB officers on the other side.'

'Christ,' Punch said. 'Right. Eh, I mean good work. Good, good.' He looked to his deputy. 'When the last ferry goes, we're on our own. It's us. Just us.'

'Right, Sarge.' Cluny looked as though it was a detail he hadn't yet considered.

'Oban?' Sonia walked in circles. 'Fucking Oban? She's never been to Oban without me. Never had the *chance*!'

43

'And head office are primed for local media, Sarge,' Cluny said. 'Description circulated. ScotRail too.'

Cluny reached to give Sonia Hislop another tissue from the box on his desk; it was housed within another box like they did in hotels. He had even introduced houseplants to the station; to Punch it was like living in a rainforest. Maybe Sting and the other Police really *were* on their way.

'I'll call the bus company now,' Cluny said.

'Eh, no. I'll do it.' Punch gestured. 'You go back to the school now. We need to establish timeframes and . . . eh . . .' He glanced at Sonia. 'Such as whether there's been anything unusual or anyone unexpected on site. New faces or the like. External, weekend staff. Even deliveries from the mainland.'

'Sorry, Miss, eh, *Mrs* Hislop,' Cluny tried, 'is there anywhere else she could possibly be? Favourite spots?'

'Iris!' Sonia shouted, sitting again and slapping her hand on Punch's desk. 'Her. Name. Is. Iris!'

'Yes. Of course it is,' Punch said, casting daggers at Cluny. 'Uh-huh.'

Sonia held the tissue to her mouth.

'Okay. We'll, eh, we'll find her,' Punch assured, noticing the delicate stud of her nose piercing for the first time.

'Changes in behaviour? Anything at home?' Cluny pressed, his arms folded. 'Tiff with a friend maybe?'

Punch took this continued line of questioning as an attack on him, on his act of – as Cluny seemed to have perceived it – prematurely assuring the woman that her daughter would be safely found.

'Tiff with a friend?' Sonia said. 'You mean me or her?' She jumped to her feet again, dropping the tissue. 'I don't have any.'

Punch leaned quickly to pick up the tissue; it was his shorter arm and so he was down longer than he wanted.

'Leave it!' Sonia snapped.

Punch eased back up. He felt a strange sense of competition with Guinness. But he was unsure whether it was professional or otherwise. He hadn't felt *otherwise* in years. Was sure folk talked all sorts about the things he got up to alone in the station house. The Clock uses *both hands*, *rings his bell*, and the like. Stuff about inviting in horses' heads too.

'God,' Sonia said, shaking her head and trying to catch her breath. 'I ... I need to get out and ... and ... *search* ... I ...'

'Look, is there anything else you can think of?' Punch said, standing, offering and then withdrawing the used tissue. 'At all?'

'Right, I'll decamp to the school, Sarge – A-SAP,' Cluny said, peering into his screen like he might find the girl or an international stock market crash in there. 'There first, then I'll report back on co-ordinating searches of the town thereafter. This is going to blow open then.'

'No,' Punch said, staring at Cluny as though his deputy was on fire. He was disgusted with the man's use of *A-SAP*, if not his choice of words at the expense of decorum. 'I'll notify wider with the descriptions, lines of enquiry. Boots on the ground if needed. Search of the missing person's home address always comes first.'

'Yes, anything at all could help enormously. Especially from the home,' Cluny said in staccato fashion in the direction of them both, which made Punch want to take the

45

man's jaw clean off. His forebears had form in this department. Giving rise to his adopted surname.

'Yes. Okay,' Sonia said, breathing heavily. 'Thank you. I'm sorry, sorry, it's just ...'

'No need,' Cluny said.

He grabbed his scarf, sped for the door and closed it behind him.

Punch was relieved they were finally alone. He appreciated now just how exhausting it was for the man Olivier. How deft he must have been at making made-up things appear believable.

'Did they check the golf course?' Sonia said, more sheepishly, running her hands through her hair. 'I didn't hear anything about it, the golf course. Sorry. You know ... for badgering him,' she said, gesturing to the door.

Punch attempted a half-smile. Felt the need to raise his hand to cover his temple.

'It's fine. He's a walking flipchart, but aye, means well ... I, eh, checked all likely places. I did. If that's what you want me to say. I'm not sure what to say. What you want to hear?'

Punch was aware of her checking if he was looking at her. He wasn't. She breathed loudly in and out, taking regular small sips from the glass like the snooker players he had seen on the TV. She leaned into the back of the chair. Punch imagined the glass – now placed between her legs – might explode in her cupped hands.

'I feel as though my ... my *suitability* for parenthood is being questioned ... all the time. Every day. Here,' she explained. 'Even from the bay. But I can't seem to leave. Despite what the locals probably think, I haven't touched a drug in years. My God, me and Sean swapped Ibiza for here? "Just *island hopping*," he called it. And then they both ... left. They left me here.' She brushed her hand over the glossy leaves of one of Cluny's plants. 'Within two years – how?'

Punch dropped to his desk. He lifted the handset.

'Sergeant Punch to PC Cluny. Do you receive? Over.'

There was a crackle and then: '*Receiving, sergeant. Over.*'

'The girl has thankfully been found,' Punch said. 'Call off all ground investigations. Over.'

They both heard Cluny's confused, self-important, adrenaline-fuelled voice coming back over the speaker. A hint of disappointment.

'The girl has been found, PC Cluny,' Punch repeated, interrupting his deputy. 'The desired outcome. Head office notified. Please stand down all other search satellites. I'll do transport. Over.'

'*Message received, Sergeant Punch. A relief. Will carry out as instructed. Over.*'

Punch thought he might as well give Cluny his day in the sun with the local special constables. Head office, too.

'I'll explain to him later,' Punch said to Sonia. 'More police nous in one of his pot plants.'

Punch dialled a number and was aware of Sonia listening as he told a CalMac representative that the search was a false alarm.

Punch moved a little closer to Sonia, as though he might not have been properly heard where he had been.

'We just needed to get word out quickish.' He spoke more softly. 'You know, in case folk started searching, eh, wider. Properly.'

47

'To save my face, you mean. I get it.'

'Don't want you going through all that again. You know.'

'*All that*? One way of putting it.' Sonia rested the glass against her forehead. She looked at the constable's photos.

'I've a picture of Iris on my bedside table. It's alongside the one of Sean on a stage at some festival in Europe. Wearing a t-shirt of Kurt Cobain in a wheelchair. Who had died on Sean's birthday. A sign all along? I don't have one of them together, of course.'

'No.'

'Sean's end wasn't at all, well, *him*: it was far too quick, too quiet, too hard to draw creativity from.'

'Right,' Punch attempted.

'It was him who wanted to move here, he'd taken family holidays on Mull as a kid. Had become estranged from his mother, a bit of a nutcase, and the island provided a sanctuary. At first. Or more like a place to block things out.'

'I believe he was very successful. In the charts too, they say?'

'He won a Brit Award and a loyal following. But wanted to escape the attention, the increasingly bonkers fans. I joked he was doing his Paul McCartney farm bit. I remember at the time of Iris, you know, I'd been so fucked up I wondered if I could blame it all on one of them.'

'It was a hellish thing.' Punch gulped heavily. 'I can understand you not wanting to leave.'

'Nothing could've prepared me for being a parent without Sean, or for what was to follow. He would've been a great dad. Maybe then she wouldn't have ... It's like a loss of myself, of *significance*. The sight of all his recordings in carrier bags next to old mattresses and kitchen appliances. All those stories. Fuck.'

'Sounds like he was a big loss to a lot of people.' Punch felt as though he was reading from a manual again.

'It was his heart that finally took him. The same thing that kills everyone else. Still can't get my head around that – they used to say his music was full of it. Heart.'

'And it's been harder of late, has it?'

Sonia paused, her breathing intensifying, her head bowed as though a cloak of darkness were being thrown over her again. 'You never found out!' she said, her voice shifting, rising. 'Never did your fucking job?' She looked at Punch for the first time. 'All that time ago – and we still don't know who pushed her over the bloody cliff edge?'

TRACK 5

PUNCH STOOD FROM HIS DESK and walked to the window. Cluny would have been a welcome distraction. But nothing. Just the sea.

'Look, Mrs His—'

'I mean, it's been almost six years!' Sonia interrupted. 'Were you too new to the job? Was that it?'

'Look, we went over this at the time ... accidents do not killers make. I'm sorry. But that hasn't changed.'

Sonia turned her head. Her breathing became more aggressive.

'And I ... I ... *was* a good mother. Despite what this island thinks! Or any other fucking island.' She gulped heavily and slammed the glass down on Punch's table. 'I'm the one who's left looking like a fool. Hanging about the school gates, for crying out loud. On a Saturday! Pathetic. Just to keep her alive. Just because you couldn't find a killer.'

'Look, people don't, they don't think that, I'm sure. Some folk don't really know grief. We ourselves don't even

50

recognise it at the time it's happening to us, because it's wrapped up in ... well, things like shock.'

'Yes,' Sonia said, deadpan. 'We learn to "live with it".'

'Try to,' Punch said. 'Try to.' Sometimes he felt more like a sergeant of the dead than the living.

'But twice,' Sonia said. 'Twice, to me?'

Punch nodded, turning his head.

'Aye,' he said. 'I know.'

'He asked me to marry him days before the end, his hand on my womb. Sometimes I think he knew something I didn't. He was breathing like an old man. Empty shelves where his music had sat proudly.'

Punch nodded; cleared his throat.

'Only weeks after, I'd wanted it all back,' she said. 'Went walking out the Glengorm Road past the Sgriob-ruadh Farm – their Mull Cheddar we'd seen on a menu in London and taken as a sign – to the dump. I wanted the framed picture of him with David Byrne of Talking Heads. Sean was so fucking proud of that. The bottle of Chateauneuf-du-Pape with the handwritten note taped on: 'To Sean, I wanted to get you Buckfast but this will have to do. All the best! Michael and R.E.M.' But it was all gone. And when I got back to the house he was too. Like an empty room, already mourned.'

'I'm sure it felt like that. It does, I know.'

'And then ... my precious Iris, two years later. Letting go of my hand on the Lighthouse Path. "*Boat! Mummy!*" Running away around the next corner. Out of sight. "*Mummy! Boat!*" The sound of the gravelly verge. Giving way. Rocks falling. A scream. Shrieks, shrieks down below.'

51

'Christ.' Punch stood. At the time, only weeks into the job, he had wondered if the little girl was running off to join the father she'd never known. 'Not sure this is helping you,' he told her. 'I can get you home.'

'All over in seconds: motherhood.' Sonia raised her hands out in front of her. 'Sean's *real* legacy. I knew I could never be a good mother again. Was sure I'd leave Mull afterwards; leave the, well ... the memories were everywhere. Are. But my wee girl was here. *Is* here. I'm caught between the past and present ... between him and her, the cliff edge and the rocks below. Sometimes I feel like I'm hanging in mid-air.'

Punch realised the words could have been his own.

'Even Calve opposite ... sitting there in the sea? As if fucking, fucking gawking! Her.'

'Who?'

'Oh everyone!' Sonia took another sip. Ruffled her hair. Gazed blankly out of the window. 'Sorry ... I know you did all you could. I do. It was just we had a kind of Morse Code between us – Iris and me – I'd squeeze her hand and she'd repeat the pattern back to me. We didn't need words. But that day it didn't work ...'

'Those are the good memories, eh? It wasn't your fault.' Punch remembered as kids how he and Randy, then still Alastair, would cycle out along the Lighthouse Path, seemingly unaware of the sheer drops to the sea. His silver Grifter. Walkie-talkies and fake accelerator twist grips. 'Silver Fox', his radio handle. Charlie on stabilisers would be left waiting for them at the path's beginning. Too young for the ride. Punch pushed a hand through his salt and pepper and sighed, aware the radio handle was becoming more accurate than ever.

'I know you did all you could,' he heard again.

'I was new in the role, but I felt I did.' Punch cleared his throat. 'There was nobody else on the path or the surrounds.' He understood her desire to apportion blame, whether that be to individuals or whole countries, entire continents or small towns; to people in Libyan deserts who didn't speak the same language, use the same alphabet as you. 'We checked all likelihoods and possibilities. It was ... well ... a tragic accident. Folk here know that.'

'Not everyone.'

Punch opened his drawer and took out a bottle. He took her glass gently from her and tipped its remains into Guinness's plant.

'Best keep Alan Titchmarsh here happy.' He poured from the bottle into the emptied glass. 'It must be strange for *you* to be the one waited on.' He half-smiled, a little hopelessly he knew. Forced smiles were the only ones he could do really. He placed the malt in front of Sonia.

She held it with both hands, lowering her head to her knees as though to concentrate, to summon something alive from the past.

'I took my eye off her for ... just ... well ...' She swallowed deeply. 'I haven't admitted that to anyone else.'

Punch nodded.

'It's like she was really there this morning. More than ever. Really with me. I wanted to make it real. You know?'

'I do.' Punch recalled the sight of her passing by earlier alone, how you never really knew what was going on with another person. Even on an island, maybe especially on an island.

53

'It's just that it's soon to be Christmas,' Sonia said. 'And tomorrow, you know, the anniversary.' She took a sip from the glass.

'Lockerbie?' Punch blurted. 'Eh no. No. Of course. Right.' He poured a measure for himself. He still couldn't fathom the chances of the little girl falling on the same day, a mere four years later, as Charlie.

'It's still a blur,' Sonia said. 'Like a film running on mute and you keep hoping for a different ending.' She looked up. 'For some reason I thought you lived in *this* side.'

'No,' Punch said, draining the glass.

'And the cell? *Is* there a cell?'

Punch nodded to a robust blue door at the far end of the room, opposite the back door.

Sonia slowly nodded, as she said, 'More compact than the old prison with the creels outside.'

'Uh-huh. As well ghosts can't be locked up.'

'Many bookings?' she asked.

'Not this month. The Christmas rush is still to come.' Punch forced a cheekbone a tad higher. 'I blame catering. Or Cluny's aftershave. Dare say toilet roll would help attract the crowds.'

She smiled. 'I find it easier … easier to picture Iris on canvas, to find her there. I used to make theatre sets. Costumes too. In Glasgow. That's how me and Sean met. On a Children in Need BBC show. It was November the seventeenth. I was good at it.'

'Right?' Punch was pleased to hear the lass open up, though the costumes disclosure arrived like an exclamation mark.

'That's what the counsellor said. To try and paint her. But I only ever see her on that path. Haven't been able to walk

54

out there again. Even the sight of the little lighthouse keeper and his dogs sets me off. Morse Code again.'

'I see him too.'

'He ties the dogs outside the Co. They sit so obediently.'

'I've thought that too.'

'Why don't I paint her? Really *see* her. Too busy pulling pints, turning beds . . .'

'Have you tried the Little Theatre in Dervaig?' *Was she capable of the effigy?* She clearly harboured a motive.

'Recruitment too?' She smiled.

'Just add it to the job spec. You've seen *Local Hero*?'

'I shouldn't be here talking away.' She stood. 'All these poor folk with *actual* people missing.'

'You are missing somebody.' Punch downed the remains of the glass. 'People.'

'I'm a nutcase. Officially,' she said. 'Walking to school with an empty schoolbag . . .'

'I'm sure you're not that at all.' Punch stood and walked to the window and then back to his desk. 'It affects everyone differently. It was a hellish trauma you suffered. Both times. That's a lot. More than most could take.'

Punch felt the brick in his stomach again. He recalled the ashen-faced tourists being taken off the Kilchoan ferry. One minute they had been spotting minke whales, the next witnessing a wee girl fall one hundred feet to her death. They had all been asked to stay on the vessel until questioning could be carried out. When they finally disembarked, most looked straight ahead, avoiding eye contact with the makeshift tarpaulin covering. The cliff face unmarked, dark granite as nature intended, before those white letters appeared.

'Does anybody here *not* know everybody else's business?' Sonia asked, sipping. 'I do my best but ...'

'I'm sure you do. You are not under investigation here. It's just that goldfish don't have far to swim in a bowl, it's the same on an island.'

He couldn't help wondering, was she walking this morning on her way back from the Gally Goo? It would certainly have to be done early, before prying eyes surfaced. Could the kiddie alert have been a cover?

Sonia dabbed the tissue around her eyes. She seemed battered by life and Punch reached to take another from the floral box on Cluny's desk.

'All the bugger's missing is a cosmetics counter.' He tried to smile, handing the tissue box to her. 'Like John bloody Lewis in here.'

'Cheers,' Sonia said, becoming a little lighter, nodding repeatedly. 'Sorry. I usually keep some kind of a lid on things. On them both. Today, though, feels like a doom-loop.' She took a deep breath and pressed her hands on her forehead. 'It's just all the other wee girls you see going into the school. Growing bigger.'

'Understandable,' Punch said. He had heard she sometimes hung around at school drop-off and pick-up times. Thought as much when Cluny had first radioed through. He saw an image of Charlie waving from the gangplank as he boarded the ferry that last time. A Christmas trip to New York, for Christ's sake. Craignure Pier like a gateway to the world.

'There are people you can still talk to,' Punch offered, looking up to the posters sent from Control pinned to the

56

board. Now uniformly aligned, thanks to his deputy. 'I'll run you home,' he added. 'Have you a shift?'

'At the Western. But they're used to me taking off. Some of them probably actually believe she *is* still alive.'

He wondered if news of the effigy was out, and whether that had been the real reason for his search of the town earlier, given he had known the missing child in question was buried up in Tobermory graveyard, where Charlie wasn't. Before leaving Mull, they had lived in the house right next to the graveyard. They would play around the graves and one in particular always stood out to him, the one with the words 'Unknown Sailor' engraved into the stone. A German U-boat commander washed ashore to Mull during the Second World War without any identification on him, a lost man whom the islanders had buried. It never occurred to Punch then that parts of everyone were unknown in a way. But who on the island could think of him now as deserving to be hung? As a saggy arse? As heartless; as a stuffed creature literally without a heart? Surely not her?

He did have a heart.

There had been Janice for a while, in Inverness, a primary school teacher from Elgin. His posting back to the island had conveniently put paid to her becoming too close. Janice, who had been the first to contact him when she heard about the plane – about Pan Am Flight 103 – despite never having met Charlie; Janice, who by then had married and who no doubt now had an army of wains each sporting her dark curls. Before, they would ride up to John o' Groats in the second-hand soft-top he briefly allowed himself. Her blasting Bach, for Christ's sake, into the Highlands; he

57

making the case for Bolan, sporting the old-style motorcycle helmet she had given him for his thirtieth birthday, and hoping not to get pulled over by Tulloch, his first sarge in the Highlands, all six-foot-four of him stuffed like a giraffe into a Panda. Janice with engagement on her mind, and he knew it. He trying not to be playing a part; attempting to be like other, normal people; trying to lie in her bed surrounded by her school marking and not be thinking of the German family who, unbeknown to them, had one of their own lying in Scottish soil without his name on a stone.

'No. Thanks,' Sonia said, her face paler. 'I better walk. People talk enough around here.'

'No need. I'll drive you. Nobody will hear about this from me.' Punch looked to Cluny's desk. 'From us. Just need a match for that computer.' He wondered if a scout around her place might reveal material scraps, failed mismatched arms, a discarded foamy truncheon.

Sonia smiled. Punch noticed how it fair lightened up the girl, a whole room even.

He put his hat on and opened the door, motioning for Sonia Hislop to walk out first.

'Actually. Take me round the town please,' she said, stepping towards the Ranger. 'I need to see for myself . . .' Her voice broke.

'That she's definitely not missing?' Punch said, wishing he hadn't.

'No. No. I know she's not missing. I meant, to make sure that nobody is out searching.'

'Best I get you home. The few who know will understand. Beyond that, bugger them.'

Punch moved quickly after her to open the passenger door and Sonia stepped apprehensively into the Ranger, which he noticed all people instinctively did, even if just being given a lift up the hill with their messages. He hurried to the driver's side, briefly under the illusion that John o' Groats or some other end point of a land might be waiting for them.

They drove past the tarmac tennis court – which Punch remembered in his youth had sheep acting as line judges and not a true bounce on it – and the football pitch. Cries of children having fun. He felt the burn of Sonia Hislop's stare cutting across him towards the park. The newly levelled-off surface of the pitch appeared almost futuristic and other-worldly to him, a far cry from the ski-sloped affair of his childhood. As difficult as it would be for her, he hoped the sight of the children playing was a clear sign to the lass that the town was operating normally, that no harm was done.

'Stop,' Sonia said.

Punch pulled the Ranger over.

Sonia jumped out, crossed in front of the vehicle and stood at the park railings. Punch watched as she stared down towards the play area. A young mother was pushing her toddler on swings. A local lass. Punch recognised her but didn't know her name. He could barely keep up with the turnover of kids; he was still recovering from an old classmate having just become a grandmother.

He noticed Cluny's Ranger on the other side of the park, next to the school, and then Cluny himself, his shock of blond hair, arms folded, deep in conversation with a female special constable.

'Unfold your arms, man,' Punch muttered. 'You're not a fucking football manager. Be chewing gum next.'

He remembered the yellow RAF helicopters that used to land on the football pitch. Charlie always enjoyed that. Sometimes they would be allowed to leave class to watch one take off. Once there was a rumour it was a famous Hollywood actor arriving for a film being made locally. Donald Sutherland or somebody. As a child, he always saw it as the mainland arriving. He turned back, but Sonia Hislop wasn't there. He looked to the park and she was running across it, clouds of breath escaping from her. Punch gulped heavily, seeing an image flash of Charlie running there, about to break the finish line in the cross-country on a trip back to the island; he was always first, even to death.

Punch jumped from the Ranger and sped towards the road to the park. A car horn sounded. The sound of skidding. Punch thrust an arm out and the car stopped a foot from his hip. He forced a smile and waved to the local, tapped their bonnet. The wave was returned and the car slowly took off.

Cluny was walking towards Sonia on the other side of the pitch and Punch knew he needed to get to her first. He had hoped to avoid this for the lass.

'PC Cluny!' Punch shouted urgently, crossing the pitch.

Cluny swerved to her like he was attempting a rugby tackle.

'Fuck, man,' Punch wheezed.

He watched Sonia Hislop sidestep his deputy towards the school building. She continued up through the car park towards the upper school gates.

'The child is found or not found, sergeant?' Cluny demanded.

'Aye. Well, no. I'll explain,' Punch said. 'Wait here, please. Both of you.'

He progressed around the school building. Sonia Hislop was walking in circles up at the gates. He saw the heavy-coated figure of Tinsel approaching her, plumes of smoke surrounding him. They fell deep into conversation as Tinsel rubbed his hands together to warm them. How much did Tinsel know? The old man had spent time in the London rag trade if you believed his shite – was he an accomplice?

As Punch got closer, Tinsel peeled off and walked quickly away down the hill.

Sonia was still now, gazing in the direction of the new nursery building next to the school gates. It was eerily quiet, little welly boots neatly stored upside down on specially made rounded wooden stumps.

'Mrs Hislop,' Punch said, when he arrived, his gaze taken by the infants' sandpit. 'Let's get you home.' He could see she was lost to him again. 'We, eh, have everyone looking for Iris.'

'We do?' Cluny said, catching up behind.

Punch turned to him, grimaced hard and shook his head.

Cluny simply looked confused.

Punch walked Sonia back down across the pitch to the Ranger. Had half a mind to fly by Tinsel's in search of a needle and thread; then there was his twin, the local oddball. Were either of them capable? He had taken Tonsils in for questioning a few times over the years. There was the knick-er-knocker case, and even recently he had brought the man over in connection with the tennis couple from away who had been spooked by the air rifle. There was always the talk of Tonsils spending too much time around kids too, plonking them up on his old motorbike, a post-war model. Making them wooden swords and the like. Punch had benefited himself in the past. On the latest occasion Tinsel had arrived at the station not best pleased. Punch had threatened them both with the cell but knew he had nothing concrete. The man's poetry wasn't quite criminal enough.

Looking at her walking in front of him, Punch thought again of Sonia Hislop's reckoning that he had failed her daughter. Was there a different answer, an alternative motive?

He drove her down the Western Road and turned left onto Memorial Road, then pulled up at the hotel.

'I'm not sure God has anything to do with it anymore,' Sonia said from the passenger's side, facing the hotel entrance, as he reversed into the car park. 'You know, on the cliff face . . .'

Punch gulped. He took off his hat, turned to her and then away again, briefly catching that her earrings were small silver crosses. He remembered first seeing them in the aftermath of Iris. Hadn't pegged her as the religious type, but he guessed it had comforted the woman.

'That's what I wanted at the time,' she said. 'Those words. Strange how a girl returns to Catholicism when, well, everything else fails. But I'm not sure now.'

'I just saw it in Iris's obituary in *The Oban Times*—'

'God Is Love. I know. I began to walk with God again, but not in a church way. But even that's gone now.' Sonia put her hand on the door handle. 'But thank you for painting it. I knew it was you. You didn't have to do that. I haven't been able to go and look at it.'

Punch nodded. 'I saw your man's lyric too,' he said, 'you know, in the paper.'

'Yes.' Sonia brought her hand up in front of her. '*I'll share my loss with you* ... Not enough room for that, on the cliff.'

He thought she might sing.

'I wanted to paint like the painters who really moved me,' she said, as though seeing something other than the arched hotel entrance. 'The ones who made us really *see* ourselves, you know?'

'Right.'

'I felt a terrible disappointment when I realised I was in Sean's shadow. That all the things in my head were not on the canvas, the way his were in his music. And I felt guilty about experiencing some small relief from that feeling when he ... well ... But then Iris. Who made it all less heart-breaking. Made him sing again in a way. And me. But even that couldn't last. I haven't admitted that out loud before.'

'The letters on the cliff will,' Punch heard himself saying, knowing it wasn't close to enough. 'Last, I mean.'

Sonia Hislop jumped from the Ranger and left the door open.

Punch watched her take the steps to his left and release the latch on the gate that led up to the chalets overlooking the hotel. The handset sounded with information from Oban that no sightings of the missing girl from Mull had been made at either the bus or ferry terminals. He reached for the device and reprogrammed the broadcast channel, setting it to LB sub-division, meaning the ears of Oban

Lochgilphead, Dunoon, Rothesay and Campbeltown would be tuned in, as would the case controller situated in either Glasgow or Edinburgh. *God* himself, for all he knew.

'Silver Fox to all divisions: the girl has been found. Over.' He realised what had come out of his mouth. 'Eh, this is Lima 519 requesting talk through. Over.'

'*Receiving. Request granted, sergeant. Over,*' came the controller's response.

'The missing child on Mull has been found and is safe and well. No criminality involved. Search called off. Repeat: call search off. Over.' He took his finger off the talk button. 'And fuck.'

The handset replied, but he didn't hear it. If procedures were being correctly enforced, he was supposed to carry the device with him at all times. But he wasn't feeling very procedural. He opened the driver's door and put his hat on. Jumped out and closed the passenger door. Stepped up to the gate.

The door to Sonia's prefab chalet was already open when Punch reached it. He walked inside and removed his hat. Heard female voices. He turned into the small sitting area where there was no child, nor hint of a child, nor of Dave the Grave, nor a short coffin laying in wake as there had been the last time he was inside the home of Sonia Hislop in 1992.

That was a relief.

Punch nodded to the two women who were rubbing Sonia's arms. Both attempted desperate smiles in his direction. The older of the two closed her eyes knowingly, her skin dark and wrinkled. Punch noted her big square head, which looked too heavy for her neck, like it had been carved from stone. Tattoos up her arm.

'No. No,' the woman said, her accent Eastern European.

'No good come of this Sonia ...' said the other.

'Right ... Right ... Course ...' Sonia said, nodding rapidly and wiping her eyes. Seeming to come to again, she looked around the sparsely furnished room. 'Did you finish your shift at least?'

'No worry about shift,' the first woman said. 'Poor baby Sonia.'

Punch turned away and walked out. He hadn't looked for materials for outfits. Sleet was falling, forming a steel-grey light on the surface of the earth. He had a sense of walking through a kind of fairy tale. As though, just fleetingly, anything was possible on Mull. Even resurrection.

'*Sergeant Punch, are you receiving?*' The voice floated up. It was Cluny, sounding excitable and short on breath. '*Over.*'

'Can't escape the fucker ...' Punch grumbled, looking out to the welcoming flatlands of Calve Island and the solitary white house on it. It belonged to a family called Damask. Occasionally you would see the old lady rowing in for her messages, like a cotton bud given oars.

Punch grimaced towards the faded green slide outside the chalet opposite Sonia Hislop's, and the little yellow welly boots discarded haphazardly beside it, poking through the light snow covering. Not easy for her, he thought. It looked too much to him like a child had fallen to Earth. He wrestled with his own motives in having followed the barmaid the night before, after Tinsel had left her alone. He was still unsure whether it was police work or more. Whether *more* was even possible for him now. Certainly, Janice had given up. He wondered, had he *wanted* to be discovered rustling in the foliage? He wasn't usually that clumsy. Maybe he was losing his touch. Sonia Hislop had looked to him like an image from a movie poster with the bay glistening below her. Propped above the clock tower. There was a 'straight to video' quality to the scene, which he was fine with.

'*PC Cluny to Sergeant Punch. Over! Are you receiving? Station to Sergeant Punch!*'

Punch took the steps in twos, dispersing the squawking seagulls from the hotel bins by the Ranger. The gate latched behind him.

'Want me to hook you up to a microphone and a set of speakers too, Cluny? Ronnie Wood on guitar?' he said into the handset, wrapping the cord around his hand. 'Punch. Receiving. Over.'

'*Sarge, I've received reports of a Mull plane. Missing. Over.*'

Punch pressed on the handset but couldn't speak. Felt part of him retreating. Was he inside his dream again?

He dropped the handset, but the voice persisted from the floor.

'*Repeat. A plane missing, Sarge. Over.*'

TRACK 6

PUNCH PULLED INTO PEBBLEDASH HQ. He was in no rush to go inside.

Cluny had confirmed on the way that a woman was going to call back shortly with more information on the plane, from the Lussa Falls Hotel apparently. The hotel sat just outside Salen, situated ten miles from Tobermory under the chin of the sleeping bear of Mull, nestling in the shadows of Ben More. Punch had toyed with heading there directly, but didn't want Guinness making an arse of things. The hotel had the only airfield on the island.

He felt his collar tightening again and was certain the grip was also something to do with Sonia Hislop. It had just turned 3 p.m. but it felt like the day had already lasted a month. He recalled his first posting after police college in Inverness, before Janice, before the badger temples set in, and Sergeant Tulloch telling him just how quickly police work could move. On Mull he was more used to showing face at Monday's Farmers' Market, or informing the council of deer carcasses needing clearing and the like; helping old

Kitty MacLean with her messages up the Aes Brae or checking on teenagers arsing about after school on the Main Street. In fact, he had half a mind to arrest a few of them, who he'd noticed had formed a covers band called The Lovesick Zombies. He was less used to his daily routines transitioning between cases of grief-stricken mothers and missing planes. Planes didn't go missing. They landed on hillsides; fell on towns. It was people who went missing. Never to return.

The Lussa Falls hosted the island's annual light aircraft show every summer, on a field alongside the Sound of Mull with goalposts at each end, which, when it wasn't a football pitch, was cleared of sheep and doubled as a landing strip. Punch recalled Pink Floyd's Dave Gilmour landing there several times. Randy claimed to have his autograph, but Punch maintained the squiggle could just as plausibly have come from Stevie Wonder or one of his Hebridean rams. Randy had asked how he knew Stevie Wonder kept rams and Punch had nearly arrested him there and then.

He removed the keys from the ignition, locked the Ranger and walked to the station. The afternoon light was failing and the air feeling heavier. He couldn't look to the sky for evidence. The sky couldn't be trusted.

Punch entered and Cluny was already on the phone, leaning forwards in his chair, typing as he spoke—

'And are you a resident in the hotel, Miss Lauder? Please – please speak slower. Sleet, yes, you mentioned sleet already . . . Take your time . . .'

Punch motioned for the phone.

'Take a breath, ma'am, that's it,' Cluny said, wrapping the cord around his fingers and leaning away from his superior. 'Is there staff to comfort you right now? Okay. We'll be with you in twenty minutes and we'll assess requirements for wider searches.'

'The Lussa Falls? We'll be there in twelve, man. And fuck.' Punch looked into the computer screen on his desk as though it might have mice turning on wheels inside it. All he saw was his reflection.

'Okay, Miss Lauder, sit tight and we'll be with you forthwith. *Over*. I mean, goodbye. Bye.'

Punch wondered if the man even said 'over' when he had finished doing the business between the sheets.

Cluny let the handset drop from the vice of his neck and shoulder, catching it elegantly with his hand. He hung it up and slowly eased his neck in short, staged jerks back to centre, gradually increasing the speed of this action to a pendulum motion. Punch watched incredulously, his mouth ajar.

'All we need is David fucking Attenborough whispering over this ... So?'

'Sorry, Sarge, I thought I should continue on the call, you know, continuity of evidence.'

'The clue's in my title. Next time, hand it over.'

Cluny leaned intently into his keyboard and rattled his fingers furiously on the keys as he spoke. 'A light aircraft, last known location is the Lussa Falls Hotel, a Cessna F150H, registration N-Number G-AVTN, left the airfield at approximately 21.03 last night. Hasn't returned.'

'That's not very approximate.' Punch looked at the wooden-framed station clock on the wall, *Tobermory*

69

Highland Games inscribed on it. He had won it in the Games raffle, was sure it had been rigged. 'It left last night and we're hearing this now?'

Punch lit a cigarette. Puffed quickly. Glad for the cover. He wanted to hide from the memory of ten years earlier, when, just a few days after he had seen Charlie off on the ferry – both of them having been back on the island visiting their mother – news of the disaster came via a live broadcast during a poker game with Randy and his Forestry cohort. Randy had drained his can, unaware of the connection to come, and said 'poor bastards' in the direction of the little TV set in the corner. Punch had felt the blood draining from his face as he tried to play his hand. Unable to say anything; trying to estimate how many planes likely took off for New York each day. And later, sitting in the car park in the darkness of Calgary Beach, on the island's Atlantic coast, grief clinging to him like salt from the ocean. Trying but not succeeding to make sense of the emotional disconnect he felt to a global news story that apparently involved ... *him*? Or was it only news in Randy's house, on Randy's portable TV set; was it confined to there? It felt like a black blanket had been thrown over Mull. The ocean was so dark the island could have been the mainland. His mother unaware, out at a whist drive. He had kept a poker face ever since.

Now, Punch gulped, his Adam's apple acting like it wanted to escape. He took several deep draws and blew out. Cluny made a small drama of coughing and wafting away the smoke drifting towards him.

'Taken for an intended short flight, Sarge, hasn't been seen since.' Cluny nodded to his screen.

70

'To New York?'

'Eh?' Cluny looked like he was explaining snow to a Martian. 'From Lussa Falls? You okay, Sarge?'

'Eh, aye. Aye. A Cessna. Right.' Punch studied Cluny's screen.

'Apparently, this model, the Cessna 150, is known in flying circles as the Needle.'

'Okay.'

Cluny continued to pound his keyboard and Punch stared at the little plastic Christmas tree now resident amid his deputy's shrubbery. He never put a Christmas tree in the house, though he had gained a buck or two from a fair few falling off the back of Randy's Forestry truck over the years. He could still hear the roar of the ocean at Calgary that night, as though the Atlantic was conveying the news from the other side. The constant surge of waves confirming the tragic loss of thirty-five college kids from Syracuse, New York. He had sat until dusk, just a PC himself, having chosen the destination as much for the dead radio signal, half expecting daylight to reveal bodies washed ashore on the sands. He had needed to see the ocean, to feel its protection. To experience the distance from the outlandish news that his younger brother Charlie – athlete, islander-in-the-city and newly qualified lawyer – was not in fact on the landmass of America, at the far side of the sea, just in time for Christmas. But instead was no more.

Punch hadn't been able to drive off, had known then he had to work towards a posting back on Mull, to be nearer his mum, or to one of the islands at any rate, where the borders were at the mercy of timetables. He could only now think of his brother as being at best permanently stuck inside Randy's little TV. Long since discarded out at the dump. Analogue, when the world was turning digital.

'Do we know who the pilot is?' he managed.

'Boyfriend of this Miss Lauder. A Xander Lowry. In his mid-fifties. Was expected to land back at the hotel. Mr Lowry is officially a missing person, as of . . .' Cluny looked up through his round rims to consult the station clock. 'Precisely 4.12 p.m.'

'There isn't a clock on the computer?' asked Punch. 'Who says he's missing?'

'The lady. Miss Lauder. Fair shaken she was.'

'No.' Punch puffed. 'As it stands, he just hasn't returned. Big difference from that to missing. Lovers' tiffs do not a crime make.'

'But he's been gone all night?'

'Very possibly just another turkey trying to escape the gravy. And fuck.' He looked to the clock. 'And in any case, he's been gone since he left the hotel airfield Friday night. Not since we received the call.'

Punch cupped his hands and sparked another match.

Cluny stood quickly, anticipating the thrown match. In so doing he knocked over his name plaque: *PC Jonathan Ambrose Cluny*.

'What you waiting on, constable?' said Punch. 'Table service at the Ubiquitous Chip? Better get out there.'

'The Lussa Falls?'

'Uh-huh. I'll start the ball rolling here.'

'Me? Right? Okay, Sarge.'

'We need to call Dave the Grave. You haven't met Dave yet,' Punch said. 'The local undertaker. He'll want good

72

warning to clean up his table in case he's needed. Keeps a clean table, does Dave. You could eat your organic salmon off a corpse's undercarriage by the time Dave's done with it.'

'Should we not call Oban Div, Sarge? Check if they've had any reports their end? Sightings? Control room at head office? Alert the coastguard? Ambulance services?'

'Those too. All in good time. If needed. Volunteers might be required too. Randy will gather the Forestry Commission boys. Handily, they're based at Aros Mains near Salen. But nothing is achieved by jumping the gun.'

'Aye. Of course, Sarge.'

'I'll make the calls. You get to the Lussa Falls smartish to make sure this Miss Lauder isn't selling us a turkey. You play good cop; I'll be along with the Al Pacinos in a bit.' Punch could almost picture Lowry. Another toff from the mainland no doubt with a jumper tied around his shoulders. 'Most likely the man ran out of Viagra.'

'Aye, Sarge, very good, Sarge.' Cluny jumped from his seat and pulled his uniform jacket over his waistcoat. He wrestled his coat, hat and scarf from the stand and returned to his desk for his glasses case. He took the wipe from his pocket and placed it inside. Punch thought the better of saying it, but had his suspicions that this kind of behaviour might be one reason for the poor performance stats.

'Right. I'll update you from the hotel.'

'Hold on, Columbo.'

Cluny turned to him.

Punch pointed his longer arm in the direction of the computer.

'Better clear a space on the back seat for your case notes.'

73

Cluny, flustered, stopped, but then turned to the door, swiping his hand through his hair as he exited.

'Angela bloody Lansbury's on a loose peg right enough. And fuck.'

Punch sat at his desk and opened the drawer. Took out the bottle and poured a finger measure the size of King Henry VIII. It was probably just another crank call. It would be unusual for light planes to fly from Lussa Falls at this time of year. He licked a rolling paper and got a bit of tobacco on his tongue. He manoeuvred it to his premolars, enjoying the feeling of grinding something. *What is ten years anyway but a number?* A drop of the good stuff, Ledaig, eighteen years matured, and the needle on Rod, would see him through till January. Possibly a local or two needing to cool off in the cell for the night over the festive period would be a handy distraction too. Then December would be over for another year. And planes would stop falling.

The phone rang. He knew it couldn't be Cluny from the hotel yet, not unless Michael Schumacher had flown in for the Mull Rally.

Punch leaned to pick up the phone.

'Station. Tobermory.'

A female voice was going ten to the dozen.

'Speak ... Eh, speak a little slower, please,' Punch interjected. 'Take your time and I'll understand you better.'

Was it Maggie May? He couldn't be certain. If it was, then this time she was without the orchestra.

'Yes, yes ... right,' Punch said. 'It took off just after nine you say and then ... not been seen since ...' He leaned forwards, trying to keep up with the voice, relieved it wasn't

74

a call from the owner of the Forestry estate out near Bloody Bay. He had no idea how Guinness could do this *and* type. 'Please take your time, ma'am, I have a constable on the way. We're alerting appropriate services. So, no landing has been reported since taking off from Lussa Falls last night?'

'That's what one is telling you, isn't it? You say a constable is coming here? I shan't think so.'

'Sorry? You're at the hotel now, ma'am?'

'The feeble man tells me they used a torch to guide it as it took off. A torch! Can you imagine? Ghastly! I'm stuck here waiting!'

'Mr Lowry?'

'But he hasn't come back!'

'And you waited until now to report it?'

'Well, I called you earlier, didn't I?'

'But you said nothing of the plane.'

'One was still ... still *hopeful*. That he'd, well, remember which side his bread was buttered on. Oh, he is such a genius but the frightful, heartbreaking shame is nobody knows it!'

'Is he?'

'This is Sergeant Punch I'm speaking with? *Ivor* Punch?'

'It is. And your relationship to the pilot, Miss Lauder?'

'Who said I was Miss Lauder?'

The phone line went dead.

TRACK 7

ALL AN ARTIST REALLY WANTS is an audience, and this particular artwork received an audience. The Gally Goo was a good choice in the end by the feeble man, being the only road in and out of Tobermory. Maximum effect. Local knowledge is good for something. Effigy I was the gatekeeper, the prototype. The kingmaker. It is against EI that all future creations will be measured. Though it is hard to think so coldly, so impersonally, of it – when it is in fact an extension of oneself. It is impossible not to see yourself in your creations. Even one of him. The island would never detect such subtlety. Let alone Punch. All he would see is himself.

It is time to engage the needle and thread again. To prove the success of EI was no fluke. The game needs to be upped. The Atlantic wind has lulled, the elements turned mute, as if out of expectation, like an anticipatory crowd awaiting what is coming next. It is strangely comforting to feel significance again. To be wanted. To touch, and be touched, once more. Like a part of you reawakened. The blood-inducing pinpricks from the needlework are a thing of the past now;

a defter approach has re-emerged. Only experience gives you that. It is all about learning to do something well one way, and then repeating it. That is what all good art is about. Repetition of practice. Inspiration is for fantasists. What was it David Bowie said? All his best work was stolen. Oh, to have dressed Ziggy!

There isn't a picture to go on for this one. This oh so sweetly special one. But the face is less important; it is more about location. And a loving touch. Because *she* couldn't provide it; she let her fall. Though hanging it from the Co-op entrance is a prospect hard to fend off. But that would not be accurate. Placement is everything for maximum effect; it will seal the deal, as will the size, of course. Dressing the body will be easier too. Touching and being touched by one so special, finally. Healing, really.

The prospect of a conversation is less likely this time. Not if you are being properly authentic about things. But words have been said between us – sweet, kind, lasting words. There is a sensation of experiencing a power more godly than human. Of touching one's own, when it had been so cruelly denied you. Closure? Ultimately? One hopes.

Now for the stitching around the neck, following the intimacy of the pen guideline, joining the face to the torso. The master tailor at work. Enough room left for a hairline. The wig readied for application. The legs laid out in position on the floor giving the impression the fireplace might get up and walk. But something is missing this time. The shock-wave of adrenaline? Too calm a night. Should there be music playing again? Miles Davis would talk about music as *only framing the perfection that is silence*; that you had to be careful how you filled it. And maybe the same applies to a body. There is the sense of a conductor operating without an orchestra. A little lost, like Punch would be without his island. Maybe the subject is just too close? Sweet, sweet thing. But one must finish what one starts. No matter the pain to one's heart, the brick in one's stomach.

Time now to really test not only Punch, but the woman, the island too. For all she, and they, and he, has done. Time to give EII the gift of life, the triumphant chance of a different ending. Maybe she will thank me?

Time to play the grace note: to secure the rope around Punch's neck even more tightly. For trying to replace what is irreplaceable.

TRACK 8

PUNCH PUSHED ON THROUGH THE dunes and reeds. Heard the waterfalls nearby, as though demanding the urgency he didn't feel. Driving here, along the Gally Goo, he had been thankful for the cover of darkness, the nightfall taking the effigy with it, but had been alarmed at his sense of, what was it, *pride* in the hanging acknowledgement, as though wishing for the entire island, if not the watching mainland, to notice it. He wondered if that was really why he had stopped Randy from cutting it down. This feeling of acknowledgement was one he associated with the sensation, the weight of the brick in his stomach, which in actuality he had first felt before Charlie. It was ego. Uniform. The need for significance.

He sometimes wondered if the origins of this were to do with his father, who he had never known, only that he originated from the Oban area. As her time off the island lengthened, his mother seemed to have let go of whatever it was she carried with her, and had increasingly missed Mull as well as her nursing post. She'd returned from their

79

Inverness sabbatical not long before the plane went down. She'd stayed on the island thereafter, believing her younger son was more there than anywhere else; to such an extent that, in the early days, she would walk the cemetery, looking for Charlie's grave.

Punch shook his head free of the past. His torchlight took off ahead of him onto the Sound of Mull like an illuminated, skimmed pebble. He turned it off. Behind him he could see a blanket of frost glistening as though jewels had been sewn into the landing strip. The Christmas lights of the Lussa Falls Hotel poked through the tree covering. Greens, reds, blues and yellows. Garish, all of it. He turned to the Sound again and, in the darkness, he could appreciate how easily even an experienced pilot, let alone this man Lowry, might wrongly assume the dark film of water was land. He had drawn as much out of the mysterious woman, who was or was not Lauder, as he could on the call, and now he preferred to proceed solo. It usually worked for him. He hadn't as yet entered the hotel, allowing Guinness to carry out the stagehand tasks.

The sky was bereft of stars and the moon non-existent. Sleet was falling softly, turning more of Punch's pepper to salt. He flicked the torch back on and stepped cautiously. He had ignored his own advice to make calls for support, jumping into the Ranger shortly after Cluny had called with the news – confirmed by Nigel Townsend, the perennially burgundy-cords-wearing hotel manager, of whom Randy often said 'if he was chocolate cake he would eat himself' – that a plane had indeed taken off from the airfield three minutes after nine on the evening before, and had not returned.

But no one reported it until the next day?

For Punch, that was the starting point, the first groove on the vinyl. Every case had to have a starter note, a place to drop the needle. If it were down to Guinness, they would still be setting up the speakers.

Punch needed to see the lay of the land for himself, and to feel the weather this plane was out in, before hearing the account of a breathless woman-scorned, or any of Townsend's bullshit, not to mention Guinness's. He reached down to the edge of the water and broke the limey seal with his forefinger. He shook slightly at the thought of touching the face of a body submerged in the reeds. There had only been one dead body in his time on Mull. The coffin the diminutive length of Iris Hislop.

'Baltic,' he puffed, cupping his hands and blowing hot air on them. He pulled the collar of his coat up to his chin, *to the rope*. 'And fuck.'

Punch checked his watch: 9.03 p.m. Exactly twenty-four hours since the man Lowry had taken flight. If he was still anywhere out here then he was surely a goner. The still night, only disrupted by the cries of a few late-season birds, had something unknowable about it. As though nature had been disturbed, or could offer a glimpse of the answers. That was the thing: Punch knew the truth of a case was always out there to be discovered, just as long as someone, some*thing*, was watching closely enough to notice, to correctly order the pieces.

His torchlight found a large blue buoy. He jolted the beam off it; momentarily fooled into thinking it was the plane cone of Flight 103. He thought of the journey he had made from the poker game to his mother that night, before realising she was of course at the whist drive. And then to Calgary, trying to fathom how he was now connected to an event playing out on the TV and radio; connected to terrorism, subterfuge, the ebbs and flows of the global quest for retribution, and to acts of aggression taking place in the name of world order. The following morning, he delivered the news to his mother. That night he slept in her bed with her. Felt the mattress trembling. Her screams of the day still echoing in his head. In the years since, he had witnessed the toll on her, a kind of geopolitical fog – not unlike the conflicted expressions you saw on the faces of world leaders, who inwardly knew they had picked a wrong war, seeming to age by the hour – that served to put a distance even wider than the Atlantic between her and the business of properly grieving her dead lad.

His mother had descended deeper into this emotional vacuum and was now resident in the Glen Iosal sheltered housing buildings beside the Scout Hall, where her whist drives had once taken place. Reminders, everywhere. She was now being nursed where she herself used to nurse, only leaving home to go to church each week. Some days now she didn't recognise Ivor; he was sure he could just as well send Cluny.

Having seemingly followed his mother there from their old house, Tinsel and Tonsils lived next door to her. Which was one way for Punch to keep an eye on them. Tonsils' motorbike was sometimes positioned outside, which all his life he had been unable to ride due to a medical condition. Scattered around it still, were wooden swords.

Punch put those memories firmly away – for now, anyway.

The few lights of the mainland seemed almost touchable. He kneeled to view the sea from a landing position; had the notion he could yodel across the Sound to the hills of Morvern and some bugger might yodel back. Possibly even this joker Xander Lowry. There were no obvious signs of wreckage, or skidding, on the airfield. Briefly, he saw the expanse of the Sound as a still blanket of Ledaig, eighteen years matured, and him diving in. All they would find of him would be his hat, like a cork floating on top. Maybe a Rod sleeve drifting alongside. All his Christmases come at once. His cleaner, Mary MacBeth, who lived in Creagan Park near the station, was forever placing empty bottles by his bin, intended as warning signs to his liver, as well as matching the correct circles of vinyl with their corresponding sleeves. Punch patted himself down. She would be doing well to get these stains out of his knees.

He got to his feet and turned to walk the airfield again. This was good thinking time without bother from the expectant world and its desire for answers and performance targets; quick conclusions were not on the evening's agenda. He stamped a boot on the frozen, lumpy surface of the airfield, imagining the shouts of footballers past and the flight of the sawdust line markings taken into the air, swirling in the field's hopeless exposure to the coastal wind. Back when he still got involved in games he had often preferred to referee, the cover of the uniform again. *Or the ego?* Charlie would return from university for a quick game and still make the last ferry, having bagged a hat-trick. Punch could almost see him now, legs like springs. The joke when Punch took the whistle was always *two yellows and it's a night in the cell.*

83

Goalposts emerged through the thickening snowfall, positioned where on the mainland you might have expected landing lights. He shone the torch over the glistening grass, looking for the old penalty spot. Of course the bastards called him The Clock behind his back; continually asked him how long to go. It was always a potential embarrassment for him when pointing to the corner flag or signalling an offside. But all that had stopped after Charlie; all the fun and games; all the breaking of records. The sky looked more like a ceiling. And now there was another plane not in it.

Punch reached the point where the airstrip-cum-football-field gave way to the hotel's rear car park. The landing area and the hotel were separated by nothing more than a wooden fence. There were no irregular tyre marks at this point either. Nothing left behind; no abnormalities to speak of. Just an orange windsock waving at the mainland, as though signalling it too knew more than he did.

Punch came across a brass plaque on the airfield gate:

Built by the Royal Engineers between May and August 1965.
15 Field Park Squadron, 38 Engineer Regiment.

Nothing about Lowry. But why would there be? He turned back to face the strip. Everything was lost to a blanket of sleet. As he walked towards the lights of the Lussa Falls, he shone on an item on the ground. A deerstalker. Possibly the lady Lauder's? Who knew the fashions of these city toffs? Unless Sherlock Holmes had got here before him. He pulled out a clear evidence bag from his pocket and a glove with it, placing the hat inside. Forensics, otherwise known as Dave the Grave, would do the once-over on it.

He reached the hotel building, which was a construction of stacked logs you might have expected in a land where folk really did yodel, and took a moment to sniff the pine in the air. He thought of the black nights when tree-scavenging off the Forestry estate. Randy and he under a starry sky with a few cans of McEwan's for company. He listened to the silence now, save for the falls and the wind speaking through trees. Two small planes were parked where the fence ended, positioned like resting toy models in the gloom of the night, awaiting Rod's gigantic hand to swoop down and propel them skywards. Punch felt huge too. Bigger than the night. As though blown out of scale before tomorrow's annual diminishment.

He reached the two police vehicles parked at irregular angles near the entrance of the building. A smattering of residents' cars were dotted about too – perhaps one of these belonged to this man Lowry. He spotted a little sports car – white with a soft top; this had to be the one, though it didn't quite go with the deerstalker. There was a skid mark leaving the car park. He hadn't spotted it when arriving. Possibly it was a local, having cut short a few festive drinks at the sight of the uniform. A dash for home rather than risk a local fine, otherwise known as twenty notes under Punch's hat.

He kneeled at the skid mark. Somebody had clearly put a lead foot on the accelerator, but to make more of it at this stage could be unhelpful. He eased himself up and walked to the hotel entrance. In the big window he could see Cluny sitting with a blonde lady around the forty mark. She wasn't unlike the blonde in *Cagney and Lacey*; he never knew which was which. Cluny's flash of even blonder hair was made festive by the glistening lights. Opposite the lady was a nodding Nigel Townsend. Punch had noticed the man waved a bit too keenly when passing him on Tobermory Main Street, but that wasn't technically a crime. Everyone on Mull had a wave. Punch reckoned he could identity most of the island's inhabitants from their hands alone. He had noticed Cluny's wave needed work. A tad Third Reich. His deputy was sitting up in the lounge in a way that did not encourage confidence, too eager, his back straight like a red setter waiting on a walk.

Punch killed the torch. He pushed open the front door, keeping the deerstalker safely hidden in his coat pocket, for now. His first thought was whether Townsend's rather pathetic-looking Christmas tree – it wasn't one of his own, Randy had been instructed to keep them out of public spaces – was worth the effort. He wiped his feet – Mary MacBeth had him well trained – before turning into the gents. Handily the single cubicle was empty. As he relieved himself, he read a sign above the urinal:

WANTED! GOOD WOMAN. Must be able to clean, cook, sew, wax aircraft and navigate. Must have airplane and hangar. PLEASE SEND PICTURE OF PLANE AND HANGAR.

He imagined Xander Lowry looking at it, possibly a mere twenty-four hours earlier, standing exactly where he was now. He was fairly certain the sentiments weren't progressing the work of Germaine Greer. Nor Mary MacBeth.

Punch washed his hands and rubbed them dry on his backside.

'Nothing saggy about it,' he mumbled.

He heard the toilet making an unusual gurgling sound. He turned back into the cubicle and noticed his flush had filled the bowl. Punch worked the handle to see if it would drain. But nothing. He lifted the lid of the tank to inspect.

'You fucker!' He jolted backwards.

A hand was floating in it.

TRACK 9

PUNCH WIPED THE SWEAT FROM his brow. With his own hand in a glove, he carefully fished out the severed hand. Nostrils flaring, he plopped it into another evidence bag. A left hand. A real hand.

No jewellery or unusual markings were evident. Despite the effects of the water, it was unmistakably elegant. If the hand was a local's, then he didn't recognise it without a steering wheel attached. Kirsop's the plumbers would certainly have had their work cut out.

With both the hand and the deerstalker in his coat pockets, Punch hurried through the Lussa Falls foyer and out the door. Thankfully, reception was not manned. He darted to his Ranger and unlocked the driver's door. Then he hid the contents of both his pockets under his seat. Locked up. This was no longer the work of sponge stuffing and fabrics, dress-up and make-believe; a game of silly-buggers rivalry or small-town vendettas – this was next level.

He returned to the hotel and took a quick right turn at reception to the wooden steps leading up to the lounge, where PC Cluny and the others were sitting. Before emerging at the top, he could see the blonde woman jumping to her feet when she heard his footsteps; she took a deep intake of breath and then collapsed into herself when she saw Punch wasn't this Xander Lowry. There was a whiff of cologne, the origins of which he couldn't yet detect. It was either Miss Lauder or Nigel Townsend. There were four other guests drinking and chatting on sofas around a table in the corner; Punch's first, macabre, instinct was to check everyone for two hands. Townsend was engaged in a conversation with the guests. Acting a bit of a tool, Punch thought. He was pretty sure there wasn't much about people and planes going missing that would enhance the hotelier's festive business; not to mention human digits in the plumbing. Or maybe folk would queue up to gawk. But body parts, for fuck's sake – on Mull? He tried to remove the limbs littering Lockerbie from his mind in favour of attempting to detect whether Townsend did or did not realise he was presiding over the Hammer House of Horror.

'Eh, hello. Evening,' Punch said, his hat held to his chest, making sure to do the clichéd thing first. It was a tactic to ensure he was underestimated. *Columbo*-like. He was in no doubt that any room he entered was a potential audience, the crime scene his stage. Townsend broke away theatrically from the group of guests, who looked suitably uncomfortable, doing a fine job of being TV extras.

'Sergeant,' said Cluny.

He noticed his deputy's mainland accent was even more refined here, as the man rose to his feet too quickly for

Punch's liking, like an inflatable version of himself given sudden air.

Looking at Cluny's uniform, Punch briefly saw the image of the effigy hanging.

'This is Mrs Lauder, sergeant. I've taken preliminary statements. And descriptions of Mr Lowry. Eh—' he looked puzzlingly down to his notepad, as though it was missing a keyboard, '—green Barbour jacket, thick, white hair, medium build, at least six foot.'

'God!' the lady sounded, her hands to her mouth; two of them.

'Miss. She's Miss,' Punch said, looking diffidently in the direction of the woman. 'Thank you for the update, constable.'

'Indeed.' Cluny turned to the woman. 'Apologies.'

'Ruth Lauder.' Miss Lauder nodded in Punch's direction, her eyes closed. Punch noted the Arran jumper and tweed jacket – they would go well with a deerstalker, he mused; hard at this juncture to detect whether she was Maggie May or just any other damsel in distress.

He turned to the emerging Townsend, quick to wrong-foot him by deploying the overly familiar Christian name.

'Nigel. Hellish business. What do you know?'

'It's just . . .' Cluny started. 'There's been a development, Sarge.'

'Right?' said Punch, pulling back in case Townsend should actually try to shake his right hand. He needed rid of the other guests and gave them a stare to that effect.

The party gathered their things and made to leave, each taking their glasses of various amber-coloured liquids.

'If there's anything we can do,' said one, a woman wearing a pained smile.

'Thank you,' Ruth Lauder said, proffering something approaching a matching smile. 'Very kind, yes.'

Punch nodded to the guests as they passed to acknowledge their decorum.

'Terrible, terrible, sergeant ...' Nigel Townsend clasped his hands as though about to deliver a sermon. He looked worriedly, but sympathetically to the Lauder woman. 'But all will be fine, Ruthie. It will. Must.'

He was wearing a decorative red Christmas jumper above the offending burgundy cords. Punch had already detected pink socks. He took particular offence to the green reindeers flashing on the jerkin. He had no idea how the world produced such things and why folk would wear them. Factories full of starving, exploited children if you believed the reports.

'Do you have more details about the plane, Nigel?'

'Yes, as I told your very fine deputy here, sergeant, the Needle was hired by Mr Lowry and Miss Lauder at nineteen-hundred hours. Give or take, one would say.'

'The Needle is the plane, Sarge,' Cluny interjected.

'I remember.' Punch cast a blank glance to his deputy; he could tell Townsend's flattery had gotten to Guinness, if not the pink socks and pyrotechnic reindeer. Punch braced himself; there was a risk it might sing too.

'I didn't hire it, Nigel,' Ruth Lauder managed, speaking through a tissue.

'Well, in any case I'd say, seven p.m.?' Townsend said. 'I remember putting it in the logbook. I keep one at reception. Goes back to dear Papa's days. Really, just awful this.'

Townsend spoke in an accent removed from Mull, but familiar enough by now to Punch, and with a confidence that Punch had always found questionable. The kind of assuredness folk who had inherited their parents' wealth possessed. The hotelier had struck up a friendship with the composer, Andrew Lloyd Webber, after the latter had flown into Lussa Falls in the early seventies. Folk said if you stood still long enough around the hotel or even the Salen branch of Spar you would have Townsend bending your ear about his trip to accompany the impresario to the Oscars in Hollywood. That 'Bonnie' herself – Faye Dunaway – had gestured for him to light her cigarette. Again, annoying, but not technically a crime.

'Why the Needle?' asked Punch.

'That's what we call the old Cessna,' explained Townsend. 'Papa christened it. Really a rather sleek beast, you know.'

'Uh-huh. I see.' Punch tried not to feel unworldly, parochial. 'And the colour?'

'Red and white I'd say. Yes.'

'Right. So, this is a given name for this plane, rather than a more widely used term for this model?' Punch walked to the wall. Classical music was playing softly, coming from downstairs.

He thought of the legend of the Grey Lady, who was apparently housed in the old jailhouse. The pale lady before him now seemed to be in a prison of her own. 'You said the *old* Cessna. What kind of shape is it in?'

'All checks and servicing are completely up to date, sergeant,' Townsend said. 'Has to be really.' The man looked to Cluny. 'One must.'

'Of course, Nigel,' Cluny said.

Punch tried to hide his irritation, could tell his deputy was already mentally in tuxedo-land, cruising the Hollywood

Hills with Lloyd Webber and Townsend in an open-top. The gong for *Jesus Christ Superstar* on the dash. Punch had fantasised himself about putting cuffs on not Faye Dunaway but Warren Beatty, for his treatment of Carly Simon alone.

The shock of the discovery was still on him. He'd had some odd fuckers in his Ranger, but a detached hand? He walked the length of the wall; on occasion he had taken his mother for a lunch here at the hotel, before realising it was a form of torture watching her stare at the plane memorabilia. At least she had been spared body parts. He surveyed the framed pictures of planes; many of them signed. You could have the autographs of half of Pink Floyd up here, he thought, but it wouldn't take away from the fact that a man – *another* man, for Christ's sake – might have fallen from the sky; that the advancement of technology came hand in hand with human jeopardy.

'The Needle?' Punch brought his right arm up to gesture at the photographs. 'Would it be here?'

He noted the woman had turned to him, tissue still readied. Didn't seem completely crushed about her man. But then you never knew with toffs. Stiff upper lip and all that.

But is she or is she not Maggie May?

'No. Unhelpfully,' Townsend offered. 'Though Papa must have taken some. Mummy claimed it was situated further up the rankings than herself . . .'

'Uh-huh.' Punch took a roll-up he had already prepared from his top pocket. It was amazing what you could do while driving the Gally Goo. 'And so it belongs to you? The plane?'

'That's correct, sergeant,' replied Townsend. 'And all papers are in good order.'

'Have to be,' echoed Cluny.

'He said,' Punch pointed out.

'Yes,' Townsend said, 'service checks all up-to-date and whatnot on all of them.'

'Whatnot?' Punch raised an eyebrow.

'Eh, well . . .' Townsend looked to Ruth Lauder, and then to the darkness in the big window and waved his arms out at it. 'I mean, all our fleet are regularly serviced.'

'Fleet?' Punch couldn't quite keep the scoff out his voice. He noticed the indented line that came straight down from the bottom of Townsend's nose to his lip, giving the impression of a fleshy moustache. John Major, he thought, had the same indentation, giving the same effect.

'Well . . . all three.' Townsend sat down again, placing his glasses case on the table. Blue.

'Aye.' Punch wondered if it was Townsend who was responsible for the attempt at humour in the gents. He was curious whether the ladies' toilet had a stereotypical equivalent of the male psyche. The other hand, too?

'And you hired it to your guests Miss Lauder and Mr Lowry. A *Xander* Lowry, I believe?' Punch enquired.

He glanced at her as he spoke. She looked as though carved from marble, as though Michelangelo's hands were still warm on her. Not beautiful. Handsome.

'Well, sergeant, I hired it to Miss Lauder.'

The woman removed the tissue from her lips and turned sharply to Townsend. Punch noted her ongoing dispute with this detail.

'That is technically, erm, true, Ruthie?' Townsend said. He patted down his cords, which Punch had noted were thickly ribbed. 'I hired it to them both. But the hire was for Mr Lowry to fly. Erm, yes.' He looked into the blackness of the window again. 'Darling Xandy. I mean ... nearly one hundred metres of runway *should* be enough.'

'Oh God ...' Ruth Lauder stood and walked to the window. 'He said he had something for me when he returned. I don't know what. Will I ever?' She put her hand to her forehead. 'But enough with this pettiness! Why aren't we doing more?'

'We'll be searching from first light, Miss Lauder. I can assure you of that,' Punch said. 'But it would be helpful if you can provide more details, so that we can establish what is currently known. It will help us plan the search operation. You were understandably alarmed during the phone calls to us, and so we need to take a pause to clearly ascertain facts. Would you consider it out of the question that Mr Lowry could have flown elsewhere, intentionally? To get this thing for you?'

'Sarge,' Cluny said eagerly. 'Miss Lauder claims she did not in fact call the station. At all.'

Punch angled his left-side badger to the woman.

'Claims, or didn't?' he said, thinking it best to conceal that he already had information to this end. The discovery of the hand was pressing on him. It would need to be transported to Dave the Grave pronto. But he turned cold at the thought of taking it there, to that place of death. It had felt like holding Charlie's own.

'I did not ... call,' the woman said, swapping the tissue between hands; Punch thought of Sonia Hislop earlier, her mentioning the letters on the cliff. That was the kind of police work that couldn't be measured by head office. That wouldn't turn up on a computer league table.

'Bloody hell, Xand!' Ruth Lauder moved to the window. 'You've had your fun! Whatever the hell this is!'

'Then, if it wasn't you, do you know who *did* call to report the missing person?' Punch asked, moving closer to Townsend and the lady Lauder. 'And the plane?'

'She doesn't know,' Cluny said.

Punch stubbed out his cigarette in the nearest ashtray. Guinness was becoming quite the ventriloquist, but he wished the lad would shut the fuck up and let potential suspects tie themselves in knots.

Cluny moved to Punch and dropped his voice.

'Should we swap swim lanes, Sarge?'

'Eh?'

'I go bad cop?'

'No.'

'Risk matrix, Sarge? Should we assess the level of the missing person's vulnerability?'

'What do you think I'm doing, PC Cluny?'

The next question was going to up the ante. Punch knew it. He looked to Miss Lauder.

'*Why* didn't you?' he said.

'What?'

'Notify services?'

'Well ...' The woman gestured to the darkness a little exasperatedly.

Punch noted the long boots up to her knees. They were muddy at the bottoms, at odds with the rest of her. Red lipstick. 'Xandy wouldn't want a fuss . . . I thought he would return, you know, today. There's his reputation to consider. And Nigel said he had reported it.'

Townsend looked to Punch like he had just lost the Oscar for Best Supporting Hanger-On.

'One did try, repeatedly,' Townsend said, turning to Cluny instead of Punch and back to the window again. 'No one home, I'm afraid. Bloody heck, Xandy, where the devil are you?'

Punch tried briefly to fathom when that could have been. During his Rod and Tobermory Malt hours – he hoped not. Instinct – or was it something deeper, something to do with the brick in his stomach – was stopping him from mentioning the hand for now.

'You alluded to Mr Lowry's reputation?' Punch said, regaining the conversation.

'Yes,' she sniffled. 'Xander is one of our finest violinists.'

'Oh, right?' Punch said.

'Would that be him playing downstairs?' Cluny said.

This was better, thought Punch.

'Eh, no,' scoffed Townsend, losing the marbles in his timber. 'That is superior in my view.'

Punch saw how the woman Lauder cast daggers at the hotelier. There was a hidden edge to her, no doubt.

'Eh, I mean, *different*.' Townsend attempted to salvage. 'No, no, the answer is it's not him. No.'

'Would he often take off so unexpectedly? For this long?' Punch said. 'In the dark of night? In an unfamiliar plane? From a field?'

'Airstrip,' Townsend corrected.

Punch raised an eyebrow. He made a mental note to request a fuller case profile of the musician, especially now he was being told the man was noteworthy.

'You said he was an experienced pilot, Miss Lauder?' Cluny pitched in.

'Well, yes. Yes!' the woman said, turning back and resting her backside on the window ledge. She put her blonde head in her hands. 'Anyone who has seen Xandy perform knows "expected" is *not* in his repertoire.'

'Made a career out of it I'd say,' Townsend added. 'In a good way, in a good way.'

Punch turned to the image of burgundy in his periphery, the colour now surging to the man's face. He had nothing to lose.

'And would you consider Mr Lowry a better pilot than musician, Nigel?'

'Oh my giddy aunt! Now what kind of question is that, Punch?' He gestured to Ruth Lauder. 'I mean – *really*?'

'So, let's try this one. Are Miss Lauder and Mr Lowry *paying* guests?'

'Well, eh, no.' Townsend wiped his brow with a spotted handkerchief. Red spots, Punch observed. 'Xandy and I go back a long way, I'd say. To our conservatoire days. But of course, for Xandy, Juilliard in New York soon beckoned.'

'Right.'

'But Xandy was fully qualified, as a pilot,' Miss Lauder added. 'Is. *IS*. Goodness, Nigel. So generous. I was quite unaware ...'

'Come, Ruthie.' Townsend moved to her and offered his handkerchief. 'Of course. Of course.'

But no blood on it, Punch noted. The flashing reindeer was reflecting in the window unhelpfully, creating an impression not unlike an approaching plane.

'Erm, can I ask you some more questions on your own, Miss Lauder?' Punch said.

'Anything I have to say to you, sergeant, I can say with dear Nigel in attendance.'

'Indeed. So, who do you suspect called the station?' Punch said. 'A staff member, Nigel?'

'I doubt that, sergeant.'

'Do you really?' Punch asked, adding, 'You seem very calm, Nigel.'

'Why does it matter who the bloody hell called your crummy little station?' Ruth Lauder declared, standing upright. 'A man, an *exceptional* man, is ruddy missing out there!'

'Come, Ruthie. Sergeant Punch is here to help,' Townsend soothed, stroking her arm. He looked to Punch. 'I can assure you I'm churned into corned beef inside, sergeant. In this game you learn to keep a brave face on.'

'So, had you been intending to join Mr Lowry on his flight, Miss Lauder?' Punch studied her hair and decided he couldn't quite see a deerstalker sitting atop it. Such headgear was more Townsend's style.

'Well, no,' said Miss Lauder. 'I wasn't feeling tip-top. I'd a nagging head. Now I wish ...' She put a hand to her mouth.

'Take your time.' Punch motioned to Cluny, who then dashed so speedily to the woman with tissues that he startled her. 'Has Mr Lowry ever flown into Lussa Falls before, Nigel?'

Logs collapsed in the fire and Punch turned. That was a better place for a severed hand, if you *really* wanted to dispose of it. The Sound too. The hand was becoming increasingly problematic to him in a deeper sense.

But whose was it?

'Yes, yes. I'd say.' Townsend nodded. 'God, Xandy knew the airstrip well enough. Often took in the show in summer.'

'I've notes to that effect here, Sarge,' said Cluny, now sitting. Punch was of half a mind to offer the lad a menu.

'You see,' Townsend explained, 'our annual light aircraft show sometimes draws as many as a hundred and fifty aircraft over the bank holiday weekend.'

'The end of May?'

'Yes, sergeant.'

'No flight communicative apparatus or ways of contacting planes?'

'Lussa Falls operates a ground-to-air advisory radio service only during the show period, Sarge,' Cluny read.

'I'd say, microlight frequency of 129.825,' Townsend confirmed, before adding, a tad inconsequentially, in Punch's view, 'Famous air visitors to Lussa Falls have included Russell Harty, Robert Wagner, David Coulthard, Donald Sutherland, Dave Gilmour, Phil Collins and Tom Cruise, to name but a few. Ireland is not far away as the crow flies, so we welcome many visiting aircraft from the Emerald Isle, too.'

'Quite the cast list. Don't remember the hotel featuring in *Top Gun* right enough. So, Mr Lowry was considered famous, in your view, Nigel?' Punch stepped closer to the man. He heard the classical music rising.

'I'd say, yes. Well yes,' Townsend said – reluctantly, Punch noted.

'Talented?'

'Erm, yes, he was. Is this relevant, sergeant?'

'So, he knew the terrain,' Punch pivoted. 'But has he flown at night before?'

'God, well, I'd *think* so. Ruthie?' Townsend turned to Miss Lauder, who was working her hands like she was crocheting. Punch noticed two plasters on her fingers. Maybe from searching, *or more*? 'A slight hazard is a five-hundred-foot hill a couple of miles from the 06 threshold. When taking off to the west, pilots must make a climbing turn to avoid this, and a similar turn when landing to the east. But he wouldn't, shouldn't, have been troubling that direction.'

'And what did he take to air *for* exactly?' Punch said. 'One-upmanship, Nigel, eh?'

'Xandy just loves to fly?' the woman said, seeking confirmation with a glance at Townsend. 'Just the other night I said he should have been born with wings. Oh, dear God!'

'Ruthie ... please.' Townsend put his arms around her. 'He'll be fine. You know Xandy, always pushing the envelope, I'd say ... Same at the conservatoire, same on stage. He just mistook the sky for an auditorium last night. That's all. We'll hear from him ASAP. I'm sure. Certain I'd say.'

Punch noted how Townsend's airs and graces were escalating. His general demeanour was by now heightened to that of a person running the Ritz rather than a glorified log cabin with bad jokes in the pisser. Not to mention the irregular plumbing. He still felt the touch of the spongy hand. Clearly, nobody was displaying obvious knowledge of it.

'And you were to guide him back with two torches, ma'am?' asked Cluny. 'Was that a likely method?'

Punch nodded approval to the constable.

101

'Yes. I thought so too,' Ruth Lauder said. 'That it was *unlikely*, I mean. But Xander thought the torches sufficient. Said he had learned that way. I'm afraid I bowed – *bow* – to him when it comes to aeronautical matters.' She breathed in heavily through her nose.

Punch pressed his forehead to the cold glass of the window and cupped his hands at the sides of his eyes. The view was at first black, but gradually presented itself as more nuanced. The Sound emerging.

'Do you think two torches as landing lights was the strategy of a man who really *wanted* to re-land?' Punch asked.

'Oh, now come, sergeant!' Townsend said, losing more of the chocolate in his timbre. 'What kind of question is that? We have a man, a beloved man, hugely respected the world over, missing here and you're casting aspersions on his integrity, not to mention being more interested in who called your poxy little station!'

'Emotions can run high when this kind of thing happens, Nigel.' Punch stepped back from the window, still felt the cold night on his forehead. 'We all need to keep a brave face on, eh?' He looked the man in the eye. 'Maybe rest is a good idea. We have enough to be going on with tonight. Do you have a mobile phone number in case he ...'

'Rest?' Ruth Lauder yawned. She appeared to shiver, then hugged herself. She took a phone from her pocket and shook her head as she looked at it. 'No signal. Nothing since we got here.'

Punch had noted there were a few more of the new phone devices on the island. Apparently, Ben More was causing some hiccups with signal coverage. Doing its job.

Ruth Lauder looked up and noticed Punch gazing at her hands.

'You've cut yourself?' he said.

'Oh?' Miss Lauder said. 'Well, I ran down to the bottom of the airfield, searching . . . You know . . . Must have caught myself . . .'

'Right,' Punch said. *The muddy boots.*

She moved from the window and Punch saw how she looked for the bad actors in the corner, now long gone. There was value in questioning them; he would need to do that himself.

'Look,' started Townsend, changing tack once more, 'I've deployed this technique with the torches for ever, sergeant. Years, I should think. Going back to Papa's time in the sky. My children used to do the same for me when I flew. Damn cataracts have put paid to my flying days. Alas.'

'Aye, alas,' Punch said. He let silence roam.

Ruth Lauder almost ran across to the big window overlooking the airfield; it took up much of the front wall.

Punch walked to her, noting her blonde head reflected in the glass, the visual embodiment of a Bob Dylan album title.

'Xandy, you bastard . . .' she said.

'Ruthie . . . come on . . .' Nigel Townsend moved towards her with her drink, but she shunned him away with her elbow – a little aggressively, Punch thought – before slumping down onto a sofa by the window.

Punch moved to sit next to her, placing his hat on the table.

'I'm sorry to ask again, Miss Lauder, but this is potentially more important than you might realise: did you or did you not make the calls to the station?'

'I didn't.' Her hand was shaking. 'First I'd heard of it was when your colleague turned up. As I said, I assumed Nigel had called you in. I can't remember the order of it all. It's so bloody cold out there ... God. To think I suggested the Bahamas!'

'Right. Right,' Punch said. 'Any clue as to who did make the call?'

She shook her head in bewildered fashion.

Punch couldn't be sure if the two voices *did* belong to the same person. The woman before him now certainly appeared calmer, more rational, than Maggie May; possibly even *too* calm for someone who might have lost their partner. But, as he knew himself, everyone housed loss differently. Then there was the classical music playing downstairs. He turned to look at the blackness. Sonia Hislop was still nagging at him. He hoped the snow might have covered those yellow wellies from her view.

'Everything okay with you and the man?' Punch said, more softly. 'Mr Lowry, I mean.'

'Who else would you mean?' Ruth Lauder said, a little defensively Punch felt. He watched as she patted her tartan skirt down on her lap. Toffs were forever claiming castles and clan symbolism; no doubt it was made by some designer or other. His own tartan would by rights have been MacInnes, but it had long been sidelined in favour of 'Punch'.

Ruth Lauder reached for her handbag before realising it wasn't by her side. Punch took out his cigarettes, opened the packet and pulled one cigarette forwards. He offered the packet to her. She took the one he had intended and put it in her mouth. She leaned to Punch, and he lit it. The filter had already taken some of her red lipstick.

'Any other reason for him to take off?' Punch said, moving away. 'What was he going to bring you?'

Miss Lauder reset her leather boots on the floor.

'Well ... no.' She turned to Punch and away again. 'No idea.'

'You've been an item long?'

She pulled the drink Townsend had left for her a bit closer; she cupped it securely with both hands. Punch thought maybe all women did this in a crisis.

'We work together,' she said. 'You know ... I'm a musician too. Well, not in his league. More an administrator now.'

Her long fingers. Punch had suspected as much.

'Your role?'

'I organise an orchestra.' She turned longingly to the window, as though it might be playing out there.

'The name of it?'

'The London Philharmonic.'

'Oh right?' Punch nodded. 'Serious then.'

The woman sighed into her drink.

Punch got up and walked to Cluny.

'Go to the car, PC. Update Control with descriptions and alert Oban and wider LB. Lochaber too. We'll need backup on the other side. First light.' He decided to keep the hand out of it, for now. He knew what it represented. It was a reminder of the biggest crime he couldn't solve.

'Aye, Sarge. *Assets*, on it.'

'Lingo. This is not happening on a flipchart now, PC Cluny. The local coastguard should be alerted, sniffer dogs too. All this should have been done yesterday had we known. But, despite the darkness, better later than ...'

105

'Oh Christ!' Ruth Lauder said, bringing the tissue to her nose. 'And me just sitting here!'

Townsend descended on her again.

Punch felt numb. He knew he was only barking out the orders now because it would appear odd if he didn't, or that he hadn't already. It was the same with the hand. Couldn't face it right now. Like it had fallen from the sky.

'Nothing more we can do tonight, Ruthie.' Townsend placed his hand on her arm. 'It's all in hand. I'd say think positives. Only positives.'

Punch moved closer to his deputy; he had to get a grip. 'Control room decide the case grading, PC. High, medium, low. An incident must first be created by Control. You have DOB and full name, address?'

'Affirmative, Sarge.'

'Okay. Get to it. Preparations for first light.'

Punch felt he was playing a part; doing the right thing; doing what Tulloch would have done in Inverness.

Cluny grabbed his hat.

'PC – update the divisional inspector too. Oban,' Punch said. 'Tell them I'm in questioning.'

'You are?' Townsend said.

Cluny scurried towards the wooden stairs. His descending footsteps reminded Punch of ones he had heard before, when Charlie used to come down from the attic from his bedroom, in the house in Inverness; the last one they lived in together. He would study up there for school, then university, as he subsequently did for the bar in Glasgow, only breaking for their mother's toast and marmalade, asking about such things as football results like a god returning to the banal.

106

'We have to cover all bases, Miss Lauder,' Punch said, returning to the living. As he looked at her sitting there, he sensed something of Lady Di about her, as though she too enjoyed being watched but was pained by it. Just a year had passed but even that death in a Paris tunnel had added some density to the fog separating Punch from his brother. His mother had even hung the princess's portrait in her hallway as some form of comfort. Now, the hand had brought it closer again, *all* death.

'We're alerting all services now, Miss Lauder,' he said. 'At first light we'll begin a thorough search.'

'Thank you, sergeant,' she said. There was sleet now evident in the window. 'It's the shock ... Xander isn't just *any* soloist ... I can't ... can't imagine the orchestra without him.'

'*Music*, even.' Townsend moved to take her glass.

'Any details, anything you can remember, no matter how insignificant, could be crucial. Here is the station number again.'

She nodded, taking the note from Punch.

He found himself taking notice of the fine stitching on the scarf around her elegant neck. Could she have made it herself?

'Here ... Ruthie. A little brandy.' Townsend placed it in front of her. 'Perhaps he got into trouble and landed somewhere further afield.' He waved the phone extension. 'He'll be in touch.'

'Exactly,' Ruth Lauder said, nodding purposefully. 'Think positive.'

Tomorrow Punch was supposed to take his mother to church, to reawaken all the ghosts again for another year.

107

But he might have to put that on ice now. The hand too. Christ.

'He was an assured pilot, by crikes. I'd say,' Townsend offered. 'I had no qualms about letting him go up.'

'Really?' Punch said. 'At that hour, in darkness?'

'Well, there was no stopping him,' Townsend said.

'I thought you didn't try to?' Punch said.

'I'm not inclined to tell paying guests what to do with their holidays, sergeant.'

'But he wasn't paying,' Punch said. 'Was he?'

'No.'

'And you can confirm nobody has heard word since Mr Lowry took off – friends, family?' Punch moved again towards the window.

'No.' Ruth Lauder shook. 'I informed your deputy already. I've called as much as I can.'

'As you can?' Punch repeated.

'Well ...' Ruth Lauder shifted uncomfortably. 'I don't know his, you know, *close* family ...'

'You see, he took off and then circled back over me,' Townsend said, joining Punch at the window.

'And you guided him with torches, you said on the call, Miss Lauder?' Punch looked over his shoulder at the woman.

'I did not. I don't believe I did.'

'You didn't use torches or you didn't make the call?'

'I didn't make the call!' She looked to Townsend for support. 'And Nigel went out with him with the torches. I had a light head! I'm not a drinker at all.'

'Had Mr Lowry been drinking?' Punch asked.

'A glass with dinner,' Townsend replied. 'The good stuff. He was perfectly compos mentis. Look, I'm not sure what you're getti—'

'Right,' Punch interrupted. 'And so, then he turned out over the water again and he just vanished into the sky?'

'Yes.' Townsend waved his arm recklessly to the night. 'I could hear him ... but no longer see him ... until he was ... well, just sky.'

Townsend moved to nudge the brandy closer to Ruth Lauder and she lifted it to her mouth. As he did so, Punch noticed there was mud under Townsend's fingernails. He hadn't spotted it earlier.

'Dear Nigel.' She smiled. 'Such a friend.'

'Can I ask how long you have known each other?' Punch looked to Ruth Lauder and then Townsend.

'Us?' asked Townsend. 'Well, this is Miss Lauder's first visit with Xander. But ...'

'We met in Edinburgh,' she interjected. 'I'd heard so much about Nigel and Mull. Xander was – Christ, *is, IS* – very fond of Nigel. He couldn't wait to show me the aerial view ...' She nodded. '*Is*.'

'Then why didn't he take you?' asked Punch. 'In daylight?'

'My head,' Miss Lauder said, standing. 'I told you, my head didn't feel so ... tip-top.'

'Come now, Ruth.' Townsend inched himself closer to the woman and rubbed the tweed of her jacket.

'He was only sitting just ... just *there*.' Ruth Lauder pointed to a sofa.

Observing Townsend up close, Punch could appreciate how readily the man would be able to switch from the surrounds of Lussa Falls to a Beverly Hills awards season. A gift, really. But a severed hand? That was more the stuff of Hannibal Lecter.

They heard footsteps coming up the stairs.

Punch turned, half expecting Charlie, study papers tucked under his arm, pen in mouth, Inverness Caley Thistle strip on.

Ruth Lauder rose expectantly. Then slumped down again.

'Sarge,' managed Cluny, desperately trying to find enough oxygen in his lungs, his glasses steamed up. 'There's been a development. Tobermory. A body.'

'Eh?' Punch said, wishing the lad hadn't announced it to all and sundry.

'Hanging.'

'Oh Christ!' Miss Lauder shot to her feet. Her glass smashed onto the table.

Townsend moved even closer towards her. Punch moved to Cluny.

'But it doesn't fit the description of Mr Lowry,' Cluny said, gulping for breath. 'And a dinghy washed ashore below it, Sarge. Oars. Lifebelt. Still inside.'

'The effigy?' Punch said. 'I know about the—'

'No, Sarge. A child's body.'

TRACK 10

PUNCH SPED OUT OF THE Lussa Falls car park, making a blur of the 'Otters Crossing' sign. He had instructed Cluny to stay with Townsend and Ruth Lauder in case of developments there. He couldn't imagine anyone was going to sleep a wink at the place. Air and water support would be brought in at first light. Below him still, the hand.

He looked at the clock. Charlie's anniversary was looming. The probability of planes falling again, of bodies hanging – children, for fuck's sake – was pressing, a weight he hadn't expected. What sick bastard had brought all this on him? It had turned from an out-of-season Guy Fawkes prank to something much more sinister. More personal. What was next – the other hand?

Punch turned right out of the Lussa Falls driveway, swerving onto the dual carriageway and off towards Salen. He flew through the sleepy village and then on past the two ruined, barnacle-encrusted boats marooned by the roadside on Salen's outskirts. The boats sat as they always did, decayed monuments to the past, as though an artist's

111

impression of slow death. One day they would simply not be there anymore, no trace.

He made light work of Aros Mains and the next few miles of darkness and soon reached the Gally Goo, where he caught a brief outline of the effigy depicting him, silhouetted in his headlights against the sky. He felt a chill looking at the clumpy thing, at what might be waiting ahead. A grab from the floor at his ankles would have had him veering towards the Sound.

The lights of Tobermory came into view, nothing festive about them. Punch pressed harder onto the Ranger floor. This was when he knew he had the loneliest job on the island.

The Main Street could not have been more benign, the Christmas lights glistening on anything that would take them. He imagined bodies hanging from the seafront gutters of the chemist's, Elizabeth's Hair Salon, as they had from houses in Sherwood Crescent, Lockerbie. Cluny's World Wide Web would make sure nobody ever fucking forgot. He drew in regular breaths in anticipation of what awaited him at the far end of the street. He remembered his two-year probationary period in Inverness and Sergeant Tulloch telling him days like these could come in the life of a police officer; the main thing was to be prepared for them, and to trust your instincts. *Go with your belly*, Tulloch always said.

The hand, for now, he just couldn't touch again. Best to keep the mainland out of it until he shook off the numbness. But it wasn't sustainable, he knew that.

At the end of the seafront, he drove by the New Pier to the Kilchoan ferry car park bays below the Lighthouse Path.

His headlights revealed a man standing near the ferry slip. Puffs emitting from him. There was the temptation to drive on past the man, to the sea. To not have to be a part of what came next. On the way in, he had radioed for air, land and sea searches to commence at first light. Cluny had been briefed to stay on top of it. It would only make Punch look good as one of the world's delegators. The call handler at head office had created an incident log, sending prompts to Control who had allocated localised call signs to him and Cluny by way of their rank and shoulder number. Punch felt increasingly wrapped up in red tape, as though hung from a tree by it. Apparently, the wider media had not caught wind of anything from Mull. A relief, given that Lowry was of note in his field. But if the man and his plane didn't come knocking soon then a briefing would inevitably be fed to the media. That was the part of the job Punch most disliked: drawing attention to cases meant drawing attention to himself, to what he had lost, to his remove.

Cluny had said the call reporting the child's body had come in from the Pier Master, Bob Noon, universally known as Palindrome. The man was waiting in Punch's headlights now, his white hair illuminated.

Punch swung open the Ranger door and Palindrome approached him.

'Pal,' Punch said. He looked around seriously to the desolate car park. 'Thanks for keeping this one quiet.'

'Sergeant,' Palindrome said. 'No bother. Irish fishing boat. Irish lads. Spotted the body hanging as it left Tob earlier. Certainly fair sent the shits up them.'

'Right.'

'Would anyone. Certainly. Aye, Irish fishing boat, as I say.'

'Uh-huh. Time?'

'Eight o'clock it was. I know that for certain,' Palindrome said. Punch noted the sweat on the man's brow, at odds with the cold. 'Eight chimes luckily. Though that certainly presents a problem ...'

'It does?'

'The clock is chiming one hour more than it actually is. I mean than it's supposed to. Certainly.'

'Right,' Punch said. 'So, nine p.m.?'

'Aye, right enough. Fair sent the shites up them.'

A small but powerfully built man with a prominent pot belly, Palindrome was noteworthy for lacking in the neck department and having nimble feet; Punch was well aware of his prowess as a handy caber-tosser in his day come Highland Games time. He was an approved celebrant at the church, and nobody gave him a hard time about it. Though, as a result, he had many a time been asked to walk across the water to Calve, usually after a few, to make sure he wasn't Jesus. Calve was the jewel on Tobermory's crown, the man was given to saying.

'Called the station soon as it was reported. Hellish business.' Palindrome motioned the torch he was holding towards the slip, which presented itself now to Punch as something more than cement, more like the gateway not to the mainland, but Hell. 'You better go see it?'

'Aye.' Punch nodded. 'Have you, eh, been around yourself?'

Palindrome shook his head. He looked distractedly to the sea. Seemed agitated to Punch, but the man was never an easy read. Probably shock. He daren't show him the hand with no body attached to it.

Instead, Punch moved swiftly to the Ranger to collect his torch from the boot.

'Christ, what a fucking day,' he mumbled.

Both men walked to the slip.

'Careful, Sarge.' Palindrome waved his torch down ahead across the flat stone. 'She's greasy.'

Punch walked down the slip and then veered sideways and up over the black granite rocks that followed the coast around to the left at the foot of the promontory. He shone the torchlight, trying as best he could to map out a route away from the lapping sea. Seemed like everything was after him. The sound of boat rigging came from the bay. Punch looked out and Calve Island might as well have been the Sound. He could hear Palindrome behind him, appreciated the man's decorum in keeping back a bit. It would have been awkward to tell him such a thing.

Punch turned the corner and stopped. It was so peaceful save for the ripples of swelling waves. This was when the uniform was at its heaviest. He heard his own breath. Cast the torch gradually up the rock face. The light danced too playfully. He saw it. About thirty feet above his head. Suspended in front of the white 'GOD IS LOVE' lettering.

A little body hanging.

Punch steadied his longer arm on the rock face.

'Christ,' he said, taking the torch off the thing, remembering he had that power over proceedings at least. 'And fuck.'

There was some relief. It wasn't a real body.

Punch shone upwards again. The rope holding the effigy was tied to a tree overhanging the cliff up on the Lighthouse Path.

It was another reproduction. And no doubting the identity.

It was her. Returned. Reimagined.

Little Iris Hislop.

Punch heard footsteps. Saw a second torchlight arriving on the body beside his own.

'Oh, you bastard,' he heard.

'Uh-huh,' Punch managed.

'Thought it was real,' Palindrome managed. 'Terrible. What? What sick fucker, eh?'

'Aye.'

'Irish boys said they couldn't be sure right enough. Certainly.'

Punch turned and his torch beam caught Palindrome's eyes. The man had a hand on his breast and Punch knew it was because a bible was in there.

'Death is the door to glory,' Punch summoned. 'I heard that once. Fuck knows where. I wonder if whoever said it had ever lost anybody. A child.'

'God grants to the living, *grace*. To the departed, *rest*,' he heard from beside him. 'Is that not how it should be?'

'And fuck.'

'When I came round just now ... I didn't know whether it was going to be real or not. I thought it would be,' Palindrome said, his eyes watering. 'Irish boys had a hell of a scare. Hellish. In the literal. Certainly.'

Punch sensed the man was uncharacteristically flustered, but then this was unquestionably beyond his general odd-a-job, Pier Master remit. He stepped up to the last layer of rock and shone the torch directly above him, catching the effigy's face. He moved the light slowly onto the strands of red hair. Wool. Possibly.

'Whoever it is, is no artist.' He knew he was speaking for effigy number one too. 'Though I've seen they have pickled sheep in glass casing on the TV now, so fuck knows . . .'

'Selling for a million notes I should think. Certainly!'

'I'm sure I could set one up in a tank in the lockup after the slaughter season and make a few bob myself.'

'Should I notify the county boys, Ivor?'

'You think they're interested in installation art?'

'No. To cut it down?' Palindrome nodded up at the cliff face. 'Poor lass. As if she hasn't had enough.'

Punch suspected the man was referring more to Sonia, than to Iris Hislop. But it didn't really matter.

'No.' He shook, lighting a match on the rock. He puffed the roll-up alive furiously, which only set off the wild cravings for a drop of Tobermory. Rod. Ronnie. Anything. Anywhere but here. 'It's evidence. Needs to be done properly, Pal. But a good thought.'

'Aye, certainly. Right you are, Ivor.' Palindrome looked away to the sea as he spoke. 'Think it's the same person who does the letters?'

'Doubt it.'

'I hear there's another one hanging, out the Gally—'

'Aye,' Punch interjected, still craning his neck upwards. 'Half a fucking mind to throw them in the bastard'n cell for crimes to crocheting . . .'

'Some joker, certainly,' Palindrome offered. 'That's what they're saying anyway.'

'Oh, I bet that's what they're saying all right . . . and fuck.' Punch knew the man still lived with his mother, who was not short of a willing tongue to wag. 'Except. It's not. A joke. This one's gone too far.' Punch stepped back off the highest rock, his boots taking in some of the water. 'Bastard.' He pointed his torchlight to the sea. 'And the dinghy? Reports of a dinghy and oars below the thing I believe?'

'Aye.' Palindrome slotted his hands into his high pockets. 'Around at the slip. Easier to get in there, you know. Felt quite spooked here on my own to be totally honest with you.'

'Understandable,' Punch said. 'Colour?'

'Well, I was pale. Don't mind admitting.'

'No, the dinghy.'

'Oh? Black, black, I think. Dark, certainly.'

Punch pointed his torch back in the direction they had come; he couldn't quite see around the corner to the car park. He wondered if Palindrome's air of efficiency was something to do with his overuse of the word 'certainly', which, on occasion, served as a second nickname for the man.

'I'll need to survey from above,' Punch said. He shone back up to the hanging body. Briefly, he imagined that he saw Sonia Hislop.

'As if the poor lass hasn't endured enough. Aye,' Palindrome said. 'Certainly terrible. We'll do an extra pull or two on the church bells tomorrow. For your mum; Charlie, too of course.'

'Aye,' Punch managed.

He wasn't sure how it was really possible to keep Sonia Hislop from knowing. 'Containment' and 'island' were not words that easily coalesced. He looked back and couldn't quite see the lights of Macgochans, but they were evident on the bay, casting a serenity that was about to be destroyed. Palindrome had reminded him that at midnight the tenth anniversary would arrive. An hour too soon.

'Aye, this is between us and the sea for now, Pal.'

'Certainly, sergeant.'

Punch's torchlight caught the man's cherubic face. The sweat on his brow and his small, ferret-like teeth, redness evident around his darting eyes; the little boy in there underneath all that mid-fifties blubber.

'You'll need it down, sergeant, before the boys go off fishing in the morning of course. First light is considered half a day wasted for those buggers. Hardy.'

'Aye.' Punch hated to admit it, but he knew his next call had to be for Forensics from the mainland. To inspect the hand too. Still under his seat, for fuck's sake. This had gone from an exercise in pissing off the local bobby to something significantly more sinister.

'First Kilchoan ferry is six forty-eight a.m.,' Palindrome said.

'Right.'

'No idea what CalMac have got against six forty-five, but there you are.'

'I've handcuffs if you need them.'

'Happily go back to the days when the paper boat into Grass Point was the only sailing on the Sabbath. Mother used to say what use was a boat made of paper.'

Punch's eye was snagged by a single light on the sea, but it wasn't clear where. Any light out there could be Lowry, but it didn't seem likely. Punch felt watched, the noose tightening.

A faint call. Punch looked up to the path, listened hard. It was from the car radio. Cluny.

'Eh, wonder who's next?' Palindrome mused. He turned like a barrel on legs. 'Mother is available. They'd need some bloody rope to hold me.'

Punch shone the torch up again. The effigy was starting to lightly swing. Causing the little red skirt to blow. Almost giving life. It suddenly plummeted straight towards him. Punch stumbled to the rocks as it crashed down on his head.

'Christ!' Palindrome moved to help Punch to his feet. 'You okay, Ivor?'

'Aye. Aye . . .'

Palindrome leaned down and saved Punch's hat from the tide. He wiped it and handed it to him. Punch leaned to retrieve his torch. He felt an unsettling, strange discomfort at having actually come into contact with the thing, as though it was a coffin lid opened, a grave dug up, a hand shook.

'For the love of—' Palindrome shone on the effigy, now lying on the rocks beside them, the limbs positioned at an inhuman angle, the woolly hair lapping gently in the sea.

'And fuck,' Punch gasped. It was on the same spot where the real Iris Hislop had landed. 'Have you an unused plastic bag or bin liner?'

'Aye, Sarge. Back in the pier office.'

'Take these . . .' Punch wrestled two blue surgical gloves from his pocket and handed them to Palindrome. 'Put the thing in a bag. Careful not to contaminate it further. I'm certain I saw someone moving up there before it fell. Tallish. Sure of it.'

Punch stepped away as quickly as he could in the direction he had come. Still he felt watched. He wasn't sure if it was the eyes of the mainland or the island on him.

Go with your belly.

TRACK 11

SO, NOT EVERYTHING GOES TO PLAN. It wasn't intended for dearest EII to fall from the cliff. Somebody cut it down. That lovely red skirt. How could they? Spiteful Muileach lot! But the audience never knows the performance the artist had in their head. And there is comfort in the knowledge that all public art is vulnerable to tampering, to contamination. Like the booing of the pantomime villain, or the abuse dished out to the opposition's best player: in actuality, the meddling or condemnation of others could be taken as a compliment; a sign of a job well done, up to a point.

EII was more impactful than EI, even if it did not quite experience the same audience exposure, or, sweet thing, sympathy. But then, some of the world's greatest works were not publicly claimed or appreciated in the artist's lifetime: Robert Burns, Johann Sebastian Bach, Vincent van Gogh, Emily Dickinson, Claude Monet, Jack the Ripper, Bible John, and dear *him*. And is not all creativity a work in progress? It is becoming apparent that sometimes you have to let go of it; allow it into the world. The real work is about process: oh yes, everybody knows about starting points – births – and end results – deaths – but nobody much speaks of the creative journey from one to the other, the space in between. The pain and the struggle of that place, of not being properly recognised; the toll it takes on people. On families. Were the Charlie Parker recordings worth the suffering of Charlie Parker's life? But then that is where the beauty lies, too – in the creative journey. A man like Punch could be plonked in front of Michelangelo's *David* and only see the slab of granite from which it began. Or two snug bollocks and a cock. A man like Punch is no replacement for *real* quality. That is his, *their*, mistake. Why they must suffer.

But still, the desire remains, for recognition. For one to have their rightful place. To claim what has been cruelly taken from one. Which is of course fuelled by the fear all artists harbour, while still knowing it can be their undoing: the need to satiate their ego, for them to come out from behind the work. But do people not then only see the artist, at the expense of the work?

In any case, it is time to stop making other people look good. It is time to show the island what it has taken, to show her, him, that they aren't the only ones suffering. They have not been spooked sufficiently.

It is time for EIII.

Half the body is done. With this one it is proving harder than expected to nail a coherence of narrative, to accurately *find* the protagonist. It could be something to do with knowing them so well. There isn't much room for whimsy or self-expression in the work. Most abstract art comes from a debate about what is necessary in the mind of the artist, rather than what is arbitrary. Meaning, not only does EIII have to feel like it is physically authentic, more than the others it also has to exist in the present rather than memory. It is required to be almost *beyond* lifelike. Like it could bleed. There is still some shame in the guesswork involved in conjuring EII, alas. That one didn't really know her, precious thing as she was.

There is even more thrill this time in having a naked torso lying on the living-room floor, more so than with EI. EII could not be thought of in this way. Oh no. But with EIII there is a greater intimacy. As though the creations are becoming closer to the creator.

The largest needle is readied, the thread left over from the dear sweet girl. Stabbing it into the skin is becoming a form of occupational therapy. As is the act of stitching, though it is slow and still bloody at times. EII had very obviously been the girl: its size, sex and location manifest. But a more refined approach is required this time. The fingers must be just right, long and elegant. The handsome jawline has been a challenge.

I have a leg straddled on either side of the body, in order to stitch them into the crotch. There is the notion you could be playful with it, in the way you might laugh intimately with a lover. Drinks have been poured! The eyes are glued in place, staring up as though expectant of life, of love. That is the biggest sensation: knowing you can both give and end life, disseminate and withhold grace, project or withdraw intelligence: and all just by the placement of a line of thread, by the direction of the needle, the choice of fabric. Fabric can be relied on. It is people who let you down.

It is time to make the Royal College of Fashion truly proud, time for the dawn of replica number three. Undeniably one's best work yet. The first two have earned a certain amount of creative kudos, freedom. EI and EII worked hard to draw viewers in. This time, though, the audience is waiting, which brings expectation, excitement and a sense of the artist revelling in their world created. But with that come pressures, responsibilities. All artists lay themselves open to public scrutiny of their work, that is the risk, the bravery, the one thing Emily Dickinson and Bible John couldn't do; but the acclaim can be blissful. I wonder, is that what dear Sean felt, in his moments of musical recognition?

And what is it they say? Nobody ever created a statue of a critic. Effigies are another matter, though. And this one has to be different from EI and EII. It has to be more original. You do not make art from art. You make art from life. And, occasionally, from death.

Shoes have been placed on the feet. The music soars. The drink shimmers in its glass. I have allowed the mastery of Lowry, tonight. The man is well known for playing with his back to the audience, the act private and public at the same time. And that is the feeling tonight as the violins soar and the cellos attack: of multiple parts working as one, of the innermost thrill married to the knowledge that Punch is out there waiting for an encore. His island subjects witness to his public ridiculing. A reclaiming of sorts. And dear Xander providing the soundtrack. All the greats living in his head.

But not all greats last for ever. Or are recognised. Soon *he* will be here. With the instrument. And there is talk of the famous score, the original manuscript.

The sea is lapping outside, the wind building expectantly like a well-rehearsed chorus. A famed conductor I once fitted said he could tell after listening to just one note whether a musician would ever play in his orchestra. So maybe it is the same with one stitch, one body, one death, one island? Maintaining one's high bar is paramount. Your creations are only as strong as the sum of their parts. Much like an island, or a symphony. And Punch, and she, and *he*, are low bar. Weak. Lowly.

Looking down at the creation, the same question occurs now as it did when one was trying to capture the unique features, the unrepeatable essence, of the others: *What makes you original?*

Soon it will be time to have EIII rowed over. By my help, feeble man. To travel the space in between. To Punch. To bring the two elements together: not the island and the mainland – but his two disparate cases.

TRACK 12

A HEAD. ONLY A HEAD. Lying on the bedroom floor. A sheep's head?

No. The face was like his own. But not quite his own.

'Duncan!' he yelled. His body was fixed in a vice. 'Duncan!' He struggled to break free. He tried again – jolted free and bolted up, soaking in sweat.

It had been the head of his ancestor. Duncan Punch, a coal distributor-cum-coffin-builder-cum-postie, known as An Gnuis Dubh – *the Black Face*. The man who had given the family their nickname as a result of having once punched a horse on the muzzle for disobeying him. The horse was felled by the force of the blow. The man was said to be of mountainous proportions, but was subsequently beheaded in a building accident. And so he was forever cast in the island's mythology as the Headless Horseman, which even now could result in a pale teenager or two arriving at the station door with claims to having seen the beast on the outskirts of the town. 'Punch' had since stuck over the years, down his mother's side of the family. Though it sat better on him than it ever did Charlie.

Punch rubbed his eyes awake. Nothing was on the floor. No head. Just the mess of his life. And two bags: a black bin liner and a Co-op carrier bag.

He dropped his head back. The sound of scratching was reassuringly familiar, the seagulls too. He fell into the fog of sleep once again, his head landing on something unfamiliar. *The Lighthouse Path?* It was there he had fallen the night before. Having tripped over a raised root at the turn by the cannon, which it was claimed had once sunk a Spanish Armada ship in the bay. Puzzles everywhere. *The hand? What did I do with the hand?* Punch brought his longer arm up to investigate. Flinched. Stopped. It might be; it might be the body of the girl. *Am I lying on her body?* He saw her again behind his eyelids, falling to him. The painted white letters on the rock face starkly replaced by the words: 'YOU'RE NEXT'. He snaked his hand slowly up to the hard object.

'Fuck,' Punch croaked, coming to. He sighed heavily. His head was lying on an album sleeve. He took hold of the offending casing and peeled open his eyes. The Faces' *Snakes & Ladders*; could've been worse. Punch turned wearily on the mattress; his body felt like it was on one of their US tours. He took in the full disarray of the room. The Stones on the same bill apparently. He closed his eyes again; imagined the music coming through the sleeve. The year: 1976. He and Charlie jumping through the summer air, anticipating a hard, sandy landing. The claps rippling down from the expectant crowd on the grassy banking. The scent of Ralgex. MacTavish – a large man, failing in the teeth department, who was the only other athlete who could get close to them – watching on, his mean, narrow eyes fixed on the measuring tape, swigging from a flask, shorts hiked up, jockstrap in place, clangers the size of medicine balls. Everyone knew the MacTavishes hated the Punches. The grudge was in effect all year round, but reached its zenith on Games Day. The different generations of MacTavishes were known for illegality on several counts. Since returning to the island Punch had ensured the new generation regularly featured in the Courts section of *The Oban Times*.

He looked to the bin liner. There were a few likely suspects, the twins possibly. Tonsils had always seemed resentful of Ivor and Charlie for – in his delusional mind – taking their mother's attention off him; and Tinsel, despite his retirement from Argyll & Bute's roads department, certainly had the tailoring skills. And then there was MacTavish, who still had a beef with the Punches for taking his triple jump record, Ivor breaking it first, and then Charlie having taken his. It was always Charlie flying higher. Punch could almost see MacTavish as he was then, his shorts hiked up high and dangerously close to his nipples even by the standards of the Hebridean crofting community. The MacTavishes had farmed the land around Salen for generations and the elder was sure Punch had a vendetta against his law-bending sons. Hardly a brain cell between them, thought Punch, they were past winners of the annual Mull Rally and he had regularly cautioned them for thrashing around the Mull roads as though it was rally fever all year round. Pulling out the breathalyser wasn't beyond him either.

He lifted his head to check the overnight damage to the bottle, having stopped counting in glasses. It was officially the anniversary. No wonder the nightmares. Ten years since Charlie took his final leap, which didn't bear thinking about really; ten years since Punch had stared into that black night out at Calgary, the Atlantic about as wide as a puddle. He wished he could sleep right through it.

The hand. He remembered now putting it in the specialised cooler unit he used for the mutton in the station lockup after slaughtering. Maybe Dave could do something with it?

He was still in uniform and his fingers touched, then worried briefly at a rip by his elbow. Mary MacBeth was handy with repairs; never wanted paying, but he insisted. It was an arrangement that suited them both. They both knew it was more; impossible to equate in crocheting terms. Or maybe that's all that was left. *But she couldn't be – could she?*

He had seen nothing conclusive on the Lighthouse Path after leaving Palindrome, having then instructed Randy to go out and bag the Gally Goo effigy. And strangely, no sight of the dinghy either in the bay. He felt a chill up his spine at the recollection of Palindrome delivering the Iris Hislop effigy to the station, after he had dealt with the hand. Just a Co-op carrier for the size of the little thing. Palindrome had turned away with a gimlet-eyed fear, barely a word from that ferret mouth of his, and sweat still slick on his brow. Punch had never seen the man look so pale, even with a felled tree trunk in his hands.

He rolled onto his feet, shook his head and walked to the window, bracing his eyes for the shock of daylight, making a gap in the blinds.

'Christ,' he croaked.

Two Rangers. Guinness was already watering his conifers no doubt. Tobacco. If only a computer could locate tobacco. Punch began a salvage operation but stopped when he arrived at the carrier bag on the floor. Lying there innocuously, it might just as well have contained a six-pack and a pizza were it not for the string of red wool escaping along the carpet. It didn't look right discarded so haphazardly. But he couldn't face picking it up. Not today.

He made his way wearily through to the toilet and dared a look in the mirror. Keith Moon came to mind. In fact, he had a kit boxed out in the lockup, but he had no clue if he could still play. Charlie's guitar too. Playing it, like everything else, came easy to his little brother. A sheep was out there too, readied for the slaughter. *'Pull it up high so the mice and rats don't get to it,'* his uncle would say. Words that could apply to the hand too.

Punch unbuttoned his trousers and let them fall to the floor. Sat on the toilet and rubbed at his forehead. He picked up the opened book from the floor where he had left it, a Tackle & Books place-marker within. *Great Naval Fleets*. He had never bought another kind of book. There was something about massive structures moving people through the sea from place to place he admired; vessels like floating islands in a way. He imagined how good it would feel to be the captain, standing alone in the bridge, a nudge of your knuckle steering thirty thousand tons wherever you wanted.

When he was done, he put the book down, flushed and stood to push the window open, noticing it was already off the latch. *Clumsy, Ivor.* He turned to slide open the door to the shower.

'Bastard!' He stumbled backwards, grabbing the towel rail. 'Jesus. Jesus fuck!'

There was a body curled on the base of his shower.

He reached to pull the door closed. Turned to the window and back to the shower. The effigy was dressed like a country gent, deerstalker and pilot's goggles. The handiwork implied a more refined affair. Thankfully, a saggier arse. It was Lowry. Missing only a sky, a plane and a violin. Punch, the audience. He looked more closely: two hands.

'Fucking bastards!' Punch dropped to the floor and rummaged in his shirt pocket for smokes and a light.

This was personal on top of personal. Breaking and entering? A fucking police house – while he was in it? The bathroom, of all places. But, who? *Randy?* Couldn't be, surely. He was a tool of the highest order but he wasn't this stupid. Punch looked to the curled body again. Then double-checked the window latch. *Careless, careless.* Now he had three effigies in the police station. One more and he had a band.

A double knock on the front door.

'Fuck.' Punch rose quickly and turned out of the toilet. Closed the door behind him. A single knock. He crossed the room in his Y-fronts, cigarette in mouth, but didn't make it in time.

A key turned and the front door opened.

'Oh?' she said, trying not to look to his lower half, her eyes dancing over the rest of the room. 'I thought you were in the station?'

Mary MacBeth was unusually pale. Punch knew why.

'I just . . . I just thought I'd come over, you know . . .' She shifted her handbag from one wrist to the other.

'You're dressed up?' he said.

'I see you made an effort too.' She looked to the room. 'So, Rod's visited again. Half the seventies, in fact . . .'

'You didn't see the TV in the garden?' Punch moved to take the needle off the vinyl; 'The Killing of Georgie (Part I and II)'. He forgot he had gone to the darker side of the repertoire in the early hours. Death was everywhere; he wondered sometimes if it was a drug. He bent to turn off the stereo amp. 'Distraction, you know. Takes the steam off . . .'

'Yes.' She nodded solemnly. 'I know.'

She waved a hand through the smoke and moved to draw the blinds. Punch felt disloyal for looking for plasters on her fingers.

'The briefing rooms don't look much like this on *Taggart*,' she said.

'He doesn't have Randy bloody Fleming visiting.'

Punch grimaced to the light, to the world closing in on him as he stood, a forty-five-year-old man in his underpants, with not a hair on his legs and a badger crawling up each side of his head. She had seen it all before, but still he felt exposed.

'So, eh, didn't want to try you at the station but you've got an unscheduled, eh *Sunday* visit . . .' she said, as though suddenly embarrassed and needing to overly justify her presence. The significance of the timing was not lost on either of them. He knew she felt as he did, that a singular cloud was hanging over their part of north Tobermory.

'Doing your own repairs now are you?' Mary MacBeth said.

'Eh?'

'On your doorstep.' She was holding a clump of red wool.

'Oh? Right. Eh ...' Punch looked to her and then away. 'Council boys are not what they were on the bins. Somebody's rubbish blown over last night likely.'

He watched Mary put part of Iris Hislop in her jacket pocket. She leaned down to pick up an empty bottle.

'I'm not here for the cleaning of course,' she said, 'but well, now I'm in Dodge ... the place smells more like a distillery than a distillery. You might get another measure wafting a glass through the air.'

'I'm sure we tried it.'

'Tobermory founded 1788 and the distillery 1798 – they waited ten years ...'

'Aye. Thirsty buggers.'

'Feeling sorry for yourself won't bring, well ...'

'Aye. And fuck. I know.'

'Ivor ... The Sabbath.'

'And it will be all day.' He took a long, final drag. 'Sorry. So, it's finally here as well. The tenth.'

'Yes.'

'Feels longer.'

'It does.'

Punch stubbed the cigarette butt into one of the two empty glasses on the table. A flashback of Randy proudly showing him his new Forestry ID in the early hours returned to him: a photo of him wearing a chainsaw, a broad toothy smile and nothing else. And he himself with two live cases and a person's hand in the lockup.

Mary cracked a window. She was wearing a black raincoat to match her hair, though it too – like his – was greying a little around the fringe; it was easy to think of her as from another era. He noticed the black line up the back of her tights. The smell of talc. He had thought only babies and old people wore talc. Though he remembered her mother had smelled the same when he went over after school.

Mary picked up both glasses and walked to the kitchenette. Her handbag still on her wrist. He recalled her in the primary school; he fixed to her side and trying to make it look the other way around, and how she had seemed this age even then. Aloof, an island herself. That being the allure. She bent to take out a cleaning product from under the sink. The only thing of note down there to Punch was an insurance bottle of Bell's, which he kept should the Tobermory Malt – a steady supply of which fell off the back of a distillery truck into the boot of his police Ranger once a month – ever run out.

He looked in the direction of the toilet and then to Mary MacBeth, hoping she wouldn't go in to inspect; the last thing he needed was gossip about him and blow-up dolls going about town. Though he doubted it would be a surprise to anyone. Not that she was a gossip. Like him, she was far too solitary a beast. He often wondered if a police sergeant should be *more* interested in other people's business. It was a well-oiled line that if you farted in Tobermory they could tell you what you had for breakfast by the time you reached Salen.

Punch viewed her now as a woman separate from him, from their shared history, separate from cleaning products and menial tasks – which he knew were really self-imposed barriers to her allowing herself more from life – separate even almost from, *no* – not that. The thought persevered whether Mary MacBeth could have entered in the night? She wasn't a woman ever stuck for a needle and thread, after all. But that was ridiculous. Such a thought he knew was symptomatic of his own failing, which had fallen on Janice, too: when anybody got too close, he made a suspect of them.

'That should take care of the worst of it,' she said, spraying air freshener around the room. 'Do you *have* trousers?'

'Uh-huh. Course.' Punch looked down and turned quickly towards the toilet. He stopped and instead grabbed a pair from the floor.

'Better than nothing.' Mary leaned to pick up the carrier bag. 'No doubt there's cold items not refrigerated.'

'Leave it!' Punch almost fell as he moved in haste to the bag, one foot still out of his trousers. He hopped towards her, and she moved away. 'Eh, I'll do it. Aye. Sorry.'

'Rightio, Hopalong,' Mary said, widening her eyes. 'Message received. Is that how you talk to your guy?'

'Fawkes?'

'Eh? The new fellow I'm talking about. Blondie ...'

'Oh, *Guinness*? Aye. Eh. Sorry.' Punch fastened his trousers and stored the carrier bag by the side of the bed.

'Cans, is it?' she said. 'You'll need better hiding places than that.'

'Guilty as charged, Miss Marple. I should issue you a badge and handcuffs while I'm at it.'

She transferred her weight from one leg to the other. Punch knew now came the real business.

'So. I, eh, wondered . . .' she began. Punch saw her tongue lubricate her lips the way it did even back when; he had noticed George Harrison did the same, all shy people possibly. 'If you'd like me to take your mother to the church – today? You know . . .' She took a cloth and distractedly wiped the sink surface. 'Well. Given you'll have a lot going on, that's why I'm here, asking this, outwith my usual cleaning day. Just thought it might help . . .'

'What have you heard?' Punch said, wishing it hadn't been his first response. He knew she would know he didn't want to face any of it; that she was substituting herself for him. He did up his buckle and stepped into his shoes; the shirt would have to be fine.

She looked at him and he wondered if she was seeing the noose. If she too was feeling even more stuck in that black winter's night in 1988. She was like the big sister Charlie never had. He always had the feeling she had taken it better than him. Knew what to do with it, where to put it: grief. That being the other loss, the one they *didn't* talk about.

'Just that you'll have been busy.' She took a deep breath. 'I hear you have a doppelganger.'

'One name for it. Randy's cut the thing down.' He stopped himself gesturing to the other bag on the floor. He rubbed his face and then slapped his cheeks with both palms.

He was relieved she didn't seem to know about Lowry and the missing plane. He didn't want his mother getting a hold of that.

137

'Anyway,' she said. 'I'm happy to take her. Well, not *happy* . . . But I'd like to.'

'Right. Well, that'd be, eh, appreciated. She'll be fine with that.' Punch took the sleeve from the bed. Walked it to the record player.

'Oh, that one you *do* put away?'

Punch looked up as he slotted the vinyl into the sleeve.

'Wasn't much cop as a pillow anyway.'

'Okay. That's sorted. I'll take her.' Mary transferred her handbag again. 'Feels like yesterday and like a lifetime away all at once. Why do round numbers matter more?'

'They do. And I don't know why. I'll drive you over. I suppose she might not register – Mother. Can only hope.'

'I mean the other thing too.'

'I know you do.'

Mary moved to take his rolled-up uniform jacket from the brown sofa.

'If God himself screwed a hook by the door you'd still choose the sofa,' she managed.

'God didn't have Randy turning up at two a.m. Pretty sure he didn't work in the Forestry either.'

'No. Carpentry.'

'Aye.'

More of it was returning to him now; Randy arriving at the door, demonstrating a rare discretion saying he had parked the Forestry pickup down at the park in case any neighbours stirred. A bottle in hand and the effigy under an arm. Looking like a particularly malnourished stagehand on *Noel's House Party*, whose next stop was a Guns N' Roses convention. Randy confirming the Hislop lass hadn't been on shift. One relief, Punch had thought. He had taken his likeness and tossed the thing into a bin liner, putting it alongside the smaller effigy in the carrier bag. Something of drowned cats in a sack about them. Randy had then blown all previous attempts at discretion by letting slip that Punch's doppelganger had been propped up in his passenger seat on the way back from the Gally Goo. That it was better company than the real deal. Punch had had half a mind to run the thing through the intoxicator.

He rubbed his eyes fully awake. Behind his lids he could still picture the gangly body he was sure he had seen up on the Lighthouse Path. A flat cap, he was certain. And the dinghy aspect was still bothering him. Palindrome verifying it had been there one minute and then gone by the time he returned after phoning in. The Irish boys by then halfway to renditions of 'Danny Boy' and tomorrow's hangover.

Punch turned to the mirror and made the best with taming the badgers.

'Here,' Mary said, offering his police jacket. 'Maybe it is as well to be just any other day, you know, if that's where she's at.'

'Sonia Hislop?'

'Eh? No, your mother.'

Punch saw the effects on her of him mentioning another woman. But couldn't do anything about that. He took his jacket from her and noted how she had turned up the sleeve of his shorter arm. She was only a few doors down in Creagan Park, but it felt further away than the mainland. Not a weed in her garden. He knew she had had to throw herself into something after; that faith alone wouldn't do it.

139

And so, it was to the earth and the sky that Mary MacBeth had gone, to gardening and God. Her own little patch of north Tobermory a sort of heaven. And Punch a few doors down, living in his own kind of hell.

A streak of light arrived like a blade on the worn carpet. Punch narrowed his eyes to the door, where the sky was grey, expectant of bigger weather. They both looked to the floor and knew what the other was thinking. That it was she, or he. Returned. They never knew the sex.

'Well . . .' Mary MacBeth said, her voice failing but trying to rise through the word. She moved to open the door.

Punch followed her out. Made sure to lock the door behind him. It felt strange knowing he had company in there, a human hand out the back. He wasn't sure for how much longer he could fly solo with it.

He turned to survey Cluny's Ranger, realising it was actually possible to park a vehicle self-importantly. People took planes to places all the time for different reasons, this close to Christmas; he knew that, unfortunately. But a break-in to police property was something else. Wider search teams were primed – he had left the mainland to Cluny, for him to liaise with Control first thing – and now localised searches would need to go out on Lowry. Punch preferred to do his own work on the ground, but this was bigger. There was also something about the woman Lauder and Nigel Townsend that needed more prodding, to do with how they were together. A man did not fly off from his lover, a cosy log fire and a drop of fine wine in his hand – not to mention a stellar career – in the dark of a winter's night because he

140

was enjoying the company. Reluctantly, Punch was going to have to cast the net wider.

There were questions only he knew to ask:

Whose hand did he have?

And who was Maggie May?

TRACK 13

THE CHURCH BELLS WERE RINGING, bringing a sense of calling. Punch wasn't sure if it was the job, the dead or God pulling on him.

But no doubt it was Palindrome on the ropes. It was strange to think of the man making music. Of the town moving to his tune.

The puzzle of the past two days was pressing on Punch. He stood outside the station and looked beyond his little patch of green on the other side of the fence, and then over to his lockup where the hand was, enclosed in an evidence bag. He took a glance up Erray Road towards the golf course. Fighting the image of it too having bodies strewn across it. His mind landed on Sonia Hislop, on her family of three that did not happen. He had heard her man was like a shadow of a person that last time coming back on the ferry. Barely able to strap a guitar on him, they said. Poor lass carrying his baby as well. There had been talk that that was why the wee girl had fallen, that she *wasn't right*, that she had been damaged in some way by the rock

142

and roll lifestyle. Punch would happily lock the cell on folk for gossip alone.

He shook his head free, turned towards the station door but stopped at the sight of the motionless head and shoulders of Mary MacBeth already in the back seat of his Ranger. Facing in the other direction. Something about her remove spoke of Sonia Hislop. They had both lost a child, after all.

He had intended to check in on Cluny, to ensure search calls had gone out, but a quick dash to the church and back couldn't really be avoided. The lad would never learn how to wipe his own arse unless he let him.

Punch heard the rhythm of a ceilidh band. Getting louder. It was Randy's Forestry pickup, racing towards him down through Creagan Park.

'Christ . . .' He sighed.

The pickup approached and proceeded to drive past Punch into the driveway opposite. Randy made a fuss of a three-point turn and drew up alongside. He lowered the music and wound his window down.

'It's you? Yip yip,' Randy said, the serious look on his face at loggerheads with the music; Punch could tell he was still carrying something of the night before. 'Hellish business, Ivor.'

'Who were you expecting, man? A footman in livery? And fuck.'

He looked towards Randy's stereo.

'I'm no Pete Waterman but I'm not convinced it goes with the church bells.'

'There's a present in the boot for you, yip yip . . .'

'Christ, not now, man. And fuck.' Punch looked around the neighbouring bungalows. Pebbledash. Everywhere.

143

'Got six with your name on them. Now or never, Sarge,' Randy said, signalling his head backwards. 'Me and a couple of the boys did a tree run this morning. Still folk making last-minute orders.'

'Anything to get away from this music.'

'One for your mum, you know . . .' he heard.

Punch walked to the rear of the pickup and opened the back door. There was a case of Tennent's alongside dust sheets that looked like they were concealing bodies. He reached in tentatively and removed a sheet to reveal thankfully not more human parts but rows of fir trees. Next to them was a box of CDs. Each CD had the same photo on the front, which was of Randy standing holding his bagpipes outside the Mishnish Hotel. The text – *RANDY MEETS HIS PUBIC* – was set above the hotel entrance in an unfortunately bright, purple font. It was a dismal attempt to make it look like the text was actually neon letters fixed onto the hotel facade. Not even Rick Wakeman had tried purple on yellow.

Punch gently closed the boot of the pickup. He returned to Randy, who had a can on the go, kept low.

'Don't say it, I know. Typo,' Randy said. 'Got three hundred of the fuckers.'

'I thought Edna was in charge of business affairs and promotions. Unless she *is*?'

'The long-haired general?' Randy puffed. 'Striking for better pay. Yip yip.'

'Better tunes too, if she's any sense.'

'Costliest fucking *L* in the history of the bloody recording industry. Oh . . .' Randy reached to his passenger side and handed Punch a small white sock.

Punch took it, gulped.

'Must've fallen off the wee girl last night—'

'Right, uh-huh.' Punch stuffed the sock into his trouser pocket.

'Right, I'm off to see an elf about a tree or two. Yip yip.' Randy pulled his hood down. He nodded back to Punch's Ranger. 'Thinking about you. All of you.'

Randy drove off and Punch brought his hand to his mouth as though he might puke. He steadied himself, then walked speedily to the Ranger.

'I see you're still keeping fine company . . .' he heard, upon opening the driver's door. 'The man was trouble in the school and it won't change now.'

'You don't want to be in the front?'

'No. I'll leave that for her. The optics are preferred.'

'Right.' Punch nodded ahead. 'I'll take my hat off at least. Always knew I was just one notch up from a chauffeur.'

They drove down past the play park before he could think against it. Tongues would be wagging; they both knew it. He was thankful for the tint on the windshield. He had made his fair share of enemies but couldn't think of one who would go to this kind of trouble. An insult to his fiefdom was an insult to him. Whoever was doing this knew that, was trying to get under his skin, his fleece. Rip it open. Sew a needle and thread along it. Like the slaughtering of a sheep in his lockup.

But why?

They emerged from the top of the Back Brae, where the bells were more dominant. A small gathering of folk was visible below the church.

145

'Busy,' he heard from the back seat.

'Already. Aye.'

He swung the Ranger to the right and up by An Tobar, the new arts centre, which before had been his old primary school building. It was there he first became aware of Mary MacBeth, and that, physically, he was not like all the other kids, pools of urine gathered on the wooden floorboards below his chair. She running for toilet roll.

He took the sharp, steep left up Breadalbane Street in an attempt to avoid the watchful eyes at the church. He recalled the excitement of weddings when they were kids, how all the children would gather outside the church for what they called *scrambles*, which was the tradition of a pile of coins thrown to the ground by the best man.

Punch pulled into Glen Iosal and parked up. No effigies. A bonus. If he himself were the culprit, this was where he would go next. You had to think like a criminal to catch one. He looked to the Scout Hall and the steep little incline in the grassy bank in front of it that used to be a makeshift bike ramp. Before his mother took him and Charlie to Inverness. It had all happened so quickly. He never understood why. Only that his uncle remained. The man had been a whaler in the Arctic, hands like fish scales.

'Right. I'll go in?' Mary MacBeth said, as though speaking in a code they both understood. She stared straight ahead: 'Will she know?'

'Maybe not. Or maybe she knows everything, more than we do. I'll get her ladyship's carriage ready. She likes the back seat on a Sunday.'

'Well, you can't be meaning me.'

Punch heard the back door opening and then closing. He watched her walk to the red-brick building. The line in her stockings stretching as she progressed. The woman he knew but didn't.

He jumped out. Opened the back door. There was a need to show some sense of haste, given he was in the middle of several live cases and on public show. Lowry was pressing on him. But he knew he had to be here now. Though the timing stank. He felt caught between the ugly past and the urgent present. He plumped up the pillow she liked. It was hard to know which version of his mother would emerge. Often she thought he was the uncle now.

'Sergeant Punch, this is PC Cluny. Come in, Sergeant Punch, this is PC Cluny. Over.'

Punch reached for the handset.

'Come in, PC Cluny. Punch. Receiving. Over.'

'Mr Lowry has still not made any contact with Lussa Falls, or anyone else as far as we know, Sarge. No changes to the status as of last night. We still have a missing person as of this morning. Over.'

'Aerial backup and coastguard deployment? Over,' Punch said. He couldn't stop himself looking to the befuddled sky for clues.

'Affirmative, Sarge. Awaiting your instruction for activating additional boots on the ground. Over.'

'Right, PC Cluny. I'm following a line of questioning first, will update forthwith. Await instructions. Keep me informed of developments. Over.'

'Received, sergeant. I'll notify Control and stay positioned at the station. Over.'

Punch took the small sock from his pocket. It had been burning a hole. He extended his reach to the glove compartment and pulled out an evidence bag. Placed the sock inside and put the bag back in the compartment.

The two women emerged from his mother's doorway. Punch felt guilty now for not going inside. His mother's folk were originally from Lewis, and it showed on a Sunday.

He stood by the back door of the Ranger.

'I wasn't sure about the slippers ...' his mother said, without looking at him. 'You know, on a Sunday?'

'As long as you're comfortable,' Mary MacBeth reassured.

'That's it, Mum, easy now.' Punch smelled the familiar odour of perfume. He eased his mother into the back seat of the Ranger.

'My escort again, eh, son?'

'Aye, Mother. That'll be it. What's good enough for the Pope, eh?'

'What's the Pope got to do with it? Too much bleach. Bleach!'

'Eh, Mum?' Punch looked distractedly to the top of the Prison Brae opposite; his following of Sonia Hislop the night previous seemed like a lifetime ago, and more than a little dodgy. Though nobody would have suspected much of his Ranger parked at Glen Iosal. 'Bleach? I'm not wearing anything with bleach, Mum. Barely had time to shave, by Christ.'

'Same!' His mother let out a fit of laughter. 'No, the new Pope's jerkin's too *white*. Doesn't suit his pallor. And that's not just a Protestant talking.'

'Right. I'll put a ribbon in the typewriter later, Mum. Better still, I'll have Guinness fire an email straight to the Vatican.'

148

'Oh! Friends in high places, that's my boy!'

There was a short pause. Punch heard his mother's chest wheezing, like an accordion warming up. He caught Mary's eye as he eased his mother onto the pillow in the back seat.

'Tell me, son. I've been meaning to ask. What is this *fax* thing I keep hearing about?'

'Eh? Oh, it's a kind of carrier pigeon in the future. We're in the future now, Mum.'

'Do you have a fax machine, dear?' she said, turning in the direction of Mary MacBeth, who was now symmetrical with a handbag on each wrist.

'No,' she said. 'Just a doorbell.'

Punch fastened her seat belt and then closed her door. He dropped into the driver's seat and Mary joined him in the front.

'Aye, nice to have an escort, Charlie lad,' he heard from the back.

Ivor gulped. Reversed slowly, catching his mother's contented look in the rearview mirror, which was at odds with how it had been ten years ago to the day, after he had come back from Calgary. She already bent over in her kitchen, grabbing at the fridge door for support. He dropping next to her on the linoleum.

'Did you hear there's another hike?' his mother said.

'Eh, Mum?'

'In the price of monkfish. Heard it on the *Fishmarket Report*.'

'Recession's always next.'

They crossed Albert Street, near his old house next to the graveyard. His and Charlie's bedroom had been the closest room to the graveyard, and he would lie in bed at night aware he could almost reach out and touch it: death.

'They produced the caviar of dung.'

'Eh, Mother?'

'Your uncle's sheep.'

Punch thought of the two brown armchairs by the fireplace that he and Charlie would be plonked on as children. Each chair with tears in the leather. He used to think he might fall inside and discover a new world, maybe even his father. Often during shearing season, he had witnessed his uncle stuffing wool into the chairs to buff them up with his cattle-swollen hands. The few Hebrideans Punch kept even now could be traced back to that first flock.

The windscreen became full of the bay as they turned right off Breadalbane Street and steeply towards the church, the morning apricity landing on their faces.

'Everything changes, except the sea,' his mother said, tilting her face a little into the warmth.

'Aye, Mum.'

He looked to Calve Island plonked out there like a battleship on a board game. Reached to turn up the handset and heard updates over the loop between Cluny and a case manager at the Control room. News of the Tobermory RNLI and a police helicopter primed to go out if needed at *thirteen hundred hours*. Talk of backup officers to follow at *the sergeant's request*. But the sergeant was going to church, to visit the other sergeant, if not the past.

'Has Charlie been killed again?' his mother blurted, realising where they were.

'What? Christ, no, Mum. No.' Punch lowered the handset.

They pulled in alongside the church. A hearse was parked in front.

'Just a spot of local bother on the airwaves, Mum. Remember, I wouldn't have a pay packet without it.'

'Like transporting a desert – a desert!' wheezed his mother, shaking her head.

Mary MacBeth smiled.

'Eh, Mum?'

'Last night, the nurse was doing the rounds, you know, with the nightcaps. And not a single malt among them!'

'Medicinal, that's what they say, eh?' Mary MacBeth smiled.

'They said the man was a bloody artist!' his mother declared.

'Uncle?' Punch turned.

'Hitler. And shoe-leather steaks of course.'

'Hitler?' Mary said.

'No dear! The Co!'

'Should we go in?' Mary MacBeth said, opening her door and closing it behind her.

'I have never told you, son, but I'm telling you now,' he heard. The timbre of his mother's voice sounded like she was more in the present. 'Don't live a lonely life. Not all your life. Not like me. Let him go.'

'Rightio!' Mary announced, having opened the back door.

Punch watched his mother riffling through her handbag.

'Hankies. *Uh-huh*. Lipstick. *Uh-huh*. Bible. *Uh-huh*,' she said, nodding her approval each time.

'Okay,' Mary said. 'All present and correct, eh? I'll get your handbag.'

'Thank you, Mary. Och, tissues mostly. You know the thing. Clean, though. A few mints on the loose.'

'I've a few myself ...' Punch said.

Smatterings of people were approaching from different directions. Each wearing clothes of various colours, as though a paint palette had taken off in the wind.

Punch saw the gangly Tonsils pass. He was walking as usual on the tips of his toes, as though made of feathers. The fancy flat cap in place. The look on his face like a man who had delivered himself onto the wrong stage.

'Och, there he is!' Punch's mother wheezed. 'I swear that man will be behind me at the Pearly Gates!'

Punch turned to see the man walk through the church gate. The image up above him on the Lighthouse Path from the night before came to him now. Surely, if it *were* the old twin, he couldn't have got out of sight so quickly? He would need to follow up.

Punch eased his mother up and Mary MacBeth took an arm too.

'God waits for nobody ...' his mother said. 'And me in slippers, Charlie!'

Punch felt a hand on his back. Mary MacBeth walked past him and quickly caught up with the old woman and looped her arm.

Their secret language, he thought.

'Eh, Mother ...' he called, but neither she nor Mary turned. He had forgotten to tell her he couldn't go in; that matters in the present were overtaking those of the past.

'Aye-aye, Punch,' came a voice behind him.

He turned to see the overalled legs of MacTavish; his wife Sheila was already through the church gate, assisting Mary MacBeth with his mother.

152

'MacTavish,' said Punch, standing fully out of the car. Still a few inches in arrears. He closed the door on the radio updates. He recalled the first time he had felt this diminished, when visiting the MacTavish croft when both men were small boys, when his mother was making a house visit to the old MacTavish woman. The day was made memorable, if not traumatic, when one of their rams ran at him and rolled him several times. MacTavish's father, a man they called the Three Wise Men, had come to his rescue, grabbing the beast by its horns, laughing loudly. Insult was only added to injury when it was revealed the ram was also named 'MacTavish'.

'Sergeant,' said MacTavish. 'Cold getting. I see the uniform's out on a Sunday.'

'Come to repent?'

'Christ, the balls are itching today,' MacTavish said with a swift shake of his head. 'Herpes waits for no man. Even on the Sabbath.' He bent both legs at the knee as he scratched his crotch. 'Could do with a shoulder under them.'

'Or handcuffs?' Punch said.

'Aye.' MacTavish chuckled as he made some further adjustments below. 'Don't remember you cuffing that little ram that made a fool of you back in the day, Punch . . .'

'It's "Sergeant" when I'm in uniform. And out of it too, come to mention.'

'Anyway. Shame about the saggy arse . . .'

Punch watched MacTavish, who was a few years older than him, creaking off slowly towards the church, then stopping to lean on the gate, the man's head a mass of unruly hair fixed to his torso as though the sculptor had run out of clay. He was sure the man could be rotated ninety degrees in any direction and he would essentially look the same.

MacTavish appeared closer now to falling into a grave than he did a sandpit.

Punch slammed the back door closed. Walked around to the driver's side, reapplying his hat. It was time to get his head back on Lowry. He knew he should also have alerted wider about the station break-in, but he was embarrassed by it. He looked to the church again; the past was pulling harder on him. He took his hand off the door handle, reasoning there was possibly more to investigate inside the church than out of it. He locked the Ranger and walked through the gate. Maybe it was best to send the town a dual signal of normality as well as surveillance. All he would see was a church full of suspects. He needed to take a closer look at Tonsils' stitching.

Inside, Punch waited for his eyes to adjust and then smiled in the only way he knew how in the direction of some of the congregation gathered in the back pews. He wondered if folk felt like criminals when they looked at him, even here. Up ahead, he saw MacTavish taking a pew in instalments.

The organ began. Punch spotted Mary MacBeth and his mother, still in her headscarf, packed in near the front. He caught the eye of Dave the Grave at the back, sitting next to the spouse of Phil the Pill, the island's doctor – the tall Victoria.

Punch slid in next to Dave.

'Sergeant,' came the whisper.

'Dave.'

'Oaf, the uniform I see.'

'Aye.'

Dave was in his usual attire of black trousers and black mac, with black shiny shoes that Punch could see made Guinness's look like those of a homeless person.

'Spot of bother out the Gally I hear, Sarge?' Dave said.

Punch rubbed his stubble, shifted on the pew. There had been talk of a clean-shaven policy being introduced across all divisions. No doubt Tulliallan were already stocking up on razors and bog roll. Next, sniffers would be given aftershave.

'Aye,' Punch said. 'Wouldn't call it bother, but aye.'

'Cold case?'

'Well, there's a breeze on it, no doubting ...'

'Oaf, you'll have Monteith at Craignure pulled in?'

Punch turned to Dave. 'No. No need. Anyway, she's on holiday.'

'She'll likely have the speed gun on holiday with her.'

'Could come in handy. Looks like she might break a few records between the sheets.'

'Echo's late today,' Dave said, in reference to the reverend, so nicknamed because of his habit of repeating himself. He blinked his fish-like eyes to the altar.

'Aye.' Punch stared at Dave's leg, which was moving up and down rapidly, causing the whole pew to reverberate.

'Oaf, I'm a maelstrom of tics,' Dave informed him, unnecessarily. 'I never approach an opened coffin anticlockwise. Haven't touched a door handle in twelve years. New pants twice a day. Always black. Exhausting.'

'Right.' Punch noted two of Dave's fingers had plasters on them. Not like the man, given his high bar for precision

155

and presentation. *Could he be in the frame?* He was a dark bastard, no mistake.

'Oaf, you should know I've a new lad helping me,' Dave said. 'A William Urquhart. Billy the Box they're calling him already.'

'Promising ...'

'Can I let you into a secret, sergeant ...' Dave leaned into Punch. 'Sometimes I come here to observe who might be ready, you know, to croak next ... Helps with coffin orders, you know. I even park by the gate to encourage them.'

'Bloody hell, Dave.'

Punch was about to deliver news of the severed hand when the sound from the organ grew louder. The truth was, he enjoyed dealing with criminals as much as Dave relished the dead; it made him feel better about himself. He had even once spent the night in the cell, going through the rigmarole of turning on the heating fan outside and relieving himself in the porcelain toilet with no paper.

'Terrible business for you and your mum ...' Dave said.

Punch turned to him.

'The anniversary, I mean.' Dave sighed. 'Saw it on the news earlier. Of course, it was in the calendar. Thinking of you all. Wish I'd had the chance to box him for you.'

Dave leaned right into Punch, who tried his best not to take in too much of the man's aftershave, which smelled more of TCP than anything else.

'Despite the respectability of the pearl set and golf club membership,' Dave whispered, nodding his head in the direction of the doctor's wife, 'they say she's got a tongue

156

on her like an anteater. A lesbian apparently. The doctor's wife charade, oaf – just a cover, I hear.'

'Not technically an offence, Dave. On either count.'

'No.' Dave brought his hand with the plasters out in front of him. 'A few nicks from the scalpel. Repairing the floor lino I was. Funny, never happens with a body.'

Punch knew he needed to get back to the station and onto the Control officer. Though making another trip out to Lussa Falls was pressing on him. Control were running background checks on Lowry, to assess whether they corresponded with the accounts of Lauder and Townsend, as taken by Cluny. It wouldn't be hard to find out more given Lowry's prominence as a musician.

The organ stopped and Reverend MacLean in his white robes stepped up to the altar.

'Hung like a bull I suspect,' whispered Dave.

'You'll find out eventually.'

'Please stand! Please stand!' came the voice booming out from the pulpit, filling the church.

'Here goes,' Dave said, 'his weekly fight against the humanists.'

Reverend MacLean nodded to the organist and motioned for the congregation to stand. He then led them through the opening hymn, 'The Lord Is My Shepherd'.

When the organ played its last, resounding notes, the reverend motioned to the congregation to take their pews.

'Luke. Luke,' he announced crisply, bringing his arms out wide on either side as though about to take off.

Punch saw something of a Vegas-period Elvis; all that was missing were the sideburns, a row of fruit machines and

157

three gospel singers. He suspected the line doing the rounds was that he had the same set-up in the station house.

'I doubt Lowry could have lasted more than an hour up there with a fuel tank that size,' Dave hissed. 'Surviving the water temperatures wouldn't be much different. Thirty minutes tops.'

So, word was out. Punch had hoped to brief Dave first.

'The Gospel according to Luke!' Reverend MacLean summoned. 'According to Luke! Companion of St Paul the Apostle, the Apostle ... erm ... oh ...?'

The reverend's gaze had become fixed towards Punch in the back of the church. His arms slowly fell to his sides, as though accepting he was mortal. A circumspect look arrested his face. Punch felt the man's gaze going through him.

Fuck – is he going to say something about Lockerbie? Is this what it feels like to be guilty?

Punch watched as, pew upon pew, heads turned to him. He wanted to duck down, to make sand dunes of the pews just as he and Charlie used to do for cover at Calgary Beach. Even Mary MacBeth had turned to face the rear, a kind of horror on her face.

'Friends – we have not ... we have not seen a ghost, a ghost!' Reverend MacLean proclaimed, having arrived in the upper pulpit, an air of condescension in his piercing voice as he gazed out.

The heads all swivelled back to the altar.

Punch felt as though he was wearing *real* badgers.

'Erm, friend, friend. Please, *please* join us ...?' Reverend MacLean flattened what remained of his combover.

'Is it my dandruff or yours?' Dave whispered to Punch, his leg levitating into overdrive.

Punch fiddled with his hat on his lap, felt his breath tighten; the noose was taking hold. He instinctively reached for his radio but had left it in the car. He was just about to stand. To try and say something. Then he heard somebody breathing deeply behind him.

'Who did it?' the voice said.

TRACK 14

PUNCH SWIVELLED IN THE PEW.

She was standing directly behind him, as if carved from stone. In a black and white chambermaid uniform with the Western Isles Hotel logo on her left breast.

Sonia Hislop.

Punch couldn't stop himself looking to her hands, imagining the trail of blood from the church door. Both were present.

Waves of murmurs travelled the church. Punch gazed along his pew and the doctor's wife boggled like she'd been caught on a fishing hook. Dave the Grave was perfectly still now, staring efficiently forwards, not unlike one of his bodies. Punch recalled the man saying Iris Hislop was the hardest corpse he'd ever had to box. The shortest, too.

'Is there a matter, a matter – friend?' questioned Reverend MacLean.

Punch felt a knee alerting his own.

'Oaf, Echo's met his match here.' Dave folded his arms and nodded to the altar, his leg now spelling out Morse Code.

'Erm ... we have ample room for you, my friend, my friend?' the reverend said, raising his arms angel-like again. 'But if we might make some progress? Please sit among us, among us?'

'Choking on the inconvenience of having to be humble in his own house,' Dave said. 'Oaf, nothing surer.'

Punch didn't know whether to rescue the woman in some way. He had experienced in the station yesterday just how powerfully she could hold a room. How her double grief – doom-loop, as she called it – could almost break you. He knew about that.

'I don't know who did it ... sir?' Sonia Hislop said.

'Did what, dear?' Reverend MacLean held his chin up by his fingers.

'It's just ...' Sonia Hislop began, 'did she really fall?' She spoke in a high, pure voice as though it too came with organ pipes, reeds and a person seated at a console playing it. Punch now saw something of the Irish singer Sinead O'Connor about her – her power, her composure and vulnerability.

'Help me ...' Sonia said.

MacLean removed his round-rimmed glasses and held them away from his eyes to imply his own, *given* eyes, his eyes as a representative of God here on Mull, were more adequate for the task.

'We will ...?' he said. 'Then we will!'

'But I have nothing, nothing left to offer you,' Sonia Hislop said.

'You *have* offered us something. You have brought yourself, brought yourself.'

161

'You ...' Sonia began, waving her arms in front of her as though flinging imaginary confetti over the congregation. 'You have taken her from me. And him. This island. And I am at war with ... with, even ... even the *view*. So, I ask again, who did it? Who helped her?'

Punch wanted to stand, to lift this woman away from the tide of staring eyes, but couldn't seem to stand himself. He wasn't certain whether Sonia Hislop was asking for a response about the effigy, or the original incident in which her daughter was lost. MacLean appeared stumped for words, unsure whether to leave the altar or not. Punch had the sense the man's status as Jesus's shepherd on Mull was in some way abandoning him, causing him to question whether everyone here was still his flock, and the kirk still a pen. Punch realised the same could be said of himself.

He noticed Tonsils leaving his pew and clumping up the aisle to exit the church.

The reverend opened his arms out wide and smiled.

'Oaf, he's at it with the angel wings again,' whispered Dave. 'Never seen him challenged in this way in his own kirk. But to show a lack of understanding would be to lose his authority. Nothing surer.'

Punch could see his mother now, folded like a penknife next to Mary MacBeth. Aligning both her slippers on the stone floor no doubt. As she had since the final days of 1988. Looking for order in anything. Hoovering day and night. He didn't know whether to move to the front or to the Hislop woman behind him. Felt silly sitting back here away from his mother, as though reneging on his duties as a son, a brother, let alone an authority figure.

162

'*Amazing Grace, how sweet the sound, that saved a wretch like me . . .*'

Sonia Hislop's faltering voice attempted to fill the church.

Punch felt it filling him. He watched all the still backs of heads, facing the altar. As if all saying in one singular movement: *we accept this. You.* Dave the Grave settled his back against the pew and placed his palms to silence his jittering thighs. Punch saw that even the doctor's wife's eyes were closed as though she too was being soothed.

'*A mortal life shall cease . . .*'

But none of it drowned out the screaming Punch heard in the silence of his mother. As though Sonia Hislop had transferred something to her on this day of all days. Anniversaries for them both. For two people who had fallen out of the sky.

Punch turned around to Sonia, to her clenched hands hanging at her front. There was a tuft of red in them. It wasn't wool. She was looking down to it as though it were a lyric sheet.

'*Was blind but now I see . . .*'

Her voice then faded away to the rafters.

'Well? Well?' MacLean smiled, trance-like, as if it was the sheepdog Punch had noticed tied up outside who had just sung out the hymn.

He heard footsteps. Turned and Sonia Hislop was walking out of the church as Tonsils had done, becoming more sandpiper to silhouette with each quickening step.

'Eh . . . right . . . right. We'll go to God's songbook, God's songbook!' the reverend said. 'His messages, his messages come to us in all ways, all ways. We must be open to receive!'

MacLean's voice rose to one high note: 'Your Bibles! Good people of Tobermory! Luke. The Gospel according to Luke. Companion of St Paul the Apostle. Companionship. Yes. Yes! We'll go there, there!'

Punch had noticed how, as Sonia Hislop sang, his mother brought a tissue from her cuff to her eyes. And now he saw the way his mother turned in Mary MacBeth's direction. Knowingly. Assuredly. Proudly. Without care of being cautioned by the past, or by her faith. It made her seem further away to him, and the ocean never-ending. Briefly, he knew it: she didn't need him. Nobody did. Not even the dead.

There was something else he was certain nobody else had noticed – because nobody watched the island and its inhabitants as closely as he did – and that was that, when Sonia Hislop had sung about grace, her fingers were bleeding.

The organ piped up again and the congregation stood. Punch saw it as his exit music. He scurried out of the pew and hurried to the door.

Outside, he applied his hat and squinted his eyes to the light. He looked left to the church hall where he had attended nursery and in the other direction to the roadside. No sign of her. He moved quickly ahead to the iron railings; as a child they had seemed as high as the clouds. He gazed down the Post Office Brae. Over to the entrance of the Back Brae. Nothing. He looked to Calve Island and the celestial shard of light arresting half of it. *Of course*. Light from a dead star.

Punch felt an even stronger presence behind him. He turned to the sound of the congregation singing. Then fell back on the bars to steady himself. An effigy was hanging above the church entrance.

It was Charlie.

SIDE B

TRACK 15

PUNCH REACHED WITH HIS LONGER arm and pulled the effigy down from above the church door. Charlie deserved more decorum; but needs must. He ran to the Ranger, looking around him as he carried the effigy under his arm. He had the feeling of a ventriloquist escaping the Pearly Gates. He opened the boot and – it hit him. It was like touching a part of the past, a part of him. Long gone. He laid the soft form gently inside, one hand under its head, slowly letting it rest on the carpeted flooring. He folded the limp legs in, the legs that once could jump for miles. Slowly, reluctantly, he gently closed the boot as though it was a door to the past, or the lid on a coffin.

He kneeled. Put one hand on the road. Gagged. The thought of how beautifully Charlie could jump overcame him. Now reduced to this sack of foam. He stumbled up and wiped his mouth. The culprit had got exactly what they wanted. He looked to the church; thankfully, nobody had emerged. At least this effigy had done another job, it had pretty much ruled out MacTavish and everyone else in the congregation. But the twin had exited with uncharacteristic intent; could he really have hung it in time?

Punch opened the driver's door and dropped inside. The vehicle felt different now, as though he was driving Dave's hearse. The radio crackled like commentary from another planet. He thumped the wheel. Swallowed heavily. It felt too personal to call it into the Control room. He decided against heading to the station. As hard as it was to admit, Cluny was doing a decent job of assisting with the disappearance of Lowry. Punch's nose was leading him somewhere else.

He turned the key in the ignition. Dave would take his mother home. She would understand. He couldn't have her in the car with this in the boot. Though the hearse wasn't much better. There was something else setting in, now that he had this version of Charlie back there: it was a strange sense of resolution, of reclaiming. Might finally having a body, something to hold, to mourn, to bury, be a comfort?

He had to find Sonia Hislop; she had said somebody had helped *her*, but whom, and with what? The rogue twin? Sleet began to fall as he drove off towards the Back Brae. Halfway down, he refused the left fork leading up towards the Western Isles and her chalet, concerned that if he did discover her, he might accuse her of something she hadn't done. To drive to the twins could risk coinciding with his mother arriving back. He wondered, could Sonia Hislop have worked that fast with the hanging? Or had it already been there when she entered? The lass was in such a fog of grief he suspected she wouldn't have noticed.

At the bottom of the brae, he turned right at Tackle & Books onto the Main Street. The sea was choppy and the familiar sandbags were in place at the foot of the doorways. The street was gloomy and deserted. No sign of her, or him. The Christmas lights were already activated. Punch turned up the handset. He would need to check in with Cluny and the Control officer soon. Fishing boats were pulling on their rigging at the Old Pier as he passed the clock, seagulls fighting to maintain familiar pathways. Everything was struggling to hold on. The dinghy Palindrome had reported came to mind; it hadn't been there at the slip. There was any number on the seafront. But light would surely have been needed to navigate? It would take someone who knew the bay. Could somebody else – other than the Irishmen – have seen something?

'*Come in, Sarge. Do you read? Over.*'

Punch reached for the handset.

'I read you, PC Cluny.' There was a pause at the other end. Punch shook his head impatiently. 'Yes, over.'

'*Been trying to reach you, Sarge. Over.*'

'I was following a line of, eh, questioning.' Punch inhaled as he looked to the rear of the Ranger; that was one way of describing religion. He set eyes on the glove compartment; just yesterday the severed hand had lain by his feet. So elegant it was hard to be sure if it was that of a male or a female.

He felt surrounded by ghosts; had the notion it was Peter Cushing at the other end of the radio. He hadn't wanted to face any of this today, but now, weirdly, he appreciated the distraction.

'Any word from Lussa Falls? Background searches from Control? Over.'

'*I can confirm the incident report number: LR42XRAY. I've just heard from the Control officer. Background checks on Lowry are in. Over.*'

'Good work, constable. And?'

'*Right . . .*'

Punch heard typing on a keyboard.

'*Flying enthusiast, musician and property developer. Fifty-five years old. Huge shock of salt and pepper hair, prominent eyebrows and sallow skin.*'

'Right.'

'*The best hands in his game they say, Sarge. Over.*'

Punch felt this last detail lodge in his gullet. He cleared his throat. *Had it been noteworthy?* Fished out of a bog?

'*They say he brought rock and roll to the classical music world, Sarge. Over.*'

'Who says?' He suspected the Women's Institute, Bearsden.

'*Apparently, he pulled a few tricks on stage. Such as letting loose a bag of live grasshoppers during a performance. Over.*'

'Sounds more like Paul Daniels we're looking for. And fuck. What about flying experience?'

'*Yes, I spoke with Miss Lauder this morning. More distraught I'd say. No word of reported contact with family or friends, ones who she is aware of anyway. One thousand two hundred civilian flying hours are registered to his name. He is half-Irish too. The Republic. Over.*'

'His car?'

'*A Jaguar. An XJS convertible. He was on the island intending to buy the Western Isles Hotel. He's been looking at property in the Hebrides generally. Skye too. Over.*'

'Okay. Certainly more than we got from Lauder and Townsend. A Jag. Right.'

'*Additionally, there have been no sightings or intel reported relating to irregular landings at any Scottish airports. Over.*'

'Ireland?'

'*Ireland, Sarge?*'

'Try Ireland. East coast. Can't rule anything out. Can't imagine his fuel would take him much further.'

'*I'll get Control on it. Over.*'

'The RAF?'

'*Just waiting on your instruction. Over.*'

'I thought we'd pressed go on that? Do it now, PC Cluny. They're always deployed with the coastguard. This is a missing persons investigation. Polsa will be appointed on my next call.'

'*Pol?*'

'Police search advisor ... Christ, Tulliallan need to take a good look at themselves. Lowry has been gone for forty hours.'

Punch knew he was really referring to himself, having still not acted on the hand. He wondered if its owner felt as numb as he did. *A hand in a Mull bog?* Such a thing made every guest a suspect.

'*Okay, Sarge. Over.*'

'I'm going to Lussa Falls to carry out further questioning.'

'*Retrospective policing. Got it, Sarge. Over.*'

Punch raised his eyebrows at the jargon as he pressed on the accelerator. He sped past the distillery and up the Aes Brae. Turned left at the top and was soon careering along the highest point of the Gally Goo. He didn't know whether to look to the sky or the surrounding fields for this rock star of the classical world. It now felt like a greater loss, or a more valuable find.

Twelve minutes later he was approaching the sign on the dual carriageway for the Lussa Falls Hotel. Opposite was the island's abattoir, which now seemed appropriate in some way. Gravel spat up as he turned.

Punch instinctively feathered the brake as the 'Otters Crossing' sign came into view. At the fork in the road there were two signs: 'LUSSA FALLS HOTEL', pointing left, and: 'AIRFIELD: NO ADMITTANCE' to the right. Punch half expected one more:

'BERMUDA TRIANGLE'.

He took the fork for the airfield, bumped his way through and parked up. Best to keep the Ranger clear of the hotel. He got out and put his hat on. Looking to the rear of the vehicle he felt a strange reluctance to leave, as though he couldn't walk away from it, the past.

He took in the few cars. No Jaguar of any type. Maybe the woman Lauder was out searching. He would need to think about raising a team of volunteers. Randy was an obvious choice. It was a stretch, but new guidelines did talk of 'Policing by Consent', which he took to mean using the public. On an island it was the only way. Monteith at Craignure would at least approve of the jargon, if not the interpretation.

Punch walked through the hotel entrance. Nobody was at reception. He approached the door to the gents. He made some checks around the doorframe and surrounding walls, but nothing was obviously amiss. No irregular markings. He looked down the Scandinavian-style corridors, nothing brewing there either. He took the wooden stairs. Up in the lounge he saw the residents who had been there the night before. They looked like they had recently finished lunch or possibly this new thing called 'brunch' he didn't understand.

Punch nodded when one of them, a jolly, red-faced man in his sixties with a musketeer moustache, caught his eye. One of the bad actors from the night before.

'Sergeant,' the man said, trying to stand as Punch approached.

Punch motioned for the man to remain seated. The man fell back in the leather sofa; something childlike about it, Punch noted, a sense of abandon. He knew it lay inside everyone.

Now the rest of the man's company turned to the arrival of officialdom.

Punch nodded, removed his hat. He was relieved he had left the handset in the car. It tended to seize up folks' tongues.

'Sorry to disturb,' Punch said.

'Quite all right, sergeant,' said the jovial man, a glass of red wine midway between his mouth and the table. 'Can we be of assistance?'

Punch noted the man had the air of a film director surveying his next scene. The Sunday papers were discarded around the empty plates. Punch knew only *he* was aware they had travelled in their own designated boat. He saw the wrecked blue and white cone of a plane on the cover of one. Even planes could be transported by boat. He didn't like headlines. He had one enough out in the boot already. No fucking escape. *Tomorrow's fish and chips wrappers*, was not much of a defence.

'You were here last night, I noticed?' he asked, taking a chair from another table and pulling it a little closer to theirs. Two women were with the man. Punch suspected a husband, wife and friend arrangement. Possibly not in the Randy construct. Too soon to tell.

'We were, yes,' the darker-haired lady closest to him said. She looked to Punch like the tall one from *The Good Life* reruns. He always preferred the smaller one with dimples. Never seen so much veg in a garden, not to mention flares.

'Would you mind if I need to ask you some questions?' Punch said, producing his notepad, relieved it wasn't a child's sock, or a severed hand.

'Of course, we're all yours ...' said the man, raking his fingers through his healthy brown beard. He placed his glass on the wooden table and sat up straighter, producing more of a belly than Punch had expected. The other lady moved the wine glass onto a coaster with a twin-prop plane on it.

'Can I start by taking your names, please?'

'I am Michael Slater – S-L-A-T-E-R – and this is my wife, Angie – eh, Angela – and my sister-in-law, Stephanie. Stephanie Price.'

The taller woman, the one with the darker hair, was the sister-in-law. Punch had guessed wrongly. Though there was a likeness between the two women now he looked closer.

'Afternoon.' Punch forced a smile. 'And you're Angela *Slater*, Miss?'

'Mrs.' The woman nodded.

'Aye, of course.' Punch noted down their names. *Unfortunate error, but recoverable.*

The man was very well spoken, like an announcer on the BBC precisely when he didn't want to be reminded of announcements on the BBC.

'How long are you staying here at the hotel?' Punch asked.

'Until the day after Boxing Day, sergeant,' Michael Slater said.

'The twenty-seventh,' his sister-in-law said. She was an attractive woman, a bit heavier than the other, armed with that thing he could never appreciate until he had left it. Presence.

'And you arrived when?' Punch said.

'Friday,' Angela Slater said.

'Via Oban?'

'Yes,' Michael Slater said. 'The four p.m. ferry.'

'Not on a plane then?'

'No, though I do fly.' Now the man ran his fingers over his moustache as though it were equivalent to flying stripes.

'So, you're obviously aware we have a potential missing person?' Punch said.

All three nodded. The jolly eyes toned down a notch.

'Gosh, yes. How could we not? Yes, terrible,' Angie Slater said, her mousy-blonde hair flapping as she shook her head.

'Terrible,' the man echoed. 'Bloody shock, I don't mind saying.'

'Did you come into contact with Mr Lowry?' Punch asked.

'We did!' Michael Slater sat up straighter, only to immediately take the edge off his own apparent delight. 'Angie and I have heard him perform, in fact. Alas. Poor fellow. What a loss.'

'He's dead?' Punch said.

'Well . . .' Michael Slater flustered. 'I mean, if it does come to that . . . but of course we pray not.'

'Yes,' his wife said. 'We do. We do.'

'Right,' Punch said. 'Where would that have been, that you saw him perform?'

'Royal Albert Hall,' Michael Slater said. He looked across the table to his wife. 'In ninety-four, I think, love?'

'About then.' She nodded. 'Definitely Vivaldi.'

'Right. Right. Of course.' The man mirrored his wife's nod. 'Would have to be. Such mastery. Yes. And always with his back to the audience. But such command.'

'Vivaldi?' Punch interjected. 'With his back to the audience?'

'Erm . . .' Angie Slater shifted. 'No. No. Mr Lowry.'

'Vivaldi is dead,' Stephanie Price said.

'Right. Uh-huh,' Punch said. 'Of course he is.' Though he doubted Dave had boxed him.

'Such a surprise, coincidence even, that he visited *here*, that he came to Mull. But a welcome one,' said Angie Slater.

'Vivaldi did?' Punch said.

'No. Mr Lowry,' Michael Slater clarified.

'Right. It's just we had the fellow Mendelssohn passing before. Out by Staffa.'

'Recently?' Stephanie Price said.

'Eh, no. No. Did you socialise with him at all?'

'Vivaldi?' Stephanie Price said. 'Or Mendelssohn?'

'Steph,' Michael Slater cautioned.

Punch could tell this was becoming a sport; he was losing valuable ground. Soon he'd be fishing himself from the bottom of the Sound.

'Well,' Michael Slater went on, 'we were at neighbouring tables, sergeant, and so yes, there was conversation and, you know, a glass of wine or two and an ebb and flow. He was not a man to miss.'

'Michael asked the maestro if grasshoppers were going to be on the menu.' Angie Slater smiled. 'You know, as an icebreaker.'

Punch thought the better of asking if they were; anything was possible in Townsend's gaff. He'd had to check twice if Sybil Fawlty was on reception.

'But what a coincidence, I say again.' Michael Slater beamed. 'Really, a fine performance in '94. I told him as much.'

Punch was naturally suspicious of the word 'coincidence' when it came to cases. He watched the man reach for his glass and then think the better of it. He liked having this kind of power. Especially to offset the Vivaldi advantage they had.

'So, you talked about seeing the man perform?' Punch asked.

'We did,' replied Angie Slater. 'And the coincidence, you know, of him being here.'

'We were cheeky enough to ask for a recital,' said the Stephanie woman, working her lips together. She sipped a white wine, leaving a trace of her red lipstick, Punch noted. He saw she had only one hand in a glove. Maybe it was the fashion with these types. They were all well-spoken.

'Right,' Punch said. 'And was one given?'

She shook her head.

'Townsend would have been selling ringside seats!' Michael Slater crowed.

'Mike ...' Angie Slater scolded. 'Respect.'

Punch nodded and smiled the way he did at times such as this, when he didn't understand the cultural landscapes of other folk. He realised he had many pre-programmed responses he could call on, possibly a way to keep people, the mainland – feelings – at bay.

'Anything unusual you might have spotted?' Punch asked. 'Before the man took to the air?' He looked away from them to the big window as a tactic to give the folk space to speak freely. Eye contact – when and when not to deploy it – he considered as part of his policing tool kit, alongside *go with your belly*.

'No.' Michael Slater shook his head. 'I mean, the man was clearly a *stage* person, you know?'

'Meaning what?'

'Well, he was larger than life in a sense,' Angie Slater said. 'Even if we had not recognised him, you would have suspected he was *somebody* ...'

'Important.' Her sister nodded.

'Noteworthy,' Michael Slater added.

'Self-important?' suggested Punch.

Angie Slater bobbed her head sideways. 'No. Commanding. Though there was something of the attention seeker about him, for sure.'

'Well, the man was used to an audience,' Michael Slater said.

'And would you connect that to him wishing to take flight last night?' Punch offered.

'Yes!' Michael Slater enthused. 'It was hard not to, sergeant, to be completely honest with you.'

'Why?' Punch wasn't a fan of people who said completely and honest together. There was only dishonesty or plain, simple honesty. As there was innocence or guilt. Unless you were talking unaccounted-for Forestry trees come Christmas.

'Well, he had most dramatically drawn attention to himself, loudly proposing the flight,' Stephanie said. 'He even had his flying boots on already, sitting at the dining table, by God.'

'He seemed to want to satisfy himself that a night landing at Lussa Falls was feasible,' Michael Slater theorised, now reaching for his wine. 'That seemed to be the gist of it.'

'That and—' Angie Slater stopped.

'He said that?' Punch said. 'About the feasibility of a winter's night landing?'

'Certainly implied,' Michael Slater said.

'Sorry, I cut you off, Mrs Slater?'

'Well, it's just . . .' Angie paused. 'Maybe you should tell the sergeant what you heard downstairs, Mike?'

'It was probably noth—'

'Anything could help.' Punch looked keenly to all three of them.

'It's just . . .' Michael Slater began hesitantly. 'I was nipping down to the gents and I heard Mr Lowry telling Townsend in the corridor that he was not *asking* permission, but out of courtesy he was letting him know. "I don't want a fuss." I heard that.'

Punch leaned into his pad.

'Townsend or Lowry said that?'

'Lowry. But Townsend seemed hot under the collar. I almost thought blows were not out of the question. I assumed they were talking about the flight ...'

'They weren't?'

'Mr Lowry said, "You're welcome to her." I thought then that he meant the Needle.'

'He didn't?'

'Well, you know Townsend has the most irritating habit of talking about planes as though they are living, breathing creatures, so it's hard to say.'

'I noticed,' Punch said. 'But you think he meant Miss Lauder?'

'That's just it.' Slater looked helplessly to the two women as though he had said too much. 'They seemed to be talking about *another* woman.'

'Well, that ties in,' Stephanie said, putting down her glass and leaning back from the table. Punch smelled the woman's perfume.

'But no name mentioned.' Michael Slater shook his head, flattening his moustache. 'But now I think on it, Lowry did mention he would put him out of business. He said that. Accused Townsend of "chronic jealousy". I won't forget that. But it was unclear what the jealousy referred to.'

'Lowry said that?' Angie turned. 'You never mentioned that, love.'

'Yes. What's more, Lowry called our hotelier "a talentless cunt". He did I'm afraid. Apologies to the ladies present.'

'But Mr Townsend was not objecting to the flight, in your view?' Punch asked. 'It was more relational?'

'Yes. He didn't seem at all happy about *some* kind of arrangement. But it wasn't completely the flight. At all, possibly – in my view.'

'Right.' Punch doodled a sunflower in his pad. It was a tactic to keep witnesses engaged, intended to demonstrate what they were saying was important; much as he imagined a psychiatrist did. Often, he would look back at his notes and wonder if Van Gogh was the culprit; the case of a missing ear instead of a hand.

'Then I came back upstairs,' Michael Slater said. 'I never saw him again, poor fellow.'

As the man spoke, Punch noticed how Slater repeatedly pulled out his jumper, an unconscious tic, to stop it hugging his belly. It was always there, someplace, the things folk were self-conscious about. It was clear to him they knew nothing of the musician's hand. The horror of such a detail to Lowry's beloved global audience now fully arrived to Punch – if it indeed *was* the musician's hand – together with the added responsibility it put on him. To some it would be like throwing emulsion on *The Last Supper*.

'One other thing we noticed,' Stephanie said.

'Yes?' Punch looked up from his pad.

'When dining, he kept talking about somebody called Archie.'

'A colleague? Friend?' Punch asked. 'Could this be the other person?'

'Possibly,' Stephanie said. 'But he seemed in love with whoever it was. As he did Miss Lauder. A woman notices these things.'

'They *were* loud.' Angie Slater nodded to her sister.

'Yes, something about this Archie,' Stephanie said.

'A man?' Punch noted.

Both women performed small shrugs. A sisterly thing, Punch thought.

'And I heard the words "man and strip",' Angie Slater added. 'As though they were teasing each other about this?'

Punch didn't say it aloud, but wondered if it was a swinging arrangement; anything was possible in Townsend's place, especially with drama types.

'Heck, I need to clean out my ears!' Michael Slater said. 'Good work, girls!'

'Did the man compose himself?' Punch asked.

'Possibly,' Angie Slater said.

'No, no. He was more in the field of reproduction, sergeant,' Michael Slater offered. 'But *what* reproduction.'

'And so, after speaking with Mr Townsend, Mr Lowry went to the airfield?' Punch said.

'No. Things went quiet then,' Angie Slater said, leaning forwards and waving a hand to the viewing window. She lowered her voice conspiratorially. 'We assumed Miss Lauder had persuaded him to come to his senses.'

'His senses?'

'Yes!' Michael Slater exclaimed, flashing his red cheeks and producing a toothy smile.

Punch noted there was something of the actor Brian Blessed about him. As though at any given moment the man could stuff a sword into his belt, spurt a Shakespearean monologue and lead men into battle.

'It was sleeting,' Stephanie said. 'Desserts had been served.'

'So,' Punch pressed on, 'Miss Lauder – did she appear concerned about the prospects of a flight?'

184

'I'd say,' Angie Slater replied. 'By now we could barely pretend to chat among ourselves for the fuss they were kicking up down there by reception.'

'But then they retired to their room, we assumed,' Michael Slater said. 'So, we thought it was off, you know?' He rubbed his belly as though comforting a foetus.

'The flight or their relationship?' Punch said.

'Well, as regards their relationship.' Stephanie hesitated a small, polite moment before divulging. 'In fact, erm, Michael has contacts in the classical world and has made a few enquiries.'

'No, Steph. Stop now,' Angie Slater said. 'We don't want to appear as gossips . . .'

'Oh?' Punch straightened his back.

'Well,' Michael Slater started, 'we really shouldn't—'

'Rumours of a child he never talks about,' Stephanie blurted.

'This is not widely known?'

'Not in any of the biographies I've read.' Michael Slater drained his glass.

'So, *reproduction* might be a wider theme here . . .' Punch offered, then wished he hadn't. 'And what did you mean earlier by,' he mock-studied his notes, 'the words "that ties in", Miss Price? Or sorry, is it Mrs?'

'Miss,' she said with a nod. 'Well, I had gone back to my room. I was watching *Kojak* of all things, you know, a rerun, when I heard an engine starting. My room is at the back there, nearest the airfield I suppose.'

'The engine of a plane?' Punch said.

'I assumed, but I'd say it was more of a continuous revving sound, like a machine. I had the TV quite loud. I threw on a coat to go and check, using the fire escape door.'

'Oh, Stephy!' Angie took her sister's arm in her hand. 'You never said!'

'I walked near the large barn back there, and the night was so black. I heard the most almighty row going on!' Stephanie Price gulped heavily and started to weep. 'Then a scream. God!'

'Oh, sissy!'

'I just haven't wanted to say, Ang! Not like me I know!'

'Dear Steph.' Michael Slater reached for his sister-in-law's gloveless hand and gave her his handkerchief. 'You've been through so much ...'

'Lowry fell out of the door of the barn,' Stephanie went on. 'I saw his face. Like a crazed animal! Then he disappeared into the night!' Her eyes filled with horror. 'Does that mean I was last to see him?'

'Did he look in pain?' Punch asked.

'Oh God, yes.' Stephanie wiped her eyes with a napkin provided by her sister. 'I rushed back to my room. Terrified actually! Then I heard what could only, certainly, have been a plane.'

'Did you see anyone else there?' Punch said.

'Well, you see, before closing my door I felt somebody in the corridor behind me. I peered through the crack. A lady had appeared. Like a vision. The back of her. But the strange thing was ... I felt the presence of evil.'

'Miss Lauder?' Punch asked.

'No, sergeant. Older. A grey-haired lady.' Stephanie gazed around at her audience. 'Then she moved. She started turning to me.'

TRACK 16

PUNCH ROCKED IMPATIENTLY. HE TOOK in some deep breaths and reflected on everything they had told him. He leaned closer to the Slaters' table.

'Why have you not mentioned this earlier, Miss Price? About Lowry? The old woman? Why have you not spoken of it even to your family here?'

'To be honest, I was thoroughly spooked, sergeant. I don't even like *Crimewatch*.'

'So did the lady knock on your door?' Punch asked.

Stephanie Price collected herself. Shook her head. 'No. I closed it quietly and heard nothing more. I stayed in for the night. Can't say I slept much.'

'You hadn't seen her before?' Michael Slater asked.
'No.'

'God, to think of you . . .' Angie trembled. 'My little sis.'

'My painkillers are very strong,' Stephanie said, looking around at them all, 'and then, mixed with the drink, I'm embarrassed to say I just didn't know if what I saw was what I saw?'

'Maybe enough for now, sergeant?' Angie Slater offered. 'My sister herself has suffered a very recent loss.'

'And you see the music had been turned right up by somebody. Pink Floyd, of course. Silly loud for a restaurant.' Michael Slater enthused his indignation, then remembered to console his sister-in-law. 'Dear Jeremy, gone too soon, gone too soon, luvvie.'

Punch looked to Slater and his wife. 'You really never heard any of this?'

'No,' Angie Slater said, agitated. 'All the while up here we were completely unaware this fracas was going on downstairs. We said that.'

'Poor Steph. Just as well you Price girls are made of strong stuff, eh?' Michael beamed his approval of their fortitude.

'Any further description of the woman?' Punch asked.

'No. It all happened so fast, and she had her back to me,' Stephanie managed. 'Just the grey hair. Bobbed. Pale, pale skin on her neck. Like an apparition; a ghost more than a real person. God, I sound crazy.'

'No, no.' Angie Slater squeezed her sister's hand.

'Also,' Michael Slater emphasised, 'upstairs we had turned out the lights to see the spectacle of the plane taking off. Fully expecting it to then re-land, of course. That was our focus.'

'It was all rather exciting I'm afraid,' Angie Slater said, gripping her sister's fingers. 'But oh, poor Stephy.'

'Did anything else strike you as odd?' Punch said. 'Well, apart from all this commotion and the man wishing to take the plane out in that weather so late.'

'Yes.' Michael Slater sat forwards. He clasped his hands together, revealing a fancy gold wristwatch. 'When he eventually did get to the plane the engine was left to idle unusually long.'

'On the airfield?' Punch said.

'Ten minutes I'd say.' Michael Slater turned to his wife. 'Dear?'

'Yes. Easily.'

'And was Miss Lauder with you or outside on the airfield?' Punch asked; he hadn't written a decipherable thing other than their names in the notebook.

'Well, she wasn't in here,' Michael Slater said. 'The wait was even longer until finally the brakes were loosened.'

'As if Mr Lowry was waiting for somebody to arrive?'

'Or for events elsewhere to – unfold, perhaps?' Michael Slater shook his head. 'I just don't know. I don't.'

'And it took off at approximately nine p.m.?' Punch looked to the Stephanie Price lady. 'How far into *Kojak* were you?'

'Oh, only five minutes or so. He hadn't even found a body yet. Just as well . . . I was shaken enough.'

'Of course. That ties in in terms of timings,' Punch said. 'And so, after idling?'

'Finally, it drew speed for take-off. Flawless take-off I have to say, admirable in those conditions.' Michael Slater nodded. 'One can easily romanticise these things, but there was indeed a *musicality* to it.'

'But tell the sergeant what it did, dear,' Angie Slater said, now propped forwards with her husband. Punch noticed both women had perfect, almost translucent skin, like porcelain dolls.

'Well, he turned the landing lights off, on, and then off again,' Michael Slater said, turning to his left and right.

189

'Highly unusual ...' Michael continued his offer. 'The aircraft got airborne quickly. He wouldn't want to take chances with no runway lights or moon to speak of.'

'Then the lights of the plane disappeared into the inky sky,' Angie said.

'Quite extraordinary,' Michael Slater mused.

'Yes?' Punch said.

'Well, Miss Lauder was in the plane when it was idling and then she got out.'

'You saw Miss Lauder?' Punch asked.

'Oh yes,' Michael Slater said, nodding.

'Or another female?'

'Now I'm simply not sure about that, love!' Angie Slater said.

'She simply *was*, dear,' her husband insisted. 'We've been over this already. She was. And we'd heard earlier that Lowry was intending her to guide the plane back in with two battery-powered torches. I mean!' He raised his arms wide apart, revealing a flabby belly, which he hastily covered up.

'This struck you as odd?' Punch enquired.

'Verging on the bloody suicidal, to be frank! I did try to tell Townsend this. To go out and stop him.'

'And did he?'

'I don't know. I couldn't find him.'

'I should imagine his cords alone could have guided in the plane,' Stephanie quipped, blowing her nose.

Punch looked to her, his attention snagged by the sharpness of her observation, matching his own. Then he looked to the big window again, to the same sky Lowry had got himself lost in. It all appeared quite benign today. He was well aware Townsend was a musician and actor-type of sorts too – hence the cords – often featuring in the Tobermory pantomime. More of a show-off, frankly. The hotel was a stage of sorts, too, for the man, now he thought on it.

'Do you think the landing lights being turned off and on was a signal of some sort?' Punch said, returning to his line of questioning.

'Can't be sure.' Michael Slater shrugged. 'But a man who has flown a plane like the Needle before would know where such basic apparatus was. A Cessna's not a 747, by crikes!'

'Right.' Punch sketched. 'There were reports of heavy sleet at that time?'

They all nodded.

'But you saw the lights flashing through it?'

'We did. Really it was all nothing short of crazy.' Michael Slater stood and gestured with his arms. 'I mean, you would need two skilled people to guide a plane of any size onto a runway – or, *cow patch*, by jings – such as this.' He snapped his arms back to his sides. 'I've landed here myself, albeit in daylight, but it was not straightforward.'

'Two people?' Punch questioned.

'Yes, one to mark the left-hand side of the threshold, one for the right-hand corner of the strip's end.'

'Was anything amiss with Mr Lowry and Miss Lauder? You know, a tiff or anything of that nature?' Punch asked.

'Quite the opposite ...' Michael Slater turned slightly desperately to his wife.

'Let's just say despite the wooden walls—' Angie Slater started.

'Yes?' Punch said.

191

'They are not exactly sound-proofed, sergeant ...' Stephanie added.

'Right. Uh-huh. Right,' Punch said, trying not to blush. It could happen. This woman was having a strange effect on him. Like an authoritative teacher might have on a pupil.

'Which is when I heard another engine,' Stephanie said. 'From my room. A car taking off. I'm sure of it.'

'Did you see anything to identify the vehicle?' Punch said, remembering the skid marks.

'I really think you should tell the sergeant, Mike,' Stephanie said, an added crispness to her tone. 'About earlier.'

Michael Slater shook his head and inhaled deeply.

'More?' Punch said.

'I'm not a man for gossip, sergeant, but – look – we were speaking with friends who live at Connel outside Oban this morning and we told them about last night and they reported hearing a plane going over their farm at about nine-thirty p.m.'

'Of course, it could have been another plane ...' Angie Slater said.

'In this part of the world?' Punch dropped his pencil. 'You're telling me this now?'

'Well, we didn't, you know, want to appear to be interfering in the investigation. Isn't that what they say on the TV? And our friends *are* getting on.' Michael Slater struggled to pick up Punch's pencil. 'We don't even know that it was the poor fellow's plane, we just know, alas, he didn't come back.'

'I will need the details of your friends, please,' Punch said, reluctantly taking the pencil.

'Of course.'

'Mr Slater, how long would a fully fuelled Cessna stay in the air in your estimation?'

'Oh, one hour max I'd say, before it got thirsty.'

'Okay,' Punch said, doodling another sunflower. 'We'll leave it there for now. Thank you for your time. You've all been very helpful.'

'It's as though the man was set off by the conductor but alas, without the notes, lost his way?' Angie Slater offered.

'I wish it had just been *Kojak* for a Saturday night, I don't mind saying,' Stephanie Price said, flicking her dark hair.

Punch turned. He wanted to quip 'who loves you, baby?' But feared he might then have to heat up a cell for himself for the night. 'Oh, do you mind me asking what you do while here, folks, if it's not flying?'

'Searching for golden eagles, sergeant,' Michael Slater said. 'All three of us are hooked I'm afraid, would you believe? Hours go by.'

Punch nodded and got up. Each to their own. He placed the chair back by the wall. Walked away from their table towards the wooden stairs. There were too many things that didn't ring true. Could Slater be the owner of the deerstalker? And then there was Lowry: Christmastime in front of spectators seemed an odd time to try something that you would expect to be done in secret. Had the man flown off to start a new life somewhere? Possibly. But he was somebody of note, a man who could not easily hide.

Punch heard footsteps coming down behind him. He turned and it was Michael Slater. The man looked nervously towards reception, which was unmanned.

193

'Sergeant ... if I may ...' He was speaking more softly. Now Punch heard a Scottish twang; posh, possibly Edinburgh. He had put on a tweed jacket. All the man was missing *was* a deerstalker.

'Mr Slater?'

'I didn't want to spook the girls any further you know ... dear Steph still has a ... fragility, let's just say ...'

'Right?'

'Well, Miss Lauder was left at the end of the runway using two small battery-powered lights to guide him back. Useless.'

'Yes. You said. Several times.'

'But the thing is I am certain I saw *four* lights.'

'Suggesting a second person on the runway ... But not Townsend?'

'Possibly ... but ...' Michael Slater dropped his voice to a whisper. 'I saw Townsend come in looking crazed and, well, like every element of the night was on him.'

'After the take-off?' Punch said.

'No. This morning.' Michael Slater glanced around, the nervous energy clear in his eyes. 'Bordering on the melodramatic I'd say ...' Slater rubbed his moustache. 'But he didn't see me. And I heard shouting about Vivaldi too.'

'Between Mr Lowry and Miss Lauder?'

'No. Between Mr Townsend and somebody else. On the phone.'

'Any indication of who he was talking to?' Punch was thankful he hadn't suggested Felix Mendelssohn.

'No. But an inference they hadn't got something; that Townsend hadn't got something.' Michael Slater looked behind him and raised his hand, indicating he feared he had said too much.

Punch nodded. 'Is that everything?' he said.

Michael Slater puckered his lips and tried to smile.

'Right. Thank you, Mr Slater.'

Outside, it was now lashing with rain. Punch listened to the man's footsteps ascending the stairs. The low murmur of customers through in the bar coming in waves like a sea, jazz floating lightly on it.

He moved to reception and leaned over to view the register on the counter, noticed the name 'Lauder' alongside room 14. He turned around to the numbers listed on the wooden wall panels with accompanying arrows pointing to the left and right. He followed the corresponding arrow and arrived outside room 14. Put his ear to the door. Couldn't hear anything. Took his car keys from his pocket and located the extra key he always kept on the chain. He inserted it into the lock and worked gently. The lock released. He pushed open the door.

The room was untidy in the usual way of guests. Punch flicked open a suitcase, using his car key. All the clothing neatly packed, male and female underwear in separate bags. He slid his hand into the wallet on the lid of the suitcase and pulled out a *Sunday Times* article. It was about a rare original manuscript score by Vivaldi – who else? – which had recently been bought anonymously for several hundred thousand pounds at auction. Punch thought of what the Slaters had thought they overheard – 'man', 'strip' – *another piece in the jigsaw*? He put the paper back where he had found it.

The room had a strange presence, as though he was not alone. He noticed a blue glasses case. *The same colour as Townsend's?* On the floor by the bed there was a fine pair of leather shoes. Lowry felt closer than ever. Punch pulled open the wardrobe doors. Shirts hanging, coloured collars, bright socks folded; the sort these kinds of folk wore. Punch knew what he was looking for: materials acting as body parts – needles, threads, fake hair – but there was none of that. He walked into the bathroom and turned apprehensively to the shower. There was no one in it. On the sink there were two toothbrushes in a cup. This was the closest he had come to Lowry yet: the inside of the famed musician's mouth.

Punch looked to the mirror above the sink and, scrawled in what looked like red lipstick, were two words:

SEARCH ARCHIE.

An engine sounded. Punch couldn't be sure if it was from the ground or the sky. Headlights shone through the closed curtains. He parted them slightly. Outside, a car pulled up on the other side of the trees, lights killed before it stopped rolling. It didn't come into the hotel car park. He didn't recognise the vehicle. But he could see there was a woman at the wheel. Grey, not blonde. It wasn't Ruth Lauder.

Punch turned to the bathroom mirror. He examined the script more closely and now saw the words differently. Darker, encrusted and without the crayon-like texture of lipstick; they were written in blood.

TRACK 17

I LOOK ONTO THE PITIFUL TOWN. Lights lining the seafront. Somebody's creation in itself, and recently two hundred years old. Who cares? If I could erase it from the view I would. It took the one thing I had. My truest creation.

EI, II, III and IV have done their jobs. But noteworthiness, artistry, is not all it is cracked up to be. The adrenaline is gone. Why did dear Larry Olivier, Dame Kiri, Roger Moore and the others not tell me? Or even Xander? Should not Xander have told me? Because I am alone. Staring at the bottom of a glass. Well, I have the measly man with me in the other room, but he is not much more than a glorified messenger. To be done away with is the plan. But when? My knight in shining armour has not arrived?

The wind has taken a break. Ideal conditions, I should think, for flying. He said we would be rich, to keep the house in darkness. That he could land here. To have torches ready. And I have torches ready, and the feeble man to help. New batteries from Browns. Same method as Lussa Falls. *Old school lovely*, he said. It was always him. Poor, overlooked, him. But he is not here. Only his music. His fingers on strings.

I have hardly taken my eyes off the sky!

I shall have to leave. I cannot wait. I must go to the hotel. The feeble man will be of use. It is a risk, but one must follow one's heart, especially when it is so full of *his* music. As was my dear son's. But she silenced it. Stopped it playing in my heart. And Punch is her lover.

People must suffer for their actions. And I had not intended it to be me!

TRACK 18

PUNCH HEARD RAPID FOOTSTEPS APPROACHING the hotel room. A key in the door. He had made sure not to leave any trace of his search. The door opened and brushed the deep pile of the orange carpet. It was closed quietly and locked from the inside. High heels had entered. Straps up the ankles. Thin ankles. The shoes moved across the carpet and Punch made sure to keep completely still under the bed. Next to his face was a shirt. Stained in blood.

'Feeble lot. One wants something done properly, have to do it one's bloody self . . .' he heard. *Possibly Lauder? Maybe more English*. He felt his nose tickle. *Bastard dust mites*. Punch slowly raised his hand to rub his nose and the immediate danger seemed to be averted. He heard the heels attacking the floor tiles in the bathroom, then stopping. He heard the squeak of the mirror being wiped. 'Archie' being removed. Then the lid being raised. Her urinating. The toilet roll pulled and the flush. She hummed gently. Something classical. Was this an accomplice? Nobody of that name was among the case personnel so far.

Punch heard a faint voice. Coming from his breast pocket. He reached to silence Cluny on the radio. There was no escaping the fucker. He waited to discover if he had been detected over the flush. He seemed to be in the clear. The high heels left the tiles and Punch felt the light movement on his back of her progressing to, and then sitting on, the bed. Her weight was positioned directly above him, his nose touching the underside of the mattress. Her bottom right on his face. Was he just a bedspring away from Maggie May?

He heard the phone receiver being lifted and the voice asking reception for an outside line. A number being dialled then a ringing tone. A small voice answering.

'It's me,' the voice above him said.

A pause.

'Yes, been a while. I hope you're happy. He's taken off now. Or you've driven him. Another one. Can't believe my ghastly fucking luck. You're like a virus I can't be rid of. Have to have everything I have. Well, not this one!'

The woman seated so close to him appeared to be listening impatiently to words spoken at the other end. Punch could hear her heavy breath, sounding more pained or angry with every intake.

'What else am I to do? That girl was my *right*! Don't think I don't know your little games. Jealous games. Was it my career you were after too? Art School in Glasgow is hardly the Royal College? You've fucked everything up, Sonia! Fucked everyone. Again! Slut! How is that bloody possible? Not an original bone in your body! Hello? Hello?'

She slammed the receiver down. It wasn't Lauder, Punch was all but certain.

He kept still. Whoever it was, was she talking to Sonia Hislop? The notion seemed absurd. There was more rage here than he imagined Ruth Lauder capable of. But killers were often undetectable beasts.

'Archie,' she said, still on the mattress. 'But where *is* Archie? Meant more to him than his son and me put together ... but come on, get one's mind onto new loves; *real* love.'

She kicked away Lowry's fine shoes.

Punch tried not to make a sound as he watched the ankles walk speedily around to the door. She opened it. Closed it behind her and locked it from the outside.

Punch waited silently. He heard the fire escape door and soon after a car engine starting up. Wheels turning on gravel. He scurried up from under the bed. He made for the door and noticed that his notebook with its pages full of sunflowers was sticking out, just slightly, from under the side of the bed.

'Fuck!' he hissed. There was no way of knowing if he had been noticed, and potentially set up.

He grabbed his hat and worked the key from his pocket. When the lock released, he stepped into the hallway and locked the door behind him. He progressed slowly back in the direction of reception. Stopped at the fire door. He noticed a smear, a dull red, the same as on the mirror. He looked down but there were no obvious signs of staining on the carpet. Quickly, he walked the corridor through to the front foyer by the gents, but, again, there were no obvious signs of blood or an incident trail. Punch walked back through to the fire door, pushed the bar and gently released it. On the outside he noticed a rectangle indented in the gravel. Clearly a doormat had been removed.

He looked over and saw Townsend now inside the foyer, chatting to guests. The man was still with the reindeer; at least it wasn't flashing. Inside, Ruth Lauder strode by the fire door. She was wearing long, knee-length boots. Punch hadn't been noticed. A room light switched on, not the one he had just vacated. He turned and saw the Jaguar was parked near the entrance. He walked to it; the smooth metal of the bonnet was warm beneath his hand. Punch turned to the front door and, upon seeing him, the guests dispersed. They smiled nervously as they passed him, which he took as a sign his reputation was intact.

Townsend nodded towards Punch as he emerged from the hotel.

'Nigel.'

'I say, didn't see your car, sergeant?'

'Just to keep you abreast, you'll have search dogs, coastal and air assets on, surrounding or above your land in the coming hours. Take it no further updates this end on Mr Lowry, or the plane?'

'No, sergeant. Miss Lauder is beside herself.' Townsend looked over to where the airfield met the shoreline. 'Daren't let Ruthie down there again, to be perfectly honest. I fear the Needle might never return. The river mouth at the end of the runway is deeper than one might think.'

'The plane your main concern?'

'Well, no. No.'

Punch turned to the hotel.

'Have you moved her, Nigel?'

'The Needle?'

'No.' Punch angled his head. 'I meant Miss Lauder, from her room?'

'Oh? Well, yes. At her request. Look, Punch, I've got a business to—'

Punch stepped closer to the man.

'Something between you and her?'

Townsend looked aghast.

'What kind of question is—'

'Call me sergeant. And I'll have an officer outside room fourteen forthwith. I don't want it touched. Do you hear? Tempted to put one on your jerkin too.' He thought about the glasses case. 'You and her an item?'

'Simply scandalous! I mean the . . .'

'Or a lovers' tiff, between he and her?'

'Put your rod away, sergeant. I don't get involved in others' personal business. I'm a hotelier not a marriage counsellor, nor am I in the business of partner theft. That might be your game but not mine, I'd say.'

'Has he a history of such daredevil activity?'

'Well. You obviously haven't seen him play.'

'No.'

'Look, sergeant, Xandy was – *is* – a haphazard fellow at the best of times. Always. Even at the conservatoire. Poor sods at Juilliard tried to rein him in I believe. Some would say his playing has become haphazard too but . . .'

'Right.' Jealousy noted. 'And tell me, why not use car headlights?'

'Eh?'

'To guide the plane – torch batteries could have run out? Trying to make the man fail? So you could feel better about yourself?'

'Oh my giddy aunt! Now you're being beyond silly!' Townsend gulped heavily. 'Look, this is getting us nowhere, Sergeant Punch. It all happened so quickly; Xan could be so impulsive. That's what's got us into this ruddy mess ... Why are you wasting time on me?'

'So, you *did* guide him on the field?'

'I made the best go of it. Xan was in the plane as it taxied.' Townsend shifted from one foot to the other. 'Ruthie shone the other torch.'

'Not how she has it, Nigel; she said her head was giving her grief.'

'Look, the snowdrift made it hard to see; maybe she did go inside. Any organised take-off was always going to be tricky. But he couldn't – *can't* – be told, the man. Ever thus.'

'Miss Lauder has been out?' Punch pointed to the Jag.

'Yes, pathetic really, but she wanted to be productive. Thought we must search for ourselves rather than sit around. But it's like trying to find a needle in ... well. The whole ghastly scenario has taken its toll on us all. Not to mention my balance sheet.'

'I heard talk of Miss Lauder getting in the plane, only to get out?'

'She didn't. We thought her use was better deployed on the ground. At least, I thought that's what they had agreed. Wouldn't have helped were she not. Headache or no headache.'

'But Mr Lowry's flying licence had expired?' Punch had been saving this information, just acquired from the case inspector at Control before he entered the hotel. He had also officially instructed wider support assets. CID weren't out of the question now. 'We've run checks.'

'Oh?' Townsend seemed genuinely surprised. 'He said to me he hadn't taken it with him because he hadn't expected to fly.'

'I see.' Punch took out the sunflower sketches. 'And wouldn't you normally ask for a licence before dishing out the Needle as dessert?'

'Erm, well, yes. Normally I would.' Townsend tried to get back on a sure footing. 'But Xandy was a highly accomplished pilot. One found it hard to deny him. Used to getting his own way, you see. Bloody *star* and all that. Really, he ceased to be a musician is the truth. Painful though it is to say. *The Muppets* were after him, for God's sake!'

'What was he then?'

'This new thing. A *celebrity*, I fear.'

'Right. Can I just clarify when it was that you began to think something was amiss?' Punch said. 'It wasn't apparent from our chat last night.'

'I should say after twenty minutes with no sign of him returning I began to worry. Fuel is a factor. I took the Land Rover and turned down past the old cemetery. Shone the lights, dipped them onto the water and swept the Sound, in case – dear God – he had undershot the landing and came in short of the threshold as a result. But no sign. Nothing at all, no sir.'

'Engine failure?'

'It would be extremely uncommon, downright squalid luck, in fact. Dear Papa used to navigate with an AA handbook, by crikes, and would swoop down low to read road signs. Sergeant ... it was tricky to say so last night, but Xan Lowry *was* impetuous ...'

'Was?'

'Is. *Is.* What I'm saying is he liked to fly low. He sought danger on a stage *and* in a cockpit.' Townsend turned to the light in Ruth Lauder's room, as though mindful of breaking a confidence. But he was about to.

'You studied together?' Punch enquired. 'And Mr Lowry was always superior?'

'That's right.' Townsend nodded. 'Well, so they say.'

'Did that bother you?'

'Erm, not really. You know, one takes what one has been given.'

'And in your case, Nigel, it wasn't so much – not as much as him? Did that concern you – the difference between you and Lowry? Between the Tob Panto and the Proms?'

'No, no, I was proud – if a little astonished – at Xandy's rise. If truth be told, I felt our competition raised his bar!' Townsend brushed at his jumper; sleet was falling, actual sleet rather than the illusion of stitching.

'So, there was a competition – between the two of you?'

'Professional. Purely professional.'

'Did I imply otherwise?'

'Look, can I help you with anything else, sergeant? I do still have a hotel to run, guests to reassure.'

Punch flipped over and read from a blank page.

'So – it was a moonless night. Blue woollen sweater. Mr Lowry theatrically announced he was going to fly. Stated he would make one flight circuit alone. His plane took a right up over the Sound, then right again, heading south. Until it vanished. And it was sleeting heavily ...' Punch kept quiet about the hand. For now. His feeling was that any mention of it might arrive him at the wrong suspect, and too soon. Or maybe it was the numbness still on him.

'Yes, Sarge. That about does it,' Townsend said. 'And now we're none the wiser. The man was lost without a conductor to guide him. Dots to follow. You know, some used to say that back at the conservatoire.'

Both men heard the sky rumble and looked up.

'RAF,' Punch said. 'I better get on.'

'Naturally, sergeant.'

'Mr Lowry's Jaguar?' Punch turned and gestured with his longer arm towards the car. 'I might need a look around it.'

'Oh?' Nigel Townsend swiped his hair. Punch observed it was wispy and unruly at the front, styled in the way of toffs. 'Right.'

'You were out with Miss Lauder?'

'Yes.'

'And your own vehicle?'

'Parked out the back on the airfield side. We were shining it out on the Sound last night, as I said.'

'Right. You did.'

Townsend headed back to the hotel and Punch looked to the sea moving behind the trees. Had the feeling his feet were carved from lead. He was stumped as to the identity of the high-heeled lady in the room. But it wasn't Ruth Lauder. He remembered what was stored in the boot of the Ranger. And the human hand back in his garage cooler, with no identifiable markings or jewellery. Very possibly a hand known the world over. He spat to the ground. Looked to the grey sky to the soundtrack of the chattering falls. Did everything know more than him?. He couldn't think how the musician could have survived.

He looked behind him to check the coast was clear, and walked purposefully through the tree covering to the large barn near where he was parked. The account Stephanie Price had given of the events she had witnessed out here needed to be investigated. He pulled the door. Inside, there were tree trunks drying and a large heap of sawdust; he remembered how they used to spade the sawdust here into large bags to use for football pitch markings on the airfield. A transformation in itself. He inspected further and could see a form – almost human – indented into it. He sat on hay bales; noticed a chainsaw behind them, tucked against the wall. Punch bent closer to inspect the chain, careful not to lay a finger on it.

There was a red stain on it.

He pulled protective gloves from his coat and put them on. He lifted the chainsaw and walked it to the door. No obvious stains on the door or the surrounds. He looked out of the barn to make sure no one was watching, and returned to the car.

He opened the boot. In an act that felt almost inhuman, he lowered the chainsaw next to the effigy. Then gently closed the boot.

He turned up his handset and set it to a new channel.

'Sergeant Punch LB519 to Control. Over.'

'*Control officer receiving Sergeant Punch Lima Bravo. Over.*'

He had to hand it to the buggers; they were gunslingers on the radios.

'Officer, in relation to our missing person on Mull LB, identified as a Mr Xander Lowry, has there been any mention of an "Archie"? PC Cluny, do you read too? Over.'

'*I'm looking through now. So, I see nothing in our background searches or case notes here,*' replied the Control officer. '*Do you have anything else to go on, sergeant? Over.*'

'That's it for now,' Punch said. 'Might be nothing.'

'*More boots on the ground required, sergeant?*'

'Sniffers, yes. We've further investigative work to be carried out here, inspector, and will report back later. The deployment of aerial and coastal assets will determine next steps. Over.'

'*Sniffers coming off the next ferry, sergeant. PC Cluny has been notified of intel at your disposal. Over.*'

'I heard the update, inspector. I was compromised with a possible lead here. Over.'

'*What else can we support you with, sergeant? Over.*'

'Sniffers for now, inspector. Over.'

'*Anything comes in we'll notify. Over.*'

Punch realised the direct channel to Control was blocking any updates from Cluny. He altered the dial and put a localised call out to Lima Alpha. He wondered if Cluny had it in him to take the severed hand to Dave. Forensics would need to do the once-over on the chainsaw.

'*Receiving, sergeant. This is shoulder number 747. Over.*'

'You don't have to say "shoulder number", PC Cluny. Just your number. That's your call sign, man.' Punch released the talk button. 'And fuck.'

'*Anything more from Lussa Falls? Over.*'

'Nothing concrete. More details of the night the plane went missing have emerged from guests, and also about a possible Lowry–Townsend disagreement. I might be closer to Maggie May too. A bedspring away. Over.'

'*Who, Sarge? Over.*'

'Eh, I mean a potential suspect. Still piecing a few bits together.' Punch knew the existence of the effigies was compromising how much he could reveal to his deputy, given Randy and Palindrome were the only ones who knew about them and they had been sworn to secrecy; to say more to Cluny risked admitting he was being tormented by somebody on the island, by his past. 'I have some assets for Forensics. I'll notify when I return to HQ. Over.'

Christ, he thought. *HQ*: he was starting to sound like Guinness and he knew it.

'*I've a map here on the computer and have isolated potential inland search areas. Over.*'

'Right. Good work. No other notifications from the public?'

'*Oh, just an old fellow. Pockets full of golf balls. He came to the station door, Sarge. Talking of stars in the sky falling into the bay last night and the like. I sent him packing. Wasting police time. Over.*'

'Who was it?'

210

'*The old twin, I believe. At first, I thought it might be connected to, you know, the effigy business. Over.*'

'Tinsel?' Punch felt a tinge of shame at Cluny's mention of the doppelgangers. He heard the keyboard going.

'*No. The other one? The flat cap; the fellow you see foraging.*'

'Tonsils?'

'*Affirmative. Real name Archie McVicar, I believe? Over.*'

TRACK 19

PUNCH OPENED THE DRIVER'S DOOR and dropped into the seat. Turned the ignition and manoeuvred the Ranger around. He accelerated down the bumpy driveway at speed. *Fuck the otters.* He turned right in the direction of Tobermory and put his foot to the floor. Knew what he was doing. It was his attempt to drive as far away as he could from Charlie in the boot.

An RAF plane whooshed overhead and he felt a tinge of power, of the world turning to *his* tune; now it was him putting planes in the sky. He would have some trouble stopping Randy from raising Forestry volunteers on the ground. But one more night without the pilot-musician and top brass would be all over it. Turning the island into the mainland. Sniffers up the gazoo. Officers coming from Oban and even deeper into LB Div, possibly Lochgilphead, Campbeltown. He needed the missing pieces to put the case to bed smartish. The chainsaw was a bonus.

As he sped through Salen, barely feathering the brake, and then past the dilapidated fishing boats, he saw them not as rotting relics, but as things that had once lived, the barnacles as infected skin. *Two of them, of course.* He knew what was happening, what he could never disclose to a case inspector or to Guinness: he was turning Lowry into Charlie.

Back in Tobermory, Punch pulled into Glen Iosal. It was at times like this he felt the Ranger akin to an engine-powered exclamation mark in the town. Word would be getting out about the missing plane. The media sniffing about soon too, given the man was of genuine note – even if Townsend didn't agree.

No doubt all kinds of exaggerated theories would be brewing, but the old twin had previous, rumours of staring too long at folk in their houses and strange timekeeping. A rogue apple. Oddball. To be kept an eye on. Punch remained convinced he had seen the old fellow up on the path the night before. This wasn't work for the case inspector; this was local policing, off-grid.

Instinct. *Belly.*

He exited the Ranger and refused the impulse to take the adjoining pathway to his mother's front door. How could he explain to her he had Charlie in the boot? A human hand in his fridge? He left the handset in the car. As he walked the paving, he saw the array of wooden swords outside. All the kids used to hang around outside the rear of the twins' old house back in the day, in the lane between his house and theirs. Swords stacked like weapons awaiting an army; though he suspected the war was really going on between the man's ears. Punch remembered how there would sometimes be a police car passing slowly, menacingly, down the lane between his and the old twins' house, which was not often used by vehicles. Never did he think he would become one of them: the one who menaces.

He took off his hat and ruffled the top of his head. The badgers would be flat as a pancake. Turned back to the Ranger and then to his mother's front door, noticing Mary MacBeth's umbrella sitting opened outside, upside-down. Dave had got them back to mission control, if not the man upstairs himself.

Punch knocked.

He heard movement inside and then the door opened.

'Sergeant?' Tinsel almost said, compromised by a needle between his lips. *Some gall.* The man was wearing a light blue cardigan with a pencil in the front pocket. Yellow tea towel over his stooped shoulder. Below were his usual trousers. Punch saw slippers at the ends in place of the rolled-down wellies. Reading glasses hanging from his neck on a frayed string. Punch had the feeling he had interrupted Tennessee Williams in mid-flow.

'Tinsel,' he said.

Tinsel removed the needle and stuck it on his collar.

'Repairs.' He gestured his head backwards, indicating Tonsils. 'He's always getting into scrapes . . . you know, out foraging, carrying tree trunks an' the like. Sorry about the anniversary.'

'Aye.' Punch looked away, the final comment catching him off guard.

'Can I help you, Ivor?'

'Well . . .' Punch turned back. 'I'll come in off your doorstep a minute if that's okay.'

214

'Right you are. Come away in.' Tinsel moved aside and Punch saw a pair of steel toecap boots on the carpeted floor. Not hard to know who they belonged to.

'He's not long back from the church,' Tinsel said. 'Finds it hard, you know, the crowds. I think I know why you're here.'

'You do?' Punch brushed by Tinsel and into the short hallway. The design was identical to his mother's, and surprisingly tidy. A hi-vis vest hung by the coats.

'Just enough room to swing a twin,' he heard from behind him. 'Mother doing okay? Well, as can be *expected* today?'

'Aye, Tinsel. Thanks, aye.'

Punch looked to the burlap sack under the stairs overflowing with golf balls.

'Jack Nicklaus would have a hard-on. Brother spends hours up on the course. Never swung a club,' Tinsel said. 'Right turn there ahead of you into the front room. Forget your indicators. You better go first, I've a poem in there not best pleased with me.'

Punch made sure to force a cheekbone up, then fixed his hat to his chest. Nothing pigeon about it. The needle had thrown him. *Another piece in the jigsaw, or too obvious?*

'In fact, you might be jailing me for the final stanza alone.'

'Eh?'

'The poem.'

'Right. Aye, Tinsel.'

'Kettle's just spoken?'

'No,' Punch said. 'Nothing, cheers.'

The furniture in the room looked like it dated to another era. Punch himself now felt downsized, as though he had

215

knocked for a new sword. Or one for the infant Charlie. He looked to the old armchair opposite and recognised the cuts in the leather. There was a bible on the table next to it.

'Now *there's* a book ...' Tinsel said. 'If you can look beyond the messaging, that is. Aye, you have to hand it to the Prophets – *Oban Times* of their day.'

Punch realised the chair was from his old house by the graveyard. It must have been recovered from the back lane or the skip when they left the house. On it was a spool of black thread and a set of overalls. A piece of paper. The poem, he thought.

'Pull a string, a puppet moves ...' Tinsel said.

'Eh?'

'Religion.' Tinsel nodded to the book. 'Bukowski said that. We're all sheep these days. Distinct lack of shepherds. Your uncle would agree.'

'Would he? The man never said much. Anyway. I suppose you have the birthright to comment if nothing else ... on the Bible, I mean ...'

'Qualification enough,' Tinsel said, smiling: a yellow-toothed affair. 'He also said, "it's not pretty".'

'My uncle?'

'Bukowski.'

'About what?'

'The ocean.'

'Right.'

Punch thought about how he knew Tinsel's birthdate, despite never having before acknowledged it; knew how he held a cigarette; could spot the man's walk from a hundred yards, how he kept his hands in his pockets but with the thumbs always on the outside; knew where his furniture came from; how his mother had a large mole on her chin and always sat with her legs apart. He was certain that in a city such intimate knowledge would be impossible.

'Right. I'll go and round up the troops,' Tinsel said. 'Christ, sorry.' He scooped up the thread and overalls and placed them on the table. Took the needle from his collar and stuck it into a small cushion with others. 'I came back to Mull after Mother got ill, to look after her, and him,' he said. 'I measured Sean Connery in London for Christ's sake. David Niven. Judy Garland always made a beeline for the shop. You expected these folk to be in black and white.'

'Right?' Punch tried. 'And I suppose Browns would be a step along the yellow brick road too far.'

'I was a tailor. But became a council worker.'

Tinsel walked out of the room and Punch heard the stairs creak. Surprising, for a relatively new build. The needle and threads were promising, but more digging was required. He had noticed plasters on the old man's thumbs.

Could the twins be in cahoots?

He looked out the patio door to the small patch of garden, the modern door at odds with the old furniture. A pair of gardening gloves discarded outside. An empty whisky glass. Ashtray of stubs. Lines of spooled rope. *More promising.* Their mother, too, was seldom without a ball of wool and knitting needles. He saw the ancient motorbike, redundant as it always was in their previous garden, the past sitting aboard like an invisible passenger. A symbol of what could have been, of another life lived, future experienced, were it possible for Tonsils. It was surrounded by flotsam, jetsam

217

and the rest of Tonsils' found objects. Often you would still see the man walking the Gally Goo, the Dervaig or Glengorm roads, the forests at Lettermore, in all weathers, half a tree over his shoulder or rocks in his barrow. Which was in stark contrast to his old Sunday morning routine, when he would sit in his dressing gown on the garden wall awaiting sight of Punch's mother, teacup in hand, Brylcreemed and looking every inch the West End darling to his poet twin. Locking him up felt to Punch like an act too far.

He looked around the room and had the notion again to search for materials: needles, threads, wools, body parts. All the necessary ingredients were evident: the tailor and the local oddball. Fred West listed in the address book, no doubt. Letters from Myra Hindley.

'A sword?' he heard. 'Is he after a sword?'

Tonsils had entered the little room, wearing a crumpled suit and slippers. Under his jacket a string vest visible. Punch had never seen him in such disarray. Tinsel arrived behind his younger twin. They towered over the seated Punch as though carved from the past. Young boys still living in their old faces.

'Eh ...' Punch was blindsided. He wanted to stand but suddenly felt insufficient in some way, as though the uniform belonged to somebody else, older, more befitting than him – somebody more substantial than this wee boy.

'I think you liked a thicker handle – am I right?' Tonsils said, looking at the carpet, his voice like a cattle whine. 'A thicker handle? I never forget a sword order.'

'Eh ...' Punch gulped. 'Maybe, aye.'

'I'll have one for you later today,' Tonsils said. 'The supply outside will be no use. No use.'

'I think Ivor, I mean, eh, Sergeant Punch, is here about what you saw, Archie?' Tinsel said. 'You know, the other night?'

'I saw it. If that's why you're here. A star out there and then it was on the water. Blinking. Blinking like it had fallen.' Tonsils turned to his twin. 'Could it have fallen from the sky?'

Tinsel looked to Punch, who felt blindsided again. He stood and walked to the glass door.

'Aye,' Punch said, 'I'm here because you were actually spotted up on the Lighthouse Path on the night the—'

'Dummy,' Tonsils spouted. 'The dummy girl, you mean?'

'What were you doing there?' Punch said.

Several clocks chimed at once, startling him. He remembered how from outside the twins' old house you would always hear the sound of clocks. As though one wouldn't be enough – nor the church bells ringing – to prompt Tonsils when it was time for God. Punch was always fascinated at their internal workings, as he was by the people who owned them. Their mother had been the antidote to the urgency of the chimes, always propped on a chair outside, working knitting needles as though supplied with an internal mechanism herself, pink and purple veins up her legs like a map of the Ottoman Empire.

'I saw a man and the wee girl's mother at the Western Isles,' Tonsils said, staring to the fireplace. 'Not good enough for her. For my wee girl.'

219

'Och, Archie, she's not your girl now,' Tinsel said. 'Come on!'

'You know I made her a sword?' Tonsils said, staring at Punch for the first time. His eyes like olives lost in brine. 'The little redhead.'

'Sonia Hislop?' Punch said. 'You saw her with a man?'

'Yes.'

'Could you describe him?'

'Well ... it wasn't for long, but he was dressed in big, colourful clothes, you know like the ones Harry here used to make on the mainland. I dragged him away from all that. I did. My fault. From London, was it?'

Townsend, thought Punch. He couldn't tell if the puzzle was becoming easier or more complex, if pieces were being added or dropped to the floor.

'How's your mother?' Tonsils asked.

'I'm not here about that!' Punch motioned. 'Please, will you sit? I'm here to question you in relation to – well, at the very least – *irregular* activity.'

'She should never have married that man. The Obanite. Not good enough for her. Your mum,' Tonsils said. He lowered into the old leather chair, the one Punch used to imagine had a flock buried in it, a whole croft. His uncle sitting on top of it all, and not his father.

'Did you have anything to do with the dummy of Iris Hislop being hung?' Punch said. 'The effigy of the child.' He thought he would keep the hanging policeman out of it for now.

'Come on now, Ivor!' Tinsel stood.

'This is a police investigation. I'd appreciate it if you would keep out of it, Harry.' Punch kept his gaze on Tonsils. 'Can you answer my question? What the fuck have you got yourself mixed up in?'

Tonsils looked out at his motorbike. The vacant stare again. He turned to his twin.

'Was he not here for a sword?' he said.

'Cut the fucking act!' Punch said. 'While we're at it, did you have anything to do with the girl originally falling off the cliff? Have you been perving again Archie?'

'What?' Tinsel said. 'Now this is—'

'His name's written in fucking blood,' Punch said. 'The bugger's got more going on upstairs than he lets on.'

'Blood?' Tinsel said. 'Ivor, I'm not sure where you're going with this. Sonia Hislop is a friend of mine.'

'Exactly,' Punch said. 'Of *yours*. Maybe Archie here is jealous? Thinks she'll take you away from him? Or are all three of you in cahoots? And call me sergeant when I'm in bloody uniform. Out of it, too.'

Tonsils shook, like a dog removing water.

'Why were you on the path the other night, Archie?' Punch probed. He was reluctant to take Tonsils in for questioning. It would be like snaring a vulnerable animal in the back of the Ranger. Couldn't imagine the bugger lasting one night in his cell without Tinsel to wipe his backside.

'Well, I'm *always* out and about.' He turned to Tinsel. 'Amn't I, Harry?'

'At that time?' Punch said. He took out his sunflower collection for effect.

221

'He's out at all times, sergeant,' Tinsel said, moving to the window. 'Always has been. Everyone knows that. You're only just after trying to pin the knicker-knocker on him! Now this?'

Despite the evidence, Punch suspected the man wasn't capable. That he was trying to force-fit Tonsils into being the missing piece. A man and a plane were out there somewhere and here he was looking for Guy fucking Fawkes to boot.

'What were you doing there?' Punch said.

'I like to stand at the cannon there below the war memorial steps. You know we're related to the man inscribed on the memorial who didn't actually die in the war?'

'Or even fight in it,' Tinsel corrected, shaking his head. 'Bugger hid down at Ledaig for five years, and that was *before* they put Macgochans there.'

'If you could answer my question, Archie?' Punch pressed. 'Why the cannon?'

'Because I like to imagine the Spanish Armada ship it sunk. You know, out in the bay?'

'Look, did a fishing boat pass? Not a local vessel?'

Tonsils shook his head and turned to Tinsel.

'I didn't see that.' He shook again. 'I didn't. Just the poor dolly.'

'Irish vessel?' Punch pressed. 'You couldn't have missed it?'

'No. Just the star,' Tonsils said. 'Blinking. Falling.'

'Right.' Punch was dying for a puff, though he suspected from the ashtray outside that Tinsel did his smoking al fresco. There was talk of how Tonsils was some kind of health freak; he remembered the man growing his own lettuce and the like. Organic, for fuck's sake. He looked now to Tinsel's hand, for signs of further aberrations. They were yellow stained. Rough all right. Nails long like those of a guitarist. But long nails were not a crime.

'It was nine strikes of the clock when I saw her hanging. Horrible,' Tonsils said, leaning to put his hand on his bible. 'I nearly fell myself. And then I saw the blinking star.'

'Couldn't have been nine,' Punch said. 'It wasn't called in by the Irish boys until nearer ten according to Palindrome.'

'What the hell does Palindrome know?' Tinsel said. 'The man's not the full neck.'

'It was nine,' Tonsils said, daring to catch Punch's eye. 'The clock strikes ten times at nine o'clock. It chimes one more than the actual time.' He turned to his twin. 'Not like ours.'

'Christ. Course it does.' Punch shook his head, as if to escape the island's reality. 'What a fucking place ...'

'Don't take the Lord's name in vain please, lad,' Tonsils said. 'Not here.'

Punch looked to the sketch of the twin's mother on the wall. Imagined his own mother just on the other side. In fact, he could hear her TV. The whole fucking island was a goldfish bowl.

'What do you mean about this star?' he insisted. 'It couldn't have been a star. Was the sky not overcast?'

Moon in the cell for the night.

'Blinking it was,' Tonsils said, raising his hand and flexing his fingers by way of demonstration. 'Like a symbol.'

'Right.' Punch motioned to the bay, in the rough direction of the space between Calve and Aros Park. 'You know that's the Narrows out there not bloody Nazareth.'

'Please, Ivor . . .' Tinsel cautioned.

Punch looked to the window. Slowly nodded.

'Wait—' He stared straight at Tonsils. 'Was the star flashing like a light, on and off, Archie?'

'Aye.' Tonsils nodded. 'Aye, it was.' He turned to his twin. 'It was, Harry!'

'Straight out ahead of you from the path?' Punch pressed. 'Uh-huh!'

Punch turned to Tinsel. 'The Damask house. On Calve. That's what you saw flashing. Or something there.' He stood and leaned over Tonsils. 'Archie. Was it a house you saw? A light from a house?'

'Maybe,' Tonsils said. 'It was a sign for somebody. Certainly in that direction I suppose.'

'No boat? No Irishmen?'

Tonsils shook his head.

For the first time, Punch saw some correlation between the cases – given the flashing of lights on the airfield reported by the Slaters. But could Tonsils be trusted about the Irish boat? Palindrome certainly seemed a more accurate witness. And *SEARCH ARCHIE* remained part of the puzzle – a piece written in blood.

Punch heard a vehicle pulling up outside. Remembered what he had stored in his boot. Felt that brick in his stomach again. The hand also needed attending to; and the chainsaw brushed for DNA. But there were too many secrets in the lockup to have Dave go and collect the hand; he could only imagine the levels of enthusiasm for the task he would be met with.

He heard knocking at a neighbouring door. Tried to detect if it was his mother's. The TV was still blaring from the other side of the wall. Now came knocking on the twins' door. It was becoming more incessant.

'Like Piccadilly Circus here.' Tinsel rose to his feet and put a hand on his brother's shoulder. 'Used to walk through the place from Savile Row, in fact. Imagine that. Not a visitor in months and then this, Archie, eh? It's okay. Okay, lad.'

Tonsils leaned back against the wall and Punch didn't know whether to leave the man or not. He heard Tinsel greeting somebody.

The voices got closer. Into the small room walked Cluny, his hat held to his chest, his face a headline, brow sweating.

'Been trying to radio you, Sarge. Sorry. I startled your mum. Assumed you were there.'

'Must've . . .' Punch patted his breast. 'Left the handset in the car.'

'A Mr MacTavish has called the station, Sarge.' Cluny's cheeks were flushed. He gulped heavily. 'A body's been found.'

'Not another effigy?' Punch said. 'I *knew* it was Jim bloody MacTavish doing the pranks. And fuck! All because we jumped further than him twenty fucking years ago.'

'No, Sarge. Not a stuffed body. A *real* body.'

TRACK 20

PUNCH RACED THROUGH THE RAIN towards Salen from Tobermory, Cluny alongside him in the Ranger. He'd never spent so much time in the village in his life. He couldn't believe his bad luck. Of all the places on Mull or the surrounds for a body to be discovered, a real body, it had to be on MacTavish's land. The man would surely bring this fact into the ebb and flow of their families' sporting rivalry, as though it could have some bearing – perhaps even the power to rewrite the record books – on how far young men once leaped into the air before landing in rectangles of heavy sand.

Maybe everything comes down to such things?

Soon he and Cluny were flying past the spot on the Gally Goo where the first effigy had hung.

'Do you, eh, need any help with the other stuff, Sarge?' Cluny said. 'You know ... the guys?'

'Eh, no. No.' Punch turned away to his side window. It wasn't the time to divulge that the cases might be linked.

'He's identified the body as Lowry's,' Cluny said. 'Mr MacTavish.'

'We'll do the police work. MacTavish can worry about the appetite of his cows. The man couldn't pick out a haystack among his herd, let alone a virtuoso violinist.'

'Got it.'

'Had MacTavish not been inside the church at the time of the, eh, last, last hanging, erm—' Punch wasn't sure he could finish the sentence. 'Well then I'd, eh, have had half a mind to confront him there and then.'

'Yes, Sarge.'

'Though I doubt the man could coordinate such a campaign.'

A plane thundered into view and out over the Sound towards Morvern. Punch looked back to the road.

'RAF boys. Control have deployed a second plane.'

Cluny looked at his watch.

'Fourteen hundred hours,' he said. 'Clockwork.'

'Good work this week. Keep it up.' Punch nodded. He was relieved his deputy hadn't pursued his line of questioning on the effigy front. He fought the image trying to make itself known of Charlie's replica, which was now stored in the station lockup along with the other effigies, forgotten, attempting escape, like wildflowers fighting through the cracks of dead buildings; a human hand and a dead sheep for company. All that was missing was a morgue-cum-abattoir sign out there.

Before leaving Glen Iosal, he had notified Dave the Grave of the hand. Informed him of how to access the station lockup. Needs must.

Punch gestured to the handset.

'We'll keep HQ out of MacTavish's discovery just until we know it's not the man playing silly buggers with history. And fuck.'

227

Punch knew he was kowtowing to Cluny, and knew he was doing it because he had been absent to some extent from the Lowry case. There was some purpose in Cluny recognising it too. It might give his new recruit more understanding of the sergeant's multifaceted role; how on an island the job was more akin to a juggler in the round of a three-ring circus. It was impossible to please all the people all of the time. He had to hand it to Bob Dylan; the man sang a truth or two.

'Mr MacTavish reported the body is lying across a fallen tree, approximately four hundred feet above sea level up one of his hillsides,' Cluny said, reading from his notepad.

Punch was relieved to see it wasn't the computer.

'A larch, Sarge.'

'He knows not to touch it, of course?'

'Affirmative.'

'Sheila MacTavish will see it as another mouth to feed.' Punch stole a sideways glance at his deputy. 'And no sign of the plane?'

'Just a dead body.'

'*We'll* decide on whether life is extinct, not some failed athlete-cum-criminal farmer.'

'Should we not have the police doctor present, Sarge?'

Punch turned to him.

'Steady on, Rebus. There's no police doctors on islands – right? And fuck. We use Phil the Pill.'

'Phil the—'

'Our doctor.'

'Oh?'

228

'Things are different here from your coiffured streets of Milngavie, PC Cluny. But here we have something the mainland doesn't: you're a policeman *and* a jailer. You have powers of incarceration. They don't have that on the other side of the sea. Tulliallan or no Tulliallan.'

Cluny placed his hand on his handset.

'Have you ever, eh, pressed your red button, Sarge?' he asked, tentatively, referring to the emergency button on all police handsets, to be activated when an officer was in distress, so as to directly alert Control room.

'Pressed the red?' Punch said. 'That's a bit like asking a fellow how many notches he has on his headboard, lad.'

'Right. I was just wond—'

'Once. In Inverness. When an ex asked me to marry her. And fuck.'

'Oh?'

'No. I was on my tod when the shite hit the fan with two gangs of bikers around closing time off the A9. Hit the red and I'd four officers appear in a row alongside me quicker than you could say Keystone fucking Cops. Like I'd suddenly joined Boyzone.'

'That's reassuring.' Cluny gazed over the Sound.

'Have you *heard* Ronan Keating sing?'

'Yes.' He smiled. 'I'm not quite made entirely of procedure and printout.'

'You're not? I was going to check your back for a chip.' Punch cast a glance, almost a smile. 'No, no, I've not pressed the red on the island. Remember, when the last ferry's gone, it's all down to you. I told you that already.'

They flew through a cattle grid and the road changed from dual carriageway to single track, the official ending of the Gally Goo.

'Fuck. Ferry traffic incoming. Time for the blues.' Punch reached to activate the siren. He usually felt no need to display the size of his knob in public, though it was tempting when MacTavish was involved. The oncoming cortège now did their best to find passing places, some taking to the verge.

'Scares the shit out of the Christmas tourists – pull over, for fuck's sake!' Punch negotiated his way through the hastily parked cars carrying concerned faces. 'A suspect among them wouldn't go amiss either ...' The Ranger bumped up and down on the verge causing Cluny's shoulder to touch Punch's. Punch pulled further to his side. Raised his signature finger to tourists as he passed. Some returned the gesture and others clearly hadn't got the hang of it yet. 'More cooperation from one of my carcasses.'

'The festive rush,' Cluny said, nervously.

'Drop the full beams, people!' Punch narrowed his eyes. 'Like driving through the aurora bloody borealis.'

Punch deactivated the siren. 'Your first body?' he said.

Cluny's pale eyelashes fluttered.

'Uh-huh. Thought as much.'

'Could he have jumped, Sarge?'

'Charlie?' Punch turned.

'Who?' Cluny said.

Punch returned his gaze to the road. Cleared his throat. His Adam's apple performed a somersault.

'Eh, Lowry? I can't imagine that would be possible, PC Cluny. If MacTavish is close to correct, then the body is one mile from the airfield. So, no. Too hilly a territory.'

'No parachute I suppose,' Cluny said.

'Parachute? Townsend barely has two torches that work, to say nothing of the flushability of his bogs. And fuck.' He had instructed Dave to carefully inspect the hand. Knew he had waited too long on that. A call for Forensics had already gone out on reports of the body.

On the other side of Salen, the rain was heavier. Punch sped onwards, now into Monteith speed-gun territory. A mile later, he slowed down in anticipation of a right turn, the wheels lashing through the surface water. The sky was darker and the light failing, mist rolling in from the Sound. *The peak of Ben More taken in for questioning.*

He turned off the dual carriageway and drove up the scraggy lane.

'Fuck,' Punch mumbled as they rocked through the potholes. MacTavish's farmhouse and various well-apportioned outbuildings came into view up ahead. 'Bugger's had grants to erect every one of them, of course. Grants for bacon rolls, hernia operations, by Christ.' He looked ahead to the adjoining sprawling mass of generators, chickens on the loose, diggers, fishing creels, ropes, and whatever else the universe had chosen to bequeath to the MacTavishes of the world. There were two rally cars, one red, one green. *The Salen Hotel* painted on the sides.

'Hillbillies,' Punch murmured. 'Charlie bloody Manson lived in less chaos.' He licked his lips, could almost feel the sand from the pit in his mouth. 'You always came home from the Games with grit on your teeth.'

'Eh, Sarge?'

The large frame of MacTavish himself hove into view; he was wearing blue overalls and a serious sideways stare.

'Fucking skull on the bugger, think it was Easter Island we'd landed on.' Punch pulled the Ranger alongside one of MacTavish's personalised plates: MACTAV1. 'Uncouth.'

He pushed open the door and stepped into the mud.

'Whore-ish thing,' they heard.

MacTavish had appeared at Punch's side. The crofter's black, hooded raincoat looked big enough to shelter a small country.

'Saw it when I was out doing the morning feed on the moors,' MacTavish announced. Punch noted the Runrig logo on his hat. Knew that it was only a matter of time before sentimental, *nineties*-era Rod would no doubt be tackling 'Loch Lomond'. 'Rushed back and called your deputy. Well-spoken lad.' MacTavish nodded into the passenger seat. 'Well-spoken lad I said.'

'Thank you, sir,' Cluny said.

Punch was anticipating a curtsey – that was when the lad *did* finally get out of the Ranger.

'Some people would do well to have him rub off on them,' MacTavish spouted. 'Anyway, Punch, you'll want to see the body for yourself.'

Punch hadn't said anything yet; he could never return an insult from MacTavish as quickly as he would like. It was something to do with what had gone before; or what had gone. Maybe the uniform, too.

'You haven't tampered with it?' Punch said. 'We'll need a tent up smartish to avoid contamination. We don't touch so much as a blade of grass until Forensics arrive with their cameras. Can you get an update to that end, PC?'

'Aye, I've watched *Columbo* with the best of them,' MacTavish quipped with a shrug.

'Come to think of it, cancel the tent,' Punch said, wiping the rain from his face. 'Maybe Mr MacTavish's mac would do the job.'

'So, no tent, just Forensics, Sarge? *Over.*'

'No. Both. Both, PC. Fuck's sake! And why are you saying "over"? I'm standing right next to you.'

Punch walked to his boot and paused, feeling a chill up his spine that the Charlie effigy might still be inside. He slowly opened the boot and was relieved to see just his coat and his usual policing supplies: a torch, pepper spray, surgical gloves and a hazard triangle. He took out the coat and the torch and slammed the boot on the past. On playing fields. On Lockerbie.

Focus. Belly.

'PC Jonathan Ambrose Cluny,' he heard.

Cluny had walked around to shake MacTavish's hand. Punch was relieved to see the man had left his name plaque on the desk.

Cluny's umbrella sprung open.

'Sure you don't want to show him your dental records too?' Punch said. 'And fuck.'

'Didn't learn his manners from you, Punch,' MacTavish said. 'Leave the lad alone.'

'Four hundred metres up, you said?' Punch looked to the hillside.

'Are you waiting on the starter's pistol, Punch? Or the lad here to radio in a shoeshine for you?' MacTavish motioned in the direction of the moors; his hands stored high in his pockets.

It was hard for Punch to imagine MacTavish with a needle and thread. His wife, Sheila, less so.

'Radio Control to check that Forensics and additional assets are on their way. Them making the last ferry's not likely.'

'Oban can organise a rib for them, Sarge?'

'HLS better.'

'Sarge?'

'Helicopter landing site. Control will know that.'

'Right. I'll relay that now. Will I put you or me down as crime scene manager, Sarge?'

'Dave the Grave will be CSM,' Punch said, the disdain in his voice evident. 'And refer all press enquiries to Control. They're bound to be fishing soon.'

'Will do, Sarge,' Cluny managed, still nursing his hand from MacTavish's grip.

'Dave would have the man smelling of Paco Rabanne by now,' MacTavish said. He turned to Cluny. 'Our Grand Master, no less.'

'Will you want your handset, Sarge?'

'No,' Punch replied. He would have said, *listen to your belly*, but the bugger would think it was organic salmon time.

Punch moved quickly to catch up with his old foe, who had jumped the start.

'Don't mind telling you, it's not pretty up there, Ivor. All joking aside.' MacTavish shook. 'Poor fucker.'

Punch walked ahead. He liked to be alone with the scene of a crime before the dancing girls and the Red Arrows arrived. It had been the same last year with the knicker-knocker. Though he suspected a damn sight more paperwork and media interest in this one. A case inspector visit was unavoidable now.

'Sponsorship,' MacTavish said, pointing to the hotel logo on the side of the rally cars. 'Paint's still wet. Four hundred quid by fuck.'

'That should cover your boys' bail money for a month.'

They walked up the hillside and over several dykes. Occasionally MacTavish would whistle or shout a 'come by' to Drambuie, his black and tan sheepdog. The sheep and goats parted as they progressed. The land levelled out briefly and they passed an overgrown sandpit. Punch imagined them going at it again. Here. Now. One last time. Athletes made giant for a day, while a reported dead man was leaning on a tree up ahead. They turned down to a stream and Drambuie took a loud slurp.

'Learned his manners from me,' MacTavish said. The dog shook his coat free of excess water. It ran up ahead and started barking. 'Wheesht, Drambuie! I do the barking around here. Remember your training, man.'

The trees clustered as the land climbed again. Punch could now see the snowy sides of Ben More in the distance, reduced to the size of his forefinger. Birds of prey circling. They arrived at the point where any notable pathway stopped. Punch kept a lookout for the plane. He grimaced back into the rain and turned to face the hill again. They walked another fifty metres. Ahead was a small dip where the trees

235

were more sporadic. Slumped onto a tree about ten paces on, he saw it: a man dressed in a Barbour jacket. At first glance you might have thought he was urinating. Punch himself was suspicious of it actually being a real, human body, after all the replicas.

So. This is you, Xander Lowry.

'I'd think the jacket alone would be worth a night in the cell, Ivor?' MacTavish shouted, having hung back a bit, flashing his gums.

'Minus the fan heater.'

'Clever fucker apparently.'

Punch looked at his watch. Determining the exact time of life extinct was going to be a puzzle. He walked closer. There they were: the man's black flying boots. As Michael Slater's party had confirmed. And the blue jumper. Sodden. Eyebrows like sleeping caterpillars. Hair full, but wet. He had the notion he already knew the man. There was a conflicted feeling he had never experienced before with a body, a sense of remove matched only by the overwhelming feeling of intimacy. *Might an audience applaud at any moment?*

There was some sensation of relief in having real, physical confirmation.

Lowry was not Charlie.

He turned to survey the land, attempting to assess the direction the man might have travelled. There was no obvious route. Unhelpfully, he saw the hillside in Lockerbie; had the feeling he was inside Randy's TV. Often he had taken off for the ferry, intending to travel to Sherwood Crescent in the Borders town, only to turn back. His mother had been, to attend the five-year memorial service. They had never discussed it. And now she probably couldn't.

'Well, if *One Man and His Dog* ever go down the horror route . . .' MacTavish wagged a roll-up as he spoke.

'It's not the Proms, I'll give you that.'

'Aye. Looks as though he's been dropped by one of my diggers. Two-ton pecker would do the job. Terrible.'

Punch turned to him.

'He fucking *wasn't* though!' MacTavish said.

Punch stepped closer to the body, straddled as it was oddly across a branch. He peered closer to the arm that was leaning on the tree. Saw what couldn't be seen from the other side. What he had suspected but not voiced. What MacTavish had not spotted.

The left arm was missing a hand.

Something moved behind them.

MacTavish swung around.

'Oh, you fucker!' he said.

Punch looked back through the rain to see Cluny cowering under his umbrella.

'Need to up your training, Punch!' MacTavish chided. 'Drambuie here is available.'

'Sorry, Sarge. Control have been updated about Forensics, they wanted you to know. They're en route now. Helicopter.'

'Right. Good.' Punch looked to MacTavish. 'Definitely hasn't been touched?'

'No. Straight out the wrapper,' MacTavish said. 'Don't mind admitting I was spooked myself.' He turned to Cluny. 'Though he'd give you more of a conversation than some in the Lussa Falls – what?'

Cluny tried but failed to force a smile. He walked with some trepidation towards his superior. Punch didn't object to the initiative shown, but wasn't about to broadcast it.

'Erm, could he have, eh, climbed the hill, Sarge?' Cluny said.

Punch lit a cigarette. He could hear the lump of fear in Guinness's throat.

'I can see some sense in it, constable, you know, to get as high as you can to see where you are.' Punch leaned closer to detect where exactly the hand had been severed.

'Bloody hell!' Cluny noticed the wound.

'Forensics will have a job. This one was always going to bypass the Home at Salen in favour of the mainland,' Punch puffed, referring to the island's small medical unit. He had been born into the world in that building. He looked at his watch. 'Though we might need to handcuff Dave to keep him off it.'

'His left,' Cluny said. 'Oh my God.'

'Eh?'

'Apparently it was considered the best in the world on a violin . . .' Cluny looked around as though he too was expecting the Royal Albert Hall; a BBC2 announcer fine-tuning his voice to report an unexpected change in scheduling.

Punch leaned to the body and saw traces of sawdust on the back.

'Aye, well, go back and radio in that the plane is nowhere obviously near the body. But air assets should refocus their search to this area.'

Punch knew he was doing that thing again – concealing evidence, attempting to control the future and its impact on the past. He had the hunch the hand should be kept to a tight circle for now. Though the sooner Forensics got their gloves on the chainsaw the better.

'Right,' Cluny said. 'Should I notify next of kin – Miss Lauder?'

'Not yet.' Punch took a deep draw. 'We don't yet know she is that. We need to keep all lines open. You okay?'

Cluny nodded.

'Are we confirming it's Xander Lowry, Sarge?'

'It's not Tony bloody Blair. Take more than this to wipe the smile off that fucker's face.'

'Though you'd lose a hand shaking his,' MacTavish added.

'Okay.' Cluny walked off.

'PC Cluny?' Punch said. 'You really okay?'

Cluny turned and nodded.

'Fine then,' Punch said. 'But lose the brolly. It's a tad Mary Poppins.'

'Right. Right, Sarge.'

Drambuie came up to sniff Punch's leg, and then moved towards the corpse, skittering around it like a drop of water on a hot pan.

'Dog!' MacTavish yelled, running until he was alongside Punch. Punch saw some of that explosive pace of old in the man's bulk, akin to the migration of the wildebeest. 'Christ, don't think about pissing on his leg, for fuck's sake!'

'One way to kill the evidence,' Punch said. 'Could he have climbed the hill from the water?'

'Drambuie?'

'Eh, no.'

'Oh, right. Christ, Ivor, there's a continuous vertical cliff-edge wall out of the Sound the whole way down there. Impossible to climb I reckon. Boggy too.'

'He'd have to have swum ashore and climbed the hill,' Punch puffed. 'But crossed the road?' He offered a roll-up to MacTavish, who took it and leaned into Punch for a light. It was strange to be talking so loosely with the man. He was more used to everything being a competition, even the discovery of death. 'Why would he cross the road?' Punch peered closer. 'No scratches on the body.'

'I've seen men leave the Salen Hotel in worse shape.'

'Your bed too.'

'Strange right enough. In all seriousness, I've never seen a thing like it. On Mull, by fuck?' MacTavish shook his head. 'What's the craic from Townsend?'

'Hard to tell,' Punch said. 'He was a name in the classical music world, apparently. Lowry. Not Townsend. Though that part could be significant.'

Lowry's room needed further investigation. He had instructed two special constables to attend Lussa Falls and seal off the room until Forensics arrived.

Drambuie took off up the hill and then returned, circling Lowry excitedly, his big tongue lapping from his mouth.

'Dram!' MacTavish called. 'Come by, you fucker.' He looked to Punch. 'Bugger's too used to rounding up everything he sees on this hill. Bacon fat from my mouth, by fuck.'

240

Punch looked around the hillside. There was no sign of distress or incident whatsoever. It was almost tranquil in the mist. Tufts of wool were blowing on the barbed-wire fencing. Embodiment of the fact that some left the island and others got entangled.

He returned his focus to the body, positioned as it was like an ornament. The face pale, already with the weather on it. The man emptied of all that music. Eyes opened. The hair impressive, caked onto his face. Cluny had done a decent job conjuring the man.

'Definitely the man?' MacTavish wheezed, as if it needed further confirmation at this stage.

'Aye. Fits every description down to the hands. Or lack thereof.'

'Oh fuck!' MacTavish looked more closely at the severing. He walked nearer and brought his stick up towards the man's midriff. 'The hands ... was that not what *made* the man? Fucking hell.'

'You'd struggle to get a note out of the bugger now. Careful not to touch.'

Punch walked off to the surrounding land; sodden underfoot. He felt it: the mainland coming; Forensics, reporters, possibly CID. He glanced at MacTavish, now tending a broken fence. Even a dead man minus a hand hanging off one of his trees could not interrupt the workings of his land, of nature's call, a buck to be made, a potential grant form to be filed.

'I better get back and radio for updates on the circus arriving,' Punch said, though MacTavish was too far away to hear. He walked back to the tree and gazed into Lowry's face. What he saw was the mask of a man. 'They say your talent was God-given ...'

'All we need is an angel on top,' said MacTavish, now returned from the important business.

'Eh?'

'The wife. Said that this very morning about the Christmas tree ... well, we've got one now. I'll be fucked.'

Punch turned and began the walk back down the hill.

'Obviously nobody goes near it,' he said. 'I'll have Cluny tent the body. Never sure what micro-organisms you've got festering around here.'

'Aye. No bother, don't blame you,' MacTavish puffed. 'I'll brief Drambuie.'

Punch turned back and wondered how much of Lowry was still the famed musician and how much was carcass. Just as he was no longer sure how much of himself was uniform and how much was still the man. The son. The brother. The lover. In the aftermath of Lockerbie, he hadn't been able to stop being a copper. He had forced himself to read the reports of corpses found in front gardens, giving the impression they had simply kneeled or laid down, rather than having fallen thirty thousand feet out of the sky.

Wee girls.

He shook his head free, restarted another roll-up and descended the hillside. The rain was falling harder, and he questioned whether there wasn't a Bob Dylan line everywhere if you looked closely enough.

'He's getting old. His brother recently returned of course ...'

'Dylan's?' Punch turned sharply.

'Eh? No, no. Drambuie's.'

'Right. Right.'

'Aye I'd given the brother pup to a family in Salen years back. Then found the bugger lying dead in my shed just two weeks ago. He'd come home to die.'

Punch sighed, but didn't offer anything.

'If only Lowry had similar homing apparatus,' MacTavish wheezed. 'Swear we'll find a Kennedy next.'

'Aye.'

When the two men returned to the vehicles, PC Cluny was standing by Punch's Ranger.

'Control have confirmed the helicopter is on its way, Sarge,' he said urgently.

'Right.' Punch noticed how his deputy had the air of Drambuie about him, as though he needed patting and being told 'good dog'. He obliged. 'Good work, Cluny.'

Punch looked to MacTavish and nodded to the farm-house.

'Best to keep Sheila quiet about this for now, Jim. Otherwise she'll have her own chat show by teatime.'

'Nothing surer. Wogan would be finished!' MacTavish rose on his toes, the seeming size of him diminishing diggers. He nodded to the hill. 'Shame your man up there couldn't do the theme music.'

A plane sounded. Punch looked up.

'Yep, the RAF boys are onto it. The Needle becomes the primary search focus.' He took another puff of his roll-up. 'Maybe you'll get us in the top ten after all, PC Cluny.'

Another vehicle came lolloping up MacTavish's drive.

'Backup?' Cluny was clearly impressed with himself. 'Already?'

'No.' Punch shook his head. 'Well, yes. The kind I trust. Our undertaker.'

'The Grand Master.' MacTavish gestured to Cluny. 'Admire the poise, lad. Something of the billiards referee about him.'

'Certainly he's handled as many balls. And fuck.'

TRACK 21

THEY WATCHED THE FIGURE EMERGE from the hearse. The man walked knock-kneed towards them, zipping a dark mac importantly up to his chin.

'Oaf, I heard you were looking for volunteers?' Dave the Grave called out. 'So I sent for a professional.'

'Dave,' Punch greeted him.

'Sergeant.'

'Grand Master,' MacTavish enthused. 'You've got the hearse a long way from home. Sends the shits up me seeing it here, I don't mind saying.'

'Should have brought a spare coffin, Dave,' said Punch, taking another puff and exhaling towards MacTavish.

'I always have a spare.' Dave looked upwards. 'I see the RAF are getting interested?'

'The plane,' Punch said.

'They'd be better looking for Townsend's insurance papers . . .' MacTavish said.

'Oaf, I got Mum home, and Mary,' Dave said.

'Thanks, Dave.'

'Easy done, sergeant. Easy done. Nothing of it so far?'

'The Needle?' Punch shook his head. 'No.'

'Brother,' Dave said to MacTavish, nodding his bald head to the hill. 'Hellish business I'm sure, James.'

'Hellish, master,' MacTavish agreed.

A voice came over the radio and Punch dropped inside the Ranger.

'Aye, we boxed the Three Wise Men up well, James,' Dave said, pushing his transitional-lensed glasses up his nose. He was fairly certain he had the first pair on Mull.

'Eh, the Three Wise Men?' Cluny said.

'Was the name given to James here's father,' Dave said. 'Fine Brother he was. Even bigger specimen than his son. Had a well-worn practice of arriving late in the night at houses for a dram because *he had followed a bright star.*'

'He did too!' MacTavish said, chuckling. 'You saw the old bugger away good and proper. Mum was thankful.'

'Biggest knob I've ever had on my table.'

'Good of you to say that, Grand Master. As I said, Mum was thankful.'

'No wonder,' Dave said.

Cluny opened the passenger door and dropped in alongside Punch.

'What's cooking, Sarge?'

'Control confirming RAF and coastguard deployment have seen nothing so far.' Punch removed his hat and swept back his badgers. He checked the dash. 'Forensics should be here soon. But I want Dave to see the body first.'

Both men exited the car.

Dave the Grave walked around to Cluny's side and outstretched his hand. 'David.'

'Right you are, aye, sorry,' Cluny said. 'PC Cluny. Pleasure.'

'All mine. All mine.' Dave smiled respectfully, stood back a pace or two and looked the man up and down. 'Badminton player?'

'Eh, aye?'

'Thought as much,' Dave said. 'Traced your Viking origins?'

'Eh, no . . . no.'

'Just give me the nod. I've charts at home. Fingers, toes, and the like in the freezer too.'

'Eh? Okay?' Cluny was unsure whether to laugh; his eyes had become saucers.

'PC Cluny, keep your ear to the radio,' Punch said, heading away towards the hill. 'Let's walk, Dave!'

Cluny inhaled deeply and leaned back against the Ranger. Checked his finger count.

'I'll get Sheila on the teas and bacon rolls.' MacTavish turned back to the house. 'Do her well to keep busy, we've had quite the shit-scare.' He whistled and the dog ran to his side. 'Christ, Dram, what a morning. We're under siege! But no blabbering to your collie bitches now, you hear?'

'Good of you, Dave, to get here so quickly,' Punch said, navigating the incline. 'Wanted you to see it before the cavalry arrives, or night falls.'

Another RAF jet whooshed overhead.

'Sounds like they have already, sergeant.'

Dave was still dressed as he had been in the church, in his uniform of black trousers with a silk strip down the sides, the black mac and shined-to-a-moon shoes. The rain was pelting off his globe-like skull. Punch had noticed there were red lines on the man's head, giving the impression they marked out continents.

'So, I'd confirm it was the chainsaw,' Dave said.

'The hand?'

'Aye.'

'Christ.'

'Certainly something with heavy teeth.'

'Can't blame it on Freddie Mercury. Never seen anything like this is the truth.' Punch cupped his hands to relight a roll-up stub. 'I won't offer you one because I know you don't smoke.'

'Respectfully done, sergeant.' Dave strode efficiently onwards. 'One has seen the effects of nicotine on a man up close one time too many.'

'Where is it now?'

'The hand? Back in the car, safely swimming in liquid nitrogen. Can't have the mainland thinking we're medieval in our approach.' Dave gestured. 'Figured the forensic pathologist will want to shake it once or twice. I was careful.'

'Okay, thanks, Dave.'

'It's Lowry's?'

'Aye. Has to be.'

'Oaf, certainly a musician's long fingers. Long, but strong. Just missing a bow on it.'

'I've been trying to fathom how the man got here, let alone minus a hand. No plane, no obvious signs of struggle. Need your take on the body.'

'What is humanly possible and the like?'

248

'Aye. Though we'll need to be careful, Dave, with Forensics arriving.'

'Ah? The *water-colourists*?' Dave gestured condescendingly. 'Leave the oils and frescos to me, sergeant.'

'He would have needed to cross the bloody road to get up here. There's no other way from the Sound.' Punch spoke breathily, his uniform sodden; he sighed deeply and turned to consider the path they had taken. 'MacTavish confirmed as much.'

'Right.' Dave strode onwards. 'Unless he fell to the earth?'

'Seems unlikely?' Punch was struggling to keep up with him.

'I'll reserve judgement on my Masonic brother's assessment until I see the body. But first thoughts point to the possibility that Mr Lowry, having already survived a plane crash of some kind, wouldn't have seen it, the road. It was sleeting heavily Friday night. He would have been unable to think straight. Logical thought and a hypothermic man are not common bedfellows.'

'Yes. Possible.' Punch drew alongside, leaned to catch his breath.

'A hundred press-ups in the morning, hundred more at night, should do the trick, sergeant. Naked in my case. Nobody wants their pyjamas getting all sweaty. Handy for the pelvic floor at our age too.'

'Right, cheers, Dave. So, Lowry was fifty-five. Hard enough for me getting up here, but in his condition, sleeting too?'

'And if he was trying to get help then why leave the road? That's if he did see it.'

'To say nothing of where the plane is. And fuck.'

'Oaf, his sense of touch would have been shot, sergeant. His feet numbed. Like walking with feet of wood, if you can imagine that. People don't know that about the body.' Dave took a cloth from the inside pocket of his mac, removed his glasses and used the cloth to wipe the rain from them. 'Good cloth this.'

'Aye?'

'Wallace's of Oban. The man's to ophthalmology what Grossman is to sauces, Nobel to peace.'

They reached the flattening of the hillside and then dipped into the burrow where the fencing was damaged.

'Just over the next fold of land.'

'Right you are, sergeant.'

The larch tree came into view. Then the body. Still half standing, held aloft by a branch.

'Okay. Enough with the trailers, time for the main feature . . .' Dave rubbed his hands together and progressed speedily towards the corpse.

'At least the bugger hasn't moved.'

Punch watched Dave put on plastic gloves. The man became almost another animal as he circled the deceased. Clouds of his breath arriving on the corpse. Pausing every so often, leaning close into Lowry. It looked to Punch as though the undertaker was capturing X-rays of the man with his eyeballs, all to the soundtrack of not *ER*, but a deep nasal hiss. Dave reached inside his black mac and produced a slim torch. Punch saw how snowfall danced around the man's head, almost refusing to land; he saw how masterfully Dave studied the body, as though walking its internal map.

'What you reckon?' Punch said.

'Oaf, another week or two al fresco in this weather and the only thing holding the body together would be its blue jerkin,' Dave said.

'Christ.' Punch moved closer; he was conscious the sanctum of the hill was now Dave the Grave's, and Lowry's. It was like trespassing on the orchestra pit, with Dave the conductor.

'We are all creatures of the earth,' Dave said. He looked up to the sky and swivelled around. 'Facing due north.'

'I thought the same. But remarkably unharmed?'

'Good spot, sergeant. A superficial cut on the right leg visible at this juncture. Love to get the man on my table, of course; but every contact leaves a trace. I've got just the box for him too. Big lad. Though the violin might be a stretch.'

'Aye, but we'll need to leave him for Forensics, Dave. You know ... to keep top brass sweet an' all.'

'Message received, sergeant. I won't leave so much as a blast of hot breath on him. Though an hour or two more of investigation and I'd tell you his next, final movement.'

'Beethoven?'

'Bowels.'

'Can't imagine the man could have survived in the sea for long, Dave. Assuming the plane landed there, that is?' Punch knew the sawdust traces on the body – apparently missed by the undertaker – all but ruled out a sea landing. But he didn't want to prematurely influence Dave's fresh analysis. He turned to review the terrain again. 'The plane, the plane ... where the fuck?'

'You're talking a water temp of ten degrees at best, sergeant. A fit human would last forty-five minutes in that, max. And the man looks fit enough for his age. One would assume his days at the Proms seem behind him, alas.'

'That's assuming he had the strength to swim to shore. In which case, the plane is in the Sound. Christ.' Punch shook his head. 'Mystery upon mystery.'

'Poor fellow,' Dave said, stepping closer to Lowry's body.

'Put a pint in his hand and he'd almost be holding court at the Mish. And fuck.'

'Oaf, I should think the Victorian opulence of the Western Isles and a cognac for this fellow.' Dave shone the torchlight into the corpse's eyes and then over his hair. 'The eyes convey all the truths of an animal's final thoughts. Always does. Some mane on you, chum.'

Punch wondered whether Dave *did* pour his corpses a drink. There was all kinds of talk locally.

'Am I missing something in his eyes?'

'Hmm. Not a happy chappy at the end, certain of that.'

'He either swam,' Punch theorised, 'fell out of the thing or—'

'Remember the sea is not a swimming pool, sergeant. Assuming he landed in the middle of the Sound, for example, a person would take half an hour to swim to shore. Then, of course, there is gasp reflex, which usually causes drowning. But yet . . . yet . . .' Dave looked right into the face of Lowry. 'You made it, to here, my friend. You did.'

Punch expected the corpse might burst into life. He was struck with how personally Dave interacted with the dead; how the man conversed so intimately, as though expecting a response. There were rumours of Dave driving the dead around the island. Randy claimed to have encountered the undertaker one winter evening in his hearse on the Glen, the barren single-track road that cut through the middle of the island at the point of the sleeping bear's bellybutton, connecting the sleepy village of Dervaig to the Salen–Tobermory road at Aros Bridge. It had been lashing down according to Randy, and he had encountered Dave in a lay-by parked in the darkness, with the vehicle's internal light on. A man was strapped in, sitting upright in Dave's passenger's seat. Stiff as a corpse, Randy had reported. When he pulled over and wound the window down, Dave had simply uttered: 'Company.' Though, as Punch knew himself, Randy's accounts were not always to be trusted. There was likely a can or two involved, if not another man's wife. Or two.

'So, he flew, crashed or ejected, and swam or walked,' Punch said.

'A mystery only the body holds the answers to, Sergeant. Always does.' Dave leaned into the dead musician's face. 'But were you travelling *largo* or *allegro*, my friend?'

'Highly unlikely he could have swum ashore,' Punch mused. 'Or survived a crash landing.'

'More tests on the body will have to be run by the forensic pathologist. Much as a mechanic would do with a car. They'll need to heat the body up.'

'They will?'

'Can't run a postmortem on a cold body.'

'Aye, of course.'

'Oaf, there's the steady effect of heat loss bringing about disorientation to consider, too.' Dave performed a three-sixty-degree turn. 'If he *did* swim then the blood draining from his brain when he stood up could have been lethal. You should always come out horizontally, not vertically, of freezing water.'

'Right.' Punch wasn't certain whether Dave was talking to him, or admonishing Lowry. 'Postmortem will tell us ratios of fresh water to potential salt on him, you reckon, Dave? Even with the rain contamination?'

'That's not the only uncertainty; lochs can have a deep layer of fresh water on top of them, sergeant.'

As well as being Grand Master in Tobermory's Masonic Lodge, Dave was the founding – and, Punch suspected, only – member of the Mull Historical Society, and as a result considered the land, the island's people and its heritage as much of a map to be explored as he did the human body.

'Even if there's not a major in-flow from the sea, it still runs off the hillside. In winter, you can have five feet of rainwater on the surface before you'd so much as shake hands with saltwater.'

'Well, the body will go off with Forensics when they arrive.' Punch looked eagerly to the sky with no answers. 'The hand too, for fuck's sake.'

'I'd like to get the man on my table,' Dave murmured once more. 'Next of kin?'

'A girlfriend, as it stands. Staying with him at the Lussa Falls. Control are running further background checks.'

'Sure, sure.' Dave removed his glasses to wipe them again.

Punch saw how in the rain Dave was even more fish-like without the specs; the lids of his eyes were red, and by the sides of his mouth pockets of hanging skin gave the illusion of gills.

'We better get back down; top brass will be after me.'

Maggie May was on Punch's mind. The high heels; the connection to Sonia Hislop.

'Funny. Look, sergeant.' Dave motioned to Lowry.

'What?'

'It's like he's playing an imaginary violin in his final resting position, you think?'

'You'd be waiting a while on a concert tour.'

The men walked back down the hillside towards the farmhouse through the emerging sleet.

'Seeing the man reminds me of a recent story in our trade mag, *Funeral Directors' Monthly*. Decent font they use. Anyway, I read about the ill-fated musician, the Big Bopper, whose son had his father's coffin exhumed and opened up owing to unanswered questions about the musician's death. You see, the son had never set eyes on his father. Had still been in the womb when his father died in the same plane crash that killed Buddy Holly and Ritchie Valens. Tragedy.'

'Right, Dave.' Punch scanned the darkening sky.

'The son – now twenty years older than his father had been when he died – described his befuddled emotions as he looked at the remarkably well-preserved body of his father, frozen in time, in his 1950s clothes, arrived to the future. I keep a clipping of the Holly crash by the bed. The day the music died, all right. Lost to the world in a frozen Iowan field in 1959. History altered by a snowflake. By the flip of a fifty-cent coin.'

Punch had Charlie's *Oban Times* obituary somewhere. He increasingly felt there was no single future. It seemed to him there were a number of possible futures, and which one you got depended on what actions you took, or that life took for you.

Cluny emerged quickly from the Ranger when he saw them approaching. He nodded officiously and stood waiting for them.

'Funny standing position, the lad?' Dave said, leaning conspiratorially into Punch. 'All angles.'

'Pythagoras would have an orgy.'

'Almost looks like a hitch-hiking arrangement?' said Dave, stroking his cod-like jowls, as he arrived to Cluny.

'Pardon?' Cluny said.

Dave nodded back to the moors. 'Lowry,' he said. 'The resting position.'

'Oh?' Cluny said. 'Yes.'

'Oaf, I hear you're an acquaintance of the World Wide Web, Constable Cluny?' Dave said.

'Yes, aye, you have to be now, I guess.'

'Sent an email?' Dave rocked on his heels.

'Yes.'

'What dial-up speed you running?'

'Eh, not sure exactly.' Cluny looked to Punch before realising it was a wasted operation. 'I can find out.'

'I'm a Windows man all day long,' Dave said. 'Though my actual surname is MacIntosh. Funny that, isn't it?'

'Yes, thanks.'

Dave leaned in closely to Cluny and whispered, 'A few episodes of *Quincy* should do it.'

'Sorry?'

'To acquaint yourself with a dead body, lad.' Dave gave him a wise wink. 'Learn from the best. Or come over sometime. Bring your mouse. We can have some fun. Loads of dead bodies on the net.'

'Right. Okay.'

'And I can help you with that cocked foot you have—' Dave said, nodding down to the constable's muddy shoes. 'Just a quick break of the ankle and then a reset. Six-week rehab job. Can do it on my table. Four if the gods are on our side.'

'What?'

'Non gratis.'

'Oh? Right, thanks.'

'Mum or Dad the same, lad?'

'Erm, well, Dad actually now I think on it.'

'Happy to do Dad too. Okay, lad? Non gratis. Maybe a donation to the Historical Society is all.'

MacTavish emerged, peering through the rain from the farmhouse door.

Cluny saw it as his chance to move away from Dave the Grave.

'CID will be informed, Sarge?' he queried.

'Control L Div will do that. I'll set a crime scene manager when the additional boots on the ground arrive. This is too big to give CSM to Dave.'

'And CID then assign additional support?'

'Let's not get ahead of ourselves, PC Cluny. I make that call. Right now, we need to preserve our locus from the elements, keep things sterile. That's your job. Now.'

257

'And what about wider protection of the crime scene area? Closing off entrances to the moors and such?'

'Less easy. You'll learn that about an island. It's far from simple on a hill like this. At least it's private land. Less threat of contamination. Though it *is* the MacTavishes . . .'

Punch walked to the Ranger and opened the boot. He removed a police tent collapsed into a black bag.

'Not for camping.' He tossed the tent to Cluny.

'Now?'

'Pronto. Medivac might be required too. But we need to get Lowry isolated before the helicopter arrives.'

'It can land on the hill?'

'No. Tob golf course or – as chance would have it – Lussa Falls are the designated landing spots. So it'll be Lussa Falls. Just hope they have more luck landing than Lowry. And fuck.'

'Terrible business up on the hill, eh, Grand Master?' MacTavish said, moving closer to Dave.

'It'd be a waste of a Masonic handshake that's for certain, brother. Folk console themselves with the hope that a body is lighter in death, thon', "*spirit floating to Heaven*" mumbo-jumbo. But in truth there's nothing heavier than a dead body.'

'Apart from Punch's wallet.' MacTavish beamed. 'Right. Come away inside, it's like Niagara out here. Sheila's been busy frying pig. Hellish business.'

Punch reached into the Ranger and took the handset with him. Sometimes the flipchart brigade won. He had no interest in home baking, but there could be a lead to be had while he waited on backup. The island would want to get involved, but this would have to stay a police-led case.

'Call out to Polsa,' he radioed. 'Sergeant Punch, Lima Bravo. Over.'

'Police search advisor. Over,' came the crackling response. *'Immediate threat to life, sergeant?'*

'We're beyond that, inspector. Dead body confirmed. Identified as a Mr Xander Lowry. That's L-O-W-R-Y. TOD: sixteen zero two; though suspected much earlier. Location, PA72 7LB, handily near the HLS landing site, Lussa Falls, Mull. On the grounds of a privately owned farm, Ballymull, belonging to a James MacTavish. Awaiting air assets. Repeat: awaiting air assets. Update to follow. Over.'

The Polsa repeated the details and Punch reconfirmed. He then requested land registry information for a property on another island. Just a hunch, at this stage, but all lines had to be explored.

Punch walked to the farmhouse.

Inside, the three men sat around the kitchen table. Sheila MacTavish, a full-bodied woman with a ready smile and white perm, was dressed in a carnival of denim. She placed mugs and bacon rolls in front of them. The mugs had illustrations of different breeds of cows. Punch couldn't be certain they weren't family portraits.

'All right, lads, warm yourself up with those,' she said.

'Right. Thanks, Sheila,' Punch said. 'One before the helicopter arrives should do it.' He couldn't stop himself looking around for darning materials, maybe a foam limb. Nothing doing.

'Shocking business,' she said. 'I said to Jim, it was just a normal Sunday until now. We'd been at church in Tob. Seen you and your mother, Ivor. Came home for the feed rounds

259

and you could have boxed me there and then when Jim came running in. Here? On *Mull*?'

'It can be arranged!' MacTavish exploded, nodding to Dave.

'Oaf, the man didn't fall to the earth from the moon, Sheila,' Dave said.

'There wasn't one last night, GM,' MacTavish said, pig fat rolling into his beard. 'So, he's not David Bowie. The musician.'

'How many David Bowies do you know?' Dave nodded his dome-shaped head towards the microwave behind MacTavish. 'Tell me, are they effective beasts? I've heard they're effective beasts.'

'Who?' Sheila quipped. 'Husbands?'

There was a knock at the door. Drambuie barked.

'Enough, dog!' MacTavish cautioned. 'Christ, it's not Lowry, is it?' His hairy eyebrows almost jumped back over his head.

PC Cluny entered.

'You're drenched to the skin, lad,' Sheila said. 'I've seen less advanced oceans. Come away in. What's another mouth to feed?'

Dave made room for Cluny next to him; the constable looked pensive about this seating arrangement.

Shelia placed a mountain of bacon rolls in front of him.

'Gosh, you're as blond as Borg,' she marvelled. 'Minus the sweatband, mind.'

'Did you get the tent over him, constable?' Punch asked.

'Aye, Sarge.'

'And secure?'

'Yes, Sarge.'

'Och, let him eat, Ivor, for goodness' sake,' Sheila said, passing out squares of kitchen roll.

Dave blew into one and then folded it over.

'Not a bad kitchen roll, Sheila,' he said, admiring the paper cloth.

Punch had a vacant look on his face. He stared at Dave and thought about the three effigies back in his lockup. And Iris Hislop. The *real* Iris Hislop. The man had boxed only one of them.

'Costco, David,' Sheila said.

'Oh? In fact, can I use your facilities?' Dave stood.

'I'll show you, Grand Master. Gosh, I hope you left paper, Jim. And brushed after yourself. You'd think one of the cows had been in sometimes!'

'They're transitional,' Dave said, leaving the kitchen, 'the lenses, you know ...'

Punch, concerned, peered out the window. Light was failing.

MacTavish waited until he heard the toilet door closing.

'So, do you think it was a dead body or a live one in the front of the hearse, Ivor?' he whispered. 'The one Randy claims he saw on the Glen?'

'I've got enough on my plate up on your hill, man. And fuck.' Punch checked the handset was on the correct channel and looked to the clock on the microwave. 'The mainland are taking their time.'

'Randy said the fellow had a moustache like Terry Thomas,' Sheila said, returning to reclaim her domain, if not the conversation.

'Dave is a dark bastard,' Punch said. 'No doubt.'

261

They heard the sound of a helicopter approaching.

'The circus is in town.' Punch reached immediately for his hat and then his handset. 'Punch 519 BL. HES approaching landing site. Over.'

His radio crackled by way of a response.

'All Double Dutch to me ...' MacTavish said. 'Can you get Atlantic 252 on that thing?'

'Hellish business at the church this morning, Ivor ...' Sheila said, as she followed Punch to the door and took the handle for him. She nervously folded and refolded her dish towel. 'Mum okay?'

Punch stopped in the doorway, hovering with obvious irritation.

'Aye, cheers, Sheila. Fine. You know, as can be expected. Look, I need to—'

'That poor lass Hislop,' she said. 'In the church. Singing. A terrible shame.'

'Uh-huh.' Punch put his hat on and his hand on the handset. Heard the toilet flush.

'I'm sure it's not true what they're saying about her ...' Sheila added.

'The effigies?' Punch said, annoyed he had taken the bait.

'Eh? No. No,' Sheila said, turning. 'Not that.'

'Tell the man, will you, for Christ's sake, woman!' MacTavish stood.

'Well ...' Sheila rested her weight on the worktop. 'It's about her and this, this poor fellow Mr Lowry actually ...' She gestured to the hill. 'God rest his soul, of course.'

'What's that?' Punch said, aware the helicopter was closer.

'That they're ... well ...'

262

'An item,' MacTavish blurted.

'Probably just talk.' Sheila rubbed vehemently on the stove with a cloth. 'You know what it's like here, but that's what they're saying. I'm only saying what they're saying.'

'Right.' Punch tried not to react. It was a well-practised instinct. 'Right. Okay.'

He felt a vein on the side of his neck pulse. The helicopter's undercarriage swooped overhead, blowing empty feed bags into the air. Punch felt the blades closing in on him. Ready to scythe his head off. The gallbladder removed. Hung upside down by his feet and matured for not four days but eighteen years.

Stiff to cut.

'My land. My rules,' MacTavish announced. 'I'm coming too.'

Punch exited and all three men followed.

Pull a string, a puppet moves.

He had a new, as yet undisclosed theory. The sawdust had only added weight to it.

Lowry was never in the plane at all.

TRACK 22

STILL NO NEWS. ONLY MESSAGES on mirrors. What use is that? No violin to speak off? Nor score?

I am back from the hotel, back on the island. I used to think it a sanctuary here, a safe place from the world and its demands, where my truest love could run free. And he *was* free. Back then. Before he left me. A place where I did not have to make *other* people look good. A place where I did not have to hang, literally, on their coat-tails. Make *them* the star. But not now. Not now there is no news. No plane. I am mercifully cut off. Alone.

Is it all going wrong?

Despite the challenge of the materials, the effigies have been creatively gratifying. To a point. Silly games really. But Punch has not cottoned on. *Her* Punch. The man who let a child perish on his watch. I thought recreating her – the dear, sweet thing Iris – would bring one closer, you know, to my truest, finally? But no. It has only served to, to substantiate what one missed out on. Dear, sweet children. Them both! But Punch. The man could not solve a robbery in a thimble, let alone an island. Of course, he is looking on the wrong island.

Why do people leave me? Where do they go? Why does beauty never last longer than two sides of a circle of black vinyl? But he *is* coming. Surely, he is coming? Tell me he is coming. Do you know?

TRACK 23

ALL ROADS, TIDES, WERE LEADING to one place for Punch. An element of surprise was the order of the day, or night.

Lowry had been painstakingly assessed, pictures taken of the incident scene and his body removed from MacTavish's land by the Forensics team. Reunited with the hand, the body had then been airlifted from Lussa Falls for DNA identification and postmortem by the pathology unit in the Glasgow mortuary at the Saltmarket. The mainland would provide the answers. But nobody was in any doubt it was the musician. And only a few bets had been taken in the Forestry on it being Vivaldi himself. The talk was Lowry had left Mull for the final time from the same airfield as he had taken off from before his demise.

But, increasingly, Punch wasn't so sure.

His job had been made trickier trying to keep Dave from leading the Forensics team, if not accompanying the body altogether, the undertaker claiming it was essential for continuity of evidence.

The helicopter had taken off just as night fell. Its lights climbing into the dark, otherworldly sky had given Lussa Falls a bit of the Arthur C. Clarke about it, thought Punch. Ruth Lauder had wanted to be with the body as next of kin, but Punch had insisted she stay on the island for questioning. Townsend couldn't get the helicopter off his land quickly enough. Extra police support had arrived and were tasked by Punch to give the hotel the once-over.

So now it was a waiting game until the body was fully examined. But Punch had a sense this was when the real police work might come into play. Now the mainland had buggered off, for a bit at least.

It was late but he had a hunch, and made a quick call.

He had a light to follow.

Minutes later, he pulled over at the Tobermory clock, his headlights producing the chip van, the shutters pulled down on it for winter. He did something he never did: he pressed the FM button and turned the dial. A female voice. Not unlike the one he had heard from under Lowry's bed.

'Welcome to Classic FM,' she said. She said there had been very worrying news. Apologised for interrupting their 'Carols Countdown'. Punch had hoped for a *Hark the Herald* or two while he waited. He liked choirs, folk singing together, not having to speak. It made him feel less alone. Like being on an island, but not really *having* to be. The radio presenter's voice went on and what she said shrank the world to the size of his Ranger.

'*Some of you might have heard the disturbing news about the disappearance of Xander Lowry,*' the presenter said, her tone

267

considered. '*Some of you won't have known that as well as being one of our finest lead violinists, he was—*' her voice broke, '*it really is so hard to say "was" – an enthusiastic pilot . . . but I am simply stunned to report that his body has been discovered in the Hebrides.*'

Punch gulped and gripped the wheel. The lassie might as well have been broadcasting from the end of the Old Pier ahead of him.

'*Anyone who had the fortune to meet Xander Lowry knows he crammed about four people's lives into his lifetime. But let's pray for him, and return him to his music. So many of us have fallen in love with his virtuoso playing, his musicianship over the years. But he cannot be thought of without Vivaldi. So, it has to be his* Concerto in d minor per Archi e Cembalo RV 127. *Here for you now on this sad evening, the maestro, on Classic FM.*'

Punch looked to the radio and turned it up. The music began gently and gradually rose, the tide seeming to lap in accompaniment, seeming as though about to engulf him.

Archie, did she say Archie?

Was he hearing things now? The piece played out and Punch couldn't move. He felt numb, as though the music, the hand of Lowry himself, was trying gamely but couldn't penetrate him. There was nothing he could take from it that adequately explained people falling from the sky.

The music finished and an advert came on. Punch killed the radio and opened the door. He bent down to hide his keys under the mat. Couldn't be doing with keys rustling. If his inkling was of merit, the element of surprise was going to be a factor. He quietly closed the door behind him. The plaque on the clock caught his eye. He remembered being fascinated by it as a child. By the name 'Henrietta Bird', in whose honour the tower was erected by her sister, the famed explorer, Isabella; by the little door on the clock where he was sure Henrietta lived. He could happily have climbed in himself now. Nobody would look for him there. Perfect place for a criminal, in fact. Or a man hiding from war. He turned to take in the shopfronts; all were dark and the street desolate. The clock chimed once. Midnight. An irritation, but not technically a crime. He turned to the town and was glad of a new day. Of another anniversary having passed. The next big one would be the twentieth. At least his mother likely wouldn't have to suffer it. When he would be fifty-five, and Charlie would have been forty-seven.

Car headlights arrived on the Back Brae. Punch imagined the vehicle ploughing onwards straight into the corner shop at the bottom of the brae. A couple of local teenage musicians had recently suffered this fate. He had been first on the scene, out looking for car keys on his closing-time run. Amazingly, the lads had survived unharmed. Didn't stop the buggers still making a racket in the Aros Hall on a Saturday night. Randy quipped the crash could have at least taken *one* of them. Dark bastard.

A pickup came into view at the bottom of the brae and turned towards him along the Main Street. Headlights dancing on the high tide. The vehicle progressed along the seafront and slowed down at the Captain's Table, turning sharply to the clock. It passed Punch then pulled up at the beginning of the Old Pier. An area recognised as VIP parking of sorts. Only the fishermen could park there. Certainly only a pickup.

The driver got out in a puff of smoke.

'Sergeant.'

'Diehard. Good of you to help at such notice.'

'No bother, Ivor. Jumped out the scratcher when you called. Beauty sleep's overrated. Just need to look at the wife.'

This to Punch was police work of the kind no case inspector on the mainland could construct. The fisherman was wearing dark blue waterproof dungarees and a monobrow.

'New pickup?'

'Fresh out the wrapper.'

Diehard took a final draw and flicked the stub into the bay. For some reason Punch noticed the man's grace in the act; imagined a flurry of disappointed fish. The singular brow had been with Diehard since school, as well as a mound of hair that he was confident had never troubled a brush.

'Primary six looks after its own, eh?' Diehard said.

'That'll be it. And fuck. Seems an age ago now. Tell me, Die, did you know about an Irish vessel here over the weekend?'

'Irish? No.'

'Sure?'

'Aye. No boats from away likely this time of year, Ivor. Right, let's do a Rod. The speedboat's at the end.'

'Eh?'

'*I Am Sailing* . . . I know you like Stewart.'

'Aye. Course. Right, Johnnie. Not so fussed on the ballads right enough.'

They walked speedily up the pier, passing stacked creels with green, blue and white ropes tangled around and escaping from them like psychedelic snakes, orange buoys attached. Punch was trying to make sense of the 'Archie' reference; when heard out of the posh presenter's mouth it was certainly a long way from the troubled twin. How did it connect? What was he missing inside the piece? *Are not all songs puzzles?*

'I hear monkfish is on the rise, Die?' Punch said, following Diehard to the pier's end and then down the ladder descending into the sea. As kids, they would try and fish seagulls out of the sky here; search for conger eels under the pier stanchions. A hidden world. Sometimes, if you were descending the ladder, a string of spit would come down from above. Punch recalled taunts of 'Stretch Armstrong'.

'We were unkind fuckers,' he heard from below. 'Take no notice of the past. You've done well for yourself, Ivor. You're always welcome at this end of the pier. I knew your father.'

Punch progressed down the ladder towards the frothing water, leading with his longer arm. Diehard would have been just one when his father left, but Punch wasn't about to arrest him for his attempt at late-hour nostalgia, at connection. A blind eye wasn't a bad quality in an island copper now and again. He had the feeling of not only being at the edge of the island, but also at the edge of himself. He wasn't used to being part of the case.

'I hear you've got a spot of bother,' he heard from below.

Punch stepped onto the speedboat.

'Aye, could say that, Die. Why folk don't just stay on the ground I'll never know. And fuck.'

'Uh-huh.' Diehard stood assuredly as though it was the island that was floating, and not him. 'He was a fast fucker, Charlie. I knew that much. Like the bugger had an outboard

271

motor on his back.' Diehard untied the boat rigging from the pier. 'Okay. We'll make a move. Table service should be with you in a moment. Hold on, it can get a smidgeon helter-skelter. I'll not ask what your business is there, but as long as it's not investigating quotas of lobster creels ... To the Damask!'

Punch was well aware he was not the one who laid down the law on the seas. Diehard started the engine and Punch held onto the rail. They sped out from the pier leaving a large V in their wake. He noticed how his old school friend stood, legs apart, without holding onto anything, tuned to the beat of the sea. It was known Diehard couldn't swim. Punch turned back to the Christmas lights doing their best to compete with the coloured houses. It didn't seem much really. The cold air felt good against his face. He tapped his chest to make sure he had brought his radio. He hoped it wasn't a bum hunch.

Within a couple of minutes, they were approaching Calve Island, known locally as Damask, after the family who owned it.

'Can we kill the engine, Die?' Punch shouted.

'Eh?'

Punch motioned a blade across his throat and pointed to the rear of the boat. Diehard cut off the engine.

'Element of surprise? Got you, Sarge.' Diehard cupped his hands around a roll-up.

They lapped towards the rocky surrounds of the island. Punch had never set foot on Calve. The only house on the island appeared dark and forlorn. He had only ever seen it in toy proportions. Rod the town planner would no doubt create a small community with a station, rail tracks and a football pitch. The boat sidled alongside the rocky edges of the small landmass.

'Just a single fare, sir ...' Diehard said as he rowed in. 'Want me to pull up in front of the house? There's a landing spot.'

'No. Thanks, Johnnie. I'll make it on the rocks from here. Best we stay away from the house. Maybe if you can go round the back of the island. You know, when you leave.'

'Christ, was it my aftershave? Aye, no bother, Ivor. You'll be giving us code names next.' He turned serious; his eyelids at half-mast. 'Of course, Calve's gift is to shelter Tob, make it a safer anchorage. And that's actually another wee island there. Eilean na Beithe. Not part of Calve at all. What is it your man Caine says? *Not a lot of people know that.*'

Punch looked to the house in darkness and felt a pang of desperation about the lead. Following a fallen star, for Christ's sake? On the recommendation of the town's oddball?

'Of course, the divers visiting can't get enough of the place and the waters around Calve,' Diehard continued. 'The rocky walls and reefs.'

Punch, for some reason, now recalled that the Bruce Willis film came out just after Lockerbie, was sure of it. *Odd the observations you make at such times.* Cliff Richard was number one in the charts. The snooker player, Steve Davis – the guy with that overbrushed red hair who was always sipping at the water – was the BBC Sports Personality of the Year.

'The wall of rock is over forty metres in depth at the northeastern point of the island, by fuck.' Diehard puffed his chest as he spoke, as though they should take enormous pride in this geological occurrence that had formed millions of years before.

'Uh-huh. I better get on, Johnnie.'

'Forever upsetting the bastard'n creels though. Thon divers,' Diehard muttered. 'And then the Armada excavations – more treasure in my mouth's dentistry!'

'I've cuffs if you need them.'

'Right, you'll know what you need to do, Ivor.' Diehard rigged two oars in place. 'I'll go and charge a few lobsters rent while I'm here. I've creels over the back.'

'Cheers, Johnnie. I'll take it from here.'

'Will I check back in on you, Ivor?'

'Aye, on the way back, but stay in the boat.'

Diehard rowed off into the night in a cloud of dispersing smoke.

The whitewashed house was about fifty yards away. Yellow painted doors and window frames were just about evident through the darkness. A line of creels stacked along the gable end. Outhouses that weren't apparent from Tob.

Punch walked the coastline towards the house. It was a clear night with a big moon and he was surprised at how expansive the landmass was, or as much as he could see of it, now he was standing on it. They said it all stretched out to a mile at least. He remembered overhearing the local postal clerk in Tob telling a tourist that Calve Island had been issued its own stamp. Apparently with a dog of some sort on it. At the time he had feigned interest, but now was struck with the detail. By the quirks of this principality, which he had known but ignored all his life.

A small wooden boat bobbed on the slip below the house. Likely belonging to the old woman Damask who used to row into Tob. Surely gone now. Punch hadn't heard of her in some time. Was certain he hadn't actually met her. Though the house was still in her family they said. He walked slowly off the rocks and onto the grass. No signs of life at all. There was a stone wall surrounding the house and hedgerows inside the garden. Punch decided against the iron gate and sat on the wall instead, flipping his legs over. He walked alongside the stone pathway, staying on the grass. It surprised him how well maintained everything was, given its exposure to the elements and how seldom the house appeared to be inhabited. At the front door he waited. Everything was silent. On the outside of the door there was a little wooden hatch with an assortment of wellies inside. The woman had children, possibly grandchildren, by the looks of it.

Punch reached for the doorknob. To his surprise, it slowly turned, and opened. The house smelled of damp. Terracotta tiled floor. He cushioned his footsteps; turned his radio down, just in case. He came to a door, a wooden frame with ribbed glass, partly open. A light was flickering inside the room. Punch did something he never did, put his finger on the red button on the handset, but he didn't press it. He gently pushed the door. The light was coming from a TV screen. Set on pause. Above it, the lights of Tobermory were faintly evident in the window. There were outlines of items discarded on the floor. Suitcases or boxes. As though

275

somebody was packing, moving in or out. He walked further into the room.

He felt a swift movement from behind him. Before he could turn, Punch felt a sharp object prodding his spine.

'Nosy fucker.'

TRACK 24

'KEEP FACING THE WINDOW, PUNCH. Hands to your sides.'

The voice. He knew the voice.

Punch did as instructed. The paused TV screen had the musician and presenter Jools Holland on it. The man was frozen in the action of waving to a band behind him. Flickering like a ghoul.

Punch stood still. Spotted a video player below the TV set.

'Drop the handset.'

Punch obeyed.

'Kick it away. Back-heel, towards me.'

Punch followed the order.

'Move to the window and take off your uniform. Try anything fancy, Clock, and Dave the Grave will be boxing you by Boxing Day.'

'Seriously? Is that fucking you—'

'Enough chattering.'

Punch was sure of the voice. Usually a pier was attached to it; or, more surprisingly, a church bell. He walked to the window and removed his coat and then his uniform jacket.

'Shirt, trousers too ...'

'Fuck's sake?'

'Strip, man!'

Punch unbuttoned his shirt. Thankfully he had a t-shirt underneath. He unbuckled his trousers and let them drop. Stepped out of them. He felt bare. Not because he had revealed the man, but because the difference in his limbs – his disability – was on show.

'I'd say we got the saggy arse just about right,' said the voice.

'Is that fucking *you*?' Punch said. '*Really?*' The description the Slaters had given of overhearing the dinner conversation between Lowry and Lauder now came to mind: *man-strip*. Was it connected?

'Kick the clothes to the side. Walk forwards and then turn.'

Punch did as he was told, then slowly turned.

Palindrome was sitting on an armchair behind the door. He was holding a rifle, pointed at Punch.

'You look like you've swallowed your truncheon, Ivor,' Palindrome said. 'Or had it shoved up the nethers. You're the *Clock* right enough. All we need is a chime out of you.'

'Pal, what the?'

'Shut the fuck up. Heck, the arm really is shorter out of the clothes.'

'And you on the church bells too?' Punch shook his head. 'Forgot your *compassion to fellow man* bit?'

'Aye. Been practising on the tourists.' Palindrome brandished the rifle.

'The couple on the Lighthouse Path?'

'Aye. Always a teenager handy to carry the can. Certainly.'

Punch took in the items on the floor. Scissors, various piles of fabric and wools strewn in all directions. Other dress-up items hanging out of suitcases. He felt terribly exposed now. Janice was the only one who had ever seen him completely naked.

'The pier, tossing a caber ... it's a long way from this, Pal. What's got into you, man? What've you got yourself mixed up in?' Punch motioned his longer arm towards the floor and then to Palindrome. 'And fuck.'

'His name's Robert.' The female voice was immediately recognisable.

Punch turned to the silhouetted figure by the door.

'You certainly don't have your truncheon in your underwear,' she said.

Palindrome chuckled.

Now Punch was sure of it. The voice.

It was Maggie May.

She turned the lights on, and Punch strained his eyes. The full display in the room emerged. A cross between the back room of a tailor and a morgue. Spongy limbs near his feet and what looked like the beginnings of a head, one eye drawn on. There was a sense of horror to it all. Death. Everywhere.

Punch studied the woman. She was tall and thin. Grey hair.

'Camilla Damask,' Palindrome said proudly, his cheeks rosy, unable to keep it in any longer. 'My business partner.'

Punch angled his head, exposed. Now he recalled he had seen her on the Main Street once, but had never spoken to her. She was attractive – no, handsome – around the sixty mark. Red lipstick. The lady who had pulled into Lussa Falls; the lady with the ankles. Same high heels.

'Right,' Punch said. 'What's the business? Stick-ups?'

'Sergeant, you must wonder what's going on?' she said.

'It'd crossed my mind.' Punch gestured to his state of undress. 'I'd have worn boxers instead of the Ys had I known.'

'Grown an arm more like,' Palindrome said.

'Such venom, Pal? What the hell have I done to you?'

'It's more what she can do *for* me. I've a ton of cash coming my way.'

'How ghastly, Robert!' The lady walked across the room. Punch observed her pale, almost translucent skin. *The grey lady.* 'What has one told you about being a blabbermouth?'

She arrived at a record player. Vinyl already in place. Next to it he saw a blue glasses case; similar, if not the same, as Townsend's.

She lifted the arm and the record turned. She dropped the needle. The music arrived abruptly, and Punch recognised it as the piece he had heard on the phone in the background, when she had first called the station; the same as he had heard earlier on the car radio. At least some of the pieces of the puzzle were landing. But he still had no idea how this most unlikely duo fitted into it. He noticed two of her fingers had plasters on them.

'Do you like it?' she asked, facing the player. 'The music?'

Punch shrugged. He had never carried out an investigation in his undies. If Diehard were to appear now, then a photo in *The Oban Times* was a given.

'*Vivaldi* . . .' Palindrome said.

'Gosh, Robert, you sound like you might have lost a tooth in the act,' Camilla Damask said. 'There aren't many to play with!'

'I recognise the music from your call,' Punch said. 'To the station.'

'My, you're good at something!' She turned to him elegantly. 'Not an altogether bad ear!'

He had encountered this kind before, the kind that wanted to be caught, that valued their innocence less than they did their desire to highlight the perceived genius of their crime.

'Your powers of deduction are finally manifesting, Punch. Until now I thought your badge was from a cereal packet.'

'Call me Sergeant when I'm in, eh ... well ...'

'The Clock,' Palindrome enthused. 'Call him The Clock.'

'And whom do you think it is playing?' she asked.

'It's not Randy Fleming ...' Punch said.

'No!' Palindrome chuckled. Camilla Damask gave him a cold stare and he straightened up and raised the rifle again to Punch.

'Try again?' she said.

'Xander Lowry, I would think.'

She closed her eyes and leaned her head back, mimed playing an imaginary violin.

'Yes it is,' she sung, 'his signature piece.'

'Certainly,' Palindrome offered.

The movement had started urgently but now slowed down. It was hard for Punch to detect where Vivaldi ended and Lowry began. Rod was just Rod.

'But actually no,' she said. 'He is not the player.'

'What?' Palindrome dropped the rifle and quickly raised it again.

The music soared higher and filled the room.

Punch wondered if Diehard was his only bet now.

281

'It's a *far* superior musician,' she said.

'Really?' Palindrome turned.

To Punch's untrained ear, the piece sounded the same as the version he had heard on the Old Pier. But he hoped he was one step ahead.

'Nigel Townsend,' he said.

'Oh, Sergeant Punch!' she gushed. 'You've outdone yourself!' Then, 'You know I have the same name as his mother?'

'Townsend's?' Punch said.

'No,' she returned, not disguising her irritation. 'Vivaldi's.' She danced her finger in the air as though following imaginary dots on sheet music. 'Camilla Calicchio. She of Venice, me of Calve! Well, by way of Kensington. Do you know we actually lived in the flat below the Lloyd Webbers, Robert? Eccentric bunch! Mum'ma was friends with their mother. Dear Andrew and Julian were always playing away. Andrew and Tim Rice gave me my break in *Joseph*,' she declared. 'At a local school, would you believe! We started out together. I even recommended Mull to them. All before the knighthoods!'

'Who?' Palindrome said.

'*Joseph and the Amazing Technicolor Dreamcoat*, goodness!'

'Oh? Right.' Palindrome took a sip of whisky from the glass at his side. 'Quite good aye, certainly. Played in the Aros Hall, no doubt.'

'I was never talented enough to be a musician or actor, but I fitted many. Goodness, I was never *out* of the Royal Albert Hall. I made clothes for them all. James Bonds, Dame Kiri, Elaine Paige, Paul McCartney, even Ken Dodd. Wogan himself, for Pete's sake!'

'Was that where you met?' Punch said. 'Townsend, Lowry, I mean. Not Palindrome.'

Palindrome choked momentarily on his whisky, then realigned the rifle.

'We all met when they were at the conservatoire; Xander, Nigel and I. Nigel didn't have the conviction that was all, but the talent, yes. Oh yes. Xander had the arrogance. In spades.'

'So, Townsend was actually a gifted musician?' Punch said. He noticed the rifle had temporarily lost its target – in favour of the whisky – once more. To disarm Palindrome would be easy enough, but there was maybe more to be gained from staying this end of the rifle. The woman clearly found revelation equivalent to power. He still couldn't understand what the hell the Pier Master's connection in all of this was, though he knew Palindrome had assisted the Damasks over the years with odd jobs, ferrying and the like. Originally with this lady's mother, he assumed now. Punch knew he needed to act at some point. But first, more information was on the menu.

'Oh, Nigel Townsend can play like this,' she said provocatively, moving as though following stage markings on the carpet.

'Certainly,' Palindrome said.

Punch noticed the man tapping his fingers to the music as though it was being broadcast live from the Mishnish.

'I thought you said it *was* Townsend?' Punch asked.

'Well, he can,' she slurred, almost falling off her heels.

'Was Nigel jealous of Xander?' he tried.

'Well, no. No.'

'Were you?'

'Jealous? No. I loved them both.' Camilla Damask raised her glass dramatically. Some of it spilled on Palindrome's shoulder. 'We made something very special ... but that feeble *bitch* got to him.'

'*Your* bitch,' Palindrome spat.

'Mine?' Punch saw how the woman's whole face changed; her expression had become completely at odds with the music. Evil. 'Who's mine?'

'Aye. The bitch. Certainly,' Palindrome said, smiling as though he had been admitted into the same asylum.

Punch couldn't tell if the woman knew about Lowry. He had detected something deeply, dramatically delusional about her, but that – like so much else around him – was not an offence in itself.

Coincidences were piling up. But it was always better to reveal nothing. Let them do it for you. He had the feeling the night was only going to get weirder. There was something oddly magnetic about her, too. Criminals often presented this quality, especially the unlikely ones.

'Fucking cleaner,' Camilla Damask almost spat. 'I see she's got her claws into you too.'

'Sonia Hislop?' Punch said, considering the phone call he had witnessed from under the Lussa Falls bed. 'That's what you think?'

'Well – how did you know who I was referring to?' she said.

'I'm afraid I heard your call, Miss Damask. At the Lussa Falls.'

'How? How did you hear me?' She ran her long fingers, red nails, along her grey fringe. To Punch, she had the beguiling look of the actress Helen Mirren about her.

'I was under the bed,' he said, thinking it no longer mattered if he played that card. 'I was carrying out a search.'

She blinked at him, confusion clouding her face. 'Everything I have she has to have,' she murmured, as if to herself.

'Bitch,' Palindrome repeated, as though brainwashed or reading from an autocue. Punch wondered if one of the church bells had fallen on the man's head.

'Dearest Robert . . .' Camilla Damask said. 'You're not the fastest greyhound on the track but you're loyal. Mum'ma said the same.'

'So, what's the arrangement here?' Punch pressed.

'None of your bloody business, Punch,' Palindrome spat.

'Well, after Mum'ma, he started doing my upkeep and messages for me when I was away . . .'

'Uh-huh.' Palindrome beamed. 'Certainly.'

'You were going to cut him in, were you?' Punch tried.

'To what?' she said. 'The violin?'

'No,' Punch said. 'The manuscript.'

'The what? Rubbish. Rubbish!'

'Rubbish,' came her echo.

'What does the bible say about kidnapping, Pal?' Punch countered. 'I could understand all this cloak and dagger for John Lennon's "Imagine" piano . . . And fuck.'

'I don't want to hear about you calling this kidnapping, Clock!' Palindrome shook, shifting in his seat. 'Mother and I need security. I'm down to net thousands here. My own boat, finally.'

'So, what kind of stick-up is this anyway?' he said.

'Stick-up?' Palindrome said, an echo once more. 'How would anyone know your arms were in the air anyway?'

Punch moved as if to take a step.

'Sit, Punch! Sit, I'm telling you!' Palindrome pointed the rifle at Punch's head. 'Taking God into your own hands too. On the cliff face.'

'Is that not what you're doing now, Pal?'

'He said sit!' the woman instructed. 'I knew John Lennon, for God's sake. "Imagine!" What tripe!'

Punch sat down. A little opposition, followed by subservience, often loosened a criminal's tongue. He could tell she was enjoying having an audience, spilling illicit beans, here on her island. Definitely more than one screw loose.

'You know it's not my real name?' she said, now more noticeably slurring, sitting on the arm of Palindrome's chair. 'Damask.'

'No?' Punch said. His state of undress was one thing, but he felt even more naked to be without his Van Gogh collection. He wondered how long she would let him converse like this. Usually folk kept schtum, happy to take the cell option rather than talk. But this was bigger; more was at stake.

'No, it came from the trade. It was how I became known in the industry. At one point in the seventies I'd dressed half of London's West End in patterned fabric. And so, Damask I became ... only me and Branson have our own island, though.'

'What's your real name?' Palindrome asked, turning his head to her.

'Hislop,' Punch said.

'Eh?' Palindrome swivelled.

Camilla Damask reached to reposition the rifle on Punch.

'Full marks again, Sergeant Punch!'

286

'Land Registry records,' Punch said. 'Any further hidden and they'd be in Diehard's creel; have to applaud you.'

'We used to holiday on Mull. Down on the Ross,' she said. 'That was before I lost, well, him.'

'Who?' Palindrome said. 'Christ, wait, are you the barmaid's—'

'Mother-in-law,' Punch confirmed.

'Oh, at last, Mr Punch!' Camilla Damask said. 'Yes, dear Sean was my son.'

'Christ, that explains a few things,' Palindrome muttered.

'He was never keen on Damask,' she said. 'Though I tried to convince him it was an interesting stage name. Of course, I encouraged him to pursue a classical career. He was truly a fine cellist. Dear Xander even took an interest in him. But it was the guitar that won out. Sean met them all through me: Mick. Roger. Elton. Dear, sweet Engelbert.'

Punch had to stop himself enquiring about Rod.

'So, he met Lowry?' he said.

'Wait ...' Palindrome said, pulling away from Camilla and turning aghast. 'You had me hang up your dummy, erm, *granddaughter*?'

'Come, Robert,' she said, moving her hands through the air to the music. 'Don't go all soft on me now. It was a tribute.'

'Really?' Palindrome shook his head in something like disbelief. 'Was it a dig at the lassie or her mother?'

'And the house lights flashing here?' Punch said. 'A code?'

'Erm ...' Palindrome looked away from Punch; the rifle on his lap. 'Aye, well, to let me know the next E was ready.'

'E?' Punch said.

'Effigy,' Damask said.

'Bill Gates must be quavering at the intel.' Punch stayed seated, maintaining the illusion of his captivity, even though he technically wasn't captive any longer. 'So, you made them here on Calve?' It was hard for him to believe the puzzle of the last few days had led to here, to this fifth-rate operation. It seemed too random for Lowry to have gone missing at the same time as the effigies appeared.

Or do planes just keep falling from the sky?

'What does it look like I've been doing, Mr Punch?' Camilla Damask said, waving her hand at the scattergun display of fabrics and materials. 'Indoor bowls?'

'We outfoxed you, Punch, certainly.' Palindrome shifted, raising the rifle again, though Punch could tell the man was unclear of his loyalties now. As though this new identity of his on another island was confusing the one he inhabited on his own. The only one he had known.

'He's a nice player, Townsend.' Punch nodded to the record player, deciding to reinforce her delusion. 'It has to be said.'

'Even a fool like you can appreciate it . . .' she observed, turning on her heels. 'The beauty of it.'

'So is this Lowry your, eh, son's old man?' Palindrome mused.

'No. Townsend is,' Punch said.

'A hat-trick, Mr Punch!' the lady exclaimed as she swayed.

It had become clear to Punch that Townsend's jealousy stretched beyond the professional, to the paternal too. But again, that did not a killer make.

'But why me, Miss Damask?' Punch said. 'Why *my* doppelganger?'

'Well, you're sleeping with her, are you not? Oh, and I never much liked authority.' She studied his upper body. 'And a bit of fun to get you spooked; I like to keep my hand in. Think I got it about right ...'

'Why your granddaughter?' Palindrome said, persistent now.

'Oh Robert! Because Sonia Hislop needs to know what a terrible mother she was!' Camilla Damask cried. 'And wife. And daughter-in-law. Hated me from the off.'

'Can't imagine why ...' Punch murmured.

'All little Iris wanted to be was a daddy's girl!'

'Are you saying your son died because of Sonia Hislop?' Punch said.

'Yes! And my granddaughter too!' The woman wiped the sides of her eyes, causing her liner to smear. 'To think I still ... *still* keep wellies at the door for her. She never once visited with her ...'

'And why my broth—' Punch stopped himself mentioning the Charlie effigy. Now lying across the water in his lockup. 'So, after ringing the church bells you hung it outside, Pal? Nifty.'

Palindrome shifted uncomfortably.

'Well ...' he said. 'She wanted to hurt you too, Ivor. Certainly. I knew how to do that. We know you and Sonia have something going on. Pubs say as much. Pretty obvious to everyone. Lifts here and there. Beyond the call of duty, so they say.'

'No,' Punch said. 'Not likely. But nice try, Pal. Sick bastard.'

'Steady on, boys,' Miss Damask said, taking Palindrome's glass and downing it in one. 'Can't have you fighting over the Hislop girls!' She stumbled as she moved to the music. 'A hank of horsehair, did you know?'

'For Iris's little head?' Punch jolted. He felt a tinge of disgust and chastised himself for showing it.

'No, stupid,' she slurred. 'What a violin bow is made of.'

'So, you broke into the station, Pal? And fuck,' Punch said, recalling how Palindrome had asked to use the toilet after dropping off the carrier bag; he'd assumed the man needed to barf. 'And why the effigy of Lowry?'

'Aye. Waited till the bottle conked you out, Clock.'

'Why Lowry? Because I *loved* him.' Camilla Damask sighed. 'And he did me. Until that bitch got her claws into him too. Unbelievable! That was the final straw.' She looked forlornly to the darkness in the window, as though awaiting somebody. Townsend was Punch's current best bet.

'Sonia Hislop?' he said.

'No. The blondie. Lauder. Bloody pen-pusher.'

'Poor Sean took much more interest in Xander. Nigel never really knew him, felt inadequate really. Despite me trying. Both men wanted me is the truth. Two maestros.'

Palindrome looked away to the record spinning. He gulped heavily. Punch could tell the little man didn't know what he had got himself into. It was amazing what a bit of posh, the promise of treasure, could do to a man.

'Play it, Robert.' Camilla Damask-née-Hislop said, nodding to the flickering TV screen as she walked to lift the needle off the scratching vinyl.

Palindrome refixed the rifle on Punch, and then pointed the TV remote at the screen. Jools Holland burst into life. The familiar high-pitched voice. An audience cheered as he waved his arm towards the musicians behind him and walked out of shot. The band kicked in and the camera zoomed in on a man in his late twenties. Punch recognised him as Sean Hislop. He was playing a Fender Telecaster and staring straight into the camera. Handsome fellow, Punch thought. Her jawline. Freckles populating the nose. A sweep of strings arrived, and the camera focused on a string quartet. Punch was astonished to see the lead violinist was the man he had just seen dead on a hillside. Younger. Hair less grey but equally unruly – and falling out of a deerstalker. It was Xander Lowry. Living and breathing. *Moving*, by fuck. The drummer then kicked in, the bass guitar and Sean Hislop's voice soared higher into a falsetto along with a piano part played by Jools himself. The tune was definitely one Punch recognised.

'Ah . . .' Camilla Damask beamed. 'And Xandy in that darn deerstalker! He always told Sean you needed a trademark . . . as if playing with his back to his audience was not enough. Trouble was everyone assumed I dressed him in it! Sean so wanted to be *his* son. Oh, and there's Archie . . .'

Punch turned quickly to her. Palindrome was tapping the arm of the chair, barely keeping the rifle on its target. Not unless Jools Holland was a threat.

'A band member?' Punch said, trying to seize another moment. 'Archie?'

'Eh?' Miss Damask said, swaying her hips and gazing at the screen in a frenzy of pride and pleasure. Punch anticipated the woman was reaching the climax of her performance.

'Archie?' Punch tried again. 'Miss Damask . . .'

'Why it's dear Xander's violin,' she said, transfixed. 'It isn't really Lowry unless Archie is on his shoulder. Not uncommon for them to be named.'

'Cabers the same,' Palindrome agreed, as though he had flipped one on the stage of the Royal Albert Hall itself.

Punch's suspicion about the instrument had been confirmed. Though it was still unclear whether the woman was waiting on Townsend or Lowry. News of the musician hadn't seemed to reach either Damask or Palindrome.

Punch looked to the young man in his element on the screen. Who appeared remarkably together, given his mother. At the height of his powers. Before life brought him down. Unaware he was to have a little girl in the world. Briefly.

'Police! Police!'

Palindrome fired the rifle and a pellet hit the fireplace. Camilla Damask screamed. The living room door swung open, breaking the glass. Three officers hurled themselves into the room. Disarmed Palindrome. Threw him face-first onto the carpet. Leaped on his back to handcuff him. Cluny and a female officer then took hold of Camilla Damask, who was ecstatically shrieking: 'Yes! Yes! Yes!'

Cluny handcuffed the woman, and the female officer manipulated her down onto the floor. Cluny picked up Punch's trousers and jacket and handed them to his sergeant.

'We picked up your red, Sarge,' Cluny said.

'Uh-huh.' Punch nodded. He heard the TV audience applauding and looked at the screen for acknowledgement. Feather boas decorated the stage. The camera closed in on Sean Hislop. A young man looking so full of life, so in command. The camera pulled away to reveal Jools Holland back in front of the band, waxing lyrical. A pink feather boa around his neck.

'It's me, Ivor!' The voice came from the hallway. 'I know you said to stay clear but look what I've ... oh fuck!' Diehard did a brief surveillance of the room and shook his hairy head. 'What the fff ... is this an *orgy*?'

'Codename Y-fronts,' Punch said, pulling up his trousers and nodding to the other officers. 'Let's get these two back to Dodge. No fan heater.'

'Ivor ...' Diehard produced a case from behind his back. 'Found this around the other side of the house. Thought you should see it.'

Punch did up his buttons and moved towards the fisherman.

'Hidden under tarpaulin. I was checking their creels. Few of mine have gone walkabout. I've found a few surprises caught in my creels, coconuts from the Caribbean by fuck, but this takes the—'

'It's ours!' Camilla Damask shrieked; her cheek was pressed on the floor.

'Has to be the missing fellow's?' Diehard said.

Punch cast a dagger to the lady on the floor and took hold of the violin case. He had a suspicion its contents were worth even more than the considerable face value.

'So, you knew I was listening in under the bed, eh?' he said to Camilla, stepping into his boots. 'A bum steer? You were waiting on somebody else. Not fucking Lowry. Read them the Mirandas, PC Cluny.'

'Worth a few quid too I'd reckon,' Diehard said, pointing to the instrument.

'No finder's fee I'm afraid, Die. But good fishing. And fuck.'

TRACK 25

EARLY THE NEXT MORNING, PUNCH rolled off the mattress onto his booted feet. No needle scratching, no Rod. He wasn't sure if he'd even slept let alone troubled a bottle. He knew well enough it had been an unprecedented few days, but the proof was in the pudding when the reporters started calling the station. Cluny was next door dealing with those now. Craignure Pier had already been in touch about a TV broadcast truck having rolled off the first ferry. TV presenters spotted in the cafeteria apparently, Christmas parties no doubt interrupted, wearing enough makeup for a guest spot in the pantomime at the Aros Hall. Speculation that an impetuous, gifted and enigmatic man, clearly someone with an aura, simply bit off more of the Hebrides than he could chew.

Punch transported himself to the table, remembering the statement he had drafted. It was sitting in front of him, but barely did the past week justice. Now he was expected to be master of public relations too. He'd be presenting the Hogmanay show live from Macgochans on the telly at this rate.

Loose ends were pressing on him. Jigsaw pieces that needed to be recut as a result of events on Calve Island the night before. Having questioned Damask further, there was the strong suspicion that she was still in love with both men, but had fathered a child with only one. Townsend.

But he wasn't going to approach Lussa Falls until all cards were on the table, until forensic reports were in.

Bank records confirmed Lowry hadn't the funds to buy so much as the doormat at the Western Isles Hotel, but there had been a recent huge spend at Sotheby's auction house. Punch suggested the men might have been interested in Damask for her island alone, and she'd broken down dramatically. She had begged all night to see the body. Though her next gambit, albeit through a veil of tears, was to enquire whether the plane had been discovered. Punch had relayed to the case controller that it was best he didn't question Palindrome himself further, given their association. Also, that he might strangle the man, though suspected he'd be up all night looking for a neck.

'*Control to Sergeant Punch Lima Bravo. Over.*'

The voice came from the handset by his bed.

Punch moved quickly to retrieve it.

'Punch LB receiving. Over.'

'*Sergeant, this is a closed channel. We have the results of the forensic checks and postmortem on the body of the deceased, Mr Xander Lowry. Over.*'

'Punch receiving. Go ahead, Control.'

He took hold of his notebook.

When the information had been taken down, Punch exchanged the handset for the phone, and dialled.

'*Sorry For Your Loss, Limited?*'

'Dave, it's Ivor.'

'Oaf, sergeant. Christ, I thought it was another body before Christmas. I'm at full capacity. Any word? I hear the media are in town.'

'The chemist is apparently doing a fine pre-Christmas run of hairspray.'

'The musical?'

'No, Dave. Never seen anything like it. We got back at four a.m. on the rib. Palindrome in cuffs. I'm still at a loss.'

'Well, you called the right fellow. Didn't think Pal had the neck for it mind ... the stomach I don't question ...'

'And the man's violin recovered, rare one apparently ... but still no Needle.'

Strangely, setting eyes on Lowry's violin had been as significant for Punch as seeing the body of Lowry. The instrument had been brushed and returned to Punch upon his insistence it was required to assist with potential leads. He had it stored in the cell for safety, becoming more Sherlock Holmes by the minute.

'The suspects?' Dave enquired.

'Cluny and the support officers took Palindrome to the cell overnight for further questioning. CID will take Damask from Craignure to Glasgow.'

'Not often both cells are booked out. Monteith Craignure is missing all the fun. I've been thinking, could Lowry have been committing suicide? Is there a motive for that, Sarge?'

'Loss of a hand? A performer's not much cop if he can't perform. Possible addiction?' Punch thought he would keep *love triangle* and *paternity* out of it for now.

'But if he *was* committing suicide then the man surely wouldn't have ended up on the hillside?'

'Is it realistic that he could have swum that distance in those waters, Dave?'

'To Ballymull? Not likely. And if he did emerge from the Sound then why would he cross the road to another hillside?'

'The case inspector's report won't likely be fit for the toilet roll holder,' Punch said. 'This one has to be solved here.'

'And the woman Damask? Oaf, I did wonder why the grandmother wasn't at the wee girl's funeral, mind.'

'Now we know. Look, so I have the postmortem results, Dave. But I don't want to give them over the phone.'

'Oaf, the buggers don't hang around, right enough! I'm heading to the Home, meet you there?'

'Right you are, Dave. Oh, we're still waiting on the brushers to come back with fingerprint idents.'

'Yes, dactyloscopy usually takes longer. We'll find out who are whirls, loops or ridges.'

'Sure that was a Crosby, Stills & Nash album. See you pronto. Over.'

Punch gathered his things and left the statement to stew; words were not his bedfellow. There was always Tinsel if he wanted it to rhyme.

Outside, he jumped into the Ranger and pulled out of the station. This was a solo job. Cluny had enough on his plate with the media spreadsheet. He pressed onwards and when he reached the Salen road he could almost see the musician crossing out in front, bloodied wrist in the air. Numb with pain. Exhausted. Disorientated. Not knowing if he was ploughing through land, sea or lost in the wings of one of the world's ornate concert halls, the crowd expectant, unsure whether he was escaping the stage or crying for help.

When he arrived in Salen, Punch turned right at the church and soon pulled up to the Home, the island's medical building, on the Gruline Road. This small, white pebbledash block where he had entered the world. On an unusually hot spring day apparently. Given the exterior finish on the Home, the station and the station house, sometimes Punch wondered if even the womb had been pebbledash.

He had the realisation that it would have been here the difference in his limbs was first detected. The news broken to his exhausted mother. Or perhaps she spotted it for herself, determining from the first instant to make the best of it, to protect and cherish her child, to let him be sure of love and independence – come what may. Now he thought about his quiet uncle, and whether he was there or where he was that day. Possibly slaughtering a sheep for distraction.

He jumped out of the Ranger. Dave the Grave's hearse was parked at an angle in front of him.

'So, we've word from the Saltmarket, sergeant?' Dave said, as he arrived efficiently out of the Home in his trademark black, as though off to deliver a box of Milk Tray.

'Aye, Dave. The police pathologists have done their stuff.'

'Oaf, a two-dayer?' Dave said.

A young lad appeared out of the hearse and Punch nearly jumped. Black hair like one of those heavy metal freaks. There was always the possibility it could be one of Dave's corpses, given life.

'Crime scene manager presents Forensics with analytics and photographic evidence,' Dave spouted in the direction of the lad. 'Straight back, that's it. William, this is Sergeant Punch, our island's top-ranking law enforcer. This is William Urquhart, sergeant. De facto second in command, *Sorry For Your Loss, Ltd.* Mull Historical Society, pending review.'

'Right.' Punch nodded to the lad. *Billy the Box.* He knew the family from the Ross end. The lad was on his shorter arm side, which always made the prospect of a handshake a tricky proposition. The lad nodded back.

'From the knee! From the knee!' Dave enthused. 'That's how you lift a coffin I keep telling him. Oaf, Coke-bottle shoulders. We've a thing to do to beef you up, lad. A coffin doesn't carry itself. And negotiations are under way about tattoos, sergeant. Don't want a corpse asking for their money back now, do we, lad? No, we'll have you on the cover of *Funeral Directors' Monthly* smartish.'

'Right, Dave. So fatal accident enquiry. Postmortem carried out by Dr McCloy as you know—'

'Oaf, one of the best forensic pathologists in the country.'

'Eh, so, uncommonly *minor* limb injuries on the body. They would expect major land-induced injuries, even for a botched sea landing.'

'As I said, but McCloy will have gone deeper. Oaf, the musician could damn near have walked straight onto a stage. Just the fiddle, a few punters and a five-minute warning bell needed.'

'Dave, time is tight . . . Nothing to suggest he had come out of a plane flying at speed at all. Results show no traces of saltwater found on the body.'

'Now this is very odd,' Dave mused.

'Toxicological search for poisons, medicines or alcohol ...
alcohol and cocaine positive.'

'And saltwater definitely negative, sergeant?'

'Aye. Body also tested for marine micro-organisms, but
lab results are all negative.'

'But he had been standing exposed to rainwater.' Dave
turned to Billy. 'Fresh water from the sky could have washed
away any saltwater present, even in a few hours.'

'So, not conclusive is your reading, Dave?' Punch said. 'He
could still have clambered out of the Cessna after hitting the
freezing water, swum ashore, but died on MacTavish's hill?'

'But they're saying nothing in the folds of the body, or
under the fingernails, spoke of seawater or marine life?'

'Aye. Aye.' Punch thought better of mentioning the sawdust
on the body. His theory couldn't be classed as conclusive, but
he liked having one up on Dave, Glasgow too.

'Unless crashing the plane was him disposing of evidence
of some kind?' Billy the Box said, embarrassed.

'Good thought, lad,' Dave enthused. He turned to Punch.
'But losing a hand in the process? And such a clean cut?
Then there's the chainsaw?'

'Aye. Points in only one direction.'

'The Lussa Falls?'

'I need proof.' Punch checked his handset. 'Come on, you
fucking brushers. Look, I best get on.'

'Will you need me, Sarge?'

'Not right now, thanks, Dave. I'm well situated here. I'll
keep you posted.'

'Okay. I'm just four digits away,' Dave said.

'Fingers?'

'No. The phone. The phone.'

'Uh-huh. Right.'

'Oh, and have that deputy of yours call me when things die down. I promised him a look at my router.'

'Right, Dave. Christ.' Punch turned. 'My hunch is it wasn't Lowry in the plane at all.'

'Really?'

'Unconfirmed as yet. But to that end I need to get on.'

Punch nodded to the lad, walked to the Ranger and dropped inside.

The case inspector's voice from Control came crackling through the handset as he took off.

'*Sergeant Punch, DNA results on the Lussa Falls Hotel staff and guests' swabs are just this minute in. Over.*'

'Inspector. Punch receiving. The contamination on the chainsaw and fire door too? Over.'

'*Affirmative, sergeant. Are you ready to receive? Over.*'

'Go ahead, inspector. Over.'

Punch listened attentively; it was the piece of the puzzle he had been waiting on. With the information taken down, he adjusted the channel and radioed Cluny, who confirmed he was already parked in Salen. And without the world's longest computer cable. Initiative, finally.

Punch sped along the Gruline Road back towards the village. In Salen, he pulled up at the white hotel building, where Cluny's Ranger was waiting. Cluny jumped out and into Punch's Ranger.

'Sarge. There's one other detail.'

'Yes?'

'You mentioned Lowry's room number was fourteen. But a staff member has confirmed that was in fact Townsend's room.'

'Fuck. He had a suitcase packed and ready to go.'

'Officers have had to leave their positions too.'

'Forty-eight hours and no charge. Right, no time to waste.' Punch's boot hit the floor. 'Unresolved cases are like bad tunes, PC – they forever grate. We don't want this one hanging around in an unsolved case file like some bargain bin compilation.'

'So, he died as a result of the elements ...' Cluny said, as though speaking aloud a puzzle. 'The cause of death officially determined as exposure: loss of heat, of will to live, of inability to struggle on.'

'Uh-huh. Though Dave the Grave maintains that's ultimately what kills everyone. And fuck.'

'Wait ... so he had a numbered room in his *own* hotel, Sarge?'

'Good spot, constable.' Punch nodded. 'But probably not unusual in a glorified log cabin.'

'The man hadn't been far from the main road?'

'But in an extreme hypothermic state ...'

'To think how close he was to help from a passing car?'

'Shock,' Punch said, 'notwithstanding the intense pain the man would have been in, accounts for irrational outcomes. Pride too can be a powerful thing. A man who had made his name so skilfully using a hand that no longer belonged to him was not likely to want to be seen in such

302

a state. I'm sure a penny or two was lost on drugs too. Ben More might've appeared as a mountain of cocaine to the man.'

Punch sped them onwards, trying to tie it all together, to do the 'Holmes with pipe and deerstalker' bit. He wasn't convinced that CID had leaned heavily enough on Damask.

'I think somebody else took off in the Needle.'

'What?' Cluny looked to him. 'Who? A resident?'

Punch turned off the Craignure Road at the Lussa Falls sign. There was a smattering of reporters on either side.

'We'll find out soon enough. But you can't put *theories* in the cell for the night, heater or no heater.'

They arrived at speed into the car park.

'Wait here, constable,' Punch instructed. 'I'll radio if I need backup. Need you here in case of runners.'

'Eh, right, Sarge.' Cluny took off his glasses, cleaned them and returned them to his nose. 'What about Control?'

'Keep them out of it, for now. If we're calling them then we've failed.'

'Last ferry's gone; I get it, Sarge.'

'Exactly. Listen to your belly.'

Punch took the handset and exited the Ranger.

TRACK 26

PUNCH WALKED INTO THE HOTEL; he heard Townsend's voice up above. The man emerged down the stairs in a cacophony of cord. Looked to Punch as though he had put an extra battery in the Christmas jumper.

'Yes, yes, Lussa Falls airfield is still in operation ... and two planes still on the ground,' Townsend was saying to whoever was following him down. 'Please don't let the tragedy, ruddy reporters, affect your stay. I've told them to stay away from the premises. I'm afraid catastrophe can have magnetic qualities. But yes, I say, during the summer, don't you know we have fleets of vintage aircraft – and it really is the perfect place from which to admire them. I really must show you the falls out the back too. We have an *ooter-innery* from where to view.'

'A what?' Michael Slater appeared behind Townsend, eagerly nodding.

'A *veranda* in old money I suppose you'd call it, Mr Slater.'

'Michael, please, Mr Townsend.'

'Then I am Nigel.'

Townsend spotted Punch.

'Oh? Sergeant ... *another* visit?'

'Nigel. Mr Slater.'

Michael Slater nodded, pulling his cardigan over his belly, which appeared to Punch to have grown overnight. The man made adjustments to his moustache. Amazing the tics folk kept about them, like an unspoken language.

'Looks like you might be in the market for a new plane, Nigel?' Punch said.

'Alas,' Townsend said. 'Yes, any further updates? I am so distressed.'

'Aye, well, you could say that,' Punch said. 'I'll need a word, Nigel.'

'Yes, of course, sergeant. But you'll appreciate I have a business still to run. Were the cordons over the rooms really necessary? I mean, mere days before Christmas?'

'Yes, Nigel. I just need to verify what that business is exactly.'

'But dear Xandy is far more important as concerns go,' Townsend said, turning to Slater. 'Than the Needle. Of course he is. I'm ... I just can't believe ... we've lost the maestro?'

'Aye,' Punch said. *Good save.*

Heels attacked the wooden stairs and Angie Slater and Stephanie Price arrived into the foyer.

Punch reached for his hat and then realised he wasn't wearing it; too late, he suspected.

'Sergeant,' Angie Slater said.

Stephanie Price smiled and nodded. Taller than he remembered.

305

'Ladies . . .' Punch said. He could have handcuffed himself for almost reaching for his hat again.

'Busy times, sergeant,' Michael Slater said. 'Devastated about the man. And for Miss Lauder's loss. Music's, really.'

Angie Slater and Stephanie Price pulled sympathetic faces.

'Must be very hard for her,' Stephanie Price said. 'We all thought we owned a piece of him, his fingers on strings.'

Punch was keen to get rid of them.

'Hard to imagine we won't hear the man perform again,' Angie Slater whispered, taking her sister's hand. 'What a loss.'

'Well, he'll live on in his music is all one can say.' Michael Slater beamed. 'All the greats do. Lennon. Bernstein. Vivaldi himself.'

'Uh-huh,' Punch managed. He wanted to say *four seasons* could be found in a Mull morning, but wasn't about to be stung again. 'Well, I won't keep you.'

'Rightio, yes. We're off to see if those otters and golden eagles can stop taking the shy pills!'

'Right you are.' Punch gestured. 'I'd think the media scrum might be some competition.'

All three of them exited the hotel.

Punch walked to Townsend; the man was talking with a waitress, glasses on his forehead the way toffs did.

'Sergeant,' Townsend said. 'Good to get a word alone. Are the rooms out of action *strictly* necessary? And all the swabs taken? Not the greatest look for business this time of year, you know? The Mad Cow years were hard enough.'

'I'd appreciate it if they stay locked, Nigel. They could contain more evidence.'

'Sure. Sure.' Townsend nodded.

'So you've decided to stay open?' Punch asked.

'Well, yes. What am I to do? Throw out paying guests?'

'Tell me, how did the lady Damask get into Lowry's room?' Punch said.

'What?'

'Sightings of her confirmed, Nigel, in the hotel. In Lowry's room.'

'Really no clue what you're talking about.'

'Or was it in fact really Mr Lowry's room? Getting creative with your room numbers on the register, Nigel? Throwing a little spanner in the works for me, eh?'

'Sometimes the staff make mistakes; they can be a trifle loose with their tongues too, if that's what you're referring to?'

'You didn't study with Camilla Damask?'

'Eh, no. No, I didn't. Andy Lloyd Webber introduced us.'

'But you studied with Lowry?'

'Yes, I did. Xander found these parts initially, owing to his connection with Camilla Damask.' Townsend looked to the entrance.

'But your father was here at the hotel before you? Surely that was your introduction to Mull?'

'Well ... yes, yes ...'

'Things are not ringing true, Nigel, are they?'

'But I never was in their company both at the same time, Lowry and Damask. That's the point of it. Elusive lady. But it wouldn't be uncommon for Xander to befriend a lady with her own island, to be honest. If you catch my drift. Look, I haven't said, but drugs took most of his money. Dear Ruthie. I think she has succumbed too, to be perfectly honest

307

with you. But then …' Townsend turned to Punch. 'The world does throw up the strangest things.'

'As farewell symphonies go, it was a corker.'

Townsend simply smoothed the ridges on his cords in silence.

'Not sure I understand your movements exactly on the night Xander Lowry took off, Nigel. Can we go to a more private space? Your office?'

'I have nothing to hide, sergeant. You're looking at my office. Look, I am grieving too, you know.'

'Why would you assume I might think you have something to hide?'

Townsend walked behind the reception counter. Dropped his glasses to his nose. Punch had to admire the man's gall, if not his dress sense. He saw drips of sweat on Townsend's fleshy moustache line.

Punch looked to the door of the gents, thought against mentioning the very particular plumbing. Yet. 'Have to, eh, *hand* it to you, Townsend.'

'Meaning? Sergeant?' Townsend looked over his glasses. Punch saw the postcards pinned on the board behind him, mostly of planes. 'I wonder, might I get my full room capacity back at some point?'

'You gave her access, eh?' Punch walked closer to the reception window.

'Who? Ruthie?'

'The violin worth a few bob, eh?'

'What do you mean? Look, I've got a busi—'

'What I suspect you don't know is it's worth double its obvious value,' Punch said.

Townsend's head shot up. Punch noted the freckled nose. 'The manuscript?'

'No. The violin. I meant the violin. What manuscript?' Punch put his hand on his truncheon. The cuffs were hanging off his belt at the small of his back. 'Worth doing over an old friend for, was it?'

'I say, Punch, you've been watching too many movies, for crying out—'

'Or was it mostly jealousy? Didn't attain the same levels as Lowry, did you? But fuck, you *wanted* it – that status, those heights, to be the maestro . . . Proms instead of panto.'

'Oh my giddy aunt! Complete tosh, Punch!'

Townsend dropped his glasses to the desk.

'Can you stop bloody saying that. And I think it's you watching the movies, Townsend. *The Texas Chainsaw Massacre* comes to mind. Camilla Damask has turned you in.'

'What?'

'Never wanted contact with your son? Or did you suspect he was Lowry's? That the reason?'

'*Nothing* was ruddy Lowry's.'

'You and Damask planning a getaway? Or were you going to fuck off without her? Cash in the score? She was still waiting on you, was she?'

'What? Where is she now? What proof do you have of any of this? This, this bullshit!'

'Had enough of running a hotel into the ground? Needed the cash, did you?'

'Fuck you, Punch. Get out!'

'Lowry's blood was on your chainsaw, Townsend.' He moved closer. 'And on the fire escape door in your hotel. I

309

put it to you that it was you who took the plane and sunk it in an attempt to make it look like Lowry's suicide. And all for his assets. His severed hand. Animal.'

Townsend bolted out.

Punch ran around the back of reception, scattering chairs and a table in pursuit. A group at the bar screamed and one woman bent over in the brace position.

Punch leaped onto Townsend and they crashed to the floor. Punch forced Townsend's hands behind his back. He retrieved his handcuffs and clasped them on each of Townsend's wrists.

He pressed the red button on the handset.

'Nigel Townsend, you are under arrest for the murder, or attempted murder, of Xander Lowry. You do not have to say anything. But it may harm your defence if you do not mention when questioned something which you later rely on in court. Anything you do say may be given in evidence.'

Within seconds, Cluny came running into the hotel bar. He dropped to his knees and maintained additional pressure on Townsend's body.

'Got him, Sarge!'

'One for your hard drive, constable. The honours are done.' Punch leaned down to put his face next to Townsend's. 'Lowry walked off in confusion and pain, didn't want to show it. You're a bastard'n fucking animal in cords, Townsend. And a shocker of a jumper. Not to say an absent fucking father too. And Lloyd Webber didn't even win the bloody gong. Streisand did!'

'Fuck you!' Townsend attempted. 'Fuck you, Punch!'

'Damask told us the rest. Not as loyal as you'd hoped. Two sick fuckers, doing away with supposed friends for a buck – you were made for each other.'

Punch got up onto his knees. He turned to look for his hat.

'I've got just the room for you, Townsend. Though it's a cell we call it. And we throw away the fucking key.'

TRACK 27

A KICK DRUM. PUNCH WAS sure of it. *But not in time. Not in the usual places? Which wasn't like Kenney Jones.* And scratching. Again, scratching.

He rolled over on the mattress and kicked off a boot. Was he clothed? He would certainly be alone. An irregular few days it had been. It'd taken all the puff out of him. What he would have given for the usual festive scuffles outside the Mish to settle, instead of folk falling, planes going missing, bodies fake and real, severed hands, the world arriving; rifles pressed into his back, by Christ.

Townsend, along with Palindrome, had been transferred from the Tobermory cell to a custody unit on the mainland. Punch had overseen the handover. Maybe officers there would give the buggers a fan heater. Whoever's idea it was to put the switch on the outside wasn't daft. A small gathering outside the station had seen the men off, several boos and shocked faces among them. Palindrome having caused the biggest stir. Punch had quipped to Randy that Palindrome would be lost without his mother to iron his underpants;

that God himself only knew what she would make of his appearance on the BBC's *Reporting Scotland*, let alone in the Courts section of *The Oban Times*.

More kicks. Becoming more inconsistent.

There was paperwork to complete, but Cluny had picked up most of that on the computer. A prototype from Tulliallan wasn't such a bad thing. The device itself would be on a wage soon the way things were going; it would be remote policing next. *The drum went on.* Punch sat up and forced open his eyes to check the damage on the bottle of Tobermory. A heavy night. No doubting it. *The kick drum. Taking on new, intermittent patterns.* He rubbed his eyes fully awake.

Fuck.

Somebody was knocking on the door. It was Christmas Eve, but he was fairly sure it wasn't Santa Claus. More likely Randy taking tree orders for next year.

Punch rolled off the bed. Put his foot back in the boot. Ruffled his hair to awaken the badgers. Hibernation seemed like a great thing. To lay low all winter. Gather enough nuts and the like to make sure any trips to the Co were kept to a minimum. He stood and slowly straightened his back. As long as it wasn't Guinness knocking, with a bow around a cactus or a badminton racket. He tucked in his shirt and pierced the blinds. No car. A good enough sign. Better would be no knock at all. Probably a reporter with no family to visit.

He walked to the record player and lifted the needle. One of these mornings the scratching would continue in his head. He looked down to make sure he had trousers on.

No doubt after the Calve strip show the town now had him down as the policing equivalent to Jamie Oliver. *The Naked Chief* was certainly an improvement on The Clock.

He went to turn the key in the lock, but it wasn't there. He opened the door.

Sonia Hislop was standing in black. She looked thinner, if it were possible. A gust of wind would take the lass.

'Oh?' Punch said. 'Sorry I was ...'

'The girls at the house said you called round,' she said. 'Wanting to see me they said. Sorry, there was no answer at the station.'

'Eh, aye. Better come in.' Punch moved aside and looked around outside as she walked in. Coast clear. She smelled of the bar. Hops, barley, smoke.

'Another night of suffering Tinsel's poetry?' he said.

'It shows?' She smiled.

'I've a cell over there if it's needed ...' he said, closing the door.

He could tell she didn't know what to do with her body, no matter how slight.

'You'll want these.' She handed him his set of keys. 'You left them in the door on the outside.'

'Christ, right. Was a late one ... high security, eh?'

'Would you rather I come back?'

'No. No. It's fine. I'm not big on the celebrations.'

'I heard about the Lussa Falls guy.' She put her hand to her mouth, then through her hair. 'Gruesome. Is it true?'

'Well, that's what courts are for, but yes. Very likely. He's in custody on the mainland now. You couldn't write it ...' He nodded to the table. 'Aye, a late one.'

'Sorry?'

'Last night. Hence, the keys in the door,' Punch said. The lass had this effect on him, no doubting it. Questioning, even when she wasn't.

'Oh? Okay.'

He moved away from her for fear of the Tobermory on his breath. Though the lass was probably immune by now.

'Take a seat,' Punch said, quickly realising there were no clear surfaces. 'Sorry.' He moved to take the Co-op bag from the chair by the table. Couldn't be sure what was inside it. Poor lass had had enough scares. He scanned the floor in case of rogue trails of wool.

'Thanks,' she said.

Punch was suddenly embarrassed by the mess of his life. Mary MacBeth couldn't swim against that tide. He would need to go and see her. Today was never easy for them.

'You'd think The Stones were house guests ...' he said. 'Or whoever it'd be now. Oasis or the like. Or the local lads, Lovesick Zombies I see they're calling themselves ... fair racket they make. Pretty lovesick, by the sounds of them.'

'Right,' she said. She sat by the table. 'I haven't heard them.'

'The Stones?'

'No, the local boys.'

'Right. They're practising in the distillery house now,' he said. 'Drunk it dry, you'd think. Broom handles for mic stands they're saying. Heard a questionable "Jackie Wilson Said" on my rounds. Thought you'd hear it from Macgochans.'

He wondered if that would be hard for her, that she might even hear them cover one of her man's tunes; wished he would shut the hell up. There was something unsettling

315

but commanding about her. Punch was sure she could bend pretty much any day to her will, let alone any man. Even Van Morrison.

'So, no horse's head then?' she said, looking beyond him.

'Eh?'

'Oh. Nothing. Sorry.'

'Right aye, anyway, just a chat,' he said. 'To clear things up. The pen-pushers will be after me if I don't.'

'It's fine.' She continued her surveillance. She couldn't place the man in his shower now. The mystery shattered. 'I should get a season ticket at this rate.'

'Eh?'

'To here.'

'Aye.' He forced a smile, which wasn't actually that forced. 'Though we'll not give Guinness any ideas. Bugger's hooked up a printer now too. Only a matter of time until he installs a sawmill out the back for paper supplies.'

She didn't say anything. She looked at the carpet as though it might have some hidden message, headline or pattern only she could discern. Possibly the face of a child.

'I didn't know about you and the man Lowry,' he said. 'Well, I didn't know Xander Lowry existed the last time you were here is the truth. Possibly to my shame. Feels like a year ago.'

She nodded. Still to the carpet. He had never seen such threadbare get so much attention. He noticed she wasn't wearing the cross earrings.

'Or about your links to the Damasks . . .'

'I heard. She and the Townsend guy? Unbelievable, or maybe not. Where is she now?'

316

'In custody too.'

'Some relief. Sorry, what do you want to know? Not something a girl wants to advertise. The woman is a horror. Actually, ill. I honestly thought she'd sold it. The island. Or maybe I'd convinced myself.'

'Right, we'll come to that no doubt. Did you know about her and Lowry, and Nigel Townsend, too?'

'I didn't.'

'You'll know we found Mr Lowry's body two days ago and he's now in the morgue in Glasgow. Well, maybe not about the morgue bit.'

'Yes.' She nodded. 'Tragic.'

'And I suppose it's about loose ends for me. You're aware he knew your, well—'

'Sean. Yes.' She put her chin in her hand and looked up and across the room. Her face turned red. 'Falling for a bit of flattery, oldest trick in the book. I'm embarrassed about it. But here I just seem to attract either the decrepit or the virgins.'

'Right.'

'Weird, but I think really I was trying to get a bit of ... of Sean back.'

Punch looked down, bit his lips; something he had seen his mother do.

'Was it known that Sean was the son of Camilla Damask?'

'Not locally. Sean was estranged. Since he was seventeen. My nutcase mother-in-law wasn't somebody he wanted to publicise ... She's been in and out of places. The Priory – you know, in London. She never visited here much until we moved here. Sean loved Mull, and his grandmother, but

317

then she died. He loved Mull enough for his crazy mother not to put him off, but their relationship was always strained, when it even existed. He could never be what she wanted him to be.'

'Or what she wanted to be *herself*, maybe?'

Sonia raised her hand in a gesture of acceptance.

'Did he know who his father was?'

'He didn't really. I think he always fantasised it was Lowry.'

'So, he didn't know Townsend, from Lussa Falls?'

'No – can't think he was ever there. Oh, he flew in there once. The Sunday his second album entered the Top Twenty.' A wave of recognition crossed her face. 'Shit, you're not saying it's *not* him? That he's not Sean's father?'

'It's unclear right now.'

'God. I feel sick. So Lowry *could* be? So I might've slept with my—'

'Seems almost certainly Townsend.'

'Right ... Okay, okay.'

'Did you have anything to do with Camilla Damask?'

'I didn't want Iris within a million miles of her, if that's what you mean.' She shook her head. 'Calve was just too close. But she never came up then. As I said, her mother had it originally. Sean was much more attached to her. Though you can see the house from bloody everywhere ... but, yeah, I thought she'd sold it.'

'You were both in similar fields? She didn't try and use that?'

'Oh, she did, before Iris was born. But then she'd only disrupt further.'

'And Lowry?' Punch said. 'Did you know him long?'

'No. Couldn't even say I knew him at all. Well, I knew who he was. I must be a sucker for musicians.'

'When did you last see him?'

'At the Western. Few weeks ago. Folk said – and that's what he told me, too – that he was interested in buying it.'

'So you didn't know him from before? From the Jools Holland performance?'

'No. Never met him then. Sean knew him through his mother he said. But something had gone wrong between them. I think it was to do with Camilla's involvement, her doing. I always felt she resented Sean's creative success.'

'Seems she resented Lowry's, too. Certainly, that's how Townsend felt.'

'Weird, I remember the guitarist Dave Gilmour was also on the Jools Holland show. He told Sean and I how he used to fly into Mull, to the airfield. Couldn't write it.'

'Mull travels, no doubting it.'

'But Sean still loved his playing – Lowry's. I feel bad now about what's happened. *Disloyal*. Freakish. You know? Fuck, what if he *was* his father? My God.' She drew away as if again recoiling from the very idea. 'I feel sick.'

'It appears Xander Lowry and Camilla Damask had a relationship at some stage … But as I said there's nothing conclusive.'

'So,' she said, rallying a little, switching to gossip mode. 'Was she with the Townsend guy or Lowry?'

'Both, it appears, but at different times. Won't be the first ménage à trois on Mull. Can I ask, did you get any indication Lowry was on the edge, or involved in anything untoward?'

'Well.' Her eyes rose to the ceiling and then back to the safety of the floor. 'When he'd been viewing the Western, he'd stayed a few nights, earlier in the month. He asked me if I had any drugs. I didn't. I don't. And then he got back in touch last week. Said he was flying into Lussa Falls. So, we met again.' She looked at Punch. 'Wait – do I need an alibi?'

'No.' Punch sat on the arm of his sofa. 'You're not in any trouble. Or under any suspicion.' It was strangely intimate having her so close to him. He had no idea if folk were really talking about them.

What a fucking place.

'I just heard him playing from outside the room,' she said. 'I'd been walking by with a pile of used towels. I actually dropped them. When I heard him playing. The door was ajar. Never heard anything like it.'

'Where did you meet, the last time?'

'At the hotel – like I said.'

'The Western?'

'Yes. I said that.'

'And Camilla Damask? When did you last speak to her?'

'Weirdly, she called me in a frenzy two days ago. No idea how she knew about me and Lowry, but then we might have been spotted.' She sighed. 'And maybe it was reported back to her. Anything's possible in this place.'

Palindrome, thought Punch.

She took a tissue from her pocket and wiped her eyes. Punch saw the transferral of eyeliner.

'Right. That'll do for now,' he said. 'And thanks for coming in.' He stood up. 'I'm sure that wouldn't have been easy. But it helps me pull all this together.'

'It's fine. If nothing else, it's a distraction. This is not my favourite of times.'

'No. I know. I do.'

'Can I ask—' she started. She put her fingers to her lips. 'Sorry.'

'Uh-huh?'

She inhaled deeply. 'What you did with the *doll*?'

'I – eh – I got rid of it.' Punch shook quickly, turned to organise his table. 'That must have been hard for you.'

'And you.'

'Aye.'

'I can feel the voodoo pins,' she said, trying but failing to make light. She used her cuffs to wipe her eyes. 'Iris would have loved a grandmother. Just not that one.'

They both stood in the relatively small space.

'Poor guy really, Lowry. Something childlike and lost about him,' she said. 'Maybe pleasing all these people for so long. I was just so lonely. Maybe needing to be a mother.'

'Uh-huh.'

She put her hand to her mouth again, as though it might stop everything from falling out of her. Punch fetched for a toilet roll and pulled her a piece. He knew the feeling. That's what Calgary was for.

She turned to the door.

'And now I've bloody well sung in the church. They'll have me down as a witch next.'

'People understand. Well, they don't, but you know . . .'

She sighed.

'Oh.' Punch moved around her to reach for the door handle. 'Did he mention an "Archie" to you at all?'

321

'Lowry?'

'Aye.'

'*No.*' She shook her head. 'No.'

'No. Right.'

'Would it be – no.'

'What?'

'Weird maybe, but would it be possible to see where he was found?'

Punch scratched his left badger. 'Aye. I don't see why not. When things die down a tad.'

She nodded. Again, to the carpet. He cursed his choice of words.

He opened the door and she stepped out. Punch felt the cold rush in.

'I'll run you down.'

'No. No need.'

'I've, eh – let me please.'

Punch reached inside for the heap of keys and his jacket.

They drove down the Western Road past the park.

'The island's only palm tree,' Punch said, feeling the need to become a tour guide and nodding towards the garden of the house belonging to the school headteacher, as they turned down to the hotel from the bottom of the park.

The Western Isles Hotel came into view, and at the bottom he took the sharp left onto Memorial Road. Christmas lights twinkled as they passed the entrance. Punch pulled into the car park near the gate leading to the chalets. Ahead was the little path that led back up to the park, where they used to rally boggy carts. There wasn't a pram in the town safe from teenagers after the wheels.

'I hope he wouldn't mind,' Sonia said. They sat in silence. 'Sean.'

'I know who you meant.'

'He said something to me,' she said, staring ahead. 'On the bed he died on. And I can't let it go.'

Punch didn't say anything.

'He said a real artist wears a mask in their everyday life, so they don't reveal the pain of what it takes to make the art. Because if they did, they would spoil your experience as a listener, as a viewer, or as a spectator. That's when I realised what artists have to do – their sacrifice – to make others happy, or sad, or heard, or whatever.'

'To make believe?' Punch tried. 'Is that it?'

'No. *Make real*. Their art is actually their truth.'

'Uh-huh. Right. Right. He seemed to be very talented, your man. And successful. But I think making art makes *them* happy, heard, too.'

'It's when I knew I could never be one. An artist. A true one at least. I think I knew that even in art school. But Sean didn't study anything. Not formally. He just – *knew*.'

Punch nodded. He didn't detect any of this in Rod, but figured some artists were born to have fun, to not be heard but *seen*, to not suffer, or make others suffer.

Sonia Hislop exited the car. Punch did too. He walked to the rear of the Ranger and she followed on her side. He reached to open the boot. For a second, he tried to abort the action, fearing he shouldn't go ahead with what he had planned.

'Eh, I thought you and the girls might want one of these?' he said.

323

Sonia looked into the boot. She pulled her hair back with both hands and ran her fingers through it.

Punch had no clue if he had made an error or not. Nothing on her face gave any indication. If she shaved her hair she really would look like the Irish singer. All eyes. He looked away. The wind was arriving off the Atlantic coast. Calve holding firm. Calgary chattering its teeth.

'That's ... very kind.' She wiped her eyes. Looked like she was calling the wind the culprit.

'I'll get it up to the house for you then. Heavy buggers they can be.'

Punch reached in and hoisted the fir tree up onto his shoulder.

Sonia closed the boot. She walked ahead and held open the gate.

He followed her up to the chalet and lowered the tree at her door.

'I can get it into place?' he said. 'Inside?'

'Thanks, sergeant. But it's okay. The girls will help. You know what they say, it takes three women to put up a tree ...'

'And one man to knock it down. I know.'

She smiled. He noticed her whole face lit up. Dollops for eyes.

'It's for *all* the girls,' he said, copying her trick of keeping eye contact with the ground.

She pressed her lips together and nodded.

'I know,' she managed. 'I – I haven't been able to go to the grave right now. Can't even remember exactly what words are on it. Is that terrible? Am I a terrible person?'

'No. You're not. I can't imagine.' Though he could, to an extent.

'Sean, we cremated. I'm not sure which thought is worse. His ashes are scattered at the T in the Park site. His first festival appearance. He'd never been to one until he played one. Then he did the next five.'

'Maybe you'll go today?' he said.

She nodded slowly; her face impassive but thoughtful.

They stood in silence. Punch reached for his hat and then realised he hadn't taken it. Nor the handset. The buggers could give him peace for one day. For this day.

'Tell me,' he said. 'I, eh, wanted to . . .' He shifted his eyes onto objects he wasn't really looking at.

She raised her eyebrow.

'What did it sound like?' he asked.

'What?'

'His playing – Lowry's? In person, I mean.'

'Oh?' Sonia Hislop looked straight at him, though Punch wasn't looking at her. 'It was . . . *complete*.'

'Right, right.' He turned away. He felt naked, no, exposed, without his hat. But at least he was clothed. 'Merry Christmas.'

'Merry Christmas,' he heard.

He walked back down the steps and noticed the child's yellow boots were entirely visible, upended on grass now. Everything had thawed.

TRACK 28

BACK AT THE STATION, PUNCH grabbed his hat and keys. Poured the remains of his whisky into one of Guinness's plants. He unlocked the cell and took hold of Charlie's old guitar case he had scouted in the lockup; the thing surprisingly light. He pulled open the station door, locked it behind him and jumped into the Ranger.

Ruth Lauder was waiting for him in the foyer of the Western, where she had been relocated. Since Townsend's arrest the Lussa Falls had temporarily closed. She was wearing a desolate expression, gaunt and pale, in long boots, Barbour jacket and hat. A woollen affair.

Punch approached, rubbed at his five o'clock shadow. He had noted the Jag parked at the entrance. It was a good sign that she hadn't left the island as per his request.

'Miss Lauder.'

'Sergeant.'

'Apologies again about you not being able to accompany the helicopter. But contamination is always a danger. Let's go to your room if we might and have a chat.'

'Yes.'

He followed her up the winding stairs; she hadn't seemed to notice his roadie act.

'In a way I feel he is more here on the island than anywhere else now.'

'Have you anyone who can be with you?' Even though he would likely be mostly alone himself, he was suddenly struck by the thought she might be by herself on Christmas Day.

'My mother. She is travelling up the day after Boxing Day, when the ferries are back on.'

'Right.'

'The Slaters have offered. Very kind. But no.'

Inside her room, they sat on two chairs. Punch removed the guitar case from his back and laid it on the table.

'A tune?' she asked.

'Eh? No. No. Wouldn't subject you to that. More of a decoy. Keeping the contents safe.'

He noted something pathetic about the woman, the way she continued to steal glances at the sky, even here in Tob. A hint of embarrassment about her remaining expectations of hope, given the body of her beloved had been found.

'Still no plane?' she asked.

'No,' he said. 'But CID are going to lean heavier on Townsend about it.'

Punch was just awaiting MacTavish discovering it. There was already talk of him charging visitor fees and a couple of quid each to reporters for Maggie's bacon rolls.

He put his hat on the table and turned the volume down on his handset.

'I wanted to go with the – *body*,' she said, returning her gaze to the window. 'I still can't get used to that word; to *did*, to *was*. I don't think I shall be able to say *maestro* and mean it, ever again.'

'Of course.' Punch followed her gaze to the window. 'I'm sorry that wasn't possible, to go with the body. Only official personnel. Standard procedure.'

'But Nigel? I mean, can it really be true?'

'Forensics have confirmed his involvement. He is now under arrest.'

'God.' She shook her head. Tears in her eyes. Punch passed her a napkin from the welcome tray.

'Miss Lauder,' he paused. 'Townsend took the plane.'

'What?'

'Yes.'

'What do you mean? Why?'

'Jealousy, greed, evil ... take your pick.'

'Oh my—' She put the napkin to her mouth.

'We're still working out the fine-tuning. The jealousy was possibly professional *and* personal, given Mr Lowry's and Miss Damask's prior relationship.'

'Who?'

'You don't know a woman named Camilla Damask?'

Ruth Lauder blankly shook her head.

'No. Should I?'

The woman was believable enough, thought Punch. And a damn sight more likeable without the flashing Townsend mooching around her, which he now reasoned had been a cover for him and Damask.

'Should I?' she repeated, looking to Punch.

'This woman was Townsend's accomplice. But had had relationships with both of them. It seems Xander Lowry always got everything Nigel Townsend wanted.'

'Oh. Right? I mean, yes. Nigel could be mean about Xandy's clearly superior talent. The fact he was a better pilot must have grated too. But I just can't ... I had no idea. I always thought Nigel was making a play for *me*.'

'Seems he kept a lot hidden behind those jumbo cords and overly pocketed jerkins. Evil, for one.'

'I came here for a romantic break. *There's* the crime! I thought Xand was going to prop—'

'This won't be easy for you, Miss Lauder, but—' Punch stopped himself; there was no point now in telling her that her musician had a tendency to trawl for other fish in the sea. He wanted to protect Sonia Hislop, too. She had been through enough.

'If you're shying away from making reference to other women, sergeant, then I'm not an idiot. But I thought we were coming here to get *away* from them. I run his orchestra, remember.'

'Right. Aye. Sorry.' Punch sat forwards. 'Did he tell you he was going to take his violin with him on the plane?'

'Archie? No. No, he didn't. Why would he?'

'Will you go back to the London Philharmonic?'

'I don't know. Honestly don't.' He detected a flicker of pride in her eyes at the mention of the orchestra, a perceptible air of sure footing.

'I gather he was unmarried?' He paused, a little uncomfortably.

'Yes, if you don't count Vivaldi, or Archie. At first, I was naive enough to think the composer was my *only* competition.'

'But did he talk to you about a possible child?'

'*Us* having children?'

329

Punch decided not to clarify; there didn't seem any point in adding potentially more pain, more shocks for the lass.

'It was the one thing I couldn't press him on. He just wouldn't talk about it.' She crumpled into herself. 'But his hand, his dear, dear *hand* . . . I mean, how could Nigel?'

'Must be a terrible shock,' he murmured, a little hopelessly.

'A shock!' She buried her head in her own hands, the fingers interlaced. 'So brutal. Like something out of a horror film!'

'It *was* a shock, I don't mind saying.' Punch sighed heavily.

'His hands were so important. So, so beautiful, so expressive . . . Townsend. The man's a bloody monster!' She stood and walked around the room. 'Said to stay inside and he would go down to talk Xander out of taking the plane. Since we arrived, he seemed more interested in it than us.'

'Townsend?'

'That was the last time I saw hi—' She brought one hand to her mouth and sat down. 'He got so silly about flying. I think it made him feel even higher than a stage.'

'Well, it seems Townsend was manipulating something much bigger.'

'Am *I* under arrest, sergeant?'

'No,' Punch said. 'No.' At this rate he would be taking out rooms in the Western for cell space. 'But I'll need your onwards travel details. There will be further clarifications needed. You will have to give evidence in the trial.'

'Oh Christ.' She turned to Punch with tears in her eyes. 'His hand. I mean, *how?*'

'I can't share all the details with you right now, Miss Lauder. Not while investigations are under way.'

'Wait, she and Xander weren't still . . .? Did he take the violin on the plane? Was he was going to her?'

'No.' Punch shook his head. 'No evidence of that. It seems there was another motive: greed – and paternity, possibly. Remember, Miss Lauder, Mr Lowry wasn't in the plane.'

She looked sharply at him. 'But Nigel was?'

'Yes. It seems Townsend wanted Xander Lowry to disappear, but not by way of the Needle. To feign suicide. Money, too, seems to be a motive.'

'And so – the violin? In the plane, do we think?'

'Well . . .' Punch reached for the guitar case. She followed his actions as though he had just plucked the case out of a top hat. He unzipped it. Carefully, slowly, he produced a violin case from inside the guitar cover.

Ruth Lauder made a neat zero with her mouth. She put each hand on her cheeks.

'Archie?' she managed.

'Forensics are done with it. I figured better to disguise it from prying eyes.'

She took the case from Punch and inspected it. She placed it on the bed and opened it up to reveal the violin. Her hand stroked it.

'It's like touching . . . my God, *him*.'

'Was it, eh, normal to name your instrument?'

'Can be.' She slowly nodded. 'At least, in the classical world. The name comes from his signature Vivaldi piece, *per Archi e Cembalo*.'

'Ah? Right. Okay I've heard it, yes.' He saw then the stickers of all colours on the case, some torn and faded; those he could read documented, *Paris, London, Sydney, Vienna, New York* . . .

'His violin was also made by an Archibald S. Hill, as it happens. So sometimes he called it Archie Two Times. Not many would know that, though.'

Punch nodded. 'Would you have a set of tweezers, Miss Lauder?'

'Tweezers?'

'Aye. I've a thought that Forensics might have missed a trick.'

She carefully rested the violin on the bed and walked to the bathroom. She returned with the tweezers and handed them to Punch.

'Eh, no. This is your bit.' He reached for the violin and carefully sat down, resting it across his lap as though it was the world's most expensive pedal steel guitar.

Ruth Lauder looked at him, confused.

Punch gestured down to the instrument.

'I think there might be something inside for you. Just a hunch, mind.'

'What?'

'I'm sure you've a steadier hand than me.'

Punch handed the violin to her. It was the one he had seen on the Jools Holland show on TV. He was sure it had seen more of the world than he ever would.

Miss Lauder laid it on her lap. She ran her fingers carefully around its edges as though it really was the body of the man who had played it. Slowly, she moved the tweezers towards one of the two holes on the instrument. She paused to look up at Punch.

'A hunch,' he said. 'Remember.'

Ruth Lauder looked back down and very slowly manoeuvred the tweezers into one of the two holes, each shaped like small snakes. Punch's mind flashed with the memory of the Operation game he'd play with a still-too-young-for-it Charlie. He feared a buzzer sound. He watched as she paused. Moved her fingers around a little and fished deeper.

'Am I missing something?' she said.

'Maybe try the other hole?'

She lowered the tweezers again. Seemed to have found a catch. Gradually, she brought the tweezers back up. A piece of paper emerged like a newborn. Cautiously, delicately, she brought it into the room.

She took it in her hand and inhaled deeply; she nodded and gulped heavily.

'Per Archi e Cembalo. Concerto in d minor.'

Punch smiled, avoided eye contact.

'In the hand of Vivaldi himself?' she marvelled. 'He bought it, for me?'

'I'd have checked myself but didn't want to risk damaging the thing. Not sure LB, let alone L, division has the insurance to cover it.'

She turned the paper around and on the back, there was a yellow Post-it with the words:

Will you be the string to my bow?

She sank to her knees and Punch reached quickly to rescue the violin, as she hunched on the floor, the note in her hand.

Punch delved a hand into his pocket and pulled out an evidence bag.

'And, eh, there's this too, ma'am.'

Ruth Lauder righted herself, took the bag from him and removed the deerstalker. She brought it to her chest.

Punch tried to force something approaching a smile, but fell short. He was starting to feel like a third-rate St Christopher himself. He took his hat from the table.

'Can I do anything for you, Miss Lauder? Get you anything?'

She silently shook her head.

'Sorry. Sorry again for your loss. That it all happened here. Islands are supposed to be safe places. We'll be in touch of course. Season's, eh . . .'

Punch walked to the door and, before he closed it, he looked back and saw that she had the manuscript by her ear, as though lost in music only she could hear.

Outside, he crossed the road to the Ranger and jumped inside. He started the engine and eased off towards the Back Brae.

Several minutes later he pulled into Glen Iosal and turned off the ignition. Tinsel and Tonsils were standing outside their front door. A few swords were stacked on the ground, resting against their wall.

Punch closed the Ranger door and walked to the men. Both of them in cardigans and wellies, looking to him like they were off to audition for *Last of the Summer Wine*. Though the accent might have been a stretch.

He took his hat off and cast a side look to his mother's front door. Killing two birds with one stone was always helpful. There was no sign of Christmas lights on either house, unlike some of the trees twinkling in the surrounds.

'Lads.'

'Sergeant,' Tinsel said.

Tonsils, in flat cap, managed a stag-in-headlights stare. Punch saw how the rims of his eyes were bloodshot. The man was about as far from riding the Isle of Man TT as Xander Lowry.

'I wanted to clarify,' Punch said. 'You know, it was odd to me, Archie, that you were there the other night, on the path, at the same time. So I had to pry. But we've found the suspects.'

'Townsend was always an insincere bastard. But this?' Tinsel said. 'And Pal? Our preacher no less?' He outstretched his palms and turned them upwards. 'Christ, what a place. Caber should have landed on that bugger years ago.'

'Uh-huh,' Punch said. 'Takes all kinds.' He looked to Tonsils. 'So – sorry, Archie. Sorry again.'

'Thanks, Ivor,' Tinsel said, nodding to his silent twin.

'Fine, Harry. You might be the closest I've come to a decoration in ten years.'

'I *did* drop the dolly girl,' Tonsils said, grabbing Punch's shorter arm. 'I didn't like her hanging like that. Suffering. *Again.* That's why I left the church too. I feel folk's suffering. I do.'

'Right, Archie,' Tinsel said, putting his hand on his twin's back and leading him inside the house. Tonsils let go of Punch's arm.

'Oh here,' Tonsils said. He turned, bent down slowly and took hold of something and handed it to Punch.

'Right,' Punch said. He couldn't think when somebody had last touched that arm. 'Cheers. Uh-huh.'

'Merry Christmas, Ivor,' Tinsel said. 'To Mum too.'

Punch turned quickly and walked to his mother's front door. He selected the correct key and turned it in the lock. Stood the sword outside.

'It's me, Mother!'

Inside, he put his hat on the table by the entrance where the phone was and closed the door behind him. He walked the short hallway, past Lady Di, and into the small living room. His mother was sitting on her sofa, her walking frame propped in front of her. A tartan shawl around her shoulders. Punch looked to the other chair and almost pictured his uncle there. Somewhere between solicitude and the sea, still with the salt on him.

'We've been on TV!' she said, fixing her eyes on the screen. 'Mull!'

'Right.' Punch sat where he had imagined his uncle. The new show, *Who Wants to Be a Millionaire?* was on. He looked to the photograph on top of the set of him and Charlie, hair like fishermen, posing with trophies. Not long after, that strange time of vacuum would arrive: post-Charlie but before his uncle died. Inverness. Janice. Talk of children. Which he had cringingly called *an expensive hobby*.

'Oh, I've had Tina Noon on the phone. Her Robert's going to be on this show she said!'

'No, Mum. Not on this show. It's the News he's been on.' It was confirmation if he needed it that you never really knew what lay behind a person, even on an island. Maybe especially on an island.

'Shush. I like this bit. They phone somebody.' She turned to the hallway and cupped her hand around her ear. She waited. 'No. Not me, Di. Never me.'

'So, if we're not millionaires yet, Mum, then a cup?'

'We need Charlie down from upstairs; he's the studious one. Yes, lad. Two sugars.'

Punch inhaled deeply and yawned. He put his radio beside him on the chair. Supporting officers were carrying out a full sweep of the Damask house, in case of any loose ends.

'Running out of lifelines,' his mother said. 'Like me.'

Punch got up, took her plate and walked out of the living room. In the hallway mirror he caught sight of his collapsed face; the landslide of skin and bone gathering at the mouth gave the impression of someone perpetually sucking on life. Confirmation that the human face stored loss. He had gotten older and, like sunrise over the mainland, it seemed to have happened without him even noticing. He walked past the small spare bedroom where Charlie had never slept, despite a bed being always made up for him. He stepped in and sat on the bed. It felt to him like trespassing in a foreign country.

His mother yelled something about the kettle.

'Aye, Mum!'

He got up quickly and took the plate from the bed. Smoothed out the duvet to make sure it completely forgot him.

In the kitchen he flicked the kettle on. His attention was taken by the glass pane on the top half of the back door, on which he saw the re-emergence of letters in a familiar hand coming through the clearing condensation:

'*Back in 30, boys. On a home call.*'

'Who's this Philip Roth?' she said, when Punch arrived back in the living room.

'Hmm . . . not sure, Mum. Christ, I can't remember which one has the two sugars now . . .' he said, putting the cups on the coasters with the Tobermory Whist Club logo.

'You can have fifty/fifty!' his mother cackled.

'Aye. Good one, Mum. I better be going soon. Just stopped by.' In a sense he felt he was on a patrol here too, around the wasteland of her diminishing mind.

She looked him up and down, as if to make sure all the parts of this person she had given birth to in a pebbledash building outside Salen were still intact.

'You'll need the bins out next week, Mum.'

'Is tomorrow bin day?'

'No, it'll be Christmas Day. Remember?'

'Christmas? Rubbish. Then where's my tree?'

'Remember you didn't want one, Mum. The mess with the needles dropping?'

'Right. Aye.' She nodded assuredly. He had noticed how her Lewis accent had come through on turbo drive since the dementia. As though the two islands were competing. 'And you're coming?'

'Uh-huh. Though I've a case or two on the go. But yes.'

He took out his notebook and studied his scrawls. There were pieces that still needed to fall into place. He hoped the search of the Damask house might throw up more information on the whereabouts of the plane, and cast more light on the Damask–Townsend–Lowry ménage à trois, but

338

he had to prepare himself for the reality that – like symphonies, he imagined – not all cases were ever truly solved or completed.

'Do you remember what he used to call you?' she said, looking up at the photograph and groping in her cardigan pocket for a tissue.

'The hanky's under your cuff, Mother.'

'His hero.'

Punch got up. Walked out of the room. He carried on down the hallway. Took his hat from the table and closed the door.

Back in the Ranger he heard a crackle on the car radio.

'*Who is this?*' a voice said.

'What the fuck?' Punch reached for the dial and turned it up.

'Hello?' he said into the handset.

'*Hello?*'

'Mum?'

'*Who is this? I'm pointing it at the TV for the BBC and nothing's happening. What time is* Eastenders *on please?*'

'Christ.' The mobile handset, Punch realised. 'It's me, Mum. Over. I mean it's . . . me.'

'*Are you the announcer, lad? Look, I'm trying to change the channel with the dit-dit! I'm pointing it and everything! I'm hopeless! Hopeless.*'

'Mum, calm down. You've got my radio. I'll be back in to get it now.'

'*Who's speaking please?*' she said. '*Am I on the TV? Have I won anything?*'

'You have the posh voice on, Mum. Wait a sec.'

Punch jumped out of the Ranger and wrestled with his keys. He opened the door and walked back into the house.

'What's the fellow on now? Sixteen grand? Might put a dent in Randy's tab at Macgochans.'

'Oh, you're *here*?' She turned to him. 'Haven't seen you since you last did the bins. I want to watch the Londoners ... never been. Well, bring the fellow Roth away in! Kettle's on.'

Punch changed the channel to BBC1 and took his handset from her. He put the remote next to her and she turned contentedly to the screen. Behind him, sounded the familiar opening hits on the electronic drum kit.

Outside, he stopped to pick up the sword. It was as smooth as he remembered in his hand. He wondered if it might be more use than the uniform at keeping the world at bay. He walked to the Ranger, jumped in and put the sword on the back seat. Reversed and drove away.

TRACK 29

PUNCH PULLED INTO THE PEBBLEDASH. He drove around
the back and parked at the rear of the station. He was in
need of the one thing it was impossible to be on an island:
invisible.

He got out of the vehicle, leaving the handset there. He
selected the key for the lockup, opened the padlock and
pulled up the shutter door. Flicked the light switch on and
closed the door behind him. The dead sheep was lying in
the corner. He would need to get it in the cooler soon; that
was if Lowry's hand hadn't killed his appetite. The big tin
of white paint lay close by. And the brush on top of it.
A year dried from last time.

Punch pulled a round steel drum closer to him and it
scraped loudly on the concrete floor. He picked up the bin
liner he had taken in the night previous, and then a bottle
of lighter fluid. He poured it into the drum. Took a match
from his pocket and lit a roll-up. He tipped the contents of
the bin liner into the drum and took several intense draws
on the roll-up. He afforded himself one look inside the

drum: to the jumble of limbs, wool, foam and fabrics. Like a soup of life. Death. He spat the remains of the roll-up into the drum and it burst into flame.

The heat was pleasing on his face. He looked to the sheep and wondered if slaughtering it was really about something else: the urge to see inside a living thing? That if he could map the internal world of livestock, then maybe it would help him with people, cases, to better understand the internal workings of the sick fuckers of the world. The Nigel Townsends, the Camilla Damasks, the Libyan suitcase carriers; Palindrome, though, wasn't worth the fluid.

The fire began dying out. Punch took off his jacket and dropped it near the door. He walked in his white shirt to the carcass. The wool was already sheared off, discarded in a raw pile in the corner. He turned on the radio and Atlantic 252 burst into life. He redialled to the classical station.

He was stunned at what he heard.

'Two days ago, a plane suspected to be carrying the musician Xander Lowry took off from an airfield here on the Isle of Mull and promptly vanished. I'm afraid we have found the body of Mr Lowry. However, aspects of the mystery remain stubbornly unsolved. Anyone with information should contact Strathclyde Police or call 999.'

It was his own voice, his press statement from the kitchen table, now coming out of a transistor radio in his lockup. On his island. On Christmas Eve.

He looked to the smoking embers and rested both hands on the slaughter table. Sought out a bottle, but found nothing. The DJ said his name and continued to speak. Punch turned up the radio; the violin with the answers inside of it filled the space. Played by the brutally severed hand that had been stored right here.

'*Many of the tributes have spoken of how irreplaceable Maestro Lowry is,*' the voice on the radio said. '*You might have read one from Daniel Barenboim in* The Times, *which I found particularly moving. Simon Rattle hailed Xander Lowry as* "one of a kind" *and shared his sense that the loss of Lowry* "would be greatly felt with audiences around the world".'

The music soared, like galloping, headless horses, Punch thought. He rolled up his sleeves. Just as his uncle would do in the little barn between Albert and Victoria Street, where he slaughtered year upon year. Punch manoeuvred the sheep onto the table so that the head lay near the end. He picked up the axe. Raised its head and brought it down on the sheep's neck. The head fell to the floor. Punch moved to toe the bucket directly under the gaping neck. 'To bleed the beast,' his uncle always said, his roll-up wagging, while Trudy, his uncle's collie, sat to attention, his ears like furry antenna. Punch remembered thinking it was a new language he was being taught.

He struggled to lift the end of the carcass higher. The blood oozed out into the bucket making a 'shishing' sound. He turned the carcass onto its back and thought of his first slaughter, during which his uncle had spouted something he would never forget.

'*I didn't . . .*' his uncle had started from behind him. '*I didn't tell you something. I didn't tell you because your father, my brother, that prick, was still around. Or in Oban at least. Just a ferry away. What I didn't tell you is . . . I'm actually your . . . dad. Both of you. Right.*'

343

Punch did now, as he had that day, when he was not more than twelve and Charlie five – he started cutting the sheep's fleece as though nothing had been said. He slid the blade carefully down its skin lining to the foot. The music changed pace and became more urgent again. Lowry moving into overdrive. The bow an extension of the conductor's arm. It was always the stage of the fleece removal that he most enjoyed. When he was permitted to put his cold hands inside the warm lining of the sheep.

Punch now took hold of the stub of neck and worked his hands in to tie a knot in the windpipe. '*To stop the guts coming back up*,' his uncle used to say. '*You're basically cutting the arsehole out*.' Which is what Punch did now. Then he pulled the windpipe out and manoeuvred the carcass so that the remaining inners and intestines dropped into the bucket. What used to be a sheep was transformed to jelly. Or was it the effects of the maestro? The one who had the barn? Punch recalled feeling his uncle had undergone a similar journey that night: '*The kidneys are surrounded by the suet fat. That's what we used to use for frying, lad. Before your mother got posh.*'

All the fleece was stripped off now. Punch grabbed the hind legs and slung the thick rope up over the bars on the ceiling. He slowly winched the beast up. '*Smit*.' That's what his uncle used to call him. '*Smit*.' It was only in adulthood, when trying to comprehend what his uncle had said to him on that day of his first cull, that Punch fully understood why. His uncle's identification dye on the side of a sheep was always red, as it was on him now.

'Just the lungs now ...' Punch heard himself say, his mixture of breath and smoke crowding the hung carcass now transformed to maturing meat. He realised the music had stopped: Vivaldi, culled; Lowry, slaughtered. He heard his uncle's voice rising in the silence again, filling the barn like death:

'I, eh, thought you should know that, but best others don't. You know. She'll probably never tell you. You leave the kidneys in. The meat must dry and harden. Till it's stiff to cut.'

It had seemed to him like a code, a language of the high seas between only them. Shortly after, his mother took her two boys off the island and Ivor never knew why. But he always blamed himself, because of what was said to him that night. Maybe it was her shame, his mother's, that he took on: her Lewis-infused fear the church would never forgive her.

Punch reached to cut the lungs, which dropped into the waste bucket. Death falling into death. The sheep as it was now would hang for four days.

The radio was playing choral music. From the mouths of boys in places like St Paul's Cathedral he had only ever heard of, travelling to – *here*? Something was running through him. His arms like the devil's up to his elbows. He had the feeling he had returned from somewhere. Everywhere stunk of death, but to Punch it was really life, it was living, it was island. The last words of his uncle-cum-father came to him:

'10.03 a.m., 2.23 feet. Low tide.'

It had been the next day's tidal chart.

Punch turned and looked at another covered item. It wasn't a musical instrument, nor anything to do with livestock, alive or dead. It was covered by an off-white sheet, as it had been for nine years. The best he could do was sigh at it.

He bent to take the carrier bag from the lockup floor, pulled up the shutter and stepped into the morning light. He turned and saw the carcass as another effigy hanging.

Punch pulled the shutter down and locked the padlock. Walked to the Ranger and put the carrier bag in the boot.

Inside the station, he took the phone in hand and dialled.

'Glen Iosal 2057?'

'Mum, it's me.'

'Oh, Ivor. Merry Christmas, son.'

Promising, he thought, if a day out. 'Aye. And to you, Mum. No bother with the remote?'

'Oh no. No.' She paused. 'I'm not being heard by MFI, am I? Gosh!'

'Eh no, no, Mum. Crimes to furniture are more evident next door to you . . .'

'What?'

'Never mind. I'll pop round tomorrow. The nurse will be in later, remember.'

'You'll stay for the Christmas meal tomorrow? Lady Di's coming.'

'Well . . . My, my . . .'

'We're we're all sitting together! Communal. I thought that might be nice for you, you know?'

Punch didn't know whether she was referring to the effects of the tenth anniversary or the fallout from the cases. The other, under the sheet in the lockup, she knew nothing of, even before the dementia took hold.

'Now I'm a millionaire I said I'd pay for everyone,' she announced.

'Oh? Congratulations. Must be nice. Aye. I'll try my best, Mum. Been a busy spell.'

'Oh, and everyone's talking about the musician. Don't know whether to be proud of you or to wish the whole thing away. Did a plane go down once before, Ivor?'

'Best to wish it all away, Mum. As I said, I'll be a bit late maybe, but I'll be there. Sorry. It's work.'

'Right, son.'

She hung up. Now he knew where he got his brevity.

He took his coat and hat. The keys and a flask of tea. Tipped a drop of Tobermory into it. Kicked off his shoes and kneeled to pull his boots on. He'd need them for this. He walked past the cell and fought the strange urge to turn into it and close the door behind him. His bloodied shirt was still on the floor.

Smit.

He opened the back door of the station and locked it behind him.

Punch drove down towards Creagan. He pulled the Ranger over opposite the first house. Jumped out and glanced around conspiratorially. It was something he did when he suspected others – behind curtain blinds, in Co-op queues, passing through ferry cafeterias, perched on their bar stools on Mull – were watching.

He opened the gate and moved up the gravel path. Everything here had a sense of order, which in turn seemed to help with his thoughts. He reached to knock on the door, but it opened before he touched it. Mary MacBeth smiled and nodded.

'I won't come in,' Punch said. 'Been a busy few days.'

'I heard,' she said. 'Always best to be invited first, mind.'

She was wearing a green velour tracksuit, like a TV fitness coach. The morning light played a dance with her blue eyes.

'Aye, fair point. I wondered, though you might be busy, but ...' Punch looked down to the steps.

'What with wrapping your present?' she said, licking her lips.

He almost smiled. A cheekbone gone rogue. It could happen. Now he felt guilty about not bringing her a Christmas tree.

'No, it's just my mother asked me to ask if you might like to join for the Christmas lunch the morrow, you know over at Glen Iosal. Can't promise excitement on the scale of the Mish karaoke, but there'll be a sherry or two on the loose I'd imagine.'

'Are you going?'

'Aye. I've a bit of work first, but yes, I'll show face.'

'She'll be pleased,' she said.

'Aye.'

'And wearing the uniform.'

'Uh-huh.'

Silence fell.

'I've been thinking about—'

'I know,' she said.

'He or she would be—'

'Nine.' She nodded to the steps. 'I know.'

'That's what I always find hardest, only being able to say he or she. Not knowing.'

'Or would that make it worse?' she said. 'Not having a grave is the thing for me.'

'I still have the pram we bought.' Punch came off the step and leaned his back against her wall. 'Haven't been able to give it away to a jumble or the like. Under a sheet in the lockup. I thought you should know.'

'I thought you might,' she said. 'Still have it.'

He could only hear her voice now, rather than see her, which made it easier.

'Remember on the drive back to the Oban ferry from the hospital? I still had it visible on the back seat. The pram,' he said. 'And I stopped at the top of George Street, pulled over at the curry place that used to be the amusement arcade. I was dreading the ferry queue. I'd stopped to move the pram, to hide it in the boot. I got out and you said—'

'*Leave it.*' She sighed, her eyes closed. 'I remember.'

'Should have gone the Fishnish way. And fuck. Putting you through that. Folk gaping in the cafeteria. You're never far enough away from an island.'

'It wasn't your fault,' she said. 'Either way I would have had *miscarriage* written on my forehead. The route we took wouldn't have altered that. It all seems such a fog now.'

'Never clears. And fuck. I've spent years investigating death, but it never prepares you for it yourself. Grief.'

'The town still has me down as a loony anyway ...' She forced a laugh. 'Pushing the pram around for days after. Christ's sake.'

'You were grieving something that had been taken from you. That was okay. *Loss.*'

'*Us,*' she said.

349

Punch inhaled deeply.

'Right.' He pushed his back off the wall and made to start down the pristine path again, feeling like the disorderly component. 'We'll hope to see you?'

He heard the door shutting.

Punch pulled the gate to behind him. There were bells ringing. Folk gathering, no doubt. He imagined Reverend MacLean would be bang in the middle of his act of trans-formation. Palindrome replaced. *Is all religion a cycle?* He dropped into the Ranger and turned the ignition; he wanted to hit the wheel, punch a horse, but didn't.

He drove away from the past, from the what-could-have-beens, down by the school and then up along Breadalbane Street, past Phil the Pill's surgery. He took a right turn onto Albert Street and progressed up to his first house and slowed down. The bedroom they once shared now looked more like a floating box in the sky above the graveyard. He passed the little steps by the kissing gate where they would sit as kids, the setting for smooching games and ghoulish adven-tures. St Mary's Well opposite. Giving its name to the town. The Unknown Sailor a step or two away. Now a creature of the land.

Punch drove on. Took the Dervaig Road. Made light work of the Mishnish Lochs, passing the old, ruined house where he'd done some winching too. The bikes always stored on the inside. He passed the slate blue of Loch Tor and soon was descending the Hairpin Bends, a favourite Mull Rally spectator spot. It was here a girlfriend's father had scolded him for not knowing the difference between fog and mist.

Ten minutes later he pulled onto the bumpy track leading to the Calgary Beach car park. Thankfully nobody else had chosen to spend their Christmas Eve here. Just a few cows and sheep grazing.

Punch swung the Ranger in and turned off the ignition. Pulled up the collar of his coat and threw his legs out. Walked to the rear and took the carrier bag and a spade out of the boot. Closed it, and walked off towards the dunes where the sheep were grazing on the precious machair. Everything was protected now. Endangered.

It was surprisingly bright and the Atlantic glistened ahead as he walked the grassy pathway in the direction of the headland. But soon daylight would be an afterthought. Somewhere out there the Needle lay, discarded by Townsend; its new home the sea. He could only hope the coming days and weeks of interrogation brought more answers.

The sandy beach sprawled out to Punch's left, populated by only a few beef cattle sipping the aqua sea. It was here they used to run and jump on the sands, his mother in a deckchair holding onto her hat. He and Charlie substituting the roar of the ocean for a crowd. Imagining, as Punch did now, what it was out there that the sea arrived at next. Only Charlie had attempted to discover the answer.

He walked further out along the headland and took a turn inland, following a craggy stone wall until it lost interest and fizzled out. The land was boggy and letting him in. The ruined settlements of Inivea came into view; the village that refused to completely die. It was as good a metaphor as any. He stopped. Looked around and placed the carrier bag down. He positioned the spade and put his weight on it, the peaty earth gave way easily.

Soon he had a sizeable hole dug up.

Punch kneeled and took the effigy from the bag and carefully positioned it in the hole. He stood up, unsure of what to do next, hadn't thought about words. He started spading the earth over the fabric, remembered his uncle telling him how men on the island would arrive at a local funeral with spades over their shoulders. The number of spades signifying how popular the person had been. Whisky served off the back of the hearse.

Punch replaced the final spadefuls of earth. He ran a boot over to flatten it. He turned away and wiped the wind from his eyes.

There, you're home now. Rest, brother.

Before the wind could play more havoc, he started walking back in the direction he had come, the dark clouds following him inland. He felt lighter, or less significant. But knew he hadn't buried ego. A dog was running along the beach. He couldn't see any evidence of an owner and, as he watched the dog springing through the wind with such abandon, he thought how much it looked like a good state to be in. To be free. To put your ears back and run.

In the Ranger, he fired up the ignition and bumped down onto the road towards Dervaig. Turning the dial through the channels, he landed on the familiar voice of the DJ, Steve Wright, who said:

'Next up is Rod Stewart. "Maggie May" is a song co-written by him, with a man called Martin Quittenton. No. I hadn't

heard of him either. So, this Christmas, here's a shout out to the forgotten people.'

Punch reached to turn up the volume. He nodded in time as he looked to the deforestation around him; evidence of a moon appearing over the snowy peaks. The opening acoustic chords arrived to him as if for the first time. And was it a mandolin? The bass notes he heard as the hook, which he had never noticed before. Double hit on the snare drum and now Rod's voice. No reverb, dry as a bone, as though the man was in the seat next to him. He switched off the radio. He could hear the song without it.

It was just hours until Christmas Day. Punch looked to the sky, imagining it too had ruins floating in it like the decaying, barnacle-encrusted boats outside Salen. He wondered if anyone had ever felt as he did now. That nothing could be dead without other things being alive.

EXIT MUSIC

IT WAS DARK ENOUGH. The town would be asleep. The dead of night and Punch felt like the only Muileach awake. He had the station-house lights turned off, The Faces in full swing. The festive season was over for another year, and it was the early days of 1999. A third cell might be needed for Prince. Hogmanay had been and gone, but a more official acknowledgement of the new year was still to be carried out. Guinness would have the whole year to worry about this Millennium Bug, to make sure it didn't interfere with CalMac's timetables. That's all folk would really care about. Punch himself wouldn't have minded if the bug righted the clock's hourly chimes.

Lowry's death had caused quite the local, not discounting international, intrigue. His demise had even been worked into the storyline of the Christmas Panto in the Aros Hall, thankfully minus Townsend and his awful corduroys in the cast. Lowry's name apparently left alone out of respect. The chorus line wearing deerstalkers was not so subtle.

The tributes to the man were impressive, Punch had to concede. Still, he wouldn't be replacing The Faces with

Vivaldi any time soon. Though he suspected Mary MacBeth wouldn't have minded.

The official forensic pathologist's report into the musician's death had been filed, and the case, or any ongoing threads, was now clearly less of a priority for Legacy Strathclyde. They wanted the case closed, resources pulled, and they weren't going to wait for a plane. Punch was on his own again, which was how he liked it.

Policing – real police work – could not be done when the whole world wanted in on it. The court appearances for Townsend, Damask and Palindrome had been set, and Guinness had printed off the pathologist's findings for Punch to sign off. As he read the report, Punch of course knew the details related to the man Lowry, but for some reason digested it as an attempt at closure of his own.

Monteith had returned and Punch, Monteith and Cluny – with the aid of the Tobermory Coastguard and Randy's cohort – had searched inland lochs and the Forestry estates for the Needle. Almost as far as Ben More they took it. Monteith trying to take credit for it being a crime-free Mull before she went on her leave. Punch had to double-check the woman hadn't lifted the sergeant's three-stripe chevron from his upper arm. Other locals had become naturally intrigued and carried out searches of their own. Even down the Ross end.

Fans of the virtuoso violinist were already making pilgrimages to his final resting place. It was said MacTavish's boys were halfway through a grant application for a merchandise shop. Punch suspected a new classical music section in *The Oban Times*. First to find the plane was going to have some serious kudos for life. When, just before Hogmanay, a local clam diver, Steve the Bream, came across a likely ruin positioned some three hundred yards out on the Sound, hopes rose. But it turned out to be a false alarm. In questioning, Townsend steadfastly maintained he had no clue where it was. Now the courts would decide.

Punch took a hit of Tobermory, walked to the record player and lifted the needle. Picked up the rucksack he had already prepared from the table, then reached for the door. Locked it behind him. Left the police hat in favour of a woollen one. This was unofficial work, not to include Guinness. Though, for a cappuccino-quaffing badminton player, the bugger had done okay for his first series of significant cases. And what a series.

Punch walked straight by the Ranger. This was a foot operation. He imagined the sound of Lowry's horsehair bow as he passed the Western Isles Hotel. That was what great art could do, he realised: stay with you. Allow you into the composer's head, his heart, if not his underpants. What was it the radio DJ had said about experiencing Lowry playing in the flesh?

'*A visceral response to beauty.*'

He turned down the Western Isles steps, which led to the Lighthouse Path. Where, just weeks ago, his in-tray had amounted to the complaints of a visiting couple and an air rifle. As he stepped down, he recalled the older lads who used to ride motorbikes up and down the steps. *Down*, he could fathom. But he never thought he would see *up*. Like petrol-fuelled gods they were.

He arrived on the path at the bottom. Could almost see the frustration on the face of the young, helmeted Charlie, on his bike with stabilisers, awaiting the crackle of fake revs and walkie-talkie handles that was him and Randy returning from the lighthouse. He scurried down the banking to the Kilchoan ferry slip.

Punch walked the numbered bays and on down towards the slip. He took to the rocks by the left of the slip, just out of reach of the tide. He edged cautiously around the granite blocks below the cliff face as the sea lapped like a series of questions. Around the bend, the ladder he had positioned earlier against the rock face was thankfully intact. He put down his torch and took the rucksack from his back. Removed the items and placed them down on a flat rock. He made sure the ladder had a sure footing. Police work, solo style, was the kind Punch preferred; it couldn't be measured on charts or league tables.

He prised open the lid of the tin, took the brush and popped the torch in his mouth. Slowly, he ascended the ladder, leading with his longer arm, carrying the pot with his other. He rose until he was face to face with the large, decaying letters, each one the size of his torso. He began tracing the 'G' with the brush. The white paint released from his hand like a flare. Only now was it officially the start of another year.

He went around the 'O' next, then the 'D'. Taking as much care as he could, feeling the mainland's eyes on the back of his neck.

When he had finished, Punch stepped down off the ladder and rested the tin on the rock's flat surface. He sat, facing out to Calve, to the blackness of the night. No. *Becoming* it. He constructed a roll-up, lit it and puffed deeply. It felt good to blow the smoke towards the inferior mainland. He thought of those who didn't get to realise their potential, folk who didn't get to even *be*. He watched the smoke rise, just as Charlie used to. As he must have that final time in December 1988, from a London runway that would make Lussa Falls look like the cow patch it was.

Would he have looked for the sawdust lines?

Punch closed his eyes. Felt the gentle ebb and flow of the sea as though he was on it. He wished he could tell his brother how a man with a suitcase had ended his life. He wished he could know whether it was possible to feel even as much as a millisecond of awareness when such a thing happened to a human being. Or was it all over too quickly for that? The elements removing the clothes from you, whipping them from your body. He didn't know which scenario he preferred.

He wanted one more chance to roam free with Charlie.

Punch laid his head back on the rock and it could have been the slaughter table. He bolted up. But then settled slowly back again. Closed his eyes and drew in steady, deep breaths. Felt his body rising gradually into the night. He looked down for the first time on his patch of Mull. Maybe this was the view people like Lowry needed. Vivaldi and Rod too. To be above mere mortals.

Every moored boat was where it should be. Jacob's Ladder meandered like a caterpillar. Tobermory lighthouse rose like a finger to the sky. Stone walls snaked as though veins showing through the flesh of the land. Every house, field, grave, moor, rock pool and roaming farm animal were accounted for.

Over he passed, following the coastline. Calgary Beach came into view below. There were two people running on the sand. But he couldn't see who they were. He felt like a bird discovering the power in its wings for the first time. Below him the Atlantic frothed, warring in all directions. Birds stabbed the sky, squawking and darting over the waves. Free to roam, each one unidentifiable from the other, which made them just about the same. Punch felt held, carried by the wind, his arms not a disadvantage here. He looked down on the island. It was two boys. They were running and jumping on the beach. One older than the other. Lines in the sand marked their progress. Olympic rings drawn by bare toes. He could see the picture was really one of light.

He could see that in this moment they had everything they needed.

ACKNOWLEDGEMENTS

Thanks to Campbell Brown, Ali McBride, Emma Hargrave, Clem Flanagan, Thomas Ross, Hannah Walker, Rachel Morrell, Lizzie Hayes and Tonje Hefte at Black & White Publishing – thank you for all your support, input and editorial insight, great to be solving crimes with you; thanks to all at Bonnier Books UK; to Henry Steadman for the excellent cover image.

Thanks to PC Kevin Bonar at Salen Police Station, Isle of Mull, and to PC Daniel Ferry and PC Neil Thallon at Tobermory Police Station – your time and availability was much appreciated; Pam, Sian, Reegie, Bonnie (!) and my mum, for your unwavering support, and all my family on both sides of the Atlantic; my cousin, Didi MacIntyre, for your encouragement and considered feedback over the years; John 'Tiger' MacArthur for your ovine overtures.

Big thanks to Veronique Baxter at David Higham Associates for providing valued feedback on early work.

Thanks also to Fiona Atherton, Nicky Stonehill and Rebecca Salt at StonehillSalt PR, Charlie Caplowe, Anthea

The Lovely, Dani and Evan Cotter at Xtra Mile Recordings, Gordon MacIean, Thom Williams at Sonic PR, Jessica Hall at Radioactive Promotions, Nick Bray at Direct Promo, Stephen Kelman, Paula and David Ogilvie and all at Borders Book Festival, Duncan Swinbanks and all at Tackle & Books Tobermory, Lee Randall, Wigtown Book Festival, Bob McDevitt at Bloody Scotland, Val McDermid, Ian Rankin, Rupert Davies-Cooke and the Original Writers Group, Soren Kristensen/SOLK Photography, Marcus McEwan, Billy 'The (*real*) Box' McClymont, all those involved in the excellent BBC Radio 4 *Great Mull Air Mystery* episode of 'Punt P.I.'.

I am also indebted to the taxi drivers' community at Reading train station, who solved a mystery as to which of their cabs I had left this manuscript in late one night after attending my MHS album mastering at Abbey Road Studios, London: Sergeant Punch would have had me arrested for multitasking.

And f—inally, if there are any errors in the information gathered from any of the above contributors then they are entirely of my own, and intended to serve the fiction.

I would like also to dedicate this work to the living memories of the casualties of the Lockerbie bombing of 21 December 1988.

Colin MacIntyre is a multi-award-winning musician, producer, author for adults and children, and playwright, who has been voted Scotland's Top Creative Talent. Born into a family of storytellers and writers on the isle of Mull in the Hebrides, he has released nine acclaimed albums to date, most notably under the moniker *Mull Historical Society*, achieving two UK Top 20 albums and six Top 40 singles to date, since his Gold-selling debut album, *Loss*. He has been voted into the Greatest Scottish Artists of All Time poll, and his new MHS album, *In My Mind There's A Room*, is a collaboration with leading authors, and includes his poet grandfather, Angus Macintyre. His debut novel, *The Letters of Ivor Punch*, won the 2015 Edinburgh International Book Festival First Book Award and he has adapted it for the stage as *The Origins of Ivor Punch*. He has toured worldwide, including with R.E.M., The Strokes and Elbow, and has appeared on multiple festival and TV stages, including *Later with Jools Holland*. He has published a memoir, *Hometown*

Tales: The Boy in the Bubble, and his first book for children, *The Humdrum Drum*.

Colin is a lead tutor in Songwriting and on the MA programme at the BIMM Institute University, and he has led the children's charity Mary's Meals in London. He once spent a year with the Scottish professional football club, Queen's Park FC, and, despite his absence of a working shield, he is a descendent of the Scottish Warrior Poet, Duncan Ban Macintyre.

When The Needle Drops is his first in a new 'Mull Mysteries' crime series.